Terence Strong was br
the '
jou
bestselling novels (which h.......
copies in the UK alone) include *President Down*, *The Tick Tock Man*, *Wheels of Fire*, *Cold Monday* and *White Viper*. He lives in the south-west of England.

Visit www.twbooks.co.uk/authors/tstrong.html

Acclaim for Terence Strong

'An expert miasma of treachery and suspicion building to a thrilling climax' *Observer*

'Belongs to the action-man school of writing, backed up by hands-on research' *The Times*

'Tension ratchets up wickedly – a strong sense of reality is reinforced with powerful emotion and gritty characters' *Daily Telegraph*

'An edge-of-the-chair thriller with the chilling grip of authenticity' *Independent on Sunday*

'Well plotted and genuinely exciting' *Sunday Telegraph*

'An extremely good topical thriller' Jack Higgins

'The storylines are skilfully intermingled – the writing is fluid, the action furious and the political premise entertaining' *The Times*

This Angry Land

Terence Strong

POCKET
BOOKS

LONDON • SYDNEY • NEW YORK • TORONTO

First published in the United Kingdom by
Hodder & Stoughton Ltd, 1992
First published in paperback in the United Kingdom by
Coronet Paperbacks, 1993
This edition published by Pocket Books, 2008
An imprint of Simon & Schuster UK Ltd
A CBS COMPANY
3 5 7 9 10 8 6 4 2

Simon & Schuster UK Ltd
1st Floor
222 Gray's Inn Road
London WC1X 8HB

www.simonsays.co.uk

Simon & Schuster Australia
Sydney

A CIP catalogue record for this book is available from
the British Library

ISBN 978-1-84739-256-5
Typeset by M Rules
Printed by CPI Cox & Wyman, Reading, Berkshire RG1 8EX

FOR PRINCESS

And for the millions of innocent individuals who died or suffered the horrors of a particularly evil war that the world chose to ignore.

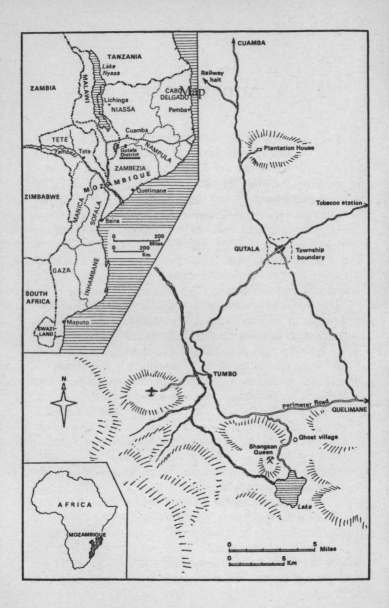

AUTHOR'S NOTE

For over ten years the former Portuguese colony of Mozambique in south-east Africa has been systematically wrecked and its people driven from their land by the shadowy self-proclaimed right-wing 'freedom fighters' of the Mozambique National Resistance (MNR) – better known as Renamo. Their army of 20,000 trained guerrillas – labelled 'bandits' – is active in over seventy per cent of a country the combined size of France and West Germany as was.

The Frelimo government struggles with 30,000 conscripts to protect the main cities and keep open the rail arteries with the outside world. To travel by train or road is to risk ambush and massacre. Air travel is the only 'safe' form of transport, and subsequently the country's fragile infrastructure is virtually held together by a few dozen motley passenger jets, cargo and light aircraft.

Renamo's deliberate campaign of destabilisation, wanton destruction and atrocity has been surpassed in scale only by the Khmer Rouge in Kampuchea. Official figures estimate a half-million civilians killed with another half-million in refugee camps. In truth these statistics can be virtually doubled.

Yet outside international political circles it remains very much an unknown war. This is due in part to the inaccessibility of the country itself and the rural areas in particular. The other reason is the extreme secrecy with which the military intelligence apparatus of South Africa has controlled the Renamo organisation, alongside an extremely effective disinformation campaign in the world media.

Recently the South African government appears to have taken some steps to sever this relationship, having belatedly recognised that the real political threat to its survival is of a chiefly internal nature. Nevertheless it is widely held that elements within military intelligence continue with – albeit reduced – support.

It is particularly saddening when it is realised that the vast majority of South African citizens have no knowledge or conception of the mass genocide that has been conducted on their behalf.

I am particularly indebted to HE – Mr Armando Penguene, Mozambique's Ambassador to London. He personifies the quiet dignity, pragmatism and patient diplomacy of the current Frelimo government under its widely respected President, Joaquim Chissano.

No doubt not all in official circles will appreciate my descriptions. But the fact is that corruption does exist (although possibly less than in many other Third World countries) and there is a decided lack of military competence, and I make no apology for speaking as I find. I have no doubt that in time both these problems will be largely resolved. Meanwhile readers may be confident that many of the incidents described are based on events and first-hand accounts experienced during my somewhat chaotic travels.

The possibility of the annexation of Rumbezia has been and remains a very real nightmare scenario for the Mozambique authorities.

All the characters – including Deputy Minister Ngoça, the da Grutas, and Brigadiers Santos and Vaz – are pure invention, although some are amalgams inspired by people I met or observed.

Again Gutala district is a fictional combination of several places visited, but nevertheless provides a realistic and typical setting.

In particular I must thank the resourceful pilots and staff of Interocean who kindly flew me to some of the more remote regions in a curious assortment of ancient aircraft. As it is the only company of its type in Beira, I can hardly deny that they inspired my Arbaérea outfit – the characters, however, are all mine.

But I am especially grateful to David Baxter of Defence Systems International Ltd, which has provided British contract soldiers to train Mozambican 'special forces' with impressive results. It was David who made the extremely tenuous upcountry travel arrangements work, and it was his wicked sense of humour that kept us going when they, frequently, didn't.

At the time of writing the Mozambique government is holding protracted and difficult talks with representatives of Renamo in the belief that a negotiated settlement is the only way to secure peace.

TERENCE STRONG
LONDON 1991

I am most thankful to the following people, each of whom has contributed to the authenticity of this story, many with accounts of their real-life experiences of Mozambique:

IN LONDON: The recent members of 4 Recce who confirmed South Africa's clandestine activities when Pretoria denied them, but who must remain unnamed; Leslie and friends for their target practice; Simone Hammarstrand for pioneering the way; Alan Rake of New African magazine; aviation adviser Ken Stubbs; Dot Keet and Ian Bray of the Mozambique Information Office, and Mark Gorden of the International Freedom Foundation.

IN SOUTH AFRICA: Mike and Sue Harper for a gold mine, hospitality far above the call of duty and an unforgettable braai on the bank of the Kamati River, and Patrick and Susan Homer for their instant welcome party.

IN MOZAMBIQUE: The indefatigable David Ankers and his chef Jean-Paul Capitaine who in a few short months were well on the way to restoring the Polana Hotel to its former glory; Graham Harper; Bill and Becky Friedman; Mark and Helen van Koevering of Christian Aid, both of whom witnessed separate Renamo attacks at first hand (and survived the ordeal, eventually to get married); pilots Mike Fogg and Malcolm Boyd. Very special thanks go to David Davies, but not forgetting good companions Lee, Faz, Robin and Terry.

I am also indebted to Frances McLeod of the British Embassy and then defence attaché, John Longman, who might very well have witnessed Maraika's return.

IN HARARE: Andy Moyse of Parade *for his revealing insights.*

PROLOGUE

It was the distant blast of the whistle that woke her.

Straight from deep sleep to instant awareness, her eyes wide and her heart palpitating with apprehension. The sweat was cold on her ebony skin.

Was it the sound of a whistle? Had she dreamed it like so many times before? There was no sound from outside now apart from the incessant cicadas and the riverside bullfrogs.

She relaxed back on the moth-eaten pillow of the hotel bed and stared up at the ceiling fan that hadn't turned for ten years.

Of course it had been the dream. The same one that had haunted her since she was twelve years old. When the Renamo *bandidos* had come to her village with their guns and their pangas. And, of course, their whistles.

Pale predawn light washed the stark plaster walls and she could now see him more clearly on the bed beside her. Sleeping like a baby, curled up in a tangle of thin sheet, blissfully unaware of anything.

If it had been a whistle he would have heard. And if it had been he would know what to do. He always knew what to do. He would protect her as he always did. Five years ago he hadn't been there when the bandits came. But now he was and she was safe.

Tentatively she reached out to touch him, afraid that she would wake him and he would snap at her. Her fingertips glanced the tousled fair curls of his beard. She loved his beard and his hair. Most white men she had

1

known before Mike Branagh had been of Portuguese blood. They tended to be short with swarthy complexions and black hair. So it had been a shock when her family came to Gutala with the other refugees and she saw him for the first time.

He had been standing outside this very hotel, the only one in the town. The only place suitable for a white man to work. Two adjoining rooms: this bedroom and a second which served as an office.

As a twelve year old she remembered clutching her mother's hand, staring up at this towering stranger with his tanned face and the sun shining on his short golden beard and hair. An angel, she had thought, sucking on her thumb. Like the pictures in the tattered Children's Bible that was her mother's prized possession.

It had not occurred to her that angels don't wear denims and bush shirts; to her childish mind he had seemed nothing less than godlike as he laughed and joked with the nervous refugees. He had brought a smile to their faces for the first time in weeks while he handed out sacks of mealie and blankets.

Her eyes travelled to the upright chair by his bedside. The bottle of Jameson was almost empty. Last night, after making love, it had been half-full.

Even angels have bad dreams, she thought, and gently kissed his cheek. He stirred. Yes, just like her he had bad dreams. Sometimes she would wake and find him standing by the window. Staring out into his past and drinking slowly and steadily until some unwanted memory died.

Maraika sat bolt upright.

It was no mistake. A single whistle trilled, then another. More whistle blasts answered from a different place.

Momentarily she was paralysed, feeling the sudden thudding in her chest. 'Mikey! Mikey!' she hissed urgently.

2

There was no response. She shook him briskly, but he merely tried languorously to put his arm around her.

More whistles. Closer. Then a solitary gunshot.

Mike Branagh was awake.

'Oh, God, Mikey!'

He screwed his eyes against the light. 'What was that?' She stared at him, not wanting to believe her own words: '*Bandidos.* I think it is *bandidos.*'

A stutter of gunfire ripped through the still dawn air like the sound of tearing calico.

Branagh was on his feet, naked and swaying slightly to keep his balance as he padded to the window. He cursed the pulsing ache that threatened to burst his skull in two.

The hazy light hurt his eyes as he tried to focus through the torn gauze of the mosquito gate. From this corner room on the second floor of the hotel there was a clear view down the main street of Gutala. The wide ribbon of ochre earth separated the Portuguese-style town centre buildings on either side. Farther down, the dilapidated Mediterranean stucco architecture gave way to the reed and wattle compounds of the civilian population.

It was from here that the gunfire and the screams came. And then the people.

Branagh could hardly believe what he was seeing as the first of Gutala's inhabitants burst onto the dusty track, running and screeching in their terror. Some naked, some half-dressed, they came in a growing torrent. Young men, old women hobbling on sticks, mothers clutching their children. Others carried whatever few possessions they could snatch. They streamed down the road seeking safety in the town centre where there was a detail of Frelimo government troops.

He switched his attention to the dirt square beneath his window. Facing him was the shuttered and pockmarked headquarters of Embamo, the state-owned company which administered the district's banana plantations. On the west side stood the crumbling façade of the long-closed row of shops which served as a billet for the small government garrison.

The first of the soldiers emerged now. Dressed in a torn vest and camouflage fatigue trousers, he stumbled through the accumulated rubbish on the sidewalk and stared down the street at the clamorous tidal wave of humanity rushing towards him. He had no gun.

Branagh drew back and threw open the mosquito gate; the glass in the window had long gone. '*Bandidos!*' he yelled down. The soldier turned, his mouth agape. '*Bandidos* for Christ's sake, man! Wake up your bloody detail! Get your weapons!'

As Branagh's voice was drowned out by the rising cacophony of screams and shouts, punctuated by gun-shots and whistle blasts, the soldier at last appeared to comprehend. He ran back into the shop doorway and returned with four companions. They all appeared disori-entated, half-asleep, two of them just wearing sports shorts. But at least they carried rifles.

They stood watching as the people scurried past, call-ing out to demand what was happening. No one had a mind to stop and explain. The detail of soldiers began a heated debate on the sidewalk.

Branagh shook his head; he could guess what the out-come would be. He knew full well that part of the detail was supposed to spend each night in the sandbagged observation post on the hotel roof; it offered a command-ing view of all approaches to the square. But he also knew that they never did for fear of being trapped there in the event of a Renamo attack.

One of the soldiers began pulling off his fatigue trousers, another tossed aside his forage cap. And as the first surge of terrified civilians passed, the soldiers joined the stragglers in their hurried exodus to the surrounding bush.

Smoke began rising from the outlying compounds as

4

huts were put to the torch. Now the earthen street was clear except for a few confused, crying toddlers who had become parted from their parents.

Then Branagh saw them.

The column of bandits strutted into view on the main street most of them with smart new uniforms and boots that glinted in the rising sun. They were led by a big officer who moved with a slow, elephantine gait. He blasted on the silver whistle in his mouth and the column immediately responded by separating into three sections. One charged into the compounds to the right and another to the left in a search for booty, while the rest advanced inexorably towards the square.

Branagh slammed the mosquito gate shut and turned into the room. Maraika hadn't moved, sitting at the bedhead with her long legs drawn up to her chin, clutching at the sheet as though it would give her some protection.

He tossed across the yellow dress he had bought for her in the Mozambique capital of Maputo. 'Put that on. They'll be here in a minute.'

'It is the *bandidos*?'

He grabbed his trousers from the bed and pulled them on. 'Well it's not a bloody carnival – although no one told that to the Frelimo troops down there.'

'Are they shooting the *bandidos*?' she asked earnestly as she pulled the dress over her head.

'Are they hell!'

He glanced round the room, trying to size up the situation. They would have no time to get downstairs before the first of the bandits reached the lobby. And there was no escaping from the window that fronted the square.

He moved to the side window. That offered a little more hope as any descent would be partly obscured by a protruding neon sign that hadn't shown a flicker of life for a decade.

'Start tying the bedsheets together,' he ordered.

'I don't understand, Mikey.'

5

'Like a rope, corner to corner,' he snapped. 'We'll climb out.' Sometimes her lack of worldliness could drive him mad. He flung open the wardrobe doors and extracted the stack of spare sheets. As he began knotting them, he again glanced out the window.

The bandits were fanning out across the square. Half a dozen women cowered on the sidewalk by the shops, having retrieved their wandering infants. He saw a bandit raise his rifle. Saw the muzzle flash. Then several of the bandits rushed at the mothers. Reflected sunlight on the bayonets shone and blinded him. The screams were piercing.

Maraika's mouth dropped and she stopped what she was doing. He snatched the sheets from her and knotted them to the ones he had tied. 'Get the side window open, quickly!'

As she rushed to obey he dragged the bed across the room until it was jammed fast beneath the sill. He secured one end of the sheet rope to a leg of the bed, and fed the other out of the window and down the outside wall.

Maraika's eyes were wide with horror. 'I can't do that, Mikey! I will fall.'

'No you won't. Just hold on tight. It's hardly thirty feet. And keep quiet. If you start screaming one of the bastards will hear you.'

She stared at the window, summoning her courage. If Mikey said she could do it, then she could. He always knew what to do.

There was a sudden crash of splintering timber from downstairs. He guessed it was the heavy front doors because the entire building seemed to shake. Gunshots followed, the sound echoing up through the stairwell.

A dog barked in the next room.

Branagh and the girl stared at each other. 'Benjy,' she said.

'Christ, I'd forgotten he was here.'

'Get him, Mikey.'

6

'Of course.' He pushed her towards the window. 'Now out you go. When you reach the ground keep down. Go to the kitchen area at the back. Hide until I join you.'

He glimpsed the worn hole in her pants as she hiked up her dress, climbed the sill and gingerly lowered herself down hand over hand. Satisfied she could do it, he ran to the adjoining door which opened into the room he rented as an office.

Maraika's younger brother was standing on tiptoe, peering out of the window in awe at the events happening in the square.

At his feet the boy's scruffy three-legged mongrel was scampering in an agitated circle. The animal had once been foolish enough to stand in the middle of the street barking at an oncoming Frelimo truck which, not unexpectedly, had defective brakes. The dog had large watery eyes and a twist to its lips that gave the impression it was smiling at some private joke. It was smiling now as it approached Branagh, trembling with restrained enthusiasm, unsure whether to be pleased to see him or scared of the noise outside.

'Come away from the window,' Branagh called.

Benjamin looked at him. 'They are the *bandidos*?'

Branagh nodded. 'We must go.'

'They look like soldiers.'

'C'mon, Benjy, now.'

'Our soldiers ran away.'

Branagh took the eleven-year-old boy by the arm. As he did so he heard heavy footsteps thumping up the stairs, then the sound of doors being kicked open. There was a sudden rattle of gunfire from outside. A stray shell shattered the last remaining pane of glass in the office window, and they both ducked.

He pushed the boy through into the bedroom.

'Where is Maraika?' Benjamin looked around, astonished, as though witnessing some conjuring trick.

'Out the window, where you're going. Quick now,

down the sheets. Hold tight. Sure I'll be right behind you.'
He lifted the boy onto the sill.

'I must take Dog.'

Branagh smiled tersely. 'You can't take Dog. You'll fall.'

'You bring Dog.'

'Even I need two hands, Benjy. Dog will be safe here. We'll get him later.'

Unhappily the boy swung his legs out and began to lower himself down.

The footsteps in the corridor were nearing fast and Branagh followed the boy hurriedly. His last sight was of the bemused dog barking, its head tilted to one side in curiosity as to why it was being abandoned.

Through the broken tubing of the neon sign he could see the milling group of bandits in the square. He prayed that they were too preoccupied to notice him. He was halfway down when the rotten material of the sheet began to give. He heard it rip and felt the friction scrape of the wall against his knuckles as the sheet tore. Then he was airborne.

He hit the hard earth, landing awkwardly in a pile of garbage. A sprained ankle was the least of his worries; thankfully he was now hidden from the bandits in the square by a corrugated-iron compound fence that abutted the hotel.

Ignoring the sparks of pain in his foot he hobbled after Benjamin who was already making his way to the rear of the building. In the yard was the open-air kitchen that served the hotel, blackened pots of burnt maize porridge still steaming on the charcoal embers. The wattle huts of the staff were deserted, except for Maraika who appeared anxiously from one of them.

'We hide here?' she asked.

Branagh shook his head. 'That smell of food will attract them.'

'There is the log-store,' Benjamin suggested.

It was a woven eucalyptus structure standing some thirty metres outside the kitchen compound. Inside the collected brushwood was piled on a raised slatted floor which allowed air to circulate. A good place to hide.

'Follow me,' he said. 'Watch how I move and copy. Keep your bottom down.'

Dropping to all fours he began a fast leopard crawl across the intervening stretch of scrub, using a slight indentation in the ground for cover. Maraika followed with a poor imitation of his movements and he waited nervously for a bandit to raise the alarm. None came. Benjamin's effort was much more accomplished.

Once they were together Branagh found a way to squeeze under the pontoons into a dark area with just enough headroom to sit. It allowed a good view of the square through the narrow gaps of the weave. Outside, the killing appeared to have stopped and the bandits were starting to concentrate on the systematic searching and looting of every building in sight.

At one point two Renamo bandits approached the log-store, opened the door and inspected the stacks of tinder with disinterest. Food or medical supplies were what they really sought. Besides which their comrades had found some cans of beer in the *cantina* and the bandits were more keen to drink that than to search for hiding villagers.

As they went away laughing, Maraika whispered: 'I wish you had a gun. Like Senhor da Gruta.'

Branagh said: 'One gun against that lot wouldn't do us much good.'

'You could kill some of them.'

'Then they would kill us.'

In the darkness of the store her eyes were bright and white as she looked at him curiously, thinking on his words. 'You were a soldier once.'

'A long time ago.'

'If you had a gun you would know what to do. Senhor da Gruta has a gun and he has never been a soldier.'

Branagh smiled. 'Jorge would be more danger to himself than the *bandidos*.'

As luck would have it for Jorge, the da Gruta family was away in Portugal to attend the funeral of Jorge's father, Dom Pedro. Branagh had never met the grand old nobleman, but he had heard plenty about him. How his unbroken lineage could be traced back five hundred years to aristocratic forebears who had dared to venture beyond Portugal's Cape St Vincent. In their fleet of fast caravelles the da Grutas had explored all the way from Angola to the Cape of Good Hope, to here in Mozambique in South-East Africa, and beyond to Macao, Java and the fabulous riches of the Spice Islands.

Those voyages were to mark the beginnings of the da Gruta dynasty and a commercial empire that once girdled half the globe, including the vast banana and cotton plantations around Gutala.

But in the end it all went wrong. Centuries of poor management, lavish spending and gambling debts saw the business empire break up and fortunes dwindle until only the Gutala estate was left. Dom Pedro apparently did what he could to halt the slide when he inherited the title after the Second World War, later sending his son Jorge to manage the estate personally.

Poor Jorge. He'd just got the estate in order when the 1974 coup d'état in Portugal toppled the fascist regime of Marcelo Caetano. The ripple effects were to be felt throughout the country's empire. With inflation rampant the Portuguese peasant economy had been collapsing under the weight of fighting colonials with 150,000 conscripts in Guinea-Bissau, Angola and Mozambique. Within a year Lisbon had abandoned the colony to the Frelimo liberation movement which had been fighting for ten years.

Portuguese landowners and businessmen fled in their thousands almost overnight. The uncertainty and upheaval of the period placed a crippling strain on the da

10

Grutas' already diminished resources. It was almost a relief to Jorge when Frelimo adopted its Marxist policy and nationalised the run-down estate, renaming it Embamo, the Mozambique Banana Company.

With all the little remaining family wealth tied up in Mozambique, Jorge and his wife had no option but to accept Frelimo's offer for them to manage the plantations they had once owned.

Now Jorge had the unenviable task of burying his father, selling off the dilapidated family estate in Portugal to meet death duties and to inherit a worthless title. An inglorious end.

But at least he hadn't had to witness this Renamo attack. One had to be thankful for small mercies.

Benjamin had been watching silently through the walls. Suddenly he turned: 'They are setting fire to the school now, Senhor Mike.'

Branagh had a sinking feeling as he looked out. It had taken local villagers a year to build the school with their bare hands under his supervision. It was Gutala's show-piece. Soon there would be nothing left. 'When the *bandidos* have gone we'll build another one. Bigger and better.'

The boy looked dubious. 'There will be no people here.'

'They'll come back.'

'You will stay?'

'I'll stay, Benjy.'

'And we will still read the stories about Jesus every Sunday? Like before?'

Branagh ruffled the coarse black hair of the boy's head. 'Just like before.'

Christ, Branagh thought, what must be going through the child's mind. Women and toddlers shot on the street, his entire world going up in flames, not yet knowing what had happened to the rest of his family – and all he's worried about is Bible stories at Sunday school.

11

Branagh had run the class every week for years. He'd started it when there was no school at Gutala, as a way of teaching the children to read. It had proved very popular, even with the parents. The country's predominantly Catholic religion had not been encouraged by the Marxist government and a lot of the people had clearly missed it.

Benjamin was fascinated by the stories of the miracles, particularly the one about the loaves and fishes. That probably came of being permanently hungry.

'He's very fond of you, Mikey,' Maraika had told him once. 'He tells me he wants to be like you when he grows into a man.'

Even now Branagh remembered his reply. 'Poor little sod.'

At the time Maraika had not heard. 'He enjoys Sunday school. He likes to learn. He says maybe he wants to be a priest one day – but he has never met a priest. When you first tell Bible stories he thought you were a priest. He wants to wear a crucifix like yours.'

In the darkness of the log-store Branagh found himself absently fingering the gold cross and chain at his throat. For a moment he wasn't there, perspiring even in the darkness with the hot African sun rising to its full strength outside. He was four thousand miles and a lifetime away on the dank mean streets of Belfast.

Under his breath he said: 'Maybe if he met a real priest he wouldn't want to be one.'

It was during that momentary lapse of concentration that it happened.

'Dog!' Benjamin shrieked.

Branagh heard the barking and turned his head to see the three-legged mongrel standing his ground defiantly against a group of laughing guerrillas in the square. Then he saw the pistol being drawn. Heard the short, sharp report of the single shot.

The barking stopped and the laughter renewed.

And Benjamin was gone. Branagh grabbed for him

but it was too late. The boy squeezed deftly between the pontoons and was out through the door before Branagh could get to his feet.

Maraika saw the youngster race across the hard earth of the square with rising horror. Her mouth fell open as she watched him run straight to the dead dog, drop to his knees and hug the limp body to his chest.

Her scream was stillborn, gagged as Branagh's hand closed swiftly over her mouth. He pulled her roughly to him.

'Quiet!' he hissed. 'There's nothing you can do!'

Her big eyes stared at him wildly above the mask formed by his hand, but he held her fast until he felt her trembling anguish subside.

Benjamin had left his dog and was now beating his small fists against the chest of the bandit with the pistol. The man and his colleagues laughed heartily at the display of innocent courage. But after a few moments they became bored with the ineffectual attack, seized the boy by the arms, and marched him out of sight.

'What can we do?' Maraika whispered.

Branagh felt the nausea rise from the pit of his stomach. 'Nothing, girl. There's nothing we can do. Just wait.'

She looked at the crucifix around his neck. 'And pray?'

It was dusk before the Renamo bandits melted back into the bush. They disappeared just minutes before an armed convoy of Frelimo government troops arrived to begin an unenthusiastic sweep of the township. There was no attempt at hot pursuit; everyone knew the night belonged to the bandits.

By the flickering light of bonfires the corpses were laid out in the square. One hundred and three of them.

With a subdued Maraika at his side, Branagh walked along the rows. There were men, women and children. Some had died by the bullet, others by the panga.

Benjamin was not among them.

As the inhabitants began drifting back from the bush

13

the word was that some sixty able-bodied townspeople, men and women, had been *raptado* – abducted to act as porters to carry away the spoils of Gutala.

They learned that Maraika's home village of Tumbo, ten miles to the south, had also been sacked by the bandits. Her parents and sister had escaped, but her youngest brother Jaime, just nine years old, was also missing.

All night long the fires burned, casting fitful, macabre shadows around the walls of the square, silhouetting the tableau of mourners who came to identify their dead.

Branagh sat alone on the hotel verandah by the light of a hurricane lamp. He could just hear the inconsolable sobbing of Maraika from his room above as sleep eluded her.

And like her he could not shake the thoughts of the two young brothers from his mind. Such gentle, happy kids, despite their deprivation in this country which seemed to know no end of suffering.

He had not seen much of little Jaime, who had spent most of the time with his parents in Tumbo village. But he had come to know Benjamin well, as the boy was often left in the care of his older sister – too boisterous for the ageing Matusis to handle. That same energy was welcomed by Branagh who found Benjamin a willing helper when distributing aid sacks or on the various building projects around the district. Or perhaps the true incentive was the chance to ride in Branagh's Land-Rover, which he seized at every opportunity.

Despite the sorrow of the day an involuntary half-smile came to Branagh's face. He had grown very fond of the boy. Although he had never married, he had often wondered what it would be like to have a son. Perhaps in Benjamin he had discovered the answer. The two of them would spend hours together in the safe bush around the village while Branagh taught him the fieldcraft he himself had learned so many years before.

Benjamin had become an excellent tracker – his

eyesight that much sharper than his teacher's – and it frequently resulted in a vastly appreciated addition to the family cooking pot. They would borrow an ancient rifle from the local militia and Branagh would teach him how to use it safely.

Once the boy had asked him why he would never handle the gun except to explain how it worked. He had simply smiled and said: 'It's a long story.'

His memory of those words and the expression of curiosity in the boy's eyes lingered with him now as slowly and steadily he drank his way through the bottle of whiskey until his burning anger was quelled.

Never again, he murmured to himself. Never ever again.

Silently he watched the moon and the stars and a giant moth battering itself against the lamp.

He fingered the small gold crucifix at his throat. It had always so fascinated Benjamin that he had resolved to make the boy a present of it for his next birthday.

Branagh had no use for it. Perhaps he never really had.

TWO YEARS LATER

1

Although she was not to know it, Kathleen Coogan was hot news in Maputo from almost the moment she arrived at the airport.

After the order and brusque formality of her brief stopover in Johannesburg she was totally unprepared for the mayhem that was Mozambique. She struggled to maintain her calm as the passengers on the short-hop flight to Maputo fought over too few immigration forms in the arrivals hall.

From the floor she managed to retrieve a crumpled, foot-trodden form that had been overlooked in the stampede. At least being a journalist she had a pen. Evidently few other passengers had and, as none were provided, a queue of new acquaintances quickly formed behind the diminutive figure in her plum-coloured tracksuit and trainers.

First in line was a florid-faced Englishman of middle age in a crumpled alpaca suit and well-travelled panama. Kathleen welcomed the encounter because the form had to be answered in triplicate and all the questions were in Portuguese. She could neither read nor speak the language.

Patiently the Englishman helped her fill in the details in exchange for the loan of her Biro which was then passed down the seemingly endless queue.

'Thank you,' she said.

The man chuckled and tipped his hat graciously. Gin-moist eyes approved the sensible urchin cut of her black hair and envied the clarity of the coffee-coloured eyes that smiled back at him. 'Smythe's the name. Ashton Smythe. My pleasure. From Northern Ireland, I see. First visit to Mozambique?'

She nodded. Despite his helpfulness there was something about the man that made her wary.

'So you're a journalist?' Smythe said as they joined the queue for the passport kiosk. He dabbed at his face with a blue pocket handkerchief. The air conditioning had failed, if indeed it had ever worked.

'This is my first real assignment. Abroad I mean.' Her enthusiasm began to overcome her reticence. 'I'm hoping this will be a lucky break for me. There's good potential here – storywise, I mean. Yet it hasn't been reported much.'

Ashton Smythe gave a kind of dismissive snort which muffled his words. 'Bloody arsehole of the world.'

'Pardon?'

He smiled disarmingly. 'This place takes some getting used to. Bit of a shambles. But you'll be all right. At least there's a buck or two to be made if you know the right people.'

'That's why you're here – business?'

He removed his battered panama and began using it as a fan. She noticed the perspiration glistening beneath the strands of thinning sandy hair. 'Buying and selling. This and that. Supply and demand. They demand and I supply. That's the beauty of the place for me. No one much knows what goes on here. And no one much cares.'

Kathleen looked up at him, uncertain. Was he trying to tell her she was wasting her time? That however good her story the world outside just wouldn't be interested. That's what her editor on the Belfast paper had told her when she had announced her sabbatical. 'Mozambique? Not a very sexy subject, Kathy sweetheart.' The next week her hairdresser had almost confirmed it in her blissful ignorance. 'A trip to Mozambique? Ooo – you're the lucky one. All that sea and sand.' God only knew where the Ulster teenager had had in mind.

Feeling a sudden, ridiculous urge to justify herself Kathleen said: 'While I'm here, I'm also hoping to trace a long-lost relative.'

'Yes?'

'An Irishman.'

He smiled politely. 'Of course.'

But as they reached the passport kiosk Ashton Smythe was no longer really listening. He knew all he needed to know to become the bearer of the hottest news in Maputo that day.

He had noted all he needed from her immigration form. Her name, her occupation and date of birth. Some quick mental arithmetic put her age at twenty-seven. Twenty-seven and an innocent abroad.

But, most important of all, he had noted her marital status. Kathleen Coogan was single.

That evening in the Maputo Aeroclub – the British expatriates' favourite watering hole – he would accept cooled cans of Castle in return for tantalising morsels of information. He would bask in reflected glory as specu-lation rose amongst the rowdy gathering of mostly bachelor and temporarily wifeless contract workers.

Ashton Smythe would fuel that speculation with a mouth-watering description of her climbing over the broken luggage carousel to retrieve her mauve rucksack. The neat backside in the snug tracksuit: 'Bum like a peach,' he would recall with relish.

By the time the bar closed, Kathleen Coogan would have become the most welcome news of the week.

But that evening, as she sat alone in the faded colonial opulence of the vast Polana Hotel dining room, Kathleen Coogan was still unaware that she had become the toast of the town.

In truth she felt anything but a celebrity as she ate in solitude at the alcove table between towering plaster

21

colonnades which supported the magnificent vaulted ceiling. With only a dozen or so other diners in the place, mostly in pairs, she was feeling distinctly lonely and isolated. The strange-tasting meat dish was tepid, presumably the result of recurring power cuts. When she tried to attract the attention of the sullen uniformed waiters they disappeared with the speed of the cockroaches she had found in her bedroom. Somewhere above her head, hidden by a balcony, an unseen musician monotonously ground out unrecognisable candlelight classics on an out-of-tune piano.

She shoved away her plate, the food scarcely touched, and lit a cigarette. A few tables away she noticed that a plump, middle-aged European in a dark tailored suit was watching her. He looked vaguely familiar and she consoled herself that at least she was not the only one eating alone. He smiled and raised his glass.

She might have responded, only she had stupidly forgotten to order a drink with her meal and the wine waiter had since vanished. So instead she sheepishly returned the smile, then averted her eyes to some fixed point in the middle distance.

Journalists abroad must frequently find themselves in situations like this, she told herself. A new country, a new assignment and no friends. Just part of the job. She would have to get used to it. It was just so difficult when alone to find the company of men without giving the wrong impression.

Like the seedy little Englishman she had met at the airport. Like a character out of Somerset Maugham. Something about Ashton Smythe had made her flesh creep. Although he'd been extremely polite and helpful she had found his appraising gaze unsettling. Despite his words of gentlemanly concern, she could believe that behind those benign moist eyes his mind had been stripping her naked. Layer by layer, like an onion.

But she could have been wrong. At this moment she

would have even welcomed his presence. After all he had kindly offered to take her in his taxi, selecting a driver he knew from the shabby crowd of Mozambicans touting for business. Even so the cab had a cracked windscreen like all the others, and the doors were held closed by loops of string.

As it had bounced over the pockmarked road which ran through the outlying shanties of the capital, Smythe had explained that he was staying at an hotel in downtown Maputo. As he had put it: 'Don't want my clients to think I'm too well-off. The buggers will want even more buckshee.' He had assumed correctly that she was staying at the Polana (the only hotel of which her travel agents in Belfast had a record) and dropped her off outside the impressive white clifftop building in the residential outskirts. 'You'll like it here. Give you an impression what Lourenço Marques – sorry, that's the old name for Maputo – used to be like under the Portuguese . . .'

It gave Kathleen an impression, but only just. The tall airy reception rooms with their potted greenery were in desperate need of fresh wallpaper and paint, and in her room the bed linen was clean but full of holes, like the mosquito-net gate at the balcony door. And only cold brown water belched noisily from the washbasin taps.

A shadow crossed the white starched tablecloth.

'Please excuse the intrusion, young lady, but I do believe this is yours.'

Kathleen glanced up with a jolt. It was the dark-suited man in his fifties who had raised his glass to her. Now he held up a Biro instead. 'At the airport, remember? Your pen got passed down the queue. I'm afraid I was the end of the line. By the time my turn came you were gone. So sorry.'

Instinctively she smiled back at the round, clean-shaven face and laughing blue eyes. The mass of tiny crowsfeet and soft pouches suggested that he enjoyed the good life; the hand-stitched suit and gold Longines wrist-watch confirmed that he could afford it.

'That's kind of you. You really shouldn't have troubled.'

'Pens are a valuable commodity in Africa,' he insisted. 'You'll find it hard to replace.' His voice was deep and rasping, indicating that he drank and smoked a little too much. She wasn't too good on English accents, but she imagined he'd once been to a good public school. His manner, however, was unpretentious and friendly.

'I've plenty of pens with me – I'm a journalist.'

His eyes lit up. 'Really? How fascinating!' He glanced about the dining room as though he were uncomfortable at being seen hovering at her table. 'Listen, truth is I felt a bit of a prat sitting all by myself – I'm waiting for an acquaintance to turn up. Then I noticed you were on your own and saw you trying to catch the wine waiter's eye . . .'

She smiled. 'I think it must be something I said.'

From his left hand, which he had been hiding behind his back, the man produced a half-empty bottle. 'I hope you don't think this an awful impertinence, but I wondered if you might care to share the rest of this? In fact share our woes as fellow travellers, so to speak. Unless of course—?'

Her smile became a gentle laugh. 'No, I'm not expecting anyone. I'd be delighted to have the chance to talk to somebody.'

Awkwardly he juggled with the pen and bottle as he shook her hand and fumbled for a chair. 'Mulholland. Vincent Mulholland.'

'Kathleen Coogan. Everyone calls me Kathy.'

'Well, Kathy, the food might leave something to be desired, but the plonk's not bad. Romeira. From the Tagus river area. That's north of Lisbon if you know Portugal.' He splashed some into her glass.

'You know a lot about wine?'

24

He chuckled. 'Drunk too much in my time not to, my dear. Almost my only vice.'

She sipped at the glass. 'Lovely – but to be honest I'd enjoy *anything* right now.'

And within moments she was chatting with the gregarious Vincent Mulholland as though she had known him for years. She was glad now she'd worn the only dress she'd packed: a simple crushproof Greek number in black crêpe cotton. This wasn't the sort of man you dined with in old slacks and a T-shirt. He was amusing and charming and clearly the sort of man-of-the-world who might be able to help her in this unfamiliar country.

'Are you here on business?' she asked as Mulholland successfully caught the passing wine waiter and ordered another bottle of Romeira.

'Not business as such, m'dear. For my sins I work for that spendidly fusty organisation known as the British Foreign and Commonwealth Office. I'm here to check that all the official government aid we've donated to this place is being properly utilised. Fat chance.'

'Oh?'

'You don't know Africa, m'dear?'

Her cheeks coloured. 'I hardly know anywhere outside the Six Counties. Except for a few trips to London, or Dublin – oh, and a holiday in Rimini once with some girlfriends.'

'A bit at sea then, eh? You'll soon get used to it. This is my first time in Mozambique, too, but I promise you some things don't change wherever you are in Africa. It's all a bit overwhelming first time.'

The wine arrived and Mulholland went through the tasting ritual to please the waiter. 'He'd be awfully offended if I didn't do things properly,' he explained after. 'Africans like to know where they are.'

'Will you be here long?'

'As short a time as possible, m'dear. Long enough to identify one fiddle – that'll satisfy my boss in Whitehall it was worth sending me. I'll be attached to the Commercial Section of the British Embassy here in Maputo. If you need any help, give me a bell.' He used her Biro to jot the number on the back of the menu.

Kathleen was grateful. 'I might take you up on that. I'm not quite sure how to go about things.'

With a refilled glass Mulholland was as content as a cat with a bowl of cream. His eyes smiled at her over the glass which he cradled lovingly in both hands. 'What sort of things do you mean?'

'Well, you see, I've never actually done anything like this before. An assignment abroad. Since I left college I've always worked on local Ulster newspapers. You know, local news, weddings, council meetings, that sort of thing. Then I got an opening on the daily as a junior reporter. But what I really want to do is feature work. You know, in-depth stuff. How and why.'

'Ah, I see, sort of stretch yourself?' Mulholland was very understanding.

'My editor agreed to let me have three months off without pay, and I persuaded a women's magazine to sponsor my trip here.'

'A commission?'

'Not really. More a promise to have a serious look at the work I bring back. The features editor and I get on. I've done some freelance stories for her before, you see.'

'But no commission?'

She pulled a sheepish face. 'A hundred and fifty pounds towards expenses. It didn't go far.'

They shared the joke as Mulholland liberally distributed more wine. 'Mozambique still seems a strange choice. Both for a women's magazine and for you. At least you could have picked a place with hot running water and electricity supplies that aren't blown up every five minutes.'

Kathleen decided that Mulholland was nobody's fool. 'You're right, of course. The magazine went along with it because it was unusual and I hoped to get a human-interest angle. You see, I'm also trying to track down one of my relatives, my step-cousin. I last saw him fourteen years ago in Armagh.'

'I'm surprised you still remember him,' Mulholland observed kindly.

She stared at the glass of wine on the table. 'Oh, I'd never forget Cousin Seamus.'

Mulholland topped up her glass. 'Tell me,' he encouraged.

Her eyes danced at the memory. 'I was the youngest of a large family, four older brothers. We had several smallholdings along the border area with Eire. The Troubles started when I was very young. The whole family was upset and divided. It was a bad time. I was very confused and didn't understand what was going on.'

'Does anyone?' Mulholland concurred gently.

Kathleen shrugged. 'My family were strict Catholic which can make it hard on a young girl at the best of times. I felt very restricted, very unhappy. I remember I would spend most of my spare time sitting in my bedroom writing poems' – a giggle – 'then reading them out to my teddy bear.'

'Were they good?'

'Not really. But I think that was when I decided I wanted to write. Some glamorous idea about being a foreign correspondent. Exotic faraway places—'

'With the strange sounding names,' Mulholland added with sympathy.

'Anywhere out of Ireland – but, as you see, it's taken a long time to get anywhere.'

'And your step-cousin, Seamus?'

'I'd hardly known him before. He'd been away serving with the British Army. But he left it and came home. I'll never forget. He arrived on my thirteenth birthday. To me he was a breath of fresh air. He was a lot older than me, of course. About my age now, I suppose. But he was so

27

much fun, always telling jokes. He would tease my brothers mercilessly.' She paused, momentarily overcome by the sudden flood of memories. It was so strange to be talking about him like this, after all those years, in a decrepit colonial hotel in remotest Africa. Like talking of a ghost, yet in her mind the images were as vivid as if it were yesterday. 'But for me he opened up a whole new world. He would take me for walks in the countryside – Armagh is beautiful, you know. He would insist that I read him my latest poems.' Again she hesitated. 'In fact I think it was Seamus who sowed the idea of me being a journalist when I grew up. He told me of all the places he'd been. Africa, Europe, the Far East and the Gulf. He said there was no reason why I shouldn't go to these places one day.'

Mulholland examined the second empty bottle gloomily. 'But something happened?'

The clear coffee eyes began to mist. 'It was very sudden when he left. One night he just packed a bag and walked out the door. Vanished off the face of the earth. Just a few days before my father and oldest brother were killed by the Army.' Mulholland looked embarrassed. 'It's all right. I've had a long time to get over it . . . Anyway, no one could trace Seamus. We heard nothing for fourteen years. Some of the family thought he must be dead.'

'But?' Mulholland prompted.

'Ma died last year. Then nine months later a letter arrived for me out of the blue. It was for the whole family really, but addressed to me. He didn't say much at all. Just how sorry he was to hear that Ma had died and that he hoped we were all well. There was no address. But the postmark was Mozambique.'

Mulholland settled back in his chair. 'Some mystery. I can maybe see the appeal to the magazine if you find him. But Mozambique is a big country.'

She nodded. 'The combined size of France and West

Germany as was, I know. That's why I need all the help I can get.'

Vincent Mulholland glanced up abruptly. 'And you know what, young Kathy, this might just be the chap who can give it.'

Her head turned as Mulholland rose to greet the dapper young man in beige tropical suit and pinstripe shirt who strode towards their table.

'Vincent! A million apologies for keeping you! Just couldn't get away. Waiting for a call from London and you know what the bloody phones are like here.'

Mulholland beamed benevolence like a beacon as they shook hands. 'Don't mention it, old stick, don't mention it. How's you, anyway?'

'As well as anyone can be in this rathole.' The young man smiled at Kathleen. 'At least I see you've been putting the time to good effect.'

Mulholland turned to the girl. 'Forgive me, m'dear. Peter, this is the lovely Kathy. We were fellow sufferers on the flight in this morning. And Kathy, this is Peter Mandrake. He's second secretary or something at the British Embassy here. Keeps an eye on the Commercial Section and looks after people like me dumped on him by London.'

Mandrake took her hand eagerly. 'Lovely to meet you, Kathy. Could do with a few more pretty faces to brighten the place up.'

'We've just finished the wine,' Mulholland apologised. 'Can I offer you a port perhaps?'

Mandrake grinned boyishly. 'Best offer I've had all day.'

Kathleen thought how pale his skin was, emphasising the short black hair with its fine sprinkling of dandruff. She guessed he spent most of his time indoors behind a desk.

Mulholland again trapped the passing wine waiter and ordered three ports.

At last the grinding monotony of the off-key background music stopped as the hidden pianist took a break.

It was like the sudden cessation of air-conditioning hum and it created an instant sense of relief.

'I've had to put up with that for years,' Mandrake said as the port arrived. 'That's why we never eat here if we can avoid it. At least there's a choice now – quite a few restaurants opening up, along with discos and nightclubs.'

Kathleen was surprised. 'I thought this country was on the verge of collapse.'

Mulholland directed the waiter to pour the ports. 'You will find, dear Kathy, that the dreaded disco appears everywhere in the world. War, famine, revolution – still you'll find the disco. Perhaps it's the need to beat the brain into oblivion.'

'Plenty to do for a young woman like you,' Mandrake assured.

Kathleen felt patronised. 'I'm a journalist, Mr Mandrake. I am not here to dance at discos.'

Mulholland laughed mischievously. 'That's put you in your place, Peter. Listen, perhaps you can help the young lady in her mission . . .'

Peter Mandrake listened attentively as Kathleen repeated her story.

'So you've written to various ministries here?' he asked when she had finished.

'The Mozambique Embassy in London was very helpful,' she replied. 'Told me who to write to. But I'm afraid there were no replies before I left. I thought that now I'm here, I might be able to see someone face to face. It was impossible to get through on the telephone from back home.'

Mandrake was sympathetic. 'And I'm afraid you can spend days waiting to get a meeting at a ministry. And then find there's no one to see you when you turn up. That's why you'll find we all swear and cuss a lot here. It's the sheer bloody frustration of this place – Sorry, see what I mean?'

'Can *you* help locate this person?' Mulholland asked.

30

'I'll see what I can do. You need someone with blat – influence.'

'Then I'm sure you're just the man, old stick,' Mulholland chortled and lay back in his chair with an air of triumph.

There was a sudden commotion at the entrance to the restaurant; all heads turned at the strident protestations of the female voice. A crowd of bemused waiters had gathered around the hapless Portuguese manager whose hands were wrung in humble supplication. Before him stood a stout, middle-aged woman in a full-length black dress, bedecked with jewellery. She was effectively adopting the air of a displeased monarch admonishing her subjects.

'Oh God, the Queen of Hearts,' Mandrake muttered. 'Off with their heads.'

'What's the matter?' Kathleen asked.

'Senhora da Gruta, that's the matter. When I saw you and Vincent sitting here I assumed she'd been in earlier.'

Kathleen and Mulholland shared expressions of total bewilderment.

'It's a sort of tradition,' Mandrake began lamely, then broke off as the woman started to walk towards their table. The manager and staff trailed timorously in her wake.

Kathleen watched the woman's approach with something resembling awe, sensing the intimidation of her presence. She moved in an imperious manner, her chin uptilted, almost creating the illusion that she was gliding on castors.

She drew to a halt before the alcove table. From beneath the short cut of henna-dyed hair, fierce little chips of anthracite glared. Her tight rosebud lips hardly parted as she spoke. 'You are, I suppose, *aware* of where you are sitting?'

Mandrake struggled manfully to his feet. 'Dama Veronique, one million apologies.'

Senhora da Gruta faltered in mid-flow. The eyes

31

squinted and the rosebud mouth puckered as she attempted to place the young diplomat.

'Peter Mandrake,' he offered. 'British Embassy. I thought you were still out of the country—'

'I've been in Maputo three days,' she snapped back.

Mandrake oozed charm. 'See how badly informed we British are? And how was South Africa?'

'It was South Africa.' Terse.

'You are looking well on it.'

Momentarily the expression softened. She inclined her head a centimetre in acknowledgement of the compliment.

Mandrake seized his moment. 'Dama Veronique, let me introduce my two guests. Kathy Coogan and Vincent Mulholland. They only arrived today. Of course they could have no idea that this alcove seat is always reserved for the da Gruta family.'

Her gloved hand was regally offered, down-turned. Kathleen felt she ought to kiss it, but resisted. Mulholland, too, made a big thing of shaking hands and smiling as though his life depended on it.

Mandrake was still pouring oil on troubled waters. Gallons of it . . . 'I've only just arrived myself. I was just saying we should move to another table . . .'

The royal hand was raised. 'It is no problem, Senhor Mandrake. You can expect nothing more from these stupid *kaffirs*, and the manager is no better. How could you good people have known?'

'Do join us for a drink,' Mulholland suggested, and earned a hard elbow nudge from Mandrake.

The rosebud blossomed into a tight smile and Kathleen could see where the lipstick had bled into the tiny lines around her mouth. 'Thank you, but no. I've just called in for a snack. And I've a headache, so I won't be good company. I'll forgo the family table for one night. It won't hurt.'

And she was gone, gliding down the restaurant with her attendant entourage of waiters.

'That was a close shave,' Mandrake breathed.

'And just who is the charming Veronique da Gruta?' Mulholland asked, fumbling in earnest for a cigarette.

Mandrake said: 'Her family is old colonial Portuguese. Used to own vast estates up Gutala way in the north of Zambezia province. Veronique's husband Jorge now manages the place for the government.'

'And the Queen of Hearts?' Mulholland asked.

Mandrake paused and all three watched as Senhora da Gruta cruised away from the buffet table clutching a plate loaded with cream cakes. Some snack. 'Oh, she spends most of her time here in Maputo or Jo'burg. Getting rid of his money as fast as poor old Jorge can earn it. She still blames the Mozambicans for what happened.'

Kathleen said: 'That's very sad.'

Mandrake grunted. 'Some might say it's no more than they deserved. The Portuguese weren't the best colonialists ever. They just bled the place dry to feed their empire. Even imported their own peasant stock to do all the menial work blacks would do in any other African country. You'll still see them driving taxis and doing menial jobs here. How many whites d'you see driving taxis in Nigeria or Zimbabwe? As a result when the Portuguese pulled out in '76, the blacks weren't qualified for anything. No one knew the first thing about running a business – even middle or lower management. There were no Mozambican plumbers or electricians. No administrators. Modern cities were handed over to uneducated blacks straight out of the shanties. Poor bastards.'

Kathleen frowned. 'I understood the Portuguese were quite liberal?'

Mandrake killed his port. 'You mean compared with apartheid in South Africa? Well, yes, in some respects. In that the Portuguese were happy to mix it with the blacks. Overseers were quite happy to have relationships with the girl workers in the fields, and South Africans used to come to Maputo – or Lourenço Marques as it was then –

33

to take advantage of the flourishing prostitution industry. It was the Bangkok of Africa.'

'That's not what I meant,' Kathleen protested.

'But that's how it was, Kathy. In theory Mozambicans could become full Portuguese citizens by adopting the Catholic religion, getting educated and working hard. *Assimulados* they're called. Well, when it came to independence these free citizens amounted to one per cent of the population. One per cent.'

'I see,' Kathleen said quietly.

'And before the Portuguese fled to South Africa or back to Lisbon, they destroyed everything they could. Burned records, destroyed factories and farm machinery. Frelimo inherited a bloody wasteland. So don't waste too much sympathy on the Veronique da Grutas of this place.' Mandrake smiled suddenly. 'I'm sorry. Getting a bit heavy there.'

She said: 'You like this country, don't you?'

'I'm going soft.' A dry laugh. 'No, truth to tell, there's a lot of sympathy for Mozambique amongst the whites working here. Despite the problems after independence, they'd worked hard to create an excellent health care and education programme. Then along came the *bandidos* – with embittered Portuguese exiles in Johannesburg planning and plotting their return.'

'Plotting for what?' Kathleen asked innocently.

Mandrake said: 'The overthrow of the Frelimo government and their own triumphant return to reclaim the old colony.'

Kathleen was puzzled. 'But I'd read it was the South Africans who back the bandits.'

'They have been, indeed, there's no doubt about that. But they had their own reasons for wanting to destabilise their black neighbours. But you'll find plenty of Renamo supporters in the Portuguese enclaves in South Africa—' He stopped abruptly and pulled a nervous smile. Kathleen wondered if he thought he'd said too much. After all, such talk hardly sounded very diplomatic. 'Listen, that damn pianist will start up again soon. I can't stand that. Let's pop over the road for a drink.'

The suggestion met with unanimous approval and, with a passing wave of acknowledgement to Senhora da Gruta, the three of them left the hotel restaurant.

What little traffic there was on the cratered dual carriageway outside the hotel comprised only dilapidated vehicles, invariably with at least one headlight missing. The air was warm and musky and Kathleen began to savour the smell and feel of Africa for the first time.

It was a short walk to the Sheik on Avenida Mao Tse-Tung, a well-appointed discotheque and bar complex run by a dour Portuguese businessman. To the strains of rap music emanating from the strobe-flashing basement, they mounted the carpeted stairs to the first floor bar where picture windows looked down onto the street.

Peter Mandrake shouldered his way through the cosmopolitan crowd to order three lagers.

He pointed out an immaculately dressed Mozambican seated with a circle of relatives and friends. 'That man's a deputy minister,' he whispered hoarsely to Kathleen above the hubbub of voices. 'A couple of those girls are his daughters.'

There was a sudden flow from the bar as half a dozen of the deputy minister's party decided it was time to dance and headed for the disco. As the bar area cleared, the man saw Peter Mandrake.

'Hey, Peter! Come and join us!'

Mandrake waved. He whispered to Kathleen: 'This might be your lucky break.' She followed Mandrake and Mulholland across the room. 'I really don't want to interrupt your evening, sir.'

The Mozambican laughed heartily. 'Not at all, Peter. I'm too old for all this discoing and all my young friends here can't wait for the chance to ditch me. They are just too well-mannered.'

As though in confirmation of his words, the rest of his party began to leave for the dance floor, feet tapping and bodies swaying to the beat as they went.

'Vincent Mulholland – just arrived from England – Deputy Minister Ngoça,' Mandrake introduced, then drew Kathleen out from behind him. 'And Miss Coogan, an up-and-coming young feature journalist.'

Her cheeks coloured at the lavish introduction as she found herself pushed forward to shake hands.

Ngoça was a tall, well-built and handsome man. The grip of his large hand was warm and dry. Friendly, intelligent eyes appraised her as she joined the others in the vacated seats around the coffee table.

'I am charmed, Miss Coogan. I trust our Ministry of Information is giving you all the assistance you require?' Ngoça said, seeming scarcely to have noticed Mulholland.

'Thank you, sir.'

Mandrake smiled to himself, then leaned forward. 'Actually, Mr Ngoça, the lady is being polite. She is having a slight communication problem with the ministry.'

Ngoça showed his teeth in a generous smile. 'That, Peter, does not surprise me – as you know. Rightly or wrongly I have earned the reputation of being a great puller of strings. Tell me, what is the problem?'

Thankful of the opening Mandrake had manoeuvred for her, Kathleen took a deep breath and outlined her hopes for the journalistic assignment.

As she talked the deputy minister relaxed in his armchair, one long leg crossed over the other, his hands linked beneath his chin. He listened without interruption. After a few minutes she began to feel more at ease, and steadily more aware of the man's charismatic presence. His black curled hair was greying at the temples, and there were silver threads in the delicate goatee beard that decorated his chin. Mid-forties, she decided. Well-educated and with a good taste in clothes. The suit was expensive: a lightweight blue-grey material with a sparkle of silk in the weave. No ostentatious jewellery, just a gold watch and a simple ring on his wedding finger.

When she had finished speaking, Ngoça thoughtfully touched his lower lip with his forefinger. 'So by tracing your step-cousin, you think you may unearth a human interest story set against the background of what has happened to us in Mozambique since we became independent?'

She blinked; it was a very succinct summary. 'I hope so, sir. But even if I don't find him, I'm sure I'll get some good material during the search.'

Ngoça nodded sagely, but she couldn't help wondering if he thought her a fool. Surely, she thought, the government would be really interested only in a story which added fuel to their case in the international propaganda war with South Africa. But he said: 'I'll have to speak with Immigration records. It won't be easy. You've no idea how long he's been in the country? It could be one month, one year or five years. Even longer.'

She felt a little uncomfortable at causing the man such unreasonable nuisance. 'I'm afraid not.'

'What kind of work did your cousin do?'

Kathleen hesitated. 'Er – he was a professional soldier.'

A ghost of a smile passed over Ngoça's face. 'Then he came to the right country. There are several European companies assisting our military effort with contract soldiers. Guarding factories and plantations, or training our special forces. They may know something of him.' Ngoça carefully cocked one eyebrow. 'Unless, of course, he is working with the Renamo *bandidos*.'

Kathleen swallowed hard. 'I hope not.'

'So do I, Miss Coogan.'

Mulholland said: 'Did he have any other special skills,

Kathy? I mean what did he do when he first left the British Army?'

That was a thought. Brightly she said: 'He helped on the family farms. In fact I believe he spent much of his childhood on the various family farms.'

Ngoça nodded. 'So he would know something about livestock or crops?'

Her smile widened. 'Oh, yes, it would be second nature to him.'

Mulholland again. 'What did he do in the Army?'

'He joined – what is it? REME? The Royal Engineers.'

'Ah,' Ngoça said, 'so he was both a farmer and an engineer . . .' He closed his eyes and whistled softly. 'That might be a qualification for working with one of the international aid agencies, I suppose . . . I'll get Immigration to pay special attention to the aid agencies.'

Kathleen's eyes widened. 'That might narrow the field.'

Ngoça chuckled. 'My dear Miss Coogan, there are only thirty government and sixty-three independent aid agencies working in Mozambique at the present time.'

Kathleen felt foolish. 'I'm sorry, I didn't realise. If I can help in any way . . .?'

The deputy minister looked at Mandrake, the warmth draining from his dark eyes. 'Well, my friend Peter here could ask his government to stop supporting South Africa. To pressure Pretoria to renounce Renamo. To halt the carnage!' Ngoça raised his hand as Mandrake was about to respond. 'Forget it, Peter, I have heard it all before. But, Miss Coogan, *you* can do something. When you write your articles and features, tell the world what has happened to us. Tell the world that the genocide here is second only to that in Cambodia. That these are the killing fields of Africa. Tell them of the million Mozambicans who have died because of Renamo, and the six million dollars worth of damage inflicted by them. Tell of the five million displaced people and the one million refugees who've fled their own land.' He paused momentarily, a wildness in his eyes. 'It has been said before, but no one listens. Say it again, Miss Coogan. Tell the world what the South African dogs have done to one of the most beautiful and fertile countries on God's earth. Please, will you do that?'

After the heat and tension of the encounter in the bar, the sweet night air was like a balm as Kathleen walked back to the hotel with Mulholland and Peter Mandrake.

'Some speech,' Mulholland observed.

'Some politician,' Mandrake added. 'A good man, but underrated. Still only a deputy minister.'

'Why's that?' Kathleen asked.

Mandrake stifled a yawn. 'He missed out on Frelimo's early struggle against the Portuguese. He was fortunate to be among the one per cent of *assimulados* who prospered. He was studying in the States while all the freedom fighters were in the bush. I suppose naturally all the 'Heroes of the Revolution' got all the plum jobs. So now friend Ngoça has to be patient. A question of dead men's shoes.'

'A shame,' Kathleen murmured.

As they re-entered the hotel lobby Mulholland glanced at his watch. 'Nearly eleven. How about a brandy in the lounge?'

'Sounds good to me,' Mandrake rejoined.

Kathleen shook her head. 'No thank you, Vincent. My head's swimming and I feel absolutely shattered. It's been a very long day. Thank you so much for all you've done.'

Mandrake said: 'Look, Kathy, I've got the morning off tomorrow. Why don't I show you round the town?'

She smiled gratefully. 'That would be wonderful, Peter.'

With his wife just returned to the UK for a holiday, he could think of no more pleasant a way of spending the day than with what he was sure would be the most sought-after girl in Maputo. 'It would be my pleasure. Say nine?'

With the walls swaying gently, Kathleen Coogan took the stairs to the first floor and wandered along the lofty corridor until she located her room. Closing the door she fell back against it and shut her eyes.

It was all too much. The new faces, the vivid colours and sounds of Africa, the people; so much to understand. But now she had some contacts, friends almost. She was beginning – just beginning – to feel in control. This wasn't like reporting back home. This was breaking new ground, *real* journalism.

Meanwhile in the solemn silence of the Polana Hotel lounge, amid the potted plants, Vincent Mulholland savoured his brandy.

'Nice girl,' Mandrake said. 'Did it go as you wanted?'

'Splendidly.'

'So what's the problem over Kathy? I don't understand.'

'C'mon, old stick, you know better than to ask. Anyway, it's all something and nothing.'

'She seemed a bit unsure of herself, a bit naïve.'

'Her first time in Africa,' Mulholland concurred. 'A girl from the bogs.'

'And you've got all you want?'

'For the moment.'

Mandrake made his move. 'Time I wasn't here. Long day tomorrow.'

Mulholland's hand landed firmly on the diplomat's arm. 'Just one small favour, old stick?'

'Of course.'

'I suppose you couldn't have a discreet word with our man in Pretoria? Young Kathy visited one of her brothers in South Africa on her way here. An engineer, works for some big outfit. Get our man to run a check, eh?'

40

For some reason Peter Mandrake resented accepting the paper napkin on which a name had been scrawled. He released himself from Mulholland's grip and stood up.

'And, Peter old stick, no word to little Miss Coogan when you take her out tomorrow, there's a good chap.'

2

'For God's sake, Branagh, it's going to happen again. We've got to get out of here while we still can!'

Jorge da Gruta's exasperated plea turned all the young heads in the Sunday school class in the mud-brick hut at Tumbo, one of the outlying villages of the Gutala plantations. A dozen pairs of marble white eyes stared in apprehension from emaciated small faces.

The Portuguese plantation manager was short with a swollen girth held in check by a thick leather trouser belt. Below the hair, which he raked in tramlines across his balding scalp, his lumpy face wore its perpetually worried expression. Today it was probably justified.

'Have I wasted my time driving fifteen miles across the plantation?' he demanded. His liquid brown eyes were magnified into muddy puddles by the pebble lenses of his tortoiseshell spectacles. 'Eh? Risked my life being shot or blown up on a mine?'

Mike Branagh scratched at his sun-bleached beard. The attentive faces of the village children awaited his reaction in anxious silence.

They knew, every one of them, from the teenagers to the five-year-old mites. They all knew what it meant if and when the bandits came. Not one had a family which had not been touched by the raid two years earlier. Someone killed or abducted, never to be seen again. Homes destroyed or possessions looted.

'Not here, Jorge,' Branagh said quietly. 'I'll see you outside.'

The plantation manager shook his head in an expression of impatient despair and stepped back out into the scorching Mozambique sun.

Meanwhile Branagh turned to the class. The children were all squatting on the floor of what normally served as the living room of the mud-brick hut that had been his home since he had moved out of the hotel in Gutala.

All eyes were on him. He cut an impressive figure, tall with broad shoulders and a tanned physique kept lean by heavy labouring work around the village and a diet no different from the natives. No one ever got too fat on mealie.

A pregnant teenage girl's hand shot up anxiously in the front row. It was fifteen-year-old Lisa Matusi, the younger sister of the girl with whom Branagh had been sharing his bed for the past four years.

'Yes, Lisa?' Branagh said in Portuguese.

'Please, Senhor Mike, is it true that the *bandidos* are coming?'

Branagh played it down; he had his reasons for not wanting the entire village to disappear into the bush. 'They won't give us any trouble this time, Lisa. We've got the militia in Gutala for protection.'

Lisa looked sullen. 'They will just run away.'

'Have faith,' Branagh said, but knew the girl could very well be right. Hadn't he himself witnessed what happened the last time? The ill-equipped militia knew that Renamo avoided direct confrontation with armed Frelimo troops unless they could achieve overwhelming superiority. So who could blame them if each just fired his rationed half-magazine before taking off into the bush with the rest of the population?

'Now listen carefully,' he said. 'I want you all to go *straight* home to your compounds. Don't go wandering in the fields or to the eucalyptus woods to play. As you have heard there are *bandidos* in the area. Warn your parents, but tell them I intend that things will be different this

43

time. It will be safer for you to stay at home rather than run into the bush because Renamo could be anywhere.' He smiled with a reassurance he didn't completely feel. 'Same time next week. God bless.'

He stepped aside to avoid the flying arms and legs as the youngsters scampered for the doorway. You didn't have to ask to know which ones had seen sights that no adult, let alone a child, should ever have to witness. Children they might be on the outside, but God only knew what dark confusion fermented inside those cute black candytuft heads.

Lisa was the last to leave, waddling under the weight of her inflated belly.

'I'll give you a lift home, Lisa,' Branagh said.

Her eyes flashed guiltily. 'I think I walk, Senhor Mike.'

Branagh could guess why. Her trip to Sunday school was the ideal chance to steal a visit to her boyfriend whom her parents had banned her from seeing.

'Not today, sweetheart, it's too dangerous. You heard what I told everyone.'

Her face crumpled as she stared at the floor.

Branagh said: 'I've got to go to the strip. Young Artur will be giving me a hand.'

Lisa's eyes suddenly twinkled like Christmas tree lights before she quickly attempted to play down her enthusiasm for meeting the father of her child. 'If you say so, Senhor Mike.'

He stepped into the sunshine to find da Gruta waiting impatiently by his dilapidated Toyota four-wheel drive.

'Well?' the plantation manager demanded. 'What are you going to do?' He jabbed a thumb at his vehicle. 'I've got your boss with me. He wants you out too.'

Branagh smiled and lit a cigarette. 'You mean he wants himself out. He gets in such a flap I'm surprised he doesn't fly all the way to Maputo.' He illustrated the point with his elbows, then stooped to wave at the pinched pink face of Leif Månson pressed against the glass.

The Swedish boss of the Direct Action relief charity wound down the passenger window. Branagh noted with amusement that he wore one of his favoured safari suits in a delicate shade of lavender denim.

'Please don't hang about, Michael. It's getting very hot in here.' Beneath the shock of cropped snowy hair the pink face was drenched with sweat.

'A flight's not due for another hour,' Branagh replied easily. 'So shouldn't you get out of there? I know you Swedes like saunas, but that's ridiculous.'

The Irishman opened the door and Månson almost fell out, dropping his small leather clutch bag. He retrieved it and swiftly composed himself, brushing at the knife-edge creases of his trousers.

'I've always meant to ask you, Leif, what do you keep in that bag?'

The Swede looked indignant. 'My credit cards, of course.'

Branagh glanced around at the primitive huts and the blue hills on the horizon. It was a hundred miles by impassable, terrorist-controlled road to the nearest derelict city. 'Sure, that's a good idea,' he murmured. 'Let's hope the Russians accept American Express.'

'The Russians?'

'The helicopter due in at lunch time is flown by the Soviets. They're doing a favour distributing aid. They're not under any obligation to fly out passengers.'

Månson turned imploringly to da Gruta. 'But surely they wouldn't leave Europeans stranded – not when there's a Renamo attack expected?'

Branagh put a consoling arm around the Swede's shoulders, knowing full well he hated being touched. 'Don't worry, I'm sure I can persuade Fred to take you out of here. I'd even pay for the privilege myself.'

'Fred?'

'The pilot.' Branagh turned to the plantation manager. 'As you're here, Jorge, perhaps you'd fill me in on the latest.'

'Three villages have been attacked this morning – over on the eastern edge,' da Gruta replied. 'That puts Renamo at no more than fifteen miles away. And it puts us in easy reach of a day's march.'

'What's the military doing?' Branagh asked.

Da Gruta shrugged. 'What they're always doing – running around like chickens without heads. The local militia is coming out from Gutala to protect all these outlying villages – if they can get their vehicles to start. And the government is sending down 7 Brigade troops from Guamba. Only our airstrip here is too short for the Antonov. So they will have to come by road.'

'That'll take days.'

Månson interrupted: 'You see, Michael, we *must* get out on that flight. And *I'll* get it in the neck from my regional manager if anything happens to *you*!'

'Charming,' Branagh murmured. But in truth he did feel a mild sympathy for his boss. Like the rest of the relief agencies Direct Action did not encourage its aid workers to work in the front line; only the church organisations allowed their people to take that risk if they were so determined.

'Senhor Månson is right,' da Gruta confirmed. 'Frelimo has ordered the evacuation of all European personnel until control of the area has been assured.'

'Fuck Frelimo.'

Colour was now flooding back into Månson's cheeks. 'And I am ordering you to leave!'

Branagh smiled thinly. 'Lucky for you, Leif, my Swedish vocabulary is very limited. But if you think about it, I can hardly leave Maraika and her family to fend for themselves and piss off with you lot, now can I?'

'She's only a fucking black tart,' da Gruta muttered with a total lack of comprehension.

Branagh's green eyes narrowed a fraction. 'But I happen to be the fella the black tart fucks, right?'

Månson adopted an aloof, po-faced expression. Curiously illiberal for a Swede, he did not approve of his staff fraternising with native Mozambicans.

Jorge da Gruta just shrugged and consulted his wrist-watch. 'The helicopter could arrive early and we don't want to miss it – we'll go on to the strip.'

The Irishman nodded. 'I'll see you up there.'

'That's more like it!' Månson said with a smile.

Branagh's patience was evaporating. 'Because someone has to bring the supplies back *here*.'

'Branagh – you're, you're—' In his fury Månson had difficulty finding the word.

'Fired? Isn't that the third time this year?' The Irishman turned on his heel and joined Lisa Matusi in the battered Direct Action Land-Rover.

By the time they reached the edge of the village, they'd already picked up passengers. Two women, each with an infant strapped to her back by means of a colourful sarong-like *capulana*, and three men. All carried various goods with which to do business at the airstrip. It appeared that Fred the Russian had established a thriving private trade on the black market.

The assortment of shacks and rondavels gave way to a patchwork of viridescent rice terraces that glittered beside the meandering river. Then the rutted laterite track turned away from the embankment, gaining height to carve its way through a bobbing sea of ripening corncobs. These were the irresistible lure for the hundreds of pigeons that wheeled overhead and awaited their moment in the branches of the flat-topped acacias.

Small crop fields of papaya, groundnut and sugar cane followed before the hill flattened out into a plateau of buffalo grass which had been scythed into a landing strip long enough to take a light aircraft.

Miraculously word of the expected flight had spread by bush telegraph and already a small crowd was gathering beside da Gruta's Toyota. Lisa spotted her boyfriend

47

and scrambled out hurriedly, leaving Branagh to scan the skies for the impending arrival.

It was twenty minutes before the ugly clatter of the Soviet Mil-8 helicopter could be heard on the breeze, although it was no more than a distant brown smudge in the noon heat haze. The machine canted jauntily above the far hills, making its approach low and fast because guerrillas could be hidden anywhere in the bush beneath it. There had not yet been reports of the bandits using portable surface-to-air missiles, but even a lucky Kalashnikov round could spell disaster. The helicopter's approach was the manoeuvre of a veteran pilot and designed to take any enemy presence by surprise.

It swooped low over the adjacent stand of upright eucalyptus trees and slowed abruptly, bucking like a tightly reined colt. With a swagger, the bulbous khaki fuselage emblazoned with the red star of the USSR lowered itself into the maelstrom of its own creation. Before the twin Isotov engines had died and the dust settled, enthusiasm overcame caution and the villagers closed in. The five rotor blades were still churning as the rear clamshell doors beneath the tailboom swung open.

Branagh called out unloading instructions while willing hands began lifting out the hemp sacks of dried fish. The two Soviet crew members made no attempt to assist, content to light up cigarettes and watch indifferently as the underweight villagers struggled with their loads.

It was a few moments before the massive bulk of the pilot, Fred Petkus, appeared at the sliding side hatch. He dropped to the grass with amazing lightness for a man of his size. The leather jacket no more managed to restrain his enormous bull-like chest than the flying helmet was able to contain the wild overgrowth of beard and moustache on the granite quarry face. When he saw Branagh, he grinned wickedly, sunlight blinking on his gold-filled tooth.

'Hey, Irish, just see what I got for you!' he boomed in heavily accented English.

He turned and dragged the heavy crate of Jameson Irish Whiskey to the hatch and dumped it on the grass.

'Fred, you're a genius.'

Petkus gave a self-congratulatory smile. 'Twelve days' supply. And maybe you need it, eh? I hear the *matsangas* are in the area.' He always used the alternative name – after the first Renamo commander – because he believed that to call them 'bandits' belittled the combat effort of his crew. 'With this lot you sleep through the next World War if you want.'

'How d'you do it, Fred?'

The Russian tapped his veined nose. 'You don't want to know. Just pay. And US or rand only. The helicopter isn't big enough to take meticais.'

Branagh dug into the back pocket of his drill trousers and thumbed through the grubby sheaf of dollar bills.

A voice said: 'If that's a week's supply, you're paying a month's salary for it.'

Hackles rose on Branagh's neck. Without turning he said: 'Fred, meet my boss. Leif Månson. And Jorge from the plantation.'

Petkus shook hands with da Gruta, then looked down at the slightly built man with his pink scrubbed face and thatch of white hair. 'Hey, a Swede! I've always wanted to meet a Swede.' He stepped back to take in the safari suit. 'And a pretty Swede at that.' He took the man's hand, crushing it carelessly in his enthusiasm until the tiny bones crackled. He looked at Branagh. 'Never I go to Sweden and always I want to. Hey, Irish, you remember I tell you my big brother, he loved Scandinavia.' He surrendered the crumpled hand which Månson withdrew with the speed of light.

It was the third time Branagh had heard the tale of the Russian's brother, and still he didn't believe a word of it. 'Listen, Fred, I wonder if you could do us a favour. My boss here and Jorge are anxious to evacuate—'

'*Matsangas?*'

'The government's advised all Europeans to get out by any means possible—'

Månson burst in: 'If we could possibly get a ride back in your helicopter?' At seeing what he took to be a hesitation, he added earnestly: 'Do you take American Express?'

Petkus blinked, and then began to smile as he saw the Swede's serious expression. He'd read fear in too many men's faces not to recognise it. He placed an arm around Månson's shoulders and applied a ferocious hug. 'Swedish, I'm afraid I only take the Visa and the Mastercard.' He guffawed at his own joke. 'But as you are a friend of Irish here, I will do it for nothing – if there is room.'

Månson pulled away anxiously. 'What do you mean, room? You have just unloaded.'

The Russian turned towards the crowd setting up their wares and provisions on the strip as though it were an impromptu market stall. 'All this – goods people want to sell me.'

Branagh stepped in before Månson had apoplexy. 'I'm sure Fred will be able to squeeze you in, Leif.'

'And you, Irish, do you want to go?'

'No thanks, Fred, I'll be having too much to do here.'

'When can we leave?' Månson pressed.

Petkus twisted an end of his moustache around his forefinger. 'As soon as I've done my business. Maybe one hour.'

Månson glared at the motley range of wares displayed for the Russian's consideration.

At that moment the Soviet flight engineer sauntered over to their group and began talking to Petkus. Half a dozen heated sentences were exchanged, the engineer jabbing a dismissive thumb over his shoulder at the helicopter.

Petkus returned to his would-be passengers.

'Sorry, Swedish, there is a change of plan. Sorry, Jorge.'

Månson's eyes widened. 'Yes?'

'Yes. I am afraid we don't go no place. Our generator is fucked.'

The Swede's mouth dropped open, and instantly he felt his heart begin to palpitate. 'Generator? But don't you always carry two? What about the spare?'

Petkus's gold tooth glittered with menace. 'That *is* the spare.' He turned to Branagh and da Gruta. 'This is what happens when you fly a rubbish airplane for a rubbish country—' He held out his palms in a gesture of helplessness. 'And to think Gorbachev wants us to compete with the West in a free market! Huh, we can't even keep spares for the few helicopters we have in this stinking place! The Soviet Union will be bankrupt and starving within five years, you mark my words, and I will be one of thousands of pilots without a job. Or sweeping the snow with the *babushkas*!' His big head shook sadly.

'From what I've seen here,' Månson observed tartly, 'you will make a fortune on your own black market.'

Petkus glowered.

Da Gruta intervened. 'How long will the delay be?'

'Maybe tomorrow, maybe days. Most of our helicopters run on their spare generators. One will probably have to be flown up from Maputo – if there are any in stock.'

'So we are stranded.' Månson just managed to keep the squeak of panic from his voice.

Branagh said: 'Then you'd all best come back to my place. I'll warn Maraika we'll be having guests for supper.'

'Ah, the lovely Maraika,' Petkus crooned.

'You've enough food?' Månson asked, dreading the thought of having to eat mealie.

Branagh stooped to lift the crate of Jameson. 'More important, we have enough drink.'

*

'Maraika,' Fred Petkus growled huskily, 'you are the most beautiful woman in Africa. I want to make mad and passionate love to you!'

He was seated in Branagh's hut with Månson and Jorge da Gruta, and watched with undisguised lust while the nineteen-year-old bent to serve the maize beer. In private even the reticent Swede would have to concede that Maraika Matusi was a magnificent creature as she blushed as deeply as her polished ebony skin would allow. She was exceptionally tall, perhaps only two inches shorter than Branagh's six feet. There was much speculation that some Somali blood coursed through her veins. It would explain her long clean limbs and high cheekbones which set off her vivacious dark eyes to perfection.

She giggled deliciously, her long lashes fluttering with embarrassment.

'Leave her alone, you godless heathen,' Branagh said, entering the spartan room with a tray of corncakes. 'Besides you couldn't afford to pay her hairdressing bills!'

Maraika's porcelain smooth brow fractured beneath the untypically long black hair which she wore pinned tightly back from her forehead. In the four years he had lived with her she had changed beyond recognition. From a gangling toothy teenager with a scalp of tight black curls to a willowy vision who would have graced any fashion house catwalk. It was not his doing; it was purely her own drive to emulate the sophisticated women she had seen in the hotel lobbies of the capital Maputo. But no matter how she strove, that sophistication eluded her. No hairstyle, no new frock, no splash of make-up would ever change that. For she had no education and no experience of Western life. All she knew came from the pictures in magazines. Sometimes she felt that she would always be just a girl from the bush.

She delivered Branagh an angry glare before continuing to distribute the beer with an assumed air of haughty indifference.

'It was my own fault,' Branagh went on. 'I once brought her back some old *Vogue* magazines from Maputo. Boy oh boy, was that a mistake. Now I have to get her down to the capital at least four times a year or else she throws a moody and life's not worth living.'

Fred Petkus saw the hurt in her eyes and decided to make a friend for life. 'Well, Maraika, I think your hair it looks bloody wonderful.'

Her face was transformed, although she failed to notice that his eyes were focused on the slender line of the taut red *capulana* rather than her hair. 'Thank you, Senhor Fred, you say very nice thing.'

As she passed behind their guests she poked a savage pink tongue at Branagh, then smiled sweetly and pushed none too gently past him.

He grinned after her. God, how he loved her naïve charm and natural grace. The way she tried so hard to understand the ways of the outside world. And her frustration when she invariably failed. Yet still she tried however angry it made her with herself or with him. And, God, how he loved her when she got mad.

Månson was saying: 'What I want to know is what we are going to do if there is a Renamo attack, I mean should we be keeping watch now?'

Da Gruta leaned forward. 'The one predictable thing about Renamo is their method of attack. It is always just before dawn.'

Petkus interrupted: 'So at least you will have a good night's sleep.' The tooth twinkled. 'Even if you do wake up to find your throat cut.'

Da Gruta added: 'The boys from the first villages attacked said they thought it was Napoleão's lot. Recognised some of the men from previous raids.'

'Who is this Napoleão?' Månson asked anxiously.

53

Branagh felt he couldn't take much more of the man's bleating. The two of them always had been chalk and cheese. Nevertheless he did his best to keep the irritation from his voice as he explained: 'He's one of the special Shock Battalion commanders from the Gorongosa region in central Mozambique. Manica province. Of course Renamo units are always on the move, but his thugs have been in this district before. Napoleão is a *nom de guerre* naturally – all Renamo commanders use them to protect their identities. But some of those who've seen him and lived to tell the tale reckon he used to be one of the Frelimo government army commanders. Every now and then he turns up here to make a pest of himself.'

Månson frowned. 'You don't sound very concerned about the possibility of another attack?'

Branagh took a sip of the milky green beer. Thoughtfully he said: 'Oh, I'm concerned all right. I've seen the atrocities they're capable of. But nevertheless they're hardly the Regiments of Guards. They pick and choose their targets carefully, preferably a village with no militia. If there is a Frelimo presence they'll attack in overwhelming numbers so that the opposition runs.'

Petkus agreed and gave a snort of derision. 'The *matsangas* are no better than Frelimo troops. They are both rubbish! If anyone shoots back at an African he turns tail and flees. Trouble is the government troops won't hold their ground – even *if* they do have ammunition. I know, I have seen this.' He turned to his rapt audience. 'And you know why, eh? Because we Soviets trained most of their officers! You see my helicopter crew earlier – they hate these black bastards, they despise them. We don't train them, we *play* at training and give them all our own worst faults. Our instructors get away with doing as little work as possible – knock off early to hit the vodka and fuck some sweet black pussy.' He thumped the roughly made coffee table with his fist, spilling the unmatched collection of glasses and chipped mugs. 'No wonder the *matsangas* walk all over them. *They* are trained by South Africans, Rhodesians and Portugeezers!'

'Portuguese,' Jorge da Gruta corrected with indignation.

'That's what I say, Portugeezers,' Petkus said, before swallowing his beer in three successive gulps without pause. He wiped the back of his hand across his mouth and belched lightly. 'I tell you, put guns in our hands and shoot back and you won't see this Napoleão's arse for dust. I tell you, I tell you!'

Månson glanced hopefully at his companions. 'Do we have a gun?'

Da Gruta grunted without enthusiasm. 'I've acquired an old Soviet bolt-action rifle. But it's never even been test-fired – I've only got the five rounds that came with it.'

Månson paled. 'We have only five rounds between us?'

'I and my rubbish crew each have a Makarov pistol for emergency use if we ditch,' Petkus added, helping himself to the pitcher of maize beer.

'What about you, Branagh?' da Gruta asked.

'I'm an aid worker, Jorge. Direct Action doesn't encourage its people to tote arms. We rely on the local militia.'

Da Gruta examined his wristwatch. 'Well, there's no sign of them yet. Perhaps the militia aren't coming.'

'But there must be some means of protecting ourselves,' Månson implored. 'Apart from running away.'

'I've been working on something,' Branagh said and stood up. He called to young Artur who was sitting with the pregnant Lisa on the porch. 'Go and fetch Francisco for me will you – as quickly as you can.'

It was ten minutes before Artur returned with the village carpenter. He was a good-looking, cheerful man in his thirties with smiling intelligent eyes and a small tufted beard that resembled black lichen. Månson noticed that there was something oddly lopsided about his face, then

55

realised that the man only had one ear. All that was left was a puckering of gristly membrane around the hole.

Branagh saw the Swede's stare. 'Renamo's work. They were annoyed when Francisco refused to co-operate. Sliced it off with a razor, then for an encore they made him eat it.'

Christ, Månson tried to say, but the word stuck in his craw.

Branagh said: 'How are the bow-traps, Francisco?'

The African smiled with pride. 'I have complete thirty sets now. Finest eucalyptus, good spring.'

'Bows?' Månson interrupted. 'You mean bloody bows and arrows? For God's sake, Michael, this isn't Agincourt. You can't fight Renamo with bows and arrows!'

'I'm talking about bow-traps,' Branagh explained patiently. 'As you said yourself, Leif, I've witnessed bandit attacks before. I know how they operate, and I can see a weakness in their method. They always approach a target village at night. It's a favourite expression of theirs: 'the night belongs to Renamo'. Ask yourself their reaction if, unexpectedly, they find that it *doesn't* belong to them after all?'

Månson was confused. 'I still don't see . . .'

Petkus began to chuckle. 'Hey, Irish, I think I understand your plan. Very funny, very good. I think this thing can work.' He scratched vigorously at his beard. 'Also I have an idea. You remember last week I deliver cans of paint?'

'The wrong stuff, the red gloss?'

The Russian laughed throatily. 'I think so – as you say in England – it is time to paint this village red!'

Månson and da Gruta exchanged glances in almost total bemusement.

The militia finally arrived in mid-afternoon having had to walk the ten miles from Gutala because they couldn't get their truck to start.

Trained only in the rudimentary use of their weapons, for which they had only been issued one magazine apiece, they were quite relieved to receive instructions from Branagh and Petkus who had begun to take a great interest in the defence of the village. It was the way that the Russian treated the life-or-death situation as one big joke which disconcerted both Månson and da Gruta. Neither had any confidence that such an improvised and harebrained scheme could work.

Everything they needed was stored together to await nightfall. It was imperative that no Renamo lookout in the hills be able to observe the defence plan being put into operation. And no spy in the village be given the chance to warn the bandits in advance. The Frelimo commissar then briefed all the villagers to go to their homes and stay there under pain of arrest and imprisonment. It was a harsh threat but necessary. Anyone wandering the perimeter of the village would invariably trigger one of the bow-sets with possibly fatal consequences.

As twilight faded the carpenter Francisco appeared with his hand-picked group of helpers and the crew of the Soviet helicopter.

It took three hours to set up all the bow-traps, driving in the support stakes that held the eucalyptus saplings horizontally above the ground, and tilted upwards to aim at the torso of any intruder. The bows were braced, restrained by an elementary toggle-release system. From this a taut cord was run around two pegs until it finally stretched across the approach to form an anchored tripwire. Only then were the arrows, with their tips of folded and beaten tin, slotted into place.

In addition two pig-traps were rigged. Saplings with twelve-inch stakes attached were bound to slender tree stems, then drawn back to full tension, just waiting for a passer-by to release the tripwire.

While Branagh supervised the work, Petkus and his crew set about digging a shallow trench. They filled it with cans of oil-based paint mixed with white spirit, avgas containers and quantities of jam from the catering tins kept in the Direct Action food store.

The Russian then proceeded to dismantle one of the helicopter's rocket distress flares. First removing the small parachute and flare-pot from the top, he sawed through the plastic casing in order to draw out the inner sleeve and buried the rocket nose first in the side of the trench. From it he ran out a command wire to trigger the pull-release mechanism.

Finally satisfied, he placed the flare-pot of magnesium-based material amid the paint pots in direct line with the buried rocket. When that fired, he decided, there would be a fireball like a miniature Hiroshima, the hot jam acting like napalm.

By the time all the work was complete the air of expectancy had become contagious; even Månson and da Gruta shared the rising sense of anticipation.

After the imposed silence of the evening's work the sudden burst of conversation and laughter in Branagh's hut was a welcome release valve for the mounting tension. Maize beer flowed and the smell of cooked meat and hot groundnut sauce added to the growing feeling of camaraderie. A daring plan shared and the die cast.

Da Gruta picked up the ancient Soviet rifle by his side and offered it to Branagh. 'You'd better have this. I couldn't shoot a buck at ten paces.'

Branagh shook his head. 'I stopped being a soldier fourteen years ago, Jorge.'

'You remember that precisely?'

'I remember.'

The plantation manager was puzzled. 'You've rigged up those deadly devices – what's the difference?'

Branagh reached to extract a bottle from the crate of Jameson. 'A big difference. I don't have to pull the trigger. If a *bandido* walks into a trap, he's killed himself.'

Fred Petkus dragged his eyes away from Maraika and

regarded his friend in silence. Maybe it was true what he had heard about the craziness of Irish logic?

Napoleão was a big man in every way.

Bodily his tall frame had long ago swollen to the proportions of an overripe watermelon, thanks to years of privileged living. His huge belly hung precariously over the belt of his camouflage trousers, which had to be made with specially reinforced stitching by the camp women.

Because of his size he moved ponderously, his tree-trunk thighs rubbing together like those of a massive black bull elephant. His face even had an elephant's benign eyes, moist and deceptively jovial with just a mischievous hint of craft. Nowadays the yellowing whites increasingly reflected his consumption of copious quantities of maize beer.

'Is everyone in position?' he demanded.

Even when he spoke in a whisper as now, his voice had a booming resonance that set his jowls quivering and the flesh of his chin bouncing around his short neck.

His second-in-command João Chande was a thoroughly efficient individual, reed thin with an eye for detail and a convinced believer in the benefits of vicious discipline. That derived from his time in Mozambique's Pide secret police under Portuguese colonial rule. Had he not been so, Napoleão might not have survived for seven years as a Renamo commander.

As it was he could rely implicitly on his aide to run the crack shock battalion like clockwork while he indulged himself in the twin pleasures of beer and small boys. His prowess was legendary amongst his followers, and he was never shy to strut naked in the camp shower with his awesome genitalia and impressively heavy scrotum proudly on view. Young men might envy, but would more wisely turn away. All was part of his fearsome reputation.

'All is ready, Colonel,' João Chande replied crisply. 'Our main column is one mile from Tumbo. They will

59

take out the main targets: the medical post, the Frelimo commissar's compound, and the Direct Action aid hut.'

The exertion of the night march was beginning to show. Napoleão mopped the pearls of sweat from his face with a handkerchief. 'Ah, the Irishman – what's his name?'

'Branagh.' Chande had a secret policeman's memory for names.

'I personally want him dead. Every time he gets involved with a village things happen. New medical posts or schools.' Napoleão cleared the phlegm from his throat and spat into a bed of ferns by his feet. 'I will come with you on the right flank attack. That will give me a better view of what is happening.'

Inwardly the second-in-command groaned. He had a grudging respect for Napoleão. They had been trained together at camps in the South African Transvaal homeland of Gazankula near Phalaborwa in the early eighties by ruthless instructors.

What Napoleão lacked in soldierly skills, he made up for in his enthusiastic and inventive terror tactics and his utter disregard for human dignity or life.

Sometimes it occurred to Chande that Napoleão might even enjoy a certain kind of orgasmic satisfaction at viewing the atrocities carried out at his command. The one-time secret policeman had come across such people before.

But tonight, to have his lumbering commander at his side in this attack was not something that Chande relished. Not one bit.

'Let's proceed,' Napoleão rasped into Chande's ear. The officer discreetly drew back from the sickly sweet smell of beer on the colonel's breath.

Chande raised his hand. Instantly the signal was acknowledged by the two other company commanders on his right. Above the monotonous rasp of the giant cicadas the rustle of movement in the undergrowth was scarcely noticeable.

The three companies separated, each following its pre-determined line of attack, each knowing exactly what was expected of it. A precision operation.

Wherever possible an approach was made using the obliging cover of a eucalyptus copse, popular for providing quick-growing building materials for the villagers. The secondary jungle that sprang up beneath their lofty upright columns provided ideal concealment for men on the move.

The main party had already left the safety of the copse and was travelling swiftly through a swaying field of mealie to join the laterite track to Tumbo. On the far flank, the second company would be advancing fast on the outlying shanties to the east.

Judiciously Napoleão had chosen to travel breathlessly on the shortest route with the third company. As the ground levelled out the going became easier. The lead bandits selected a raised track that ran along the embankment between the gurgling river and the stagnant rice paddies. Above their heads the waterside weeping bean trees whispered an urgent but unheeded warning to the sleeping village ahead.

Napoleão stopped suddenly. Ahead of him the three lead bandits shuffled to a halt; they could hardly be unaware that their commander's heavy, careless footfalls had ceased.

'What is it, Colonel?' Chande enquired anxiously.

Napoleão clutched at his chest. 'My heart is thumping!' he wheezed noisily. 'Can we slow up?'

'It's just nerves,' Chande replied, scarcely hiding his annoyance. 'We all get it. It'll stop when the shooting starts.'

Napoleão's eyes bulged with indignation. 'Nerves? How dare you! I'm a sick man.'

'Colonel, we must press on. This is a coordinated attack. We're nearly there – this is where we leave the track.'

61

'Go on, I'm all right now.'

The lead bandits smirked to each other. They'd seen Napoleão use the ruse before. An excuse to drop behind the front party and to be forewarned of any danger to himself.

They moved off at a reduced pace, turning inland from the embankment along a dusty path. It was used by village women when collecting water or taking laundry to the river.

A merest hint of lightness was appearing in the eastern sky. Inch by inch it was pushing back the indigo canopy of night; the stars were fading. The huts and rondavels of the village were taking vague form in an untidy silhouette a hundred metres ahead.

Nothing stirred, but Napoleão could detect the acrid smell of last night's wood fires lingering in the dead still air. Somewhere up ahead a cockerel uttered its strained call. It was answered by the distant yap of a dog.

Silence settled once more, broken only by the bandits' boots crunching on the dusty earth. The night closed in again. Napoleão's heart began to thud louder and louder until all he could hear was the blood rushing in his ears.

It was then that the distant fearsome scream pierced the air. A soul in the most excruciating torment. Then it ceased abruptly as though an anxious hand had been placed across the mouth of the screaming man.

Napoleão stopped. 'What was that?'

Chande's eyes were wide and white in the pre-dawn gloom. 'I don't know.' He swallowed uneasily. 'Perhaps the main group has started early. Mistimed.'

The colonel hesitated. 'We should wait,' he decided breathlessly. 'We're not far from the centre of the village ourselves. Look, that must be the Direct Action hut. We shouldn't get there before the main group.'

Then he saw his three lead men staring at him. They made no attempt to conceal their expressions of contempt.

'You lot go ahead!' Napoleão snapped angrily. 'Recce the place and report back. Pinpoint any Frelimo militia.'

They shrugged in dumb insolence and unshouldered their Kalashnikovs, then moved forward together.

Napoleão didn't quite see what happened next.

All he heard was the sharp creak of timber as though a branch were suddenly unrestrained. It was followed instantly by the abrupt rush of displaced air.

As his head turned towards the lead bandits the brief noise culminated in a thudding squelch.

His breath caught in his throat as he took in the scene with stunned disbelief. Instead of three men standing ahead of him on the path there were just two – both with jaws agape.

The third man was pinned against the pathside thorn tree by a gigantic timber stake that had been driven into his stomach by a spring-loaded sapling. It still trembled with the force.

Blood foamed from the impaled victim's mouth so that he was unable to speak. Only his eyes could plead as he struggled in vain to release the stake with his own hands. At last his fellow guerrillas overcame their paralysis and ran to assist. One held the man's torso fast while the other had to use both hands and all his strength to force the loaded sapling back. As the splintered tip of the stake emerged, Napoleão stared, mesmerised by horror, as a red snake of intestine followed it out.

The man slid down the trunk; he was unconscious before he reached the ground. His comrades stepped back warily. Fear dawned, dispelling their initial instinct to help. This was bad juju. The air of Tumbo village was beginning to reek of bad spirits.

Napoleão was still stunned by events. 'What the . . .?'

'A booby trap,' Chande hissed. 'A pig-trap. This isn't the work of Frelimo. Someone else . . . We must be careful, there may be others.'

Another sudden scream punctuated the night, this time somewhere off to their right. Still there was no gunfire.

To Napoleão the reason was obvious. His men were being picked off one by one in the dark. Silently, without warning. Booby traps. There were no shots because there was no one to shoot at.

'I'm not using this path,' he pronounced. 'We'll find another way!' And he was gone, blundering through the undergrowth.

'Colonel!' Chande called.

But his warning went unheeded. Chande turned back to the two lead bandits. Reinstate command, he decided, before this gets out of hand. 'Continue up this path,' he ordered, adding unnecessarily: 'And be careful.'

Without waiting for a response he struck out after Napoleão. Finally he caught up with his commander fifty metres into the bush by the edge of a narrow game trail.

The big man had regained his composure and a small measure of courage. 'This one is less likely to be booby-trapped,' he declared, as though it were unthinkable for the enemy to prove him wrong.

Chande hesitated. 'Colonel, why not wait here until we've secured the area?'

'Wait? What do you think I am? Yellow?'

'Of course not . . .'

'Well then! Follow me.'

Napoleão began waddling up the trail. Chande was left in no doubt that his chief was determined to redeem himself after the earlier display of panic. The second-in-command followed meekly.

At last they could distinguish the open ground surrounding the village fence.

Napoleão slowed, suddenly less keen to proceed.

Chande studied the trail ahead, his tired eyes attempting to penetrate the shadowy foliage. Then he caught a glimpse of the thin straight nettle string stretched horizontally across their path.

Napoleão took another lumbering step.

'COLONEL!'

The big man stumbled onto the string, feeling the taut resistance against his shin. Assumed it to be a bramble sucker. Jerked at it irritably. Felt it slacken abruptly. Simultaneously came the dry sound of wood clacking against wood as the primitive trigger mechanism released the arrow shaft. He vaguely registered the disguised shape of the bow five feet ahead of him. Saw the line snap rigid and the sudden movement like a darting snake. But didn't see the shaft before he felt the force of it driving between his legs. Then came the excruciating pain as he was thrown back into Chande's arms.

Both men hit the dirt, and as they did, the very earth appeared to quake. A wall of flame leapt from the open ground at the village edge. A wave of pain surged up through Napoleão's body like a tidal bore from his punctured scrotum. Through streaming eyes he could hardly discern what was happening ahead. Geysers of molten paint spewed skyward. Grotesque elongated shadows were scattered in all directions as members of the main advance group turned to run. Some appeared to be ablaze. Dancing fiery spectres that lit the compound walls in a macabre light show.

He felt their pain, his pain. Shared the flames; his whole being seemed to burn. Didn't understand, didn't want to . . .

Through the veil of his tears he witnessed the dying conflagration and saw the dark figures of menace emerge from the shadows of the huts. Yelling villagers, armed with staves and kitchen knives, poured out of the burning mouth of hell itself.

Unconsciousness closed in around Napoleão before he could witness the cries of jubilation as the men of Tumbo saw their dreaded foes take flight. Nor did he see the dazzling muzzle flashes as the ragtag Frelimo militia discharged a withering concentration of fire to speed the vanquished on their way.

And he was unaware of the exertions of his second-in-command as João Chande struggled to drag the enormous weight of his chief into the safety of the night.

Night belonged to Renamo, but this particular night did not.

Dawn came to Tumbo, and with it a sense of happiness and pride none of the inhabitants could remember having experienced before.

None of the villagers had returned to their compounds after the repulsing of the attack. And those who had not been involved in the defence plan joined in the spontaneous celebrations to cheer them as heroes. That day the rich aroma of baking bread began early. It thankfully obliterated the sickly sweet smell of charred remains around the improvised napalm bed.

Branagh had organised a burial detail to recover the half-dozen Renamo dead, but the volunteers just wanted to laugh with relief and talk with their friends. No doubt the story would be told for years around the village fires. No doubt, too, the magnitude of the victory would grow with the telling.

'Well done, Branagh,' Jorge da Gruta said flatly, his expression suggesting that a smile was in danger of breaking out. He held up his antiquated rifle. 'It worked. I got four rounds off.'

'But did you hit anything?' Fred Petkus asked as they sat down in Branagh's hut.

'How do I know?' da Gruta retorted. 'I couldn't see anything in the dark.'

Leif Månson said: 'I just hope my regional manager doesn't hear about this. Our involvement in this sort of thing is strictly forbidden.'

Fred Petkus raised an eyebrow. The Swede had spent the time hiding in the compound kitchen with Maraika. At least she had a meat cleaver to hand and looked as though she would have used it.

66

After breakfasting on maize porridge washed down with a steaming pot of Petkus's black market coffee, news reached them of the arrival of another Soviet helicopter at the strip. It carried a stick of Frelimo troop reinforcements; it also had a spare generator on board.

As Petkus's crew began carrying their kitbags out to da Gruta's waiting Toyota, the Russian himself was in deep thought. He stood by the door and stared into the middle distance.

For several minutes he appeared entranced by the vibrant colours of Tumbo. White woodsmoke from the cooling fires tumbling into the flawless azure sky. The yellow reeds of the compound walls against the red ochre of the scorched earth; the glossy two-tone green of the baobab trees shining in the sun and the long-tailed drongas sweeping lazily back and forth above the riverside bean trees.

After the horrors of the night it was a miracle of peace and tranquillity.

'A penny for them?' Branagh asked.

Petkus stirred from his daydreams and lit a cigarette. 'Tell me, Irish, am I a crazy man or what?'

Branagh laughed. 'You're crazy all right.'

The Russian exhaled a long, slow stream of smoke. 'Yes, that is what I think.'

'It helps if you live here. Helps to be a little mad.'

'That is also what I think. Fred, I tell myself, if you would really rather stay here than go home to Smolensk, then you must be crazy. Real bad crazy.'

'When is your tour of duty up?'

Petkus shrugged. 'A month, six weeks.'

Branagh was intrigued by his friend's unusually pensive mood. 'But your family, you'll be pleased to see them?'

The Russian fixed him with an angry stare. 'I have no family, Irish. My old mother died of hypothermia two winters back. There was just my brother Ustin.' Moisture softened the hard brown eyes. 'He and I, we did everything together since kids. Mushroom-picking, hunting, school and then the military. And chasing girls . . . Now he is no more. Died serving in Spetsnaz.'

'You've never mentioned a wife?' Branagh pressed gently.

Petkus sighed and stamped out his cigarette butt underfoot. 'That is because there isn't one. We divorced five years ago. My unreasonable behaviour.'

'I'm sorry.'

Idly the Russian's eyes followed Maraika as she began to sweep the soft earth of the compound. An unnecessary ritual; it was already finely raked and spotless as always.

'I envy you this life, Irish. And I envy you that woman. In Africa a man can be his own man.'

'Even here in Mozambique?'

'Maybe especially here in Mozambique. Like my country there is plenty bureaucrats, yes? But here they cannot reach you. In my rubbish country they always reach you. Everything you do is touched by them. And what happens when I go home? There are no more wars to fight. We are pulling out all over. Afghanistan, soon here and Angola. I will soon join the queue of military pilots to fly for Aeroflot, eh? We have only ourselves left to fight. And in five years the Soviet Union will not even exist.' He tore his eyes away from Maraika and faced Branagh again. 'It is all so clear.'

'Sir! We're ready to go!' It was the flight engineer.

Petkus appeared to arrive at a decision. He detached himself from the shade of the makeshift porch. With a sudden violent jerk he snapped the chain of the identity dog tags from his neck. Thrusting his hand through the Toyota's open window, he dropped the engraved metal discs onto the flight engineer's lap.

'What's this?' Bewildered.

'My tags,' Petkus retorted, 'what does it look like? Take them back and give them to Commander Peskov. Tell him I was killed in the raid last night.'

The engineer's mouth gaped. 'What?'

'You heard. I'm staying here.'

'But – sir – you can't—'

'Don't tell me what I can and can't do,' Petkus hissed. Then he drew breath and smiled thinly. 'You can have my black market concession.'

Branagh watched with fascination as the younger man hesitated. You could almost visualise the dollar signs ringing up inside his head. 'But why, sir?'

'Because I'm going to enter the free market economy. Like Gorbachev wants. But here, not there in that rubbish country. I prefer *this* rubbish country. Now, stop asking fool questions – and GO!'

Da Gruta started the engine. Leif Månson called from the rear passenger window as the Toyota began waddling down the rutted track: 'Michael, I have decided this transport situation is hopeless! I will ask the regional manager for our own aircraft. Then I can visit you more frequently. Keep an eye on things!'

The wake of red dust obliterated the Toyota from view.

'That will be nice,' Branagh murmured.

Petkus studied the receding dust trail. 'Perhaps Swedish will want a pilot for his airplane.'

Branagh gave an unenthusiastic grunt. 'Maybe. Just make sure you never leave him stranded with me again.'

Maraika had stopped sweeping, resting on her broom to watch the Toyota go. Now she straightened her back and watched with growing concern as two familiar figures emerged from the settling dust. She noticed that the village carpenter was keeping a consoling arm round the shoulders of her pregnant younger sister.

'See, Mikey,' Maraika called anxiously. 'Francisco comes with Lisa. What is the matter?'

The Irishman felt the crawl of hairs on the back of his neck. That feeling again from the dark Ulster days.

Lisa Matusi scurried ahead of Francisco for the last few paces and threw herself into her sister's arms where she promptly disintegrated into hysterical tears.

'What's happened?' Branagh demanded.

But the young teenager could hardly breathe, let alone talk, between her hot sobs.

Francisco looked crestfallen. 'It is Artur,' he explained. 'The father of her child. He lives on far side of village. Last night the *matsangas* kidnap people as they run away. Artur is one of them.'

Branagh turned away savagely. He walked to the edge of the compound and kicked angry holes in the board-flat earth that Maraika had just smoothed.

He glared at the distant blue hills. Renamo country. The hills and the night belong to the bandits. Despite everything it had happened again. Again, again, again. What it was to feel so bloody helpless.

Christ, he needed a drink.

3

The lounge of the Polana Hotel was alive with activity and the squeak of shoes on polished parquet as Kathleen Coogan searched for Peter Mandrake from the British Embassy. She found him waiting on one of the wicker sofas. He looked a lot more relaxed than he had the previous evening, dressed now in a casual shirt and slacks.

'It's very good of you to show me around.'

'Think nothing of it,' he replied lightly as he led Kathleen out of the building and into the blinding sunlight.

He pointed to a decrepit red Fiat with one wing badly buckled. 'Doesn't look much, but at least it goes, Kathy. No point in having a decent car here, it'll just get nicked. See the tail-lights are smashed? You won't find a car in Maputo with a set intact. The kids do it to steal the bulbs, then sell them on the streets.'

'That's awful.'

Mandrake shrugged as he forced open the passenger door. 'But understandable. There're tens of thousands of refugees in Maputo. Driven off the land by the bandits. No work, no food. So the kids do what they can. I'm sure we'd do the same in their position.'

It was a revealing drive. Although the houses near the Polana Hotel on the Avenida Julius Nyerere were smart and evidently occupied by the country's elite, the road itself had disintegrated into craters and potholes.

As they rattled into Avenido Eduardo Mondale the

full impact of the urban degeneration and decay hit her. The Portuguese influence was instantly recognisable in the architecture but the Mediterranean-style buildings were stained and crumbling, having long since fallen into disrepair. The mosaic pavements had lost their splendour, disfigured by holes and missing cobbles. Each house had accumulated its own individual mountain of garbage. Only the crazy branches of the fever trees, which shaded virtually every walkway, remained as testament to the original Portuguese dream of a mini-Lisbon recreated under the African sun.

'You can't blame the Mozambicans,' Mandrake said, negotiating the pocked tarmac. 'When the Portuguese fled, the people came in from the villages and were allocated the whites' old houses. Whole families in one room. These people didn't know what doors were, never had 'em. So when they needed to cook they used them for firewood. When windows were broken there were no trained glaziers to fix them. No glass even. In fact no skilled labour at all, you see. Then when things really got bad in the early eighties and Renamo got under way, there wasn't any money to import spare parts anyway. So the whole place just started to fall apart.'

'It's like a time warp,' Kathleen observed. 'As if nothing has happened for – what – fifteen years?'

Mandrake nodded. 'There's a half-built hotel along the coast. It's exactly the same as the day the Portuguese walked out in '76. Ladders and wheelbarrows just as they were left. Mind you, the Portuguese poured cement down the lift shafts first, just so the Mozambicans wouldn't benefit.'

After a while they parked the Fiat and walked the scabby streets. The few sidewalk shops offered nothing better than second-hand household appliances and a vast array of what Kathleen could only describe as useful bits and pieces. A few used screws, a piece of glass, electrical oddments, a hammer, an empty picture frame.

72

Makeshift stalls were everywhere, manned by entrepreneurial refugees trying to scrape together money for food. Individual cigarettes and sweets were neatly set out to tempt the passer-by. Black bananas and bags of cashew nuts could be found for sale between the street cobblers' stalls, the derelict-looking cafés, and garages selling petrol in lemonade bottles to those who'd had a windfall.

'God, it's depressing,' Kathleen murmured.

Mandrake nudged her. 'But then there's always something to lift the spirits. Look.'

Across the shattered pavement a family of smiling young girls was purposefully on the move, like a line of ducklings behind their mother, each with a galvanised bucket of water balanced on her head.

'And the shoe-shine boys,' Mandrake laughed as they approached the downtown district of Avenida Karl Marx. 'Must be hundreds of them, yet hardly anyone has a decent pair of shoes. A throwback from the Portuguese. The only place I've ever seen as many is in Lisbon.'

By the time they approached the central railway station Kathleen had had enough, seen enough. The area was heaving with the *affectados* – the dispossessed men, women and children who had lost everything to Renamo. Many were dressed in filthy rags; others fared better with whatever came to hand from charity distribution. One small boy proudly sported a bright red pair of ladies' highheeled boots. Adults sat around, vacant-eyed, most too malnourished and dispirited even to talk amongst themselves. Landmine victims, nursing gangrenous bandaged stumps, watched with envy the young orphans who could scavenge in the rubbish skips for scraps of food.

'This was always Maputo's pride and joy,' Mandrake said as they reached the domed baroque façade of the station. 'It's the lifeline with South Africa. For years it's meant access for the Mozambicans to work over there,

73

especially in the mines. The South Africans like them because they're less troublesome than their own Xhosas or Zulus. But now the poor bastards work like stink for a year, living in hostels, coming back by train to their families – only to get robbed and butchered by Renamo ambushes on the line.'

Kathleen experienced an involuntary shudder of abhorrence. 'What's it all about, Peter? All this terror. What is the purpose?'

He smiled awkwardly. 'That, Kathy, is a very good question.' But he didn't appear to have an answer.

Later they took an alfresco salad lunch back at the hotel, overlooking the pool and neatly trimmed lawns. While they talked, white children shrieked with laughter as they dived into the pool. Pied crows caw-cawed eerily overhead as they roosted in the coconut palms. Businessmen took their lunch breaks in swimming shorts, broiling contentedly on the white wooden sunbeds.

But Kathleen had no appetite. She couldn't rid herself of the smell of the Maputo streets nor the haunting images that kept spinning around inside her head. She pushed away her plate, the food hardly touched. 'I'm sorry, Peter, it just strikes me as obscene to be eating and drinking in a place like this while all that is going on outside.'

Mandrake said: 'If you don't mind me saying, Kathy, you can't be the conscience of the whole world. The best thing *you* can do is spend your money here. This country needs all the foreign currency it can get.' He smiled sympathetically. 'Eat all you can and save a starving Mozambican. Yes – I know it's crazy, but I guess it's a crazy world.'

She smiled; the intense young diplomat really was a charming companion. 'Thank you for everything, Peter. It's really appreciated, so it is.'

He waved her words aside. 'No problem. Listen, I've

got to look after a visiting delegation of MPs from London for the next few days, But I'll be free after that. Maybe I could show you some of the fleshpots of Maputo?'

'That would be nice – if I haven't got a lead on Cousin Seamus by then.'

He winked. 'Then I'll keep my fingers crossed that you haven't.'

'Thanks again, Peter, for everything.'

Returning to her room she changed into a pink swimming costume she'd picked up in a sale as she passed through London. She'd chosen a one-piece for modesty, but, with the taxi meter still running outside the shop, had no time to try it on. Now she found the high-cut thighs and stretch material left little to the imagination. She laughed at her own stupidity as she viewed herself in the chipped mirror. Yet she had to admit she did look pretty good in it . . .

Swathed in a gigantic hotel towel, she got as close to the poolside as she could before discarding its protection and diving into the limpid blue water. At last the smells of downtown Maputo were washed from her as she swam and ducked, enjoying the cool splashes and the tropical sunlight. She floated on her back, eyes shut, and thought of nothing but the rays caressing her body. This *was* crazy. This was Maputo. But, if she kept her eyes closed, it might just as well have been paradise.

'Miss Coogan.'

The dream shattered. She turned over and trod water. He stood at the poolside with the sun behind him, and she had to shield her eyes against the refracted light off the water.

He called again.

She swam to the edge, out of the sun's glare. Deputy Minister Ngoça was looking down at her. There was another man, dressed in a military officer's uniform, standing a pace behind him.

'I was told I'd find you here,' Ngoça said. His voice was deep, almost husky. 'Is this your towel?'

She struggled to lift herself from the pool and the deputy minister reached down to assist her. She remembered the warm dryness of his hand from the night before.

'Shall we have a drink?'

Standing before him, with a growing puddle at her feet, she felt naked as he regarded her unblinkingly. 'May I have my wrap please?'

Slowly he held the towel out. She grabbed at it eagerly, swamping herself in its thick warmth. Without waiting, Ngoça and his companion led the way to a table and sunshade and beckoned a waiter from the thatched poolside bar.

As they sat Ngoça said: 'This is my dear friend Brigadier Vieira Santos, one of our senior Frelimo generals and a Hero of the Revolution. If you want any stories about Mozambique's struggle against our former Portuguese oppressors, he is your man.'

Brigadier Santos looked almost bashful. 'I was hardly a hero, Miss Coogan. Just doing what had to be done.'

Ngoça laughed. 'You can see that he is far too modest to be a politician. He is far better suited to the soldierly arts, concentrating his efforts against the *bandidos*.'

As the drinks arrived Kathleen said: 'Brigadier, one thing puzzles me, why do you refer to Renamo as bandits?'

Santos sipped at his orange juice. 'It is a long-standing policy of this government. To deprive Renamo of the honour of calling themselves freedom fighters or a national resistance, or to claim that this conflict is some kind of civil war. Besides that is how they behave, like bandits.' He hesitated. 'But personally I think it could be a mistake. It leads the world to misjudge the enormity of the threat that they represent.'

Ngoça looked uncomfortable. 'My friend is never slow to express his own opinions.'

The brigadier smiled gently. 'Since when do bandits number twenty thousand, have satellite communications and control ninety per cent of a country?'

'Quite,' Ngoça said with a hint of impatience. Clearly he was well versed in his friend's views. 'Now, Miss Coogan, about your step-cousin, Seamus Gallagher. I've had my office check with all aid agencies operating in Maputo and no one has such a person registered. Immigration is less easy. I am afraid we have adopted the Marxist love of paperwork and bureaucracy with everything in triplicate. Basically too much information for the clerks to wade through without computers. Nevertheless they assure me that no one of the name Seamus Gallagher has been in the country during the past year and not left. I am afraid that information is not only not helpful to you, it is also unreliable.'

Santos said: 'Could he be using a different name, false papers?'

'I really can't think why he should.'

'People have been known to hide in Africa,' Santos said kindly. 'To escape their past, or to make a new start. Few countries here have sophisticated immigration procedures, so it is not difficult.'

'I am sorry I cannot be of more help,' Ngoça added.

Kathleen felt downcast but tried not to let it show. 'You've been most kind. At least now I know the worst.'

'I owed Peter Mandrake a favour,' Ngoça said simply and rose to leave. 'Besides it is my policy to help the press. You never know when you might need them. If I can help in any other way, please call me.'

She watched as they left, crossing into the lengthening shadow cast by the hotel. There were few people on the sunbeds now; it was cooler and the offshore breeze had stiffened. Despite the thick towel, she found herself shivering.

*

The next few days were long and tiring and filled with disappointment. All of Kathleen's lines of inquiry just confirmed Ngoça's words. No one had heard of Seamus Gallagher.

But when she next met Peter Mandrake he offered one last ray of hope. 'It's where the Brits hang out. If anyone knows about your cousin, it'll be one of the old hands there.'

The Aeroclub was just getting into full swing as he led Kathleen into the bar at eight thirty. The shirt-sleeved drinkers were still gathered in their separate cliques, not yet merging into the general bedlam that resembled a rugby club outing. Conversation faltered momentarily as the new girl made her entrance; faces, flushed with alcohol, turned as though drawn by some magnetic force. Some glasses were raised in greeting, several lewd grins and not a few coarse whispers were exchanged. Peter Mandrake was suddenly the most popular man in the place as the predators gathered to deprive him of his prize.

'Hi, Peter, wanna beer? Who's the little lady?'

'Hello, darling, my you're just what this place needs to brighten it up.'

'Looks like old Pete's scored there. Does the wife know?'

It was all harmless and friendly enough, although Kathleen actually found herself relieved to see the familiar figure of Ashton Smythe. He was apparently on his usual perch at the corner of the bar, cravat askew, his hand tucked contentedly down the back of the trousers belonging to the vivacious Mozambican girl by his side.

'Mustn't keep meeting like this,' he welcomed, a slight slur already creeping into his diction. 'I'm old enough to be your father!'

Mandrake bought a book of tickets and tore some off to pay for the cans of Castle. That done, he began introducing Kathleen to each group of drinkers in turn, telling them of her search for her step-cousin, whilst fending off the increasingly provocative passes aimed at her. Nobody appeared very interested in the old photograph she showed.

Despite several unlikely anecdotes involving Irishmen, nothing could be substantiated. It was mostly hearsay and rumour, and the name Gallagher wasn't mentioned. Most of these men worked in Maputo and if her cousin was here they'd certainly have known. But she began to realise that if Seamus was in any of the remote provincial towns they would have no idea. She downed the fourth can of beer pressed on her and resigned herself to the fact that she was not going to find him.

It was then that the big Russian arrived. She first became aware of a sudden commotion at the door, followed by much laughing and cajoling by the crowd as a hugely built man in a worn leather flying jacket shouldered his way through. There was an immediate sense of impending menace created by the wild black beard and contrasting close-shaven bullet head as he scowled around the bar in search of a familiar face.

He found it in Ashton Smythe. 'Hey, English! You're a member of this rubbish place. I need a beer damn quick.'

'Good Lord, Fred, you look pale,' Smythe observed.

The man squeezed up to the bar, seemingly unaware that he was crushing Mandrake and Kathleen into the corner. 'You'd be pale, too, English, if this happens to you.' He held up a big fist the size of a ham joint. 'Look, trembling like a leaf. Shaking like a damn woman.'

Smythe patted the side pockets of his jacket. 'Sorry, Fred, I'm clean out of cash.'

The man leaned towards the Englishman until their noses were almost touching. 'I don't want your money, just order me a drink and I'll pay you. I am not a member, remember?'

Mandrake nudged him and the big man turned sharply. 'Yes?'

'Fred, it's me – Peter – we met last night. Allow me to buy you a drink.'

The granite face behind the whiskers began to crumble. 'Ah, my diplomatic friend! Last night I was very drunk. Celebrating my new nationality! Now I remember you. You tell me about the airplane for sale.'

Mandrake smiled happily now that his life was no longer under direct threat. 'Did you get it?'

'Sure, sure. A nice Twin Otter. Very good. Runs as sweet as a nut. And a good price.' He tapped the side of his nose. 'Enough for me to make a little commission, eh?'

'So now Direct Action has its own aircraft.'

'And its own pilot.'

'A beer then?'

The man glanced down at his hands. They were still shaking slightly. 'And a vodka chaser.'

Peter Mandrake ordered. 'What happened to you?'

A grunt. 'I am driving into town from the lady I stay with on the outskirts. There is a roadblock, a check by the army. But I see they wear no red armbands—'

'What?'

'Official roadblocks wear red armbands. Not this lot. I do not like the look of them.'

'You mean they were Renamo?'

A shrug. 'How the hell do I know? Renamo, official Frelimo, unofficial Frelimo, I just put the foot down. Phoof! Straight through! This guy he hangs on the front of my car fifty metres before he falls off.'

'How dreadful,' Kathleen said.

The big man peered around Mandrake's shoulder at the half-hidden figure behind him. 'Ah and who is this? Not the mistress you take while your wife is away?'

Mandrake glared and motioned him to silence,

80

quickly stepping in with a formal introduction. 'Kathy, this is Fred the Russian, as we call him. Fred Petkus.'

'Fred the West German,' Petkus corrected, patting the inner pocket of his flying jacket. 'That is what my new papers say.'

'Of course,' Mandrake apologised. There was always a good market for forged documents in Maputo. 'And this is Kathy Coogan from Northern Ireland.'

A charming glitter of gold shone in the smile. 'Ah, another Irish! I think you are my favourite peoples.'

Mandrake frowned. 'Of course, you know an Irishman don't you? Where is it, Gutala? I met him once. I don't recall he looked like your photograph, Kathy. He's been up there for years.'

'Sure, Irish and me are like that!' He closed his thumb and forefinger to make a circle. 'Just days ago we see off a full Renamo battalion by ourselves!'

Behind his back Ashton Smythe gave a derisory chuckle.

Petkus lowered his head to Mandrake and jabbed a thumb over his shoulder. 'Listen to that English! He does not believe me, yet he is happy enough when I offer him flight real cheap for tomorrow now I have my own airplane. Well, the price just goes up and now I screw him good, eh?'

'You mean Direct Action's aircraft.'

Petkus's laugh was like a drain emptying. 'That, my diplomat friend, is the same difference.'

Kathleen stepped forward and proffered the Russian a creased black-and-white photograph. 'Is this the man you know?'

'Eh? What is this, little Irish?'

'My step-cousin. I'm looking for him. His name is Seamus Gallagher.'

Petkus tilted the faded print to avoid the reflection of the bar lights. 'How old is this picture?'

'Fifteen, sixteen years.'

'My friend is much older than this. And he has a beard. Besides his name is Branagh.'

'Then there's no resemblance?'

Petkus handed back the print. 'The man in your picture wears a soldier's uniform.'

'Yes.'

'My friend Branagh was once a soldier.'

Kathleen felt a sudden and irrational elation. 'How can I get to Gutala?'

Mandrake stared at her. 'You're mad. It's a chance in a million that's him. You said Ngoça said your cousin wasn't listed.'

'He also implied that Immigration's files are hopeless,' she retorted excitedly. 'Anyway, I've got to start working on my feature somewhere. So why not this place – Gutala?'

'For a start it's front line,' Mandrake warned.

'What does that mean?'

'It's a redevelopment township where Frelimo are trying to resettle refugees. That means it's a prime target for Renamo. Added to which it's bloody remote. I've only ever been there a couple of times myself.'

'How can I get there?' she repeated.

'With difficulty,' Mandrake replied without enthusiasm. 'Look, for a start it's some seven hundred miles upcountry. Halfway between the Malawi border and the coast. The roads are mined and run through bandit territory. And there isn't even a rail link. That leaves air. There are only – what – a few dozen aircraft of various types in the entire country. A few military, the LAM airline that runs up the coast route and the rest are light aircraft. Mostly run by aid agencies.'

'Could I hitch a lift?'

'Have you got money?'

She looked sheepish. 'Not much.'

Petkus said: 'I think little Irish should go. She'll find it hard to get a seat on LAM, but I am taking

English to Beira tomorrow on my way to Pemba in the north.'

Mandrake was angry at the interference. He wanted to keep the girl in Maputo, not lose her to some remote area of the bush on a wild-goose chase. 'Beira is not Gutala.'

'Where is Beira?' Kathleen pressed.

'About halfway upcountry on the coast' Mandrake answered irritably. 'It used to be a holiday resort, but now it's the pits.'

Petkus added: 'Maybe someone gives you a flight from there. Smile sweet and show your legs, eh? And tell Branagh that Fred sends you. Tell him I say to look after you.'

It may have been the effect of the drink, but Kathleen's face was glowing with the optimism and happiness she felt. 'Could you really take me to Beira, Fred? Tomorrow?'

He shrugged casually. 'Why not. I fly that English – Ashton Smythe – so now he pays for you too, little Irish.' He chuckled as he savoured the sweetness of his revenge.

She turned and kissed Mandrake full on the mouth. 'Peter, I love you.'

But it didn't make him feel any better.

It was two hours' flying time to Beira.

Inside the twin-engined Otter conditions were hot as it bumped down the runway and lifted tentatively into the air.

With her nose pressed to the sun-warm perspex of the window, Kathleen looked down on the receding sprawl of Maputo and its shanty suburbs. She tried to ignore Ashton Smythe's intimate proximity as he deliberately leaned across her to point out landmarks. To her surprise there was another passenger. This was Brigadier Santos whom she had met earlier at the hotel poolside with Deputy Minister Ngoça. He sat beside Fred Petkus who was clearly thrilled with his new toy. She found his exuberant self-confidence distinctly reassuring as the small craft was buffeted by the thermals.

'You can *see* the difference between Mozambique and other countries in the region,' Smythe was saying. 'Cross Zimbabwe or Swaziland or Malawi by air and you'll see vehicles on the road and smoke from the village fires. Out here, once we clear Maputo, you'll see nothing moving. There'll be no sign of life until we reach Beira.'

She didn't fully believe him but he was right. Below them mile after mile of silent, deserted bushveld slipped by. The amber velvet fuzz of the buffalo grass and green tufts of the thorn bushes were lit in the mellow gilded flush of the rising sun. Dark shadows from hundreds of puffball clouds spotted the landscape like a leopard's pelt. Occasionally an ochre ribbon of road meandered across the terrain, but not a single truck or car was in sight. At that altitude the thatched roofs of villages were clearly visible, as would have been the inhabitants had there been any. It was a wasteland.

The monotony of the empty plain was relieved as they circled low over the fertile Pungoe River valley. There the waters of the delta glistened like quicksilver as they flowed out into the Mozambique Channel. This was Beira – the coastal end of the militarily secure 'Beira Corridor', the lifeline railway that stretched right across the country to Zimbabwe. All of a sudden a rash of villages could be seen dotted amongst the crop fields and rice paddies; vehicles were moving, and people were going unconcernedly about their daily chores as Petkus dipped the wing on the final approach. The lush landscape exuded its fertility in a thousand vibrant shades of green.

The wheels hit the concrete strip with a jolt and Kathleen breathed a sigh of relief. Whether she was thankful for landing safely, or was just grateful actually to have got anywhere at all, she couldn't be certain.

It was a large airfield flanked by a small passenger terminal and a row of enormous aircraft hangars. Half a dozen Soviet military helicopters stood on the apron with their rotors pegged by guyropes to prevent wind damage. A collection of vintage Dakotas dating back to the Second World War stood idly alongside a line of brightly coloured light aircraft which looked like plastic toys by comparison. A huge twin-engined Antonov military transport stood apart, businesslike, and guarded by a scruffy detail of government soldiers in their familiar forage caps with twin tails.

Thankfully the passengers stretched their legs, refreshed by the breeze that gusted unhindered across the airfield. A Red Cross aircraft wound up noisily for takeoff on the distant main runway.

'Let's go get a coffee,' Petkus said, shouldering Kathleen's rucksack. 'And we see if we can get you on to Gutala.'

As Brigadier Santos strode over to the Antonov and Ashton Smythe scuttled off with his attaché case towards the terminal building, the Russian led Kathleen past the giant Dakotas to one of the hangars.

'Still nothing beats these Daks in Africa,' he explained with relish, as though he were talking about an old whore who could still do tricks others hadn't even thought of. 'Nothing is better for load and fuel on short, uneven strips. That's why they keep the old buggers going – except maybe they don't afford anything newer.'

The smell of oil and avgas greeted them as they stepped into the cool shade of the hangar. Another Dakota had been stripped and new bodywork panels were being fitted by two white engineers, sweating in just shorts and trainers. A side workshop had been converted into a crew room by the simple expedient of arranging rows of tatty airline seats around a makeshift coffee table of milk crates. A chorusline of pneumatically breasted girls smiled exuberantly from the posters on a row of metal lockers and on the wooden corner bar. Behind it stood an enormous and ancient American refrigerator, a sign on which reminded users to 'Close the Fucking Door'.

A white-haired Scot in overalls was at the bar pouring a saucer of milk for a tabby cat who viewed the new arrivals with curiosity.

'Hey, Scottish,' Petkus called, 'I got a surprise visitor with me. Making her way to Gutala.'

'I'm Kathleen Coogan – pleased to meet you.'

Ian Hagan wiped his hands on his overalls before shaking her hand fiercely. 'Nice t'see you, lass. We dunna get many visitors up here. Make y'self comfy and let's see if I can help at all.'

Petkus helped himself to two coffees from the urn that was forever on instant standby. 'Scottish runs Arbaérea for years. It is the bush airline for the country.'

Hagan grimaced. 'Was only going t'do it for a month. Now I've got a hotchpotch o' freeloadin' ne'er-do-wells and circus pilots and aircraft that take all my profits t' keep in the air. Canna afford t' pack in now.'

'What he means,' Petkus translated amiably, 'is he has the best veteran bush pilots and the most reliable airplanes in the whole of southern Africa. And they all work for him for a pittance.'

'Y' silver-tongued Russian bastard, you,' Hagan chuckled. 'But you, young lady, you're trying t' get t' Gutala?'

'I think my step-cousin may be there. The family had lost touch with him.'

Recognising her accent, Hagan put two and two together to come to a logical conclusion. 'Y' mean Branagh? Well I'm blowed! I never thought tha' bastard had a mother, let alone a wee cousin!'

Petkus said: 'I cannot fly her up just now – I have to take urgent morphine supplies to Pemba.'

Hagan scratched his chin. 'I'm thinking, Rod's taking

86

a cargo up t' Cuamba. If he can leave here early enough, he might have time t' go via Gutala.'

Kathleen felt awkward. 'How much will the fare be?'

'Fare!' Hagan found that very amusing. 'Nay, lass, it'll be my pleasure. There's never enough aid coming in t' feed these poor bastards, so there's room for a wee one. Besides, it'll be worth it just t' see the look on Branagh's face. Now, give me half an hour to finish an engine check and we'll have a wee spot o' lunch.'

Lunch was to prove an unexpected pleasure on the shaded verandah of the Aero Clube da Beira at the side of the airfield. Obviously popular, it was filling up fast with mostly European aircrew types. Ashton Smythe had already staked his claim on a table and was nursing a large gin as he engaged in earnest conversation with a Mozambican army officer.

'Hey, English!' Petkus called. 'You mind we join you?'

The Englishman seemed taken aback. 'What? Oh, Fred. Er – yes, I suppose so.'

Kathleen noticed that the Mozambican officer was immaculately turned out. When he spoke to Petkus his eyes were still keenly fixed on her. 'I should be delighted. Senhor Smythe and I have finished our business.'

Smythe dabbed at the perspiration on his face with a handkerchief. 'Yes-yes, I suppose we have.'

His battered hide attaché case was lying on the table top. As he went to retrieve it the Mozambican reached out and gripped the handle. 'Shall I move this so they can serve the food?' he suggested smoothly. With both hands he lifted the case and placed it carefully beside his chair.

Hagan and Petkus pulled up another table and more chairs. As they sat down Smythe said: 'This is Colonel Vaz. You travelled up with his chief this morning, Kathy.'

She nodded. 'Brigadier Santos. A charming man.'

'Santos is going north in that bloody great Antonov you saw on the runway. Meanwhile his second-in-command, Colonel Vaz here, is returning south to Maputo for some well-earned rest and recuperation. Eh, Colonel?' Smythe winked knowingly.

Vaz was unfazed. He fitted a cigarette to a small mother-of-pearl holder while he spoke. 'Brigadier Santos and I are sometimes like ships that pass in the night.'

'There is more trouble upcountry?' Petkus asked.

Unhurriedly Vaz lit his cigarette. 'There is always trouble with the *bandidos*. But nothing we cannot control.'

'What about Gutala?' Smythe interjected. 'Fred here reckons there was a battalion-size Renamo attack a few days ago.'

'I am sure it seemed like a battalion to your friend,' Vaz replied dismissively. 'Now allow me to recommend something from the menu. Perhaps a meat dish spiced with piri-piri?'

They had hardly begun to eat when Brigadier Santos arrived. He was clearly in an uncharacteristic temper, his cheeks puffed with suppressed rage.

'Damn those Russians!' he declared to the entire gathering.

Petkus looked up and blinked as the officer slapped his cap on the table before angrily jerking a spare chair towards him.

'Brigadier?' Vaz inquired politely.

'Those damn Russians!' Santos repeated. It was unlike him to be so undiplomatic in public. 'How do they expect us to win this war with the *bandidos*?'

Ashton glanced knowingly at Petkus and chortled: 'I don't think they're very bothered any more.'

'So it appears,' Santos growled. 'I need to get up to Cuamba urgently. The Antonov has flat batteries. So we need the Russians' starter unit to charge our engines. I sent a man to their billet and he comes back with the message that they had a hard night on the town last night! They will come out with their starter unit after lunch – *if* they are feeling better! I ask you?'

'The Russians are not always the most helpful of our friends,' Vaz agreed.

Hagan said: 'I hope t' have the Caribou going up t' Cuamba this afternoon, via Gutala. It's due in from Chimoio at any time. If tha's any good?'

Brigadier Santos sighed and smiled. 'That is a kind offer.'

'But the brigadier has men and equipment going with him,' Vaz interrupted quickly. 'So he has to travel with the Antonov.'

Santos's eyes narrowed. 'Incidentally, Colonel, some of the men on the Antonov say there's been much increased enemy activity this week. You didn't mention that to me earlier.'

Vaz smiled uncertainly and blew a perfect smoke ring. 'They exaggerate as usual. Besides it is all in my report, Brigadier. You will be able to read it when you get to Cuamba.'

'It may be too late when I get to Cuamba. And if things are as bad as they say, I will want *you* with me. In fact, I had been thinking that you should postpone your leave and come back to Cuamba with me now.'

With a deft flick of the wrist Vaz stubbed out his cigarette. 'Whatever you say, Brigadier. Meanwhile let me go personally to the Soviet billet. I will dig them out of bed. The Antonov shall take off this afternoon without fail.' He stood up briskly.

Somewhat taken aback Santos nodded his agreement and watched as Vaz marched smartly from the verandah, carrying the hide attaché case. 'How lucky I am to have such a second-in-command,' Santos murmured. Kathleen couldn't be sure if he meant it.

However, in under an hour the Soviet starter unit and

crew arrived to fire up the Antonov's huge Kuznetsov turboprops. Colonel José Vaz was not with them.

When the Arbaérea high-tailed Caribou lurched in low over the runway like an ugly flying beetle, Brigadier Santos was still standing by the Antonov, waiting impatiently for Vaz to appear.

Kathleen and the others watched him while they waited by the hangar for the taxiing Caribou.

'Vaz is a crafty wee sod,' Hagan observed. 'I reckon he's gone t' ground with his tart in Beira. He kens Santos canna wait because of the daylight. And if he stops the Ant's engines the Russians will never come out for a restart.'

As though in confirmation of the Scotsman's words they witnessed Brigadier Santos stump resignedly up the tailramp of the Antonov. With lights flashing the huge beast began to move, starting its long taxi towards the main runway.

Hagan said: 'They reckon Santos is the best commander the government's got. Some say it's about time they made him Defence Minister.'

The outbound Antonov passed the incoming Caribou as it edged noisily towards the hangar, black oil dribbling from one of its engine cowlings.

'Number Two's still playing up,' Hagan noticed, turning to Kathleen. 'Tha' means Gutala's out until tomorrow. But I'll be able to fly y' up in the Caribou in the morning.'

'That'll be grand,' the girl replied. What was another few hours after fourteen years?

Ashton Smythe watched the Antonov turn onto the main runway, the deafening crescendo of its engines demanding attention even at such a distance. 'I suppose there's no chance of any flights back to Maputo this afternoon, Ian? I can't bear staying over in this town; it stinks. I've lost more blood to mosquitoes here than any place I know.'

Hagan laughed. 'Sorry, old son, you'll have t' put up with it. Think yourself lucky. This is home t' me.'

With a roar the Antonov's turbos wound up to full pitch and everyone turned to watch as the huge shape thundered down the runway. Slowly, slowly, it began lifting its huge weight, nosing up into the sky towards Cuamba.

'Wouldna mind flying tha',' Hagan muttered in awe.

It lumbered steadily into the opalescent haze of the afternoon, shrinking rapidly from view.

No one was expecting the vivid flash that was almost blinding to the naked eye, and the rolling percussion of the explosion which followed a few seconds later.

'Gone?' Vincent Mulholland demanded. 'When for Christ's sake? I've been looking for her all day.'

Peter Mandrake glanced round the lounge of the Polana Hotel. 'Keep your voice down, can't you? She got a lift with a Russian pilot. He works for the Direct Action aid outfit.'

'Where has he taken her?'

'Up to Beira, I believe.'

Mulholland sucked furiously on his cigarette as he attempted to marshal his thoughts. 'How can I get there?'

'That could be a problem. You'll have to make your own arrangements.'

'What?' Mulholland sensed the change in the young diplomat's attitude.

Mandrake didn't reply directly. He reached inside his jacket and drew out a buff envelope. 'This is the information you requested from our man in Pretoria.'

Mulholland made an effort to hide his irritation. 'Thanks a million, old stick.'

The other man didn't respond. Instead he said carefully: 'Our ambassador spoke to Whitehall this morning. Apparently your presence here was not known.'

Mulholland shrugged. 'Crossed wires, I expect. You know what it's like.'

'London requests that you return immediately. And meanwhile I have been instructed to give you no further assistance.'

It was the next morning before the high-winged Caribou transport was allowed to take off from Beira.

After the explosion that had destroyed the military Antonov, the government authorities were in a state of near-panic. A cordon of troops was thrown around the airport building and all aircraft were grounded. Plainclothes SNASP secret police made a rare appearance, questioning airport staff and the milling crowd hoping to get seats aboard an internal Linhas Aéreas de Moçambique flight.

By nightfall the police had lost interest and everyone, including the Arbaérea pilots and engineers, was free to go. Before kindly allowing them to spend the night at his house, Ian Hagan had taken Kathleen and Petkus to one of the few functioning restaurants in Beira.

Talk in the PicNic was on one topic only – the crashed Antonov. Rumour and speculation were rife. It had been shot down by a Renamo shoulder-fired missile. An engine had caught fire and exploded. A bomb had been placed on board by South African secret agents.

'All I ken is,' Hagan said next morning as the Caribou levelled out on a course set for Gutala, 'tha' Frelimo have lost one of their best soldiers. And a very decent chappie.'

Kathleen was perched on the flight-deck steps immediately behind Hagan and his copilot. She said: 'He seemed very charming and honest, I thought. I can't believe he's dead. It just doesn't seem possible. One minute he's having lunch with us and the next . . .'

It was difficult to talk above the clatter of the Caribou's primitive engines and a sombre silence fell between them as the aircraft droned doggedly northwest. They were no longer in view of the sea; below them hundreds of square miles of deserted bushveld were again passing by. Halfway through the journey the low mountain ranges on Mozambique's western border with Zimbabwe appeared. These spartan, scrub-covered peaks, Hagan told her, were the favourite hiding place of the bandits as they moved from target to target with virtual impunity.'

Eventually the deafening monotony of the flight took its toll and Kathleen curled up between sacks of dried fish in the cargo hold. As fatigue dragged at her senses she found herself smiling. She was flying to Gutala. The biggest adventure of her life had begun. Those childish dreams in her Armagh bedroom of one day reporting from abroad were no longer dreams. She was here.

A change of engine pitch woke her. The pungent smell of fish was thick in the confines of the hold as she opened her eyes to find the aircraft losing height.

'How's the sleeping beauty?' Hagan asked as she clambered up to the flight deck. He pointed out of the cockpit. 'Tha's Gutala below. We've no communication so we approach over the town t' let everyone ken we're coming in. The airstrip's ten miles away near a village called Tumbo.'

As with the outskirts of Beira Kathleen could instantly see the difference between the protected area and the empty bushveld over which they had been cruising. Beneath the aircraft now there were swaying fields of mealie maize and the seemingly endless green swathes of the Embamo banana plantations. People walking the red dirt roads stopped and waved as the Caribou dipped low on its approach to the strip.

It was an unnerving touchdown as the undercarriage skimmed over the tops of the eucalyptus trees and the flat plateau of buffalo grass rushed at them. Kathleen shut her eyes until she felt the jolt of the wheels as they hit the ground and the forward momentum almost instantly began to slow. By the time the Caribou was able to taxi into a turn it was only metres from the edge of the strip. It didn't take an aviation expert to realise that it had been a skilful piece of flying by Hagan.

As the rear ramp was lowered Kathleen slung her rucksack over one shoulder and stepped out into the sunlight. Hagan, wearing a pair of Polaroid sunglasses, joined her and together they walked towards the small group of Mozambicans watching from the track that led down to Tumbo. Hagan put their unusual wariness down to the fact that their arrival hadn't been expected and he confirmed to them in Portuguese that there was nothing to unload.

'Someone's coming,' he observed and pointed to the trail of dust moving along a track between the crop fields.

Kathleen felt the knot of apprehension tighten in her stomach. She was probably about to make a complete fool of herself in front of a total stranger. She had no real illusions that this man called Branagh would be her stepcousin. Now that she was here she had to acknowledge the fact that she was grabbing at straws. At least if he was Irish he should have a sense of humour. She certainly hoped so.

The white Land-Rover with its buckled wing came into view, weaving between ruts that had been baked rock hard since the last rains. It slewed to a halt and one of the doors, emblazoned with the Direct Action livery, swung open.

The driver was tall and tanned, wearing a green bush shirt and khaki shorts. But it was the blond beard and tousled hair that caught Kathleen's attention first. She wasn't good on people's ages but she guessed he could be in his early forties. Perhaps that was wishful thinking because that would make it exactly right.

As he stepped closer she squinted, trying to imagine him younger and without a beard. Then she was certain. Something about his stance, the powerful strides. The

94

expression on his face, the half-smile, suddenly seemed familiar. Was it possible? God, it had all been so long ago.

'Hello, Mike,' Hagan said.

The Irishman nodded. 'Morning, Ian. I wasn't expecting a flight. Are you in trouble?'

The pilot grinned. 'Nay trouble, just dropping off a visitor. A wee lady reporter who wants t' write about what's going on here.'

The green eyes narrowed as Branagh focused on the girl. 'Reporter? No one's said anything about a reporter. There's nothing here to report.'

Kathleen took a deep breath and stepped forward from Hagan's side. She couldn't prevent the smile that lit up her entire face. 'Hello, Seamus.'

Alarm flashed in Branagh's eyes. He glanced angrily at Hagan. 'What is this?'

The girl laughed lightly, almost a giggle. 'You don't remember me, do you?'

He stared at her, long and hard. Then slowly his mouth dropped. His face began to take on an expression of sheer astonishment.

'Kathleen,' she said.

Branagh swallowed hard. 'Kathleen,' he repeated numbly.

She looked at him wide-eyed. 'Really. I was only thirteen when you last saw me. I expect I've changed.'

Anger had returned to his eyes. 'What in God's name are you doing here?'

She took an involuntary backward step. 'That's not a very nice welcome.' She looked hurt. 'Ian told you. I'm a journalist. I came to find you – and to write a report.'

'You're joking!'

Hagan watched in bemusement. He could not believe this hostile reaction. Feeling distinctly uncomfortable, he said: 'Look, folks, time marches on. We're on our way to Cuamba.'

Branagh turned on him. 'You're not planning to leave her here, Ian?'

Hagan said: 'There's nowhere for her t' stay in Cuamba, Mike. I dunna think a Frelimo barracks is very suitable.'

'Well, there's nowhere for her to stay here either!' Branagh snapped back.

Kathleen interrupted. 'Your friend Fred said you'd look after me . . .'

'Fred? What's he got to do with this?' Branagh demanded.

'He flew me to Beira. He said you'd look after me.'

'Jesus Christ!' Branagh, fists on hips, stared in turn at the sky, the distant hills and then his feet. Nothing offered inspiration or salvation. He fixed her eyes steadily with his own. 'Listen, Fred's got it all wrong, see. To be sure it's nice to see you, but there's nowhere for you to stay – and besides it's dangerous.'

Kathleen's feeling of rejection began giving way to an anger of her own. 'This is a protected area.'

'That doesn't mean we don't get attacked. Only a few days ago . . .'

Defiantly the girl squatted down on her rucksack, arms folded across her chest. 'I'm staying. Please, Ian, leave me now. I'll be all right.'

'Are you sure, Kathy?'

'Positive.'

Hagan began backing towards the Caribou.

Branagh saw him. 'Where the hell do you think you're going, Ian?'

'Sorry, Mike. I'm just the delivery boy around here. It's the wee lady's decision.' He disappeared into the Caribou.

Branagh glared down at the girl. 'Right, young lady. You can do this the hard way or the easy way.'

There was a wild look in her eyes. 'Is that a threat, Cousin Seamus?' she challenged.

'Right,' he said, and in one swift movement his powerful right arm scooped her around the waist and lifted her slight body off the ground. Picking up her rucksack in his left hand, he started carrying the struggling girl towards the aircraft.

A flailing fist caught him in the face and then, as he pulled back, her teeth found his bicep. Without hesitation she bit hard and deep.

'Shit!'

She landed heavily at his feet. 'Bastard!' she spat. 'How *dare* you do that! Who the hell do you think you are? You wouldn't treat Kate Adie like this.'

'Who?'

'Never mind!'

He stared at her, speechless, then looked towards the Caribou. Its ramp was closed now and its propellers were spinning to a blur as it taxied back onto the strip.

His anger began to ebb. He knew when he was beaten.

4

They both watched as the Caribou began its run, engines screaming as they gathered power. Ponderously the aircraft lifted into the shimmering sky, clearing the eucalyptus tops as it climbed steeply above the rolling plantations.

Branagh rubbed at the livid teethmarks where she'd broken the skin and looked towards the amused group of villagers still standing by the track. No doubt they had never seen anything like this before. The story would provide endless mirth in the district for months to come.

He said: 'You'd better get up.' There was no offered hand.

Slowly Kathleen climbed to her feet, dusted herself down and scowled after Branagh as he stalked back to the Land-Rover. The line of watching villagers broke to allow him through. With a grunt of satisfaction she hoisted the rucksack to her shoulders and followed.

The engine started as she got there. She peered through the driver's window. 'Well, do I have to walk or what, Cousin Seamus?'

He stared straight ahead through the fly-spattered windscreen. 'Get in.'

No sooner had she slammed her door than he accelerated harshly, scattering the growing number of curious onlookers.

For some minutes he didn't speak, concentrating on the hazards of the uneven track. At last he said: 'Get one thing straight, Kathleen. The name's Mike Branagh. Your step-cousin Seamus died years ago. I buried him. Got it?'

'But why?'

'It's none of your business.'

'You sent that letter after Ma's death. Or did a ghost write it?'

He swerved to miss a stray goat. 'That was a mistake. I certainly didn't expect you to come looking for me.'

'Don't delude yourself – my main reason for coming was to write the press features.'

He said irritably: 'Then you can write them someplace else. You're on the first available aircraft out of here.'

She sat back in her seat and braced herself against the irregular bounce of the suspension. There was a slight hint of triumph in her voice as she asked innocently: 'And when – Mike – is that likely to be?'

He pursed his lips but didn't answer. They both knew full well it could be days or even weeks before there was another flight in.

As the track levelled out by the river, outlying wattle huts and compounds became more frequent. 'Is this Tumbo?' she asked.

'Yes.'

'And you live here?'

He hooted to scatter a line of wandering chickens. 'There's a Direct Action station here. First aid, food distribution and elementary education. It's where I stay.'

'I think it's wonderful what you're doing,' she ventured.

He hit the brakes outside a compound that enclosed the first proper mud-brick dwelling she had seen. He turned sharply on her. 'You don't *know* what I'm doing. And the whole world doesn't know what's happening here, let alone care.'

A look of defiance returned to her eyes. 'Well maybe I can help change that.'

He killed the engine. 'Sure you can.' He made no attempt to hide his sarcasm.

She climbed out and hurried after him as he entered the compound. 'This is your home?'

He said: 'We'll get you fed and watered then I'll drive you to Gutala. There's an hotel of sorts there.'

'Can't I stay with you?'

'No.'

He offered no further reason and left her standing by the door while he went to the side of the building where a lean-to roof of corrugated iron covered the kitchen area. A very tall, beautiful young black woman, wearing a brightly coloured *capulana*, rose from beside the cooking fire.

'Maraika, this is a relative of mine from home,' Branagh said brusquely. 'She'll be staying at the hotel. I want you to give her some lunch. If she eats in Gutala she'll end up with food poisoning. I'll be back later this afternoon.'

As he turned to leave, Kathleen caught his arm. 'Can't I come with you? I'd like to see round the village.'

'You'd be in the way. Maraika will look after you until I get back.'

Then he was gone, gunning the Land-Rover into life and disappearing down the track in a choking cloud of red dust.

'Bastard,' Kathleen said under her breath.

Maraika looked on dubiously, her eyes taking in the small trim figure of the girl inch by inch. Her gaze lingered long on the boyish urchin haircut with the shaggy short mane that covered the back of her neck.

Kathleen turned to the girl who had remained timidly in the shade amid the rising steam of the cooking pots.

'Maraika, is it?' She smiled reassuringly. 'You do speak English?'

A sheepish look. 'A little speak . . . Do you speak in Portuguese?'

'I'm afraid not.' Kathleen gave a helpless shrug and smiled.

Maraika smiled back and gave a nervous giggle, unsure of what to say.

Kathleen extended her hand. 'I am Kathy. I hope we will be friends.'

The Mozambican girl shook the offered hand limply. She was not used to shaking hands with white people. No other white person had ever shaken her hand. Not even Branagh. It made her feel accepted. Important. Suddenly she smiled very brightly. 'I will make you good food! You enjoy!'

Kathleen laughed at the sudden release of tension, the ice broken. Sod Branagh, she was in need of a friend and now she had found one. 'What are you cooking?'

Maraika took her by the hand to the lean-to. Inside a pregnant teenager was preparing vegetables.

'This my sister, Lisa.'

'Hello, Lisa,' Kathleen said, but received only an uncertain smile in response.

Maraika knelt by the pot. 'Mikey call this his Irish stew.' She laughed. 'Sweet potato and goat meat. Also cowpea leaves and squash leaves. Very nice.'

'Mikey?' Kathleen queried. 'Mike Branagh?'

'Yes.'

'You cook for him?'

'Of course, I am Mikey's woman.'

Kathleen couldn't disguise her surprise. 'Oh, you're married?'

A shrug of the slender shoulders. 'Yes, we are married very soon now.' Concern clouded the dark eyes momentarily, and then the smile returned, as though she had put a troubled thought to rest. 'I must go see headman of village now. You want come with me? I show you village. When we come back Irish stew is ready.'

'Sure, why not.'

Maraika snapped a few words in Portuguese at Lisa

which drew a sullen response. Then she picked up a gourd with which to collect water from the river before leading her guest out of the compound.

'Mikey says you are a rel-at-ive?' she asked, stumbling over the unfamiliar word. 'What is that?'

'The same family. A step-cousin.'

'Ah, I have many cousin.'

'We were very close once upon a time. Kissing cousins.'

Maraika walked on in silence for several moments, turning the expression over in her mind. Kissing cousins. Suddenly she stopped dead in her tracks and turned sharply on her new-found friend. 'You do not come here to take Mikey away? You do not want to marry him?'

Caught by surprise Kathleen laughed aloud. 'What a thought! Of course not! He's just about old enough to be my father—' She stopped herself. 'Sorry, it's just that he's become so rude. Rude and boorish.'

They walked on again in thoughtful silence. Occasionally Maraika would wave at other women working in their compounds, collecting firewood and water, washing clothes or cooking. Others tended their crops with their children in the small *mashambas* or vegetable gardens. Maraika talked to some in Portuguese, proudly introducing them to her special guest.

'There aren't many men here,' Kathleen observed.

'Men work on the big plantations,' came the explanation. 'Near here are many bananas. Some miles there is cotton and sisal, too. Men come home at weekends. Others go far to coast, collect coconuts. Others a long way to work in mines in South Africa. Only come home after many months.'

She stopped outside a hut that was larger than most. A queue of women sat on the ground outside, each with a tethered chicken or small package at her side.

'This is headman of village,' Maraika said. 'I must go in here.'

'All these people are waiting?'

'Headman is also a *curandeiros*. Makes good medicine. Talks to spirits. These people bring him gifts.'

'You mean he's a witch doctor?' Kathleen asked.

'What is that?'

The Irish girl caught herself in time. 'Nothing. I'll wait.'

It took only ten minutes. Kathleen gathered that Maraika was well-respected in the village because she had gone straight in without a murmur of protest from the others waiting. She emerged carrying a green liquid in an old Coke bottle.

'What's in there?'

Maraika smiled happily. 'A good potion. So I have baby. Like my sister Lisa.'

'You want to have a baby? How old are you?'

'I am nineteen years. Then, when I have baby, Mikey will marry me.'

Kathleen stopped walking. 'Is that what Mike says? I don't believe it.'

Maraika laughed. 'Mikey doesn't say, but I know. I live with him four years. No baby. I know what men think. Who wants to marry a woman who cannot have sons for him?' She began walking again towards the river. 'I have baby, then Mikey marries me.'

Branagh was not there when they returned to the compound to eat. It was late afternoon before the white Land-Rover pulled up outside.

'Let's go,' he said simply, picking up her rucksack from the doorway to the hut.

Maraika stepped forward. 'Mikey, she can stay here. We are friends. There is room.'

Colour pulsed in Branagh's cheeks. 'It's not suitable. Besides, I'm not having two chattering women under my roof.'

He strode back to the vehicle and Kathleen followed, leaving Maraika to watch forlornly from the compound.

As they drove towards Gutala, Kathleen said: 'Do you always talk to her like that?'

'She's used to it.'

'To being treated like dirt? Well, I'm certainly not.'

He concentrated on the road. 'No one asked you to come here. And no one asked your opinion.'

She was about to retort but stopped herself. What was the point of antagonising him? She decided on a different tack: 'Look, Mike, I realise now I shouldn't have come here. I had no idea you would feel like this. I thought you'd be pleased to see me. I thought such a lot of you when I was a kid.'

'That was a long time ago.'

She stared ahead at the twisting road, now neat glossy ranks of banana plants providing a guard of honour on each side. 'So it would seem. But while I am here, can't we at least be friends? Or just be civil? After all, I really do have a job to do. I won't invade your privacy. Please.'

For the first time she caught a hint of the smile that she remembered so well. The powerful hands appeared to relax on the wheel. 'Okay, young Kathy,' he said at length. 'Maybe I have been a bit hard on you. I suppose you weren't to know. You turning up here came as a bit of a shock. You were part of another life I left behind many years ago.' He glanced sideways at her. 'But I meant what I said. First flight out. I really can't be responsible for you.'

'You're not.'

'And I can do without that stubborn Irish nonsense, too.'

'You can talk – Mike.' She shook her head. 'I can't get used to calling you that.'

After the endless banana groves, more huts came into view again. It reminded her of Tumbo, but on a much larger scale. Here the track was much wider and there were more signs of development. An entire row of mud-brick bungalows was being constructed by the roadside.

They passed a large, single-storey hospital complex freshly painted in white and blue, complete with gleaming black iron railings and gates. There were market stalls overflowing with produce, and a new galvanised shed which housed a flour mill.

Branagh said: 'This is what can be achieved with security. Two years without an attack. And a good Administrator.'

'Administrator?'

'Like a mayor or governor appointed by the government. A bad or lazy Administrator makes all the difference. The guy we've got here is an inspiration, but I'd had many run-ins with his predecessor.'

'It's so clean, tidy. Not like Maputo and Beira.'

'It used to be. I had long talks with the Administrator when he first arrived. There was no excuse for the piles of garbage in the streets, it was just a symptom. The people's spirit had been broken by Renamo. They'd lost their self-respect. The first thing we did was clean the place up. Showed the refugees they didn't have to be helpless. They could actually help themselves. Began teaching them crafts, from carpentry to engineering. Restoring a sense of pride and self-reliance.'

'Like the Army.'

He turned on her. 'What?'

'Sorry – I mean you were in the Engineers, weren't you? That experience must have come in handy.'

Branagh looked back at the road. 'It all helped.'

The Land-Rover now cruised into the busy heart of Gutala where the compounds gave way to stucco buildings of clear Portuguese influence, all vividly coloured.

'It's amazing what a lick of paint can do,' Branagh pointed out. 'Lifts the heart – and Africans love bright colours. An intrinsic part of their culture.'

The central square was dominated by the two-storey hotel.

'This'll be your home. It's got its own generator, but

105

the water's a bit spasmodic and it's contaminated. Some Italian engineers were working on a new supply pipeline, but the Renamo attack on Tumbo last week scared them off. They haven't come back yet.'

'I'll manage,' she said as the vehicle pulled up outside the heavy double doors. Even the recent coat of varnish couldn't hide the riddling of bullet holes.

'I lived here when I first came to Gutala. It's comfortable enough. Have you got drinking water?'

'I've a bottle of mineral water.'

Branagh nodded. 'Don't use the stuff from the tap – even for brushing your teeth. You can buy more mineral water in the market. *Aqua do Vumba*'s local and good. And if you must eat here stick to bread or omelettes. Certainly don't touch salads. You can have a main meal with us again tomorrow.'

Kathleen felt her earlier resentment of him start to subside. 'That's most kind of you. And thanks for the advice. I'm sorry to put you to all this trouble, bringing me here.'

He swung easily out of his seat. 'No trouble. I come here most evenings. A sundowner at the *cantina*. I hear there's some beer in.'

A broad smile broke across her face. 'I see you're still an Irishman at heart.'

He grinned. 'And liver.'

'Could I be joining you? I'm parched.'

Branagh looked at her across the scratched bonnet of the Land-Rover, and suddenly felt as though he were seeing her properly for the first time. When she had arrived with Hagan earlier she had been a total stranger. He could hardly have failed to notice the striking, typically Irish features. The milk-smooth skin contrasting with the raven hair. The dark coffee eyes and black lashes. The strong bone structure. But there had been no recognition before her sudden use of his old name had exploded in his head. A time bomb, literally.

He had been blinded since, and deaf even to his own

thoughts and reasoning. The only thing that had reeled through his head all afternoon was that the past was no longer the past. His escape had failed. The past was the present, the present the past. And it was all here in Gutala.

'Well, Mike?'

He could see it now. The beautiful wide eyes that had watched in wonder as he told her of the world beyond the dank Armagh countryside. A mouth that by turn could light the heart or pout in stubborn, fiery defiance.

'How old are you now?'

'What? Twenty-seven.'

'Of course.' His mind came back to the present. 'C'mon then. Let's get a couple of beers.'

The *cantina* was on the far side of the square. Half a dozen rusted white metal tables and chairs were scattered on the raised wooden sidewalk. The corrugated-iron overhang was supported by struts of eucalyptus. As they sat down the Mozambican owner emerged from the dark interior.

'*Dois cerveja, se faz favor*,' Branagh ordered.

The cans of Lion beer were wet from the bucket of water in which they'd been stored. She raised her glass. 'To home.'

He smiled thinly. 'Sure, home.' He downed half the contents and grimaced. 'Sorry, his fridge has broken down.'

'It's fine.' They were still strangers. The gap of the years was yet to be crossed.

'How did you find me? That letter?'

'That and a lot of luck. When I heard there was an Irishman up here I didn't really think it would be you. Not with a different name.' She accepted the cigarette he offered. 'And you, how did you know Ma had died?'

He shook his head, still disbelieving as he recalled the coincidence. 'A long shot. There was a contract worker from Londonderry working here. He was very homesick and religiously had copies of the *Irish Post* forwarded out to him. When his contract ended he asked if I'd like the old issues. Well, there isn't much to read here. I don't usually read obituary columns. Don't know why I did that time.'

'I'm glad you wrote.'

He grunted. 'It was a bad idea. I'd had a drop to drink, I was feeling mellow.'

She was sympathetic. 'You're bound to feel homesick, too, sometimes.'

He looked up from his glass. 'This is home for me, Kathy. My life is here.'

'Maraika?'

'And Maraika.'

'She seems very sweet.' Kathleen toyed with the beer can. 'Do you love her?'

Branagh stared across the table as though she'd uttered an obscenity. 'What kind of question is that?'

She shrugged. 'It's just a question. Women ask that sort of thing.'

'Not in Gutala, they don't. We don't ask personal questions like that here. And we mind our own business.'

'You know she wants to marry you?'

'She doesn't know what she wants.'

'Because she's only nineteen?'

Branagh could hardly miss the hard edge of disapproval in her voice. 'This is Africa, Kathy. Things are different here.'

'Do you mean because here no one will find you out?' She meant to leave it at that, but her sense of feminine and moral indignation made it irresistible to add: 'That you've been living with Maraika since she was a minor?'

If she'd been expecting another explosion of anger, she was to be surprised. Branagh just held her gaze steadily. Slowly he said: 'War makes people grow up quickly. Too quickly. Children become adults before their time. Renamo is full of young boys who are hardened killers and girls who are enforced prostitutes. Maraika is cared for, safe and well-fed, and better looked after than any other woman in the district. So don't come here to a country you know nothing about and start making snap judgements and moralising.'

Kathleen finished her beer. 'In your letter you said how fond you'd been of Ma. Well, have you stopped to wonder what she would have thought of your behaviour here?'

Branagh said: 'You don't give up, do you? The Pope's little edicts don't count for much here, I'm afraid. People are too busy surviving as best they can. Tomorrow they may be dead. So just get it into your head I'm not interested in your opinion or anyone else's. If you want to be a journalist with anything worth reading, I suggest you stop talking and start listening. And learning.'

She was about to retort but then thought better of it. Something in his words hit a chord. Her experience of life had been confined to a remote farmhouse and the nearby village until she had escaped to the bedsit life of the Belfast suburbs. There she herself had broken Ma's own moral code, eventually living in sin with an acne-faced young sub-editor. It hadn't lasted, and when it was over she had experienced a profound sense of relief. That night she had gone to confession for the first time in a year. God might have forgiven her, but she wasn't sure Ma ever had.

Eventually Kathleen said: 'I'm sorry, I had no right to say anything. It's between you and Maraika.'

Across the street two white men emerged from a bland two-storey office block which carried the name Embamo on a sun-faded and bullet-holed sign over the door.

'A chance for you to meet a local character,' Branagh invited. 'Your man with the balding head and thick glasses is Jorge da Gruta. If we're both in town we always meet up for a drink after work. His family used to own all these plantations until the Portuguese pulled out. Now Jorge manages them for the government.'

'Who's the other man?'

Branagh shook his head. 'Never seen him before.'

As usual da Gruta looked hot and bothered. His face was beaded with sweat and there were dark patches at the armpits of the crumpled shirt which showed the top of a string vest at the open neck.

'Ah, Branagh, I see the town is full of newcomers today. A nice change.' With effort he stepped up onto the sidewalk and acknowledged Kathleen with a brusque nod. 'This must be the young lady who flew in on the Caribou this morning. A cousin or something?'

Branagh grimaced. 'News travels. This is Kathy Coogan.'

'And this is Rob,' da Gruta introduced. 'From that new French tobacco station. The one that's experimenting with new strains of plant.'

The stranger was tall and broad-shouldered with black hair that fell in a comma across his forehead. He looked cool and relaxed in chino trousers and a short-sleeved shirt.

'Rob D'Arcy,' the man said as he shook hands. Branagh had assumed him to be French, but there was a hint of a Scots accent when he spoke. And there was something familiar about the deep blue eyes and the white scar that sliced across the tanned skin of his right cheek.

Da Gruta called for beer as they sat down. 'Rob's the boss of IAP. That's the private security company that's training troops to protect the tobacco station.'

Branagh said: 'I've seen some of the Mozambicans you've been training. They look impressive.'

'Thanks,' D'Arcy said, 'but that's down to my Number Two out here. He's been training them as a special force since last month. The tobacco company has been getting twitchy – don't want to rely on the regular troops for protection. So I'm just out here for a few weeks to evaluate the situation.'

Da Gruta interrupted: 'Talking of which you've heard

110

about Brigadier Santos? He got blown up on an Antonov last night. It was just taking off from Beira.'

The news struck Branagh like a thunderbolt. 'I had no idea.'

'There's worse,' da Gruta added. 'I was talking on the radio to Maputo earlier today. They've appointed that creep Vaz in his place. You know, Colonel Vaz – Santos's second-in-command. Making him up to a full brigadier.'

Kathleen said: 'I was in Beira when it happened. I saw the explosion.'

Da Gruta's eyes appeared to widen until they filled the lenses of his spectacles. 'You saw it?' he asked incredulously. 'What happened?'

She shrugged. 'It had just taken off. Then suddenly there was a flash in the sky. Police sealed off the airport but I don't think anyone was arrested.'

'That's why Rob and I have been talking all afternoon,' da Gruta explained. 'With Vaz in command of the region it'll make life difficult. Before we could always go over his head to Santos. But now . . .'

Kathleen said: 'I met Colonel Vaz at the airport. He was certainly lucky – he was supposed to be on that flight. I thought he seemed pleasant enough.'

Da Gruta pulled a face. 'As pleasant as a rattlesnake. Smooth and deadly – but hardly to the enemy.'

'Vaz is one of the government's Soviet-trained officers,' Branagh explained. 'And his main interest is number one. He's clueless in military affairs and was continually undermining the efforts of Santos. It's not good news that he'll be in control of this district.'

'And more bad news,' da Gruta added grimly. 'Rob tells me there are definite signs that Renamo are back in the area.'

D'Arcy said: 'I've started sending a few of our best recruits out on probing patrols. To be honest they're nowhere near ready for it, but they're on strict instructions just to look and listen and report back. And I'm afraid there's little doubt the bastards are back in the hills.'

Kathleen leaned forward. 'Which hills are those?'

Branagh pointed in the direction of Tumbo. The rolling backdrop of peaks had taken on a misty shade of purple-green in the failing light.

Perhaps it was her imagination but the air temperature seemed to have dropped abruptly, and she felt an involuntary shiver. The hills suddenly appeared to be very close.

They drank until mid-evening when Branagh left for Tumbo village and da Gruta drove off with Rob D'Arcy to the plantation house. More obliging than her step-cousin, the Portuguese manager had promised to show her round the old colonial mansion and the plantations the following day.

It was a welcome triumph after Branagh's obstructive attitude which wasn't helped by her observation that he drank too much. She'd instantly regretted saying it, but the moment was past because it was then that he left.

Now she settled down in her bedroom determined to catch up on her notes. But her mind refused to concentrate. So much had happened in such a short space of time. Her concentration wasn't helped by the ethereal buzz of mosquitoes. She decided they were most probably breeding in the bath; it had been filled with stagnant water for the purpose of flushing the lavatory, using the galvanised bucket provided. The atmosphere was hot and cloying, the air-conditioning system having long since expired. Single bulbs had been rationed to the cheap gilt wallfittings and the feeble light made it difficult for her to see what she was writing. From outside she could hear the crackle of the fire in the kitchen compound, and finally she fell asleep to the murmur of voices belonging to the hotel staff who sat around it.

She awoke with a start to find herself lying fully clothed on the bed, her pen and notepad still on her lap.

112

The glimmer of the wall lights battled against the thrust of morning sunlight burning through the window.

Someone was knocking on the door. Blearily she stumbled to open it.

To her surprise Branagh stood in the corridor, smiling. 'Good, you're dressed. Let's go.'

She was still half-asleep. 'What? Go where?'

'I'll tell you on the way. Grab your things.'

Her heart began to pound. Was there about to be an attack by bandits? Branagh didn't appear anxious, but then perhaps he wouldn't. She snatched the notebook from the bed and picked up her rucksack.

Branagh had already gone and she followed breathlessly along the corridor and down the dark stairwell to the lobby and out into the brilliant sunshine. Hardly had she fallen into the waiting Land-Rover, than it took off at speed across the square.

'For God's sake, Mike, not so fast!' she protested. 'What's the hurry? Please tell me what's happening?'

He nodded in the direction they were travelling. Towards Tumbo. 'An aircraft has arrived at the strip.'

Kathleen blinked. 'I beg your pardon?' She did not believe she was hearing this.

'Fred's flown in and he's going back to Maputo. A change of plan. It's your lucky day, you could have been stuck here for weeks.'

'You bastard!' The words exploded with anger. 'How *dare* you! Stop immediately and let me out.'

Branagh gave a brittle laugh. 'No way. We agreed yesterday you were on the next aircraft out.'

She continued her protests, which Branagh steadfastly ignored, until the aircraft came into view. The gleaming white Twin Otter in Direct Action livery was already surrounded by curious villagers.

Fred Petkus and Leif Månson stood by a stack of unloaded medical supplies.

The Russian beckoned Branagh as he approached.

113

'Hey, Irish, what do you think of my new toy? I buy her for a song.'

Månson didn't appear to share the enthusiasm. 'No wonder it was so cheap if it breaks down in the first week.'

Petkus shook his head despairingly. 'I tell you, Swedish, an airplane is like a new lover. It takes time to get to know each other. You must expect these little problems. I will radio for a spare from the plantation house.'

'My regional manager will not be pleased to hear about this,' Månson moaned, 'All that money for a heap of junk.'

Petkus was without sympathy. 'Then do not tell him,' he hissed.

'So there's no chance of takeoff today?' Branagh asked.

The pilot shook his head sadly while Kathleen grinned in triumph. 'What a shame, Mike, and I was so looking forward to getting back to the Maputo slums.'

The Russian then recognised Kathleen for the first time, shaking her warmly by the hand. 'Little Irish – you go so quickly? This man is not your cousin, eh?'

She spared Branagh a withering glance. 'Oh, he's my cousin all right. Not that you'd think so. I've never met anyone so rude and unhelpful. All he's interested in is getting me out of here.'

Petkus stared at his friend. 'Irish, you are a madman. I will give my gold tooth for such a pretty young visitor—'

'Stow it, Fred,' Branagh growled. 'You had no right to send her here without asking me.'

Leif Månson looked on in confusion. 'Would someone mind explaining to me what is going on?'

Kathleen stepped forward defiantly. 'I'm a journalist,' she stated flatly. 'I'm here to write about the struggle in Mozambique and efforts being made to rehabilitate the refugees. I heard that my step-cousin – Mike – was here, so I thought this would be a good place to start . . .'

Månson turned on Branagh. 'Is this right, Michael? You're refusing to assist your own relative? I don't believe it. What kind of person are you? Besides, don't you realise the good it would do Direct Action? Some good press stories, the publicity?'

Branagh shut his eyes. 'You mean your regional manager.'

The Swede's pinched face lightened the more he thought about it. 'Well, yes, I'm sure he would be delighted. You know, I really don't understand you, Michael. I think we ought to extend every facility to Miss . . . er?'

'Kathleen Coogan.' The impish grin was very wide.

The previous night, five hundred miles to the north of Maputo, the South African strike craft *Jan Smuts* had wallowed in the long starlit swells of the Mozambique Channel between the African mainland and the island of Madagascar.

The Israeli-built vessel had cruised the eight hundred miles from Durban over a three-day period. To avoid drawing attention to itself it rarely exceeded fifteen knots, a speed easily absorbed by the four 16-cylinder MTUs.

Among the crew only the skipper, a grizzled fifty year old from a seafaring Port Elizabeth family, knew their ultimate destination. For their part the naval officers and ratings scarcely bothered to speculate.

Almost certainly it would be a mission to infiltrate commandos of 4 Recce somewhere along the Mozambique coast. After all, they had made such clandestine voyages countless times before. Indeed that had been the reason for the removal of the aft gun turret and deck clutter – to make room for the two Avalanche racing catamarans that the *Jan Smuts* carried pickaback on two pairs of giant davits.

The gun well space itself had been converted into two aft messes where the undercover soldiers spent their time, the engine rooms separating them from the ship's crew. On this mission there were eleven commandos, sufficient to man just one of the Avalanche cats.

There was only one man new to the team drawn from 4 Recce. Anton Boyd had been a last-minute replacement for the regular lieutenant who had been struck down with malaria.

It was an uncomfortable position for Boyd. A veteran himself he was still regarded as a newcomer by this closeknit team who had trained, fought and shared the same combat experiences together over many years. Each man had grown to respect the next and to trust his comrade with his life.

To be a last-minute draft was to be an intruder. An unwelcome necessity to plug a gap. A fellow professional with equal experience perhaps, but still a stranger.

As second-in-command he would be treated with brittle courtesy. Nevertheless the suspicion would continue until he was able to prove his worth. To earn respect and fellowship in the bush. Only then would the silent hostility end and the new man be fully accepted. It was like entering a secret society in which no one was told of the unwritten rules they were expected to obey.

Anton Boyd accepted his position. He was not a gregarious man; indeed he preferred his own company and was content to select a lower bunk away from the others. There he smoked and read a dog-eared paperback, not speaking until spoken to, not attempting to force his presence. He would wait for them to approach him.

Yet all the time he observed closely, silently assessing each member of the team in turn, their relationship with each other and the unofficial pecking order. He began to make mental note of their apparent strengths and weaknesses, mindful that one day his life might also have to depend on them.

Boyd had already realised that this was a mission with

116

a difference. Always secretive at the best of times, military intelligence had kept this assignment completely under wraps. It had been made perfectly clear from the outset that there would be no general briefing beforehand, and that the orders would be revealed only when necessary by the commander of the actual five-man team who would carry out the operation.

That was Captain Nico Dracht, who had greeted Boyd warily, his ice blue eyes appraising the new man with whose military record he would be familiar. In fact Boyd could sense the calculating mind at work in the head of longish sun-bleached hair. His commander's welcome had been just warm enough to be civil, but no more.

'Glad to have you aboard, Anton,' Dracht had said in a laconic Afrikaans drawl. 'You're replacing a good man, an old friend. But I'm sure you're up to it – if your record's anything to go by. You'll soon fit in.'

The inference was, of course, that he might not.

But if Dracht was getting the measure of the lieutenant, then the newcomer was also getting the measure of his new commander. Boyd knew how to work the army system and had called in an old favour with a contact in personnel in order to dig out the service record of Nico Dracht.

It appeared that the chunkily built-blond was something apart from the average special forces soldier. Much of his career had been spent in Namibia and Angola as a white officer in the infamous 32 'Buffalo' Battalion. But his regular career had been interspersed with postings to the Directorate of Military Intelligence. Most assignments had been unspecified, but at one time he had been aide-de-camp to Colonel Willem van der Walt, a shadowy figure at whom liberal African newspapers had pointed accusing fingers on subjects such as the death squads and the notorious Civil Co-operation Bureau. That was the clandestine organisation responsible for the control of the Renamo terrorist network if one believed the press – and

Boyd didn't. Like the majority of South Africans, both military and civilian, he knew little about the Machiavellian workings of his country's secret military and intelligence apparatus. Such speculative accusations by left-wing journalists he dismissed as the usual anti-apartheid rantings from countries with no proud record of democracy or human rights themselves.

Boyd had once read in a Zimbabwe newspaper allegations of horrendous atrocities committed by the right-wing Renamo guerrillas. Accusations that they were masterminded in Pretoria. He had consigned the paper straight to the trash bin.

Sure, he himself had been ashore in Mozambique many times, mostly to blow a bridge here, a railway line there. Jobs you couldn't trust the *kaffirs* to do themselves. Forget their own arses some of them, if they weren't permanently attached.

And sure, he himself had only been witness to one small piece of the vast jigsaw of secret South African operations. But he had never met more than the occasional ragged Renamo agent or a handful of their so-called officers. Certainly he had never witnessed anything like the bandit massacres alleged in that Zimbabwe newspaper. If there was a grain of truth in it, which he doubted, it would be down to the Renamo guerrillas themselves. Typical black-on-black bloodlust. You could count on that.

The bastards might have political ambitions and the conceit to want to run South Africa, but the truth was they still had five hundred years of evolution to go.

'Fancy a game of cards, Anton?'

It was Armando da Gruta who interrupted Boyd's thoughts. Although he was a staff sergeant he didn't even hesitate to use the new officer's first name. Boyd overlooked the bad manners; rank counted for little in special forces like this.

'What's the game?'

Da Gruta's teeth glinted in the glow of the bulkhead light. Handsome bastard, Boyd thought, and doesn't he just know it. Even standing by the bunk, his natural arrogance was apparent in his body language. One hand on hip, the other idly stroking his lush black hair, his raised elbow against the bunkpost. A festoon of matching underarm hair hung exposed by the wide holes of his cutaway T-shirt. It may have been a concession to the cloying humidity of the mess, but somehow Boyd doubted it. Like the snug-fitting blue denim jeans, it was all just part of Armando da Gruta's usual peacock posturing.

'Poker,' the Portuguese commando said.

'What stakes? Matchsticks?'

An uncertain smirk crossed da Gruta's face. Was this man for real? 'Good joke that, Anton. We play for rand – or dollars of course. Upper limit of two hundred rand a game. Helps calm the nerves before an infil – takes the mind off all those black beasties waitin' in the dark.' He laughed, showing his very white teeth.

Boyd said: 'Count me out.'

'C'mon, man. Nico's team always makes a four. Sort of ritual before we go in. Bad juju not to.'

Boyd picked up his paperback. 'I don't play for money.'

Da Gruta's upper lip curled in a doglike snarl. 'That's a patsy way of thinking—' He hesitated, afraid he'd overstepped the mark. 'Not how we do things on Dracht's team.'

The newcomer met the other's glare. 'It's not patsy, Armando, when you've a wife and babe to support. Not on our wages. Got it?'

Da Gruta's snarl transformed itself awkwardly into an uncertain smile. 'Sure thing.' He forced a laugh. 'How the hell would I know? Like the rest of us I'm a fuckin' bachelor. How would we know?'

Boyd said nothing more, just watched as da Gruta backed off having made it clear that the newcomer was considered the odd man out. He went back to his book but couldn't concentrate. One eye was continually drawn to the poker game that got under way without him.

There was no doubt Nico Dracht was in control of the huddled group beneath the umbrella of coiling cigarette smoke. In sheer physical presence alone the deeply tanned blond with his huge box shoulders dominated the proceedings as he dealt with a practised hand.

Next to him da Gruta would laugh and joke – frequently with a nod in Boyd's direction – and whisper in Dracht's ear like a court jester anxious to amuse his king.

The third man hardly shared the humour. His dull grey eyes were devoid of emotion, his thin lips parting only to take the ganja roll-up he habitually smoked. That was Drummond. A sandy-haired veteran of Ian Smith's Rhodesia with fair skin that freckled and reddened but refused to tan despite a lifetime under the African sun. Like many soldiers Boyd had met in the South African Army, Drummond had seen no future for himself after the Lancaster House agreement when his country was renamed Zimbabwe. There was no way he could come to terms with his country being handed over to the Communist 'terrs' and Robert Mugabe. The very people he had spent years trying to destroy as a soldier in the Rhodesian Light Infantry. Leaving behind the vast farm that had been in his family for generations, he went in the only direction left open to him – south. To South Africa, the last bastion of the white man on the entire continent.

But like many ex-Rhodesians, Drummond's presence wasn't accepted totally without rancour. Many South Africans privately felt little sympathy for what they saw as the capitulation of their fellow colonialists. In the armed forces in particular it rankled to hear the constant recalling of military exploits of derring-do: 'When we were in Rhodesia we did this . . . did that . . .'

It had earned Drummond and others the 'Wenwee' nickname, which was only part affection. The other part was an unspoken reminder: 'When you were in Rhodesia, you fucked up.'

The game was interrupted when both da Gruta and Drummond were down some two hundred rand to Nico Dracht. It was Drummond's long-standing Shona cohort, Moses Chipoko whose grinning black face appeared at the bulkhead hatch.

'Skipper says stand by, *bass*. ETA is thirty minutes.'

The announcement came as a profound relief. Each man had been aware of the rising tension in the humid, airless confines of the mess with the condensation trickling down its steel walls. And everyone was happy to give up the pretence of concentrating on trivia.

No orders were given. The only signal was Dracht scooping in the rand and the deck of cards.

Silently each man went about the business of final preparations. Stoves were packed with 24-hours ration packs and biltong meat strips, and lightweight feather sleeping bags into a motley collection of rucksacks. None were regular South African Army issue. No uniforms were worn, just civilian denims and T-shirts in neutral colours and the traditional *veldschoen* suede boots. Belt orders carried two water bottles each, a combat knife and ammunition pouches.

'Don't worry about Frelimo scum, Anton.' It was da Gruta again, talking as he hoisted his rucksack onto his shoulders. 'I don't know what it's been like on your ops, but we've never had trouble. We once did a hit on some ANC shit in Maputo itself. Blew up the bastard in his car. Then everything went wrong. Our transport broke down and Frelimo troops were swarming everywhere. We got to our RV in the harbour hours late and we were picked up by our own dinghy. By the time we got to our mother craft the sun was up. I ask you?' He grinned fondly at the memory. 'The whole Frelimo garrison's on full alert, and there's us in the strike craft – sitting in the middle of Maputo bay in broad daylight. And there's this

Frelimo patrol boat with a 20mm cannon moored right there. We were shitting ourselves. And you know what?'

'I can guess,' Boyd said evenly.

'Yeah, we just sailed out. Straight up. Not a shot fired, nothing. Those bastards couldn't hit shit if they tried. But they didn't even try. Too busy wiping the sleep from their eyes.'

Boyd picked up his AK47 and began checking it over. All the team used the Russian-made weapons, captured in Angola, rather than the regulation Armscor R4. The exception was da Gruta who insisted on his favoured Portuguese M48 submachine-gun. 'I've had closer shaves than that, Armando. It doesn't pay to get complacent.'

Da Gruta glared resentfully at the mild rebuke. 'Yeah, sure, Anton, you're right about that.'

'Yes.'

'Doesn't do to get careless. It can happen. And you know what those black bastards do if they catch one of us?'

'I've heard,' Boyd murmured dismissively.

'First thing is down with his trousers. Bugger the white man, break his spirit.' Da Gruta winced at his own imagination.

Boyd opened his mouth to tell the man to shut it, but he was saved the effort by Dracht: 'You spreadin' horror stories again, Armando. Anyone stuck it up your arse you'd probably love it, you randy sod. Doubt it would break your spirit. Now get up on deck.'

Dracht turned to Boyd: 'Don't mind Armando. He's got a big mouth and keeps his brains in his underpants. But he's a good soldier. Ace.'

Boyd made no comment. He shouldered his pack, picked up his AK47 and followed the Portuguese commando through the hatch.

It was a spectacular night. A vista of silver stars sparkled across the enormity of the ultramarine sky and the smoky yellow moon peered down through a gossamer wisp of cloud. The soft purple radiance played on the long swells as they shrugged towards the inky smudge of coast. Finally they broke on the shoreline in an incandescent necklace of white surf. Even above the heavy thud of the engines the sound of their thunder reached his ears like distant artillery.

Boyd felt the thrill of anticipation course through his body as the deckplates began to tremble beneath his feet. The skipper was winding up the MTUs, sixty-four pounding cylinders of synchronised power. He experienced the forward surge, like an aircraft on a runway, as the screws began to bite and the salt spray whipped at his face.

'This way, Anton!'

It was da Gruta who beckoned, grinning with near maniacal glee as his black hair stood up in the slipstream like iron filings. He jabbed a finger at one of the two Avalanche catamarans resting on the deck beneath the giant davits.

As Boyd climbed in after da Gruta, he was followed by Dracht. There was now a full complement of ten men plus coxswain. All set.

Streaming eyes turned towards the coast, sweeping the ragged indigo frieze of palms where a Renamo agent should be waiting with an old American Valiant car to transport them inland. Nothing, nothing. The speed of the *Jan Smuts* increased, the slipstream and crash of water beneath the bows rising to a deafening pitch. Boyd scanned the beach again, and again. He could see nothing.

'AHOY!' A voice drifted back from the officer of the watch on the bridge.

Da Gruta nudged Boyd hard in the ribs. 'See? There!'

He followed the direction of the Portuguese commando's pointing finger. There it was. A steady blink of light amid the coastal spume of the breakers. From the bridge he heard the metallic chatter of the Aldis lamp as the signal was acknowledged.

Da Gruta's eyes had become wild with excitement and

123

his wide grin infectious. 'I love this bit, Anton, don't you? The big run in.'

Boyd smiled. 'I prefer the run out. Never was a good sailor. This is more like a bloody fairground ride.'

Grimacing happily, with spray dripping from his face, da Gruta appeared not to hear. His attention had been diverted up to the grey steel davits as the winches began cranking up the slack. The hawsers tightened, their woven steel tendrils flexing, creaking as the cat was hoisted clear of the deck. Boyd felt the wind catch and the assault craft begin to sway.

'Airsick and seasick all in one,' da Gruta mused through his set grin. 'Skip'll have to slow. Must get down to twenty-five knots. If we hit one of these long swells any faster we'll nosedive straight to the bottom.' He turned directly to Boyd and laughed harshly. 'Roll on death and let's fuck the mermaids!'

The cat began swinging out, suspended above the rush of water, and the rocking motion became more pronounced and rhythmic.

From the seat on his right, Moses Chipoko let out a howl that sounded like pure anguish. But when Boyd turned he found himself staring into a laughing black face half-hidden by a woollen skullcap pulled down almost to his eyes.

The African was loving every moment.

'That's it!' da Gruta gasped, and Boyd sensed the throttling back of the main engines to launch speed. He glanced over the gunwale. Mere feet below him the wake of the *Jan Smuts* was creaming past at an alarming rate. A whistle blasted from the bridge. Instantly the coxswain responded, firing the cat's twin V-8 Volvo inboards, and the craft began to tremble like a living thing.

The cat lurched suddenly, dipping towards the black lacquered waves as the hawsers ran out. At twenty knots the craft hit the sea in an explosion of spume. Scarcely had Boyd recovered from the impact and the drenching of salt water than he felt the bite of the cat's own power.

Already the *Jan Smuts* was veering off, a black wraith without lights, vanishing rapidly into the night to wait anxiously for the pick-up.

Now the cat settled into its own harsh rhythm, slamming hard into each oncoming roller, the dark outline of the coast edging ever closer.

Boyd relaxed and looked again at da Gruta. He had to shout into the other man's ear to be heard above the Volvos and the crashing of the bow wave. 'You look happy.'

'Sure. This mission's different. Very different. This time I'm going home.'

'Mozambique?'

'I mean home.'

'You know our destination?'

Da Gruta tapped his nose. 'Dracht and I go back a long time – but don't tell him I told you.'

'And where's home?'

'A place called Gutala.'

5

After two days Kathleen sensed that Branagh's attitude towards her had mellowed slightly. He was no longer directly antagonistic and appeared to have come to terms with her presence.

As she breakfasted in the Direct Action compound at Tumbo with him and Leif Månson, she was actually beginning to enjoy his company.

But the almost convivial atmosphere was shattered by the unexpected arrival of the village woman.

'He's gone, he's gone. My Carlos he does not come home last night.'

She was beside herself with grief and hugged her five-year-old son to her side for comfort. On her back, snugly held in place by a *capulana* wrap, a baby slept blissfully unaware that its father was missing.

Branagh looked up from his bowl of maize porridge. 'Where was Carlos working?'

'In the top field. He grows squash and *feijão* bean. Near the big baobab tree.'

'I know it.'

'He leave his tools there. I find them this morning,' the woman said between tears. 'He never leave his tools.'

'Why didn't you come to tell me last night?'

The woman looked sheepish, the skin of her face blushing to a darker hue.

Branagh said: 'Okay, I'll take a look. Go home for now. I'm sure he'll be all right.'

As the woman tugged her young son after her, Kathleen asked: 'What do you think has happened?'

'It could mean he's been taken by *bandidos*,' Månson said. 'I've heard it's something they do. Take someone from the outlying fields and make him tell them about village defences.' He had suddenly lost what little appetite he had.

'Carlos is also the village rake,' Branagh pointed out. 'That's why his wife waited until this morning before raising the alarm.'

Maraika had been listening from the kitchen lean-to. Now she came forward apprehensively. 'Mikey, you think *bandidos* are here again?'

Branagh put down his bowl and stood up. 'I'd be surprised after the pasting we gave them last time. It's more likely that they'd move on to find an easier target.'

'That man D'Arcy said he believed they were in the hills again,' Kathleen reminded.

She's a sharp one and no mistake, Branagh thought grudgingly. 'That's true. But his scouts are hardly trained yet – an unknown quantity. Besides, that French tobacco station is about twenty miles away from here.'

'Nevertheless . . .' Månson muttered, as usual anticipating the worst.

Maraika said: 'I know where Carlos sleeps with his mistress. She lives down by river.'

'Pay her a visit,' Branagh suggested. 'Meanwhile I'll go up to the top fields.'

Månson collected his safari jacket from the hanger hooked beside the porch; this one was a delicate shade of coral. 'I want to check that antibiotics inventory, Michael. So why not take Kathleen with you? You've also those hypodermics to deliver – show her the hospital.'

Branagh opened his mouth, then shut it again. Now that Månson had decided that Kathleen was going to provide him with some glowing publicity to show his regional manager, he had become a man possessed.

127

Kathleen helped Branagh load the cardboard boxes into the Land-Rover. As they pulled away Maraika was setting off to visit the mistress of the missing Carlos. The spinning wheels powdered her in an instant film of red dust. She stood for a moment, staring after the disappearing vehicle. Wearily she tried to shake the stuff from her newly washed hair. She started walking again, deep in thought, wondering when the green potion would begin to work.

News of the disappearance had spread rapidly. On the track to the outer crop fields Branagh and Kathleen passed the families of two farmers heading back into the village, all their worldly possessions stacked aboard ox-driven carts. Even the small *mashamba* family plots, usually tended by villagers, were deserted.

When they finally stopped by the big baobab tree an uncanny silence had fallen over the land. Branagh was immediately aware of the absence of the usual sounds. No grind and clink of hoes digging into the sun-baked earth; no chattering of women's voices exchanging village gossip; no laughter from the helping children. Only the whispering of the breeze in the ripening grey ranks of mealie. Beyond, the upright battalions of eucalyptus took on a secretive air about what might be found lurking in the cover they provided.

Kathleen shielded her eyes against the pounding sun. This was one of the high points of the river valley side and from here the blue-green vista of hills felt unnervingly close. It was as though she could reach out and touch them. Who or what, she wondered, might be up there? Even watching her as she looked? She shuddered inwardly at the thought.

Branagh was crouching to examine a wooden handled rake in the corner of the field.

'What is it, Mike?'

'I imagine this belongs to Carlos.' He pointed to a series of impressions in the dust. 'Bare feet here. Then boot prints behind them. Thick military-pattern tread.'

'Are you sure?'

'They were hiding in the scrub hedge at the corner. As Carlos finished his work for the day he was walking backwards while he raked. They just had to leave their cover to take two steps. He didn't stand a chance.'

Branagh kicked at the grass at the field's edge. 'This is where they sat and waited.'

'God, how awful.' She stared at the hills, venting her anger on an unseen menace she didn't begin to comprehend. 'What will they do with him?'

'Ask him questions. Find out about defences, Frelimo dispositions, numbers, that sort of thing.'

'And if he refuses to tell them?'

'He'll tell them.'

'You mean they'll torture him?'

Branagh looked at her. In her eyes he could see the confusion and the anger. He was reminded of the small girl in Armagh. And he imagined there had been the same confusion and anger in her eyes when her father and brother were shot dead by the British Army stakeout.

He said: 'We'd better go.'

No words were spoken on the drive back to the village. There was nothing for Branagh to say. They both knew the fate of the farmer. Words couldn't soothe what the imagination had already witnessed in every disgusting detail. He could sense she was shocked. Perversely he wanted to remind her that she had wanted to discover the truth about Mozambique, and now she knew it. Half of him wanted to shock her, this total stranger who had intruded from his past. The other half wanted to protect the child in the farmhouse bedroom with its Cinderella wallpaper and cuddly toys.

He stopped off to see Carlos's wife, returning to the Land-Rover after only a few minutes.

'How did she take it?' Kathleen asked anxiously.

'The same as you or I would. But they've had to live with this sort of thing for a long time now. When you suffer so much for so long you become resigned to it eventually.'

As Branagh restarted the engine she said: 'Mike, I know you're not happy that Leif Månson wants me to stay. And I realise it's my own fault. I've said I shouldn't have mentioned anything about you living with Maraika – and then about your drinking. I'm very sorry, it won't happen again. But now I'm here I really would like to get on with my job.'

He glanced at her and grinned. 'That sounds very professional and determined.'

'It is!' She glared at him. 'I am. Please don't patronise me, Mike. You seem to forget that I'm not the little girl you once knew. I've grown up, if you hadn't noticed. My father and oldest brother were shot dead by the Brits and two of my other brothers are in the Maze. I've reported on bombings and shootings and road accidents for the last five years. I've seen dead bodies and I've seen what horrific injuries ten pounds of Semtex can inflict. I'm new to this country, but not to what's going on here, Mike. It's almost home from home. Please understand that. Don't feel you need to shield me from it all.'

It was a powerful and eloquent speech. And Branagh had to admit she had come pretty close to pinpointing his feelings about her presence. But only close. And he couldn't allow her to come any closer.

'Point taken,' he said. 'Just one thing. There is a difference between here and the Six Counties. Never be fooled into believing that what's happening here is a civil war. That gives it a sort of respectability it doesn't deserve.'

They lapsed again into silence as he drove her to the hospital in Gutala which they had passed on the previous day. After depositing the syringes that Petkus had flown in, he showed her round the building. It was utilitarian but cheerfully painted and filled with simple wooden beds built by the carpenter Francisco and his workers. There

130

was little medical equipment to be seen, but the drugs shelves were reasonably well-stocked courtesy of Direct Action. Branagh found himself studying Kathleen's reaction with interest as they toured each section. The busiest of these was the maternity clinic where she quickly made friends with mothers and their offspring despite the language barrier. In the ward she shook hands with each bemused patient in turn.

'I feel like visiting royalty,' she confided as Branagh showed her to an unmarked door at the rear.

As she stepped inside, Branagh heard her sharp intake of breath. It was a large, bright room, the walls decorated with giant – Disney-like cartoon characters inexpertly drawn. A group of children looked up from a roughly made table at which they were sketching under the watchful eye of a white-robed Mozambican nun who worked for the Health Service. Three boys stood, like ballet dancers, clutching a wooden rail that ran the full width of the far wall. They grinned spontaneously at the sight of the newcomers. It took several seconds before it occurred to Kathleen that they were not learning to dance; they were learning to walk. Each one had an aluminium limb fitted to the stumped remains of a leg.

'Mines,' Branagh whispered in her ear. 'The bandits aren't too fussy where they leave them.'

He watched as Kathleen unhesitatingly went to each in turn and spoke a few words. The youngsters didn't understand what was said, but clearly enjoyed being the centre of attention.

'Your friend has a way with children,' the nun observed.

'My cousin,' he said with a certain affection. This was the girl from the Armagh farmhouse all those years ago.

When Kathleen joined them, he introduced her to Sister Graca. 'You must be very proud of Senhor Branagh and what he has done for us here.'

131

Kathleen spared Branagh an impudent smile and said: 'I'm sure I'd be proud of him if he let me, Sister.'

A fine eyebrow raised on the serene forehead. 'Ah, yes, and modest too no doubt. But he is largely the reason we have the hospital here in Gutala. Your cousin pressured the Provincial Health Directorate for funds, and when only a little money came he organised the materials and the building of it with Din Din.'

'Din Din?'

Branagh said: 'Din Din Singh – our local Indian wizard, an engineer from Delhi. God knows why he came here in the first place. He's only officially qualified as a car mechanic, but he turns his hand to anything, including aircraft repairs. Now he's trained a whole team of locals who are getting even more inventive than him. As you can see, he's a competent builder of hospitals.'

Sister Graca smiled at Kathleen. 'So you can see what peace can bring to this angry land.'

'Like the John Lennon song,' Kathleen said. '"Give peace a chance".'

The nun clasped her hands together. 'If only.'

'And the children,' Kathleen asked, 'what are they drawing? Is this an art class?'

'Not an art class,' Branagh answered. 'Psychotherapy.'

Sister Graca said: 'I will show you.' She took a sheet of drawing paper from a five-year-old girl, who looked up at them with a strangely emotionless expression on her face. Her eyes were dull, lacking natural childish sparkle. It was almost as though the mind behind the eyes had in some way died.

Kathleen frowned as she studied the crayoned scribble. 'I don't understand.'

'A picture of Mummy and Daddy,' the nun explained softly.

The red crayon mark was not earth, Kathleen suddenly realised, it was blood. The squiggles were not bushes and branches in the grass. They represented a decapitated head and dismembered limbs.

Sister Graca said: 'That is how she remembers them. It is all she ever draws.'

It was a relief when the profound silence that followed was interrupted by the steady drone of an aircraft passing overhead. Someone was coming in to the strip.

Branagh said: 'We'd better go.'

'Of course,' the nun replied, 'they will need your transport.'

At the door Kathleen paused. 'I'll be here for a while Sister. Perhaps I could come and help.'

'That would be most kind.'

On the track towards the airstrip Kathleen said: 'Thanks for showing me the hospital, Mike. I have to know, to understand. I wonder if that little girl will ever get over it.'

Branagh took a bend in a four-wheel drift. 'There's a whole generation here who will never get over it. And it won't be helped by your offer to play nurse.'

'What do you mean?'

'Do you speak Portuguese?'

'You know I don't.'

'Do you have any medical knowledge?'

A pause. 'No.'

'Then leave them be. They've nurses and helpers. All they need is to be pointed in the right direction. They've got to learn to look after themselves. To stand on their own feet and get back their self-respect. Not survive on aid and charity handouts. Like they've got to find the will to win this war for themselves.'

Her eyes smouldered with indignation. 'God, you're a heartless bastard. What's happened to you over the years?'

He ignored her question. 'You call yourself a journalist. So do what you *can* do. Write.'

'Don't worry, I will!' she snapped back. 'And don't get any more funny ideas about putting me on a plane.'

133

To her surprise Branagh laughed. 'No, Kathy, I think I know when I'm beaten. You'd scratch my eyes out, Fred would dislocate my jaw, and Månson would fire me – again.' He stopped short of admitting that he was actually beginning to enjoy her company.

By the time they reached the strip an Arbaérea Piper Aztec had landed. Ian Hagan was in conversation with Senhora da Gruta who was dressed in an ample stone-coloured safari jacket and long culottes. Next to her stood a man whom Branagh did not recognise.

Hagan smiled broadly when he saw Kathleen emerge from the Land-Rover. 'Hi, Kathy, are you okay?' He scowled disapprovingly at Branagh. 'I was a wee bit concerned when I left you. Looked like you were having a wrestling match.'

Kathleen laughed. 'We were – and I won. We've come to an understanding.'

'So you're staying on?'

Before she could reply Senhora da Gruta bustled between them, offering Branagh a powdered cheek to kiss.

'What a wonderful surprise, Veronique,' he lied. 'Jorge will be pleased. Are you wanting a lift to the plantation house?'

'Dear Michael, how sweet of you, but no. We radioed Jorge before we left. He's picking us up.' She suddenly recognised Kathleen. 'You are a long way from Maputo, my dear.'

A nervous smile. 'Mike is my cousin.'

'How interesting,' Senhora da Gruta said absently, turning back to Branagh. 'Michael, I don't think you've ever met my dear friend Willem?'

The man was in his fifties, of upright bearing and fit-looking in casual slacks and a blue blazer worn over a lemon polo shirt. The colour accentuated the tanned skin of the open face and bald crown which was surrounded by a monk's halo of silver hair. But it was the enigmatic smile and the very pale, distant blue eyes that were his most striking features.

'Mike Branagh.'

'Willem van der Walt.' The handshake was firm, the accent less harsh than that of most Afrikaners. 'And the charming young lady?'

'My step-cousin Kathleen from Ireland.'

His eyes sparkled as he took her offered hand tenderly in his own. 'Enchanted to meet you, Kathleen.'

Branagh said: 'Is this a business or pleasure trip?'

Van der Walt surrendered the hand slowly. 'A happy combination, Mr Branagh. I have known Veronique and the da Gruta family for many years. Sadly because of the civil war here I've been unable to visit Gutala since Frelimo took over. But now that restrictions are relaxing a little, it is possible that we can now examine some trading arrangements. This area has many possibilities.'

'Mostly bananas,' Branagh said.

Van der Walt looked at him curiously. 'Yes, of course. And cotton.'

Kathleen glanced between the two men, sensing an undercurrent of antagonism. Perhaps it was bad chemistry, or some other reason she did not know. The unmistakably hostile silence was broken by the noisy arrival of Jorge da Gruta's Toyota. As the plantation manager climbed out of his vehicle he did not appear overjoyed at meeting either his wife or Willem van der Walt. He gave his wife a perfunctory kiss on the cheek, then shook the South African's hand with apparent reluctance.

'It's been a long time, Jorge,' van der Walt said. 'I've seen Veronique regularly, but you never come to Jo'burg. You really should leave this place more often.'

'Someone has to do the work here,' Jorge replied stiffly. He appeared anxious to be going. 'I'll load your luggage.'

Van der Walt turned to Senhora da Gruta. 'Veronique,

135

why don't we invite the charming young lady and Mr Branagh to supper? After all, I do believe that tomorrow is your birthday – we can celebrate.'

She stared up at those blue million-miles-away eyes that she had always found so beguiling. 'Willem, you remembered!' She glared across at her husband. 'Which is more than I expect Jorge has . . . Yes, it is a wonderful idea.' She turned to Branagh. 'The two of you must come tomorrow evening. I insist. Colonel Vaz will also be there. He's flying here in the morning. But it's all very informal. About eight o'clock?'

Kathleen glanced up at Branagh, expecting him to turn the invitation down.

To her surprise he said: 'It will be a pleasure.' He didn't mention that he considered an urgent meeting with Vaz to be imperative. The incident of the missing farmer meant that time was not on their side.

There was something about the arrival of Willem van der Walt in Gutala that concerned Branagh. Yet for the life of him he couldn't think why. It was a feeling, an instinct. That weird sixth sense that makes the hairs crawl on the back of the neck. Something had caused Branagh to feel an instant distrust of the South African. Something didn't quite fit, but he couldn't put his finger on it. And the name. Van der Walt. Somehow it rang a distant bell. Had he heard it before? Perhaps Jorge da Gruta had mentioned the old family friend, or more likely it had been his wife. But if either of them had, Branagh could not recall the occasion.

He was still pondering the question when they arrived back at Tumbo.

Månson was still fussing over his hospital supplies and inventory, dabbing furiously at his pocket calculator as he tried to resolve some discrepancy. Maraika was putting the final touches to lunch and a dishevelled Fred Petkus was in the compound, nursing a ferocious hangover from the previous night.

'Hey, Irish,' the Russian croaked. 'Where you been? I need some aspirin.'

'There's some in the bedroom – I'll get them. You should have asked Maraika.'

Petkus managed to smile through his wince of pain. 'I did. These are not so good for headaches.' He held up the strip of foil with its neat row of day-numbered pills and waved it from side to side.

Branagh took them from him. 'She's not too good at reading English. I'll get you aspirin.'

Kathleen looked at Branagh curiously. 'Are those Maraika's?'

'Well they're not mine,' he answered without explanation and disappeared inside the hut.

The Russian beckoned Kathleen to join him on the improvised bench of plank and oil cans. 'I hear there is a problem in the upper fields.'

'Mike thinks a farmer was taken by Renamo.'

Petkus grunted. 'Those bastards. You think the *matsangas* learn not to come back here. Not after what happened last time.'

'Mike mentioned that too. What did you do?'

'We give them a dose of their own medicine, little Irish, that's what we do. Me and Irish. He has these booby traps made – the bow and arrow – it is not what those *matsangas* expect, eh? Irish knows these things from when he is in the army.'

'I don't think he used bows and arrows.'

Petkus chuckled. 'In special forces you use many things.'

'He was with the Engineers.'

The Russian gave an inscrutable shrug. 'If that is what he says, then he was with engineers . . .'

Branagh returned with a bottle of aspirins.

'And who was on the airplane that woke me up?' Petkus asked.

'The dragon of Gutala – and a South African friend. A Willem van der Walt.'

137

Petkus crunched on three aspirin before swallowing them without water. 'Van der Walt?'

'D'you know him?'

The Russian belched lightly. 'I know of a van der Walt. A *Colonel* van der Walt.'

Branagh recalled the man's upright stance and his immaculate turnout. It was possible. 'What about him? South African military?'

Petkus nodded. 'Two years back I am seconded to the Soviet intelligence unit in Maputo. There are files on all the peoples running the *matsangas* in Mozambique. A Colonel van der Walt was listed in the Civil Co-operation Bureau.'

Branagh frowned. 'The Bureau?'

'What's that?' Kathleen asked.

'It's part of the Directorate of Military Intelligence,' Branagh explained patiently. 'A highly secret unit responsible for both the South African death squads and running operations in Mozambique.'

'De Klerk had it disbanded recently,' Petkus added conversationally. 'If you believe what you read, eh, Irish?'

Kathleen was puzzled. 'So you mean the bandits are no longer run by South Africa?'

Branagh said: 'What Fred means is you can disband an organisation, but that doesn't necessarily stop the component parts from still operating. Even if it is without official sanction.'

The Russian began rolling himself a cigarette. 'I tell you this van der Walt and others are a law to themselves in that country. Very strong men, eh? The South African government does not control them. There it is the military and the secret ones who run their own affairs.'

Kathleen shook her head. 'I really can't believe that charming man at the airstrip could be one of them.'

Branagh said thoughtfully: 'I hope you're right.'

The bulbous old Valiant automobile finally expired on the remote dust track below the foothills of Gutala.

As the engine spluttered its last the stillness and utter blackness of the night closed in on the passengers. The Renamo agent kept his hands on the steering wheel and stared at the dials on the dashboard as though he expected them to offer a solution.

Nico Dracht said: 'They won't tell you anything. Get out and take a look.'

Perspiration began to trickle down the agent's face. 'This car's fucked, *bass*. It ain't no good goin' out there. I can't see nothin' in the dark.'

'Then take a fuckin' torch,' Dracht snapped. 'Christ to think we trained these bastards.'

From the back seat came the mimicking Rhodesian accent of Drummond: 'Are we afraid of the dark, then? Watch out for the stalking leopard – BEHIND YOU!'

The agent gulped.

'Stop pissing about, Wenwee,' Dracht ordered. 'Go with him and see if you can see what the problem is. The rest of you spread up and down the track. I don't want to run into a bloody Frelimo patrol.'

The doors swung open and the commandos climbed out, stretching their cramped limbs for the first time in hours. Armando da Gruta and Chipoko the Shona retraced the tyre tracks towards the last bend.

Dracht beckoned Anton Boyd to follow him forward. For several minutes they walked in silence, AK47s at the ready in case of the unexpected. The soft crunch of their *veldschoen* boots in the dust was muted by the rustle of the trackside banana plants and the maddening chirrup of the cicadas. From somewhere above in the looming black denseness of the hills came the deep-throated yawn of a wild cat.

Dracht chuckled. 'That'll get our agent going. Expect he's just shit himself.' He came to a halt at the crown of a rise. 'This'll do. We can see anything that's coming.'

Boyd crouched down on the opposite side of the track. The newly posted officer's noncommittal silence was beginning to irk Dracht. He sensed unspoken disapproval. 'Don't talk much, Anton, do you?'

Boyd cleared his throat. 'Only when I've something to say.'

'Been to this area before?'

'Gutala? No.'

A sardonic grin broke Dracht's face, unseen in the darkness. 'So you know where we are?'

'The whole team knows where we are. I just happen to be the last one to be told.' A brief pause. 'I'm only the second-in-command.'

Back down the track Drummond put two fingers to his mouth and whistled.

Dracht stood up. 'Let's get back.' He fell into step alongside the other man. 'No hard feelings, Anton. This team goes back a long way together, and our ops have always been a little bit special. *Extra* sensitive you might say.'

'Like this one.'

Again Dracht smiled thinly. 'What makes you think that?'

'A feeling. No proper briefing as such. Our five-man team keeping separate from the rest of the lads in the cat. A long inland haul that might normally have been made by light aircraft or chopper.' He stopped there, not mentioning that he knew of Dracht's personal connections with the Directorate of Military Intelligence.

Dracht chuckled. 'Good observations. And you're right, of course. In fact I can tell you now, this is the most important mission ever undertaken by the Bureau. It could turn the tide of history in southern Africa . . .' He paused for effect, but in the intense velvet stillness of the African night it struck Boyd as being unnecessarily melodramatic. 'So now you understand why I've been overcautious in what I tell you. I had to be sure.'

Boyd's voice was flat. 'And now?'

His commander slapped him reassuringly on the shoulder. 'No problem, Anton. You're one of us.'

They were approaching the darkened Valiant, the bonnet raised to reveal its oily innards.

Wenwee Drummond said: 'I'm surprised this wreck's got us this far. Anyway the carburettor's fucked. It needs to be completely stripped and cleaned out.'

'We'll push the car off the track and cover it up,' Dracht decided calmly. 'You come back tomorrow, Wenwee, and sort out the problem in daylight. Meanwhile get Chipoko to take a branch and wipe out the tyre tracks for half a mile. We'll go the rest on foot.'

While the Shona commando disappeared into the night the other five pushed the heavy American car to a suitable spot where the trackside earth was level but hidden by vegetation. It took an hour to complete the camouflage and for Chipoko to return.

'You sure you can get us to the camp?' Dracht asked the agent.

'Sure thing, *bass*,' the agent replied confidently, but his eyes betrayed him.

It was hard going. The hillside was steep, the ground uneven with a surface of loose rock hidden by sharp buffalo grass. Each step threatened to unbalance the unwary and sprain an ankle, while the ubiquitous thorn bushes snatched spitefully out of the dark at every opportunity. The night became hot and airless the higher they climbed, the sheer physical effort required sapping their strength.

Two false peaks were crossed before they found the first summit. There the agent halted, took a torch from his pack and flashed a signal to the next summit. There was no response from the supposed Renamo lookout.

Dracht shook his head. 'The bastard's lost.'

Dawn was almost upon them before they finally stumbled onto the sleeping Renamo picket. He awoke to find the muzzle of Dracht's AK47 under his nose. The commando snapped a few choice words of Portuguese and the terrified soldier began to radio his base camp. It took

141

several attempts before his trembling hand found the right frequency.

There would have been little indication of the bandit camp from the air, and only little more from the ground. Soldiers of the battalion were well spread out in a high pass between two summits. Wrapped in their blankets they slept blissfully unaware of the commandos' approach. The centre of the camp was marked by two DPM awnings beneath which the cooks were already preparing pots of maize porridge. Round bread pellets were being handmoulded using stolen American aid flour.

Only one battered green tent was in evidence, lopsidedly erected beneath a lone tamboti tree. As they neared, the flap was thrown back and the massive bulk of Napoleão emerged, struggling to zip up his voluminous trousers. He saw the South Africans then and lumbered towards them. Behind him the small black face of a teenage boy peered warily around the tent flap, then disappeared back inside.

Napoleão's smiling eyes were unfocused and puffed with sleep. 'You are late, my friends. I expect you at midnight.'

Dracht did not flinch back from the beer-tainted wheeze. 'Always expect the unexpected, Commander. Especially when your own agent doesn't know his way.'

Napoleão began to chuckle, then winced suddenly, one hand reaching defensively to his groin as the commando grabbed him.

'Hurts when you laugh, does it?' Dracht asked innocently, hardly bothering to hide his amusement. News of Napoleão's intimate encounter with the bow-trap had spread like a bushfire through the Renamo battalion. It was the first thing that the agent had told Dracht's team, embellishing the event with relish.

'Who said you didn't have the balls for this war?' Drummond added provocatively.

Dracht ignored the Rhodesian's interruption. 'Right,

Commander, I want my boys out of sight of the rest of your baboons before they get up for their morning piss.'

Napoleão nodded painfully and with renewed respect. 'We have a site allocated. A few hundred metres . . .'

'And on the way let's take a look at Gutala district.'

Below, the river valley was shrouded in a cool grey mist. Through the binoculars trees and huts were reduced to purple outlines, flickering yellow highlights denoting the starting up of the charcoal breakfast fires.

'That's Tumbo village,' Napoleão offered. 'Ten miles beyond is Gutala itself. Maybe you can just make out the hotel at the highest point. There is a Frelimo flag flying above it.'

Out of the valley visibility was sharp and sunlit across the glossy banana groves to the town.

'I can see it,' Dracht said, lowering the high-powered binoculars. 'But first we have to plan in great detail. There must be no mistakes. We will need to know about all the dispositions of Frelimo troops and any militia units.'

Napoleão dabbed the perspiration from his face with a handkerchief. That sounded complicated, a job for his second-in-command João Chande. He said: 'You will also need to target the man Branagh. I understand he was responsible for the booby traps in the last attack.'

'The aid worker?' Armando da Gruta asked sarcastically.

Dracht said: 'I don't think we need concern ourselves with an aid worker, Commander. Let us concentrate on getting an accurate intelligence assessment.'

Napoleão stood proudly to his full height. 'That has begun. Last night we captured a farmer from one of the fields. Chande has been with him all night.'

'Chande?'

'Yes, he was once with the Portuguese secret police here. He knows all about interrogation techniques. Some very special methods.'

143

Dracht raised his hand. 'Spare me the details.' He turned to Armando da Gruta who was now studying the scene through the binoculars. 'What do you think?'

Perfect white teeth showed in a broad smile. 'I think, Nico, that it is nice to be home at last.'

'I would never have accepted,' Kathleen told Branagh the next evening. 'Not if I'd known how upset she'd be.'

'Too late now,' Branagh replied, changing down a gear as they sped through Gutala town and took the road out again towards the plantation house.

There had been a horrendously embarrassing scene over lunch when Branagh, having put it off as long as he could, casually announced that he and Kathleen had been invited to the da Grutas. While Maraika had brusquely handed Kathleen her chicken and rice dish, she had all but thrown Branagh his meal.

She stood over him with her arms folded in magnificent defiance. 'Always I want to see the plantation house. You know that, Mikey! Always you go alone to see them. You never take me. Never, never, never! Now this cousin comes and you take *her* to plantation house.'

Branagh had tried his best. 'You just weren't invited, sweetheart. Besides you wouldn't like it. And you certainly wouldn't like Veronique.'

Maraika pouted. 'Yes I would like her. And I can put on the dress from Maputo, and I can wear my high-heeled shoes. Just like the magazines. I can look smart like your cousin. You are ashamed of me.'

The outburst left Kathleen feeling both guilty and helpless to rectify the situation. Maraika was inconsolable, retreating to the kitchen lean-to to sulk for the remainder of the afternoon. Even Petkus's lascivious attempts to placate her met with a wall of stony silence.

'Problem is Jorge would never dream of asking Maraika,' Branagh explained. 'And Veronique would just refuse to have her in the house unless she was working for them. To them she's just another black. They only tolerate Mozambican ministers and officials of Embamo because they have to. But I can't tell Maraika that.'

'Doesn't she realise?'

Branagh deftly lit two cigarettes one-handedly and passed one across to her. 'She doesn't want to. She's desperate to be accepted on white terms, but it won't happen. Certainly not with the likes of the da Grutas. Maraika's an uneducated girl from the bush and that's how they see her.'

'Her English is quite good.'

'I didn't say she wasn't intelligent,' Branagh reproached. 'She's picked up English in the few years she's known me. But her cultural background is the African village. She can't – or won't – rationalise, like the tantrum over this supper at the house.'

'You can't blame her for that, Mike. I'm sure I'd feel the same. Maybe you shouldn't have introduced her to Western ways.'

Branagh smiled at the mild rebuke. 'I haven't. I came here to get away from the trappings of civilisation. You've seen how I live and what I eat. Just like any Mozambican villager.'

'Apart from the whiskey.'

'Apart from the whiskey,' he agreed. 'But you can't stop people's aspirations. Maraika sees magazines, meets Europeans in Gutala and occasionally in Maputo. She wants to look like them, dress like them and be respected like them.'

Kathleen stared thoughtfully at the rutted track ahead. 'But she remains just the girl from the bush?'

Branagh smiled, remembering some of the precious moments he and Maraika had shared. They flashed unbeckoned in his mind's eye. Moments that would have been impossible with any other woman he had ever known. The shared hilarity and the misunderstandings; the sorrows and the innocent passion that had recaptured his youth. Their relationship was never easy. It was full of mood swings and arguments, pouts and sullen silences, but relieved by Maraika's mischievous sense of humour and her unbreakable spirit. That was what he loved about her most. And through it all had run a freedom and a crazy wildness that could only have happened in Africa.

'Just the girl from the bush,' he repeated softly. 'And all the better for that.'

They were reaching the high ground now, the neverending banana grove giving way to a large clearing of patchy turf dotted with mimosa trees and ornate umbrella pines which had been imported by the da Grutas' ancestors. In the spangled shade discoloured statues peered from behind a variety of flowering shrubs.

The orange tiles of the pagoda-style roof glowed in the sunset above the tree tops, but it was several minutes before the full baroque mansion, with its bell tower and stucco arches, came into view.

'One of the last vestiges of the Portuguese empire,' Branagh said, applying the handbrake.

'It's beautiful,' Kathleen agreed, climbing down from the Land-Rover. It was the highest point for-miles, the orderly waves of glossy green banana plants falling gently away in all directions.

Jorge da Gruta came down the stone steps to meet them. 'Thank God you've arrived, Branagh!' he greeted. 'Veronique's back five minutes and she's already driving me mad. What with that South African and that baboon Vaz!' The big eyes blinked behind the spectacle lenses. 'Now they've promoted him to brigadier we'll never hear the end of it. He's more unbearable than ever!'

The hall was vast and white and cool above an echoing floor of polished dark wood. A few sombre oil paintings hung on the walls, but failed to fill the void.

Senhora da Gruta spotted their approach through an archway which led to a dining room of more comfortable proportions. 'Michael and dear Kathleen, how good of you to come,' she said as though she had been half-expecting them not to.

While Jorge bustled obediently to keep wine glasses filled to his wife's continuous instructions, Branagh found himself face to face with the newly promoted brigadier.

'I understand congratulations are in order.'

Out of uniform Brigadier José Vaz made no concessions to informality. The pale blue suit made Branagh feel as though he himself had come straight from a day's labour in the mealie fields with his bush shirt and the only trousers he possessed that weren't torn. 'You are most kind.'

'I understand you met my cousin at Beira airport.'

Vaz delicately switched his mother-of-pearl cigarette holder to his left hand before greeting Kathleen. 'Indeed it is good to renew your acquaintance – last time was just before Brigadier Santos's sad demise. There could have been happier circumstances in which to earn promotion.'

'Santos and I got on well,' Branagh said flatly.

The brigadier inclined his head. 'And I am sure that we will too, despite the little differences we have had in the past.'

'I assume Gutala remains in your area of responsibility as you've taken over from Santos?'

'Rest assured, Senhor Branagh, I consider Gutala pivotal to my entire brigade front. You can rest easy in your beds.'

Branagh nodded politely. 'Then you'll be interested to hear that there has been a Renamo probe on the outskirts of Tumbo village.'

There was the mildest flicker of surprise on Vaz's face. 'What happened, Mr Branagh?'

'A farmer was abducted at twilight. Two days ago. The usual Renamo form, seizing a villager to assess the strength of our defences.'

Jorge looked at Branagh. 'You didn't say anything to me about this abduction.'

147

'There wasn't much you could do about it, Jorge. I thought our new brigadier might have an idea or two.'

Vaz could not conceal his pleasure at the recognition of his new status; nevertheless he appeared singularly unconcerned. 'One missing farmer is hardly evidence enough to change brigade plans.'

Branagh smiled. 'But it might be prudent to send a detachment down to Tumbo from the main garrison at Gutala.'

The brigadier raised an eyebrow. 'To act as a deterrent?'

'Exactly that.'

Vaz leaned forward and touched Branagh patronisingly on the arm. 'Do leave these matters to those of us who have a view of the broader picture, there's a good chap.'

The Irishman's retort was defused by the timely call from Senhora da Gruta for supper to be served. Vaz turned abruptly away.

Jorge said consolingly: 'I'll get you another drink.'

'Thanks, but make it a whiskey, could you? I need one.'

Senhora da Gruta waved a tiny perfumed handkerchief like a semaphore flag. 'Jorge dear – do show dear Michael and his guest to their seats.'

The da Grutas sat at opposite ends of the table in their positions as hosts. Branagh and Kathleen were placed at one side, facing Vaz and Willem van der Walt across an expanse of gleaming cutlery and cut-glass goblets.

When Jorge had passed round the wine carafe and poured Branagh a stiff measure of whiskey, van der Walt pushed back his chair and stood. He ceremoniously cleared his throat. 'Dear Veronique – dear Jorge – and my new friends. I am not going to make a speech –' Jorge da Gruta winced – 'but I feel that a few words are in order,' the heavily articulated Afrikaner voice continued, 'as it is my first visit to Gutala since the beginning of the troubles here.' He inclined his head towards Vaz. 'And I hope it is an indication of how Mozambican nationals can work together with us South Africans and the Portuguese towards a prosperous future for this land which has so much potential.' He raised his glass. 'To peace and prosperity.'

Senhora da Gruta clapped delicately as glasses chimed against each other in accompaniment. It was strange, Branagh thought, to see van der Walt and Vaz seated happily side by side. As South African and Mozambican they should at least have been wary of each other. If Fred was right about van der Walt, then they should have been sworn enemies. Perhaps Fred had got it wrong.

'We also have a birthday to celebrate,' van der Walt added. 'And if we did not know her, we wouldn't possibly guess that Veronique has reached the tender age of sixty-five.'

'Sixty-one,' came her terse correction followed by a stifled laugh from the other end of the table where her husband sat.

Van der Walt glanced down at his wristwatch. 'I mentioned a birthday surprise earlier. A very special surprise. And as a retired military man you will understand my demand for precise timing and punctuality . . .' He paused and everyone at the table heard the growl of the car outside and the slamming of a door, followed moments later by the clack of leather soles on the hallway floor. Van der Walt added: 'Nevertheless he is fifteen minutes late – but then you would expect that of your son . . .'

Senhora da Gruta's mouth fell open as all eyes turned towards the archway. 'Armando?'

Branagh had to admit it was a stylish entrance. He was tall for a Portuguese with broad shoulders and a head of sleek black hair. Even in denims with a canvas jacket held nonchalantly over one shoulder he looked as though he belonged on a fashion catwalk.

'*Mamãe*,' he greeted, stepping towards his mother. She

offered her cheek as he leaned towards her, but he kissed her sour rosebud mouth instead.

'Silly boy,' she reproached mildly. 'Is there no woman you do not flirt with!'

'Not if she is as beautiful as you, *Mamãe*. Happy birthday.' He turned, noticing Kathleen who sat beside his mother. 'Enchanted,' he said taking her hand and pressing it to his lips. White teeth and dark eyes flashed as he smiled and lingered before walking past Branagh to where his father sat.

'*Pai*.'

Jorge rose awkwardly from his seat. 'How did you get here, son? I didn't hear another aircraft . . .'

Armando shook his reluctant father's hand fiercely. '*Pai*, it is good to see you.'

Jorge remained unmoved, unsmiling. 'I did not hear an aircraft,' he repeated.

'I got a flight into Cuamba and came the rest of the way by road. It is not so bad.'

Branagh watched as Armando da Gruta was given a spare chair between Kathleen and Veronique. The Irishman could scarcely believe that anyone would risk the long road to Cuamba without a military escort. It ran through unprotected country that was susceptible to both ambushes and mines.

Veronique da Gruta echoed his thoughts. 'You really should not take such risks, Armando.'

Armando coolly raised his hands, palms up. 'Anything to see *Mamãe* on her birthday.'

'You should both be proud of him,' van der Walt declared, and looked pointedly at Jorge. 'It has been no hardship fulfilling my promise to your father, the late Dom Pedro. He would be proud of his grandson. I said that I would take Armando under my wing in the South African military and I have done so, but he himself made his career the success that it has been.'

Vaz coughed discreetly.

Van der Walt smiled benignly at the Mozambican officer.

'Forgive me, Brigadier, how indelicate of me. But I am, of course, talking of the past. Pretoria has renounced all support for Renamo and, as you know, is seeking to build new economic links with Mozambique.'

Now Branagh knew that Fred Petkus had been right. He said: 'Pretoria has promised to stop supporting Renamo since the Nkomati Accord was signed six years ago – but it never has. Why should it be so different now?'

He might just as well have thrown a hand-grenade onto the table. After an embarrassed silence Senhora da Gruta quickly called for the servant girl to bring in the first course.

But as the consommé was served, van der Walt defended his position in a reasonable tone: 'Your point is accepted, Mr Branagh. It is believed that certain elements of the South African military continued *some* unauthorised support for the bandits. But that is no longer possible after the recent clampdown and the change of political climate in the new South Africa.' The enigmatic smile returned to his lips. 'Besides I have recently retired from the military myself, so my guesses are no better than yours.'

'Retired from the Civil Co-operation Bureau, you mean,' Branagh suggested lightly.

'Branagh!' Jorge hissed, placing a restraining hand on his friend's arm. 'This is not the place . . .'

Van der Walt waved his host's protest aside. 'It's all right, Jorge. Either Mr Branagh is very astute or remarkably well-informed. Or both.'

Branagh added: 'And that is why you haven't been able to visit Gutala for ten years. The Mozambique Government would not allow you in.'

The South African, now smiling broadly, raised his hands in a gesture of surrender. 'Yes, yes, that is true.

151

But of course what you cannot know, Mr Branagh, is that I was one of those in favour of disbanding the Bureau.'

Branagh said tersely. 'We will have to take your word about that.'

'I am afraid you will. But if Brigadier Vaz here is prepared to let bygones be bygones, I think you might be charitable enough to do the same.'

Branagh glared back angrily, his fists clenched white on the table. Beside the untouched soup bowl his whiskey glass was empty. He felt a boiling fury and an utter helplessness, not assisted by the effects of too much drink on an empty stomach. He told himself to shut up, not to spoil his hosts' evening. But he'd seen too much over the past fourteen years. Seen what the likes of van der Walt had achieved. Sitting in their ivory towers in Pretoria. The untouchables. Like the untouchables in other countries and in other wars. Images of the misty green landscape of Armagh flickered momentarily in his mind. Rain trickling down the back of his neck. Cold, wet gunmetal against the skin of his fingers. The dark figure in the cross hairs. About to die because the untouchables decreed it.

He said slowly: 'Bygones aren't bygones, however much you wish they were. Visit Gutala hospital – legless victims of your mines and kids who can only draw pictures of their dismembered parents. Bygone for you perhaps, not for them. And my woman's young brothers, taken by Renamo two years ago. Alive or dead, who knows? And the farmer abducted in Tumbo – when will his wife and children see him again?'

Armando da Gruta leaned in front of Kathleen. 'I don't know who you are, Irishman, but I don't think there is a place for you at this table. If there is a war there are casualties – that's part of it. What you conveniently forget is that South Africa was left alone to defend itself against the Communist sweep through Africa. Marxists and Cubans in Angola, the Marxists of Frelimo here, and joined by that Communist bastard Mugabe in Rhodesia. Plus the ANC terrorists in our own country. A line clear across Africa. The real front line against the Warsaw Pact wasn't in Germany, friend, it was *here* in southern Africa!'

Branagh listened patiently, then he said: 'Ten years ago you might have seen Mozambique as an enemy, but you know as well as I do – with due respect to the brigadier – that this country can't even protect itself against the bandits, let alone pose a threat to South Africa.'

'Only because we kept the pressure on,' Armando retorted.

Branagh took a deliberate deep breath to quell his rising temper. 'Pressure against what, Armando? The poorest country in Africa? Against a handful of ANC supporters – Mozambique has never been a major launch pad for them? Against the Soviet presence they allowed, which Pretoria would have acted against openly if there was any serious threat?'

'There was no threat,' Armando interrupted, 'because we *kept* the pressure on.'

'Pressure?' Branagh stared at him incredulously. 'You flattened the fucking place. Then when the people were down you proceeded to kick them in the bloody head. Some pressure.'

'Don't blame South Africa for what blacks do to each other in a civil war,' Armando retorted sniffily. He looked round the table for support; he found it in the po-faced expressions of van der Walt and his mother.

But Branagh wasn't prepared to let him get off that easily. 'What civil war is this, Armando? In most civil wars the opposition tries to win. Renamo doesn't even try. It has no policies, no political views, just a load of rhetoric. It's had ten years to win the hearts and minds of the people. And it does it by cutting off ears and noses and women's tits.'

'Enough!' Veronique called from the top of the table. 'I will not hear any more of this talk.'

Branagh's chair scraped violently against the floor as he stood up. 'I'm sorry, Jorge, forgive me, Veronique, if I've spoiled your birthday celebration, but I've lost my appetite.' He glanced pointedly at Armando da Gruta. 'In fact I feel positively sick. Kathleen – are you coming?'

She was taken off guard by the sudden turn of events. In some confusion she rose to her feet. 'I – I suppose so . . .'

Branagh ushered her towards the hallway. Behind him the brittle silence was broken by the sound of Armando laughing.

As they reached the front door he heard Willem van der Walt's voice calling after him: 'Perhaps, Mr Branagh, if you didn't drink so much you wouldn't be feeling sick—'

The door slammed behind them and the cool air rushed at Branagh, serving to soothe the raging anger in his head. He reached for the wall to steady himself.

'He had a point about the drink,' Kathleen said.

Branagh took a deep draught of air. 'Spare me another lecture.'

She put her arm in his, and he made no attempt to pull away. Softly she said: 'It's good to see that you still have some principles left.'

'What do you mean by that?'

'Oh, nothing.'

Branagh halted beside his Land-Rover. Something had caught his eye. Starlight picked out the pitted chrome on the fender of the battered Valiant automobile parked under a nearby mimosa tree. A Mozambican was asleep, mouth open, in the driver's seat.

'That must be Armando's transport,' Branagh thought aloud.

'I didn't think the roads were safe.'

'They're not. But what puzzles me is how he could drive into a secure area like Gutala without being stopped?'

'What do you mean?'

'Frelimo troops or militia have roadblocks to stop Renamo incursions. Someone like Armando has got to be a prime suspect as being an infiltrator or saboteur. At the very least he should have been taken to the police post for questioning.'

As they boarded the Land-Rover, she said: 'Perhaps he bribed the guards on the roadblock.'

Branagh smiled as he started the engine. 'You're learning fast, Kathy. I expect that's exactly what he did.'

The blurred wall of banana plants whistled past the open windows as Kathleen relaxed in her seat, enjoying the warm afterglow of the wine. 'You didn't like van der Walt from the moment you saw him, did you?'

'Not much. Just instinct really. Obviously Jorge doesn't care for him either.'

'And Armando?'

'Jorge doesn't talk about him much. Takes after his mother. He was at university in South Africa when Frelimo took over here. Bit of a playboy by all accounts – fast car, lots of girls and nightclubbing. That came to an abrupt end, of course. His inheritance vanished overnight. And it doesn't sound as though he's forgiven the Mozambicans for it either, does it? He joined the South African Army to get back at them.'

'What you said to Armando back there – is it true?'

'Every word.'

'You keep saying this isn't a civil war. I don't really understand.'

'Do you know how the bandits started?'

'Not properly,' she confessed. 'Peter at the British Embassy said something about Rhodesia.'

Branagh examined the track ahead. 'It all began the same year I was at your farmhouse in Ireland. The year the fledgling Frelimo party took over from the Portuguese. It was all Marxism and the black brotherhood then. In neighbouring Rhodesia Ian Smith was then fighting a rearguard

action against Mugabe's ZANU terrorists. The Mozambicans, with their new-found independence, thought it
churlish not to offer ZANU safe havens and bases over the
border, including Soviet training camps.'

'So that's what Armando meant about the front line,'
Kathleen murmured.

Branagh said: 'The Rhodesian Central Intelligence
Organisation responded by gathering a hard core of
fugitive black and white Mozambicans who'd fled the
new Frelimo regime. They included members of the
former Portuguese Pide secret police, commandos and
paratroops. But it was never more than two thousand
strong.

'They were then launched under the cover name of the
MNR or Mozambique National Resistance. You turn that
back to front Portuguese-style to get Renamo. But it was
nothing like it is today. Then it was a proper clandestine
warfare outfit aimed mostly at ZANU bases and raiding
the Malawi-Beira rail link. As covert operations go it was
quite justifiable to the Smith regime that was fighting for
its life.'

'What happened, Mike? What changed it to the
Renamo of today?'

Branagh lit a cigarette. 'That all started in 1980.
Mugabe came to power in Rhodesia and the defeated
whites offered the Renamo setup to South Africa in order
to keep the battle going against the Marxists. The likes of
van der Walt jumped at the chance. Expanded it – they
reckon twenty thousand bandits now – poured in money,
training and equipment and developed the terror tactics
you see today.

'The Defense Intelligence Agency even chipped in
with satellite communications. Fred tells me they were
destined for the pro-Western UNITA guerrillas in Angola,
but diverted via an old World War Two airfield in Zaire.
At that time the Yanks thought Renamo might succeed
and wanted to be on the winning side.'

'But according to you,' she pointed out, 'Renamo has never tried to win. So what's the point of it all?'

Branagh gave a sardonic laugh. 'The survival of South Africa, or greed. Perhaps both. With all rail links to Mozambique ports severed by bandits, all the land-locked nations like Zimbabwe, Malawi and Zambia have been obliged to export and import everything through South Africa – at a price. I expect van der Walt would argue that it was the only way to survive against sanctions.'

'HEY!' she squealed suddenly as Branagh swerved to avoid a goat that wandered into the headlight beam. 'Are you okay to drive, Mike?'

He grinned at her. 'No one's around this time of night.'

'Except goats.'

She closed her eyes and began to hum a tune.

'That sounds vaguely familiar,' he said.

She giggled. 'It ought to. Ma was always singing it.'

'Of course. A long time ago.'

Opening her eyes again, she said: 'Don't you ever miss Ireland, Mike? Not ever?'

He drew thoughtfully on his cigarette. 'Well, some-times. But it's like a dream now. As though it never was.'

She looked directly at him. 'Mike, do I have to go back to that awful hotel? It's full of mosquitoes and cock-roaches. I wouldn't mind sleeping on that couch.'

The drink must be addling my brain, Branagh thought, but somehow the idea of Kathleen in the hut no longer seemed such a terrible idea. 'You've talked me into it. We'll pick up your things tomorrow.'

As they bounced through the rough, deserted streets of Gutala and took the road to Tumbo, she began to hum the tune again. Before they reached the village they were both singing, that and other long-forgotten ballads Branagh hadn't heard for fourteen years.

They stumbled from the Land-Rover, still singing, outside the Direct Action compound. With the headlights

157

off, the village was very dark. Only the occasional cooking fire or oil lamp still burning sent a misty aurora of light into the night sky over the woven compound walls. Somewhere a dog's howl rose above the chatter of the cicadas.

'No lights on,' Kathleen whispered hoarsely. 'Will Maraika be up?'

'Sssh!' Branagh laughed. 'No, she'll have gone to bed early in a sulk. Make sure she's asleep when I get back.' He wagged a finger at Kathleen. 'No nooky. My punishment for taking you.'

No sound came from inside the hut. The pungent smell of wood smoke lingered in the air above the embers of the cooking fire. Branagh cursed suddenly, stumbling over something by the door.

'Ssh!' Kathleen giggled, following him inside.

'I can't find my lighter,' Branagh's voice complained from the darkness.

It was like a flash of lightning. Unexpected and totally blinding, it shone directly in his face.

He shielded his eyes. 'What the hell?'

A stifled mumble and sudden scuffle of feet came from beyond the starburst of light. Then the beam shifted and he saw her. Maraika's eyes were wide with terror above the camouflaged forearm that gagged her mouth. She was twisting and turning in a relentless effort to escape from the man who held her.

Another sudden shuffle came from behind him. He spun awkwardly, wrong-footed. But Kathleen had been already seized by someone hiding by the door. Her cries of alarm were muted by her assailant.

'Christ,' he breathed, instinctively dropping into a crouch, anticipating that someone would launch at him from beyond the bright lights.

No one came. His mouth was parched and his heart was pounding, adrenalin driving the alcohol from his system. Still he squinted, peering into the dazzling array of torch beams, trying to discern the shadowy figures behind them.

Then his blood ran cold as he heard the cocking handle. One thing he would never mistake was the rasp of an AK47.

And suddenly the man was there in front of him. Like a jovial genie in a pantomime, spotlighted by someone's torch. He was big, very big with benign crinkled eyes set in a smiling black face.

'Who the hell are you?' Branagh demanded, but he really didn't have to ask.

'They call me Napoleão.'

6

Unseen hands grabbed at Branagh, forcing his arms hard up behind his back until he winced with the pain.

'So you are the Irishman?' the voice asked. The question was followed by an impatient pause. '*Answer* when I speak to you!'

Branagh had been doubled over, able only to see his own feet. Now someone gripped his hair, jerking him into a painful upright stance. The Renamo commander hadn't moved, a mountain of black flesh dressed in baggy DPM fatigues which were as new and clean as the highly polished boots he wore. If Branagh needed any confirmation of the misnomer of the word 'bandit', this was it.

'Let's try again,' Napoleão said mildly. 'You are the man called Branagh?'

'Yes.' A whisper.

'Louder!'

'YES!' Branagh roared with a sudden surge of anger.

The thick lips curled back to reveal white tombstone teeth. 'That's better, Branagh. I don't want to get the wrong man. I want the man responsible for boobytrapping this village last time. The man responsible for killing and maiming a dozen of my men. That is the man I want. It is a very personal score.'

Branagh studied the bulbous, sweat-slicked face before him. Tried to see beyond the smiling dark eyes with their beer-yellowed whites. 'Well, you've got me. So let the women go. You have no argument with them.'

Napoleão threw back his head and laughed until the

phlegm rattled in his throat. He cleared his mouth and spat on the floor. 'How chivalrous, Irishman. Your concern for your whore and this white woman is most touching. But you are in no position to give orders to Renamo.' He shuffled heavily towards Maraika, the torch beams following him as though he were the leading player in a shadowy stage set. The girl still stood immobile and petrified, restrained at the throat by one of Napoleão's bandits.

Branagh noticed for the first time that she was half-naked, the torchlight emphasising the dark lustre of her skin. Without taking his eyes from the Irishman's face, Napoleão's sausage fingers reached out and slowly, very slowly, caressed one of Maraika's breasts. Branagh watched, mesmerised, unable to look away as he witnessed the involuntary stiffening of her nipple and saw the girl turn her head away in humiliation. He refused to rise to the deliberate provocation.

Napoleão chuckled and withdrew his hand. 'You know what my men do with pangas, Irishman?'

Branagh's throat was parched, his mouth sour. 'I know.' His reply was scarcely audible.

'It only takes a word from me,' Napoleão sneered, 'to let my troops loose to have their pleasure with these women. My men have been deprived for many days.'

This time Branagh remained steadfastly silent.

'You and they are lucky this night, Irishman.' He sounded genuinely disappointed. 'I do not have orders to kill you, but to *warn* you. Warn you and the other Europeans to leave Gutala in the next twenty-four hours. My masters do not want your blood on their hands unnecessarily – a view, incidentally, that I do not share. So go away, and persuade the citizens of Gutala that it is no longer safe. If they want their old people and children to live, then they should evacuate the district. Do you understand?'

Branagh nodded. He understood full well. Renamo

was notorious for its ploy of visiting key members of society in advance of an attack – to intimidate them into setting an example by fleeing, so that the general population would take flight. It was easier to raze a township to the ground without opposition. And the bandits had no taste for a stand-up fight. If they did, they made sure they enjoyed overwhelming odds. No wonder they had been so angered by his booby-trap defence of Tumbo. At least the man called Napoleão was right about one thing, Branagh realised with an increasing sense of relief. This was indeed their lucky night. Often the bandits' methods of intimidation left the victim dead – a warning to others of what was to come.

'One thing before I go, Irishman,' Napoleão said, his voice suddenly deepening. 'I told you that this was very personal. You have caused me great hurt. Very great hurt.'

The Renamo commander nodded to the men holding Branagh. Instantly he felt the vicelike grips tighten on his biceps. A knee in the small of his back forced his pelvis forward, leaving the area of his groin unprotected. He glimpsed the big man's sudden, lumbering movement, like an overweight footballer going for a goal kick. It was all a blur as he lifted both legs from the ground in a desperate attempt to defend himself against the blow, the sudden increase in weight catching his guards by surprise.

He hit the dirt floor heavily with the excruciating pain exploding in his testicles. His mind spun in a seething red void that sparkled with myriad lights. Stabs of agony lapped like waves of molten lead from his groin, sapping his strength and his will to fight. He hovered on the edge of consciousness, only dully aware of the steel-capped boots thudding into his ribs and kidneys.

He must have passed out then for he was unaware of the bandits' departure which was followed by a flurry of activity as Maraika and Kathleen set about tending his wounds.

'Mikey, you awake?'

Double vision. Double vision and a headache the like of which he had never known before hammering against the inside of his skull like a bell.

He felt Maraika's hands cool against his face, stroking his cheeks. 'Mikey, you all right, all right? What they do to you! I think they kill you, Mikey. And I not live without you. I am sorry what I said. I love you.'

Her words resounded around his head like an echo. Then the pain in his groin began to radiate again in a gigantic drumbeat throb.

'Fred's here now.' It was Kathleen's voice, gentle and reassuring. 'He's got a medical kit – he'll give you a jab of morphine. Rest now.'

He moved his lips to speak, but no sound came out.

She leaned closer to his ear and he was aware of her hair brushing against his cheek, the smell of her skin. The smell of Ireland. 'I can't hear,' she whispered.

'I need a bloody drink.'

Mercifully he slept until well into the morning.

When he awoke it was to the sound of birdsong and the muted hubbub of voices from outside the hut. His vision had refocused, but when he moved gingerly, pain lanced at a hundred different parts of his body. He drew down the sheet to find that he was naked. No wonder his entire body throbbed in one great ache. His skin was a mass of blue and yellow bruises. His inner thighs were the colour of a Stilton cheese and he assumed that he must have involuntarily raised his legs to deflect Napoleão's vicious first blow. Thank God he had, he reflected, because his balls ached badly enough as it was. Had the full force landed as the bandit leader had intended then he'd have been hospitalised for a week.

'Mikey?' Maraika's head appeared around the door.

'Hello, sweetheart.' His mouth was arid. 'Are you all right, you and Kathleen? What they did to you . . .?'

She wrinkled her nose. 'That pig does not frighten me. They do not hurt us. But you, you hurt?'

'I hurt.'

'I get you special good coffee. With your whiskey in it.'

'You're priceless.'

Her teeth sparkled, flattered. 'I am priceless.'

He squinted against the light from outside. 'You look different. Your hair . . .'

She stepped lightly into the room and pirouetted on tiptoe. 'You like?'

He grinned. Gone were the long black tresses, now transformed into a shaggy urchin cut that looked distinctly familiar.

'Lisa cuts it for me while you and her go to plantation house.'

He laughed, and it hurt. 'How *will* I tell you and Kathleen apart?'

It was another hour before he hobbled out into the compound. A council of war seemed to be in progress with Fred Petkus arguing fiercely with Leif Månson, Francisco the carpenter and the captain of militia. The voices faltered as they saw Branagh appear.

Petkus shook his head despairingly. 'You do not manage so good by yourself, eh, Irish? Not so good without your old Russian buddy-buddy.'

'Stuff it, Fred,' Branagh replied with painful good humour.

Månson regarded the battered face with distaste. 'Don't you think you ought to visit the hospital, Michael? See if there are any bones broken?'

Petkus said: 'I checked him over. He's in one piece. Those *matsangas* do not aim their feet any better than their rifles.'

'Don't be so sure,' Branagh replied.

Månson drew himself up to his full height; it was a sure sign that he was about to announce an important

164

decision that was certain to meet with the Irishman's disapproval. 'Now look, Michael, I know your views about such matters, but I've decided it is time to evacuate.'

Branagh glared at him. 'Too right you know my views.'

'Listen, listen,' Månson added quickly, raising a hand defensively. 'Not for any length of time. Just a day or two until the situation becomes clear.'

'Your aircraft is grounded,' Branagh pointed out.

'I am aware of that.' He glowered pointedly at Petkus. 'But Fred has assured me that the parts have been located in Maputo and will be flown up shortly. With luck that might be today, or tomorrow at the latest.'

Branagh shut his eyes. How long would Månson have to be in Mozambique before he realised what life was like here? People were long on promises but short on delivery. Making things happen was an art form that even the indefatigable Petkus had not yet managed to master. Resignedly he said: 'Okay, Leif, you go. But it doesn't set a good example for Direct Action's image, does it? Bugging out to abandon our friends Francisco here and our good captain of militia to their fate. It's playing straight into Renamo's hands. All the Europeans take flight and the villagers follow into the bush. And another two years' good work is lost. We've got to lead by example, and not bow to the first signs of intimidation. We stood up to them last time. We gave the bandits a bloody nose that they haven't forgotten.' He looked to the carpenter with the missing ear and the captain. 'We can do it again . . . Besides, what would Kathleen write in her article if she witnessed you taking fright at the first indication of trouble?'

Månson blinked rapidly, sparing a glance at the girl whose presence he'd clearly overlooked in his anxiety to be gone. But he recovered quickly. 'My dear Miss Coogan, I do *actually* have an important meeting with my regional manager later this week.'

Branagh managed a smile, but it hurt his face to do so. 'And a duty to the people of the village.'

'Of course,' the Swede agreed with reluctance. 'I will naturally put that first. I was only thinking of everyone's safety.'

Branagh turned to the ever cheerful Francisco. 'Do you have the bow-traps ready?'

'More now. There are forty.' He sounded very pleased with the achievement.

'The next time it won't be so easy, they will be expecting them.' He looked to the captain of militia. 'We will need even more help from you, too Rafael.'

Rafael Costa was a small, balding man in his late thirties who wore a permanently apologetic expression on his leathery black face. He was immensely proud of his position in the community, and was always to be seen wearing his stolen Frelimo DPM trousers with holes worn at the knees. Having had the barest of essential weapons training himself, he was not best qualified as a leader of fighting men. Nevertheless, what he lacked in military prowess he made up for in a willingness to learn and unbounded enthusiasm.

This time, however, that enthusiasm was noticeably lacking. 'You want militia to deploy in Tumbo, Senhor Mike?'

'Just like last time, Rafael. You and your boys were very good.'

A momentary smile of pride flickered and then faded. 'But we now have new Brigadier Vaz. He makes many changes, he says militia to stay in Gutala as—' he thought hard about the unfamiliar expression he was searching for '—as mobile reserve.'

Branagh stared at him in disbelief. 'You're joking? Gutala's got Frelimo troops now – the militia are supposed to be in the outlying villages as a first-line defence.'

Rafael appeared baffled. 'Brigadier say mobile reserve very important job.'

'Do you know what a mobile reserve is, Rafael?'

An uneasy broad smile provided the Irishman with the answer he expected.

Branagh said: 'What transport do you have – cars or lorries?'

Rafael thought. 'We have good Bedford lorry from England. Like English soldiers. When we get engine it will be very fast.'

That truck was twenty years old to Branagh's certain knowledge and he had never seen it move from the vehicle graveyard near the hotel. Even Din Din Singh had given up on it.

At that moment the noisy arrival of Jorge da Gruta's Toyota interrupted their conversation, screeching to a halt beyond the wattle fence.

'Someone is in a hurry,' Petkus observed.

Da Gruta entered the compound, breathless and with his shirt half-buttoned. 'Branagh, have you seen Veronique this morning?' he implored.

'I haven't been in a position to see anyone. We had a personal visit from Renamo last night.'

Da Gruta noticed the bruises on Branagh's face. 'Christ, are you all right?'

'It was just a warning call. They want all Europeans to get out of the district.'

The plantation manager grunted, apparently only half-listening, his mind preoccupied. 'Damn that woman. You get a call from the *bandidos* and she's off joy-riding with van der Walt and that idiot son of mine.'

'Armando?'

Da Gruta pulled off his battered straw fedora and scratched at the thinning hair of his crown. 'I woke up late. Bloody great hangover after last night – that South African, Vaz and Veronique are a combination to drive any man to drink. Anyway, when I surfaced the servant tells me the three of them have gone off to inspect the plantation in that old Valiant motorcar. I ask you! And there's the *bandidos* wandering all over!'

167

Branagh said: 'I always knew you loved that wife of yours, Jorge.'

Behind their lenses, da Gruta's eyes stared. 'This is no time for jokes, Branagh. If anyone's going to kill her, it'll be me, not bloody *bandidos*.' He looked about him as though trying to decide in which direction to go first. 'I blame Armando. Headstrong young buck, just like his grandfather. I imagine it was my son's idea. Trying to set up some deal to sell the crop to van der Walt's new company. Got some Mozambican minister keen on the idea. Over my head of course – I'm just the bloody manager.'

'Can we help you look for her?' Branagh offered.

Da Gruta shook his head. 'No, no, it's bad enough I've got to waste *my* time . . .'

Petkus-stepped forward. 'I go with you, my Portugeezer friend. Just in case of trouble. At least I can shoot that old museum piece of yours, eh?'

The plantation manager blinked gratefully. 'Your company would be appreciated.'

As the two of them drove off down the track towards one of the remoter banana outstations, Branagh became aware that the captain of militia was tugging at his sleeve.

'What is it, Rafael?'

The crab-apple face smiled uncertainly. 'Please, Senhor Mike, they will not find the senhora.'

'What do you mean?'

'I see them this morning in the Americano car. At the checkpoint. They do not go on the plantation road, they take the road to the hills.'

'Why didn't you say something when Jorge was here?' Branagh demanded.

Miserably Rafael Costa contemplated the holes in the knees of his fatigue trousers. 'Because Senhor Jorge will be cross that I allow the car through the checkpoint.'

Branagh was exasperated. 'Why did you?'

'Because Senhor Armando tells me. My family always does what the family da Gruta say.'

'The family don't own you any longer, Rafael.'

Another awkward smile and a shrug. 'It is difficult. I remember when I am small how Senhor Armando beats me because I will not do what he says . . . Besides, I think why not let car pass? I also let Senhor Armando come through on the hill road last night.'

'The hill road?' Branagh was puzzled. Armando da Gruta had said he'd driven the road from Cuamba to the north; the hill road ran in the opposite direction. 'Why did you let him in? Just because you knew him? That's strictly against orders.'

'Oh no,' Rafael replied brightly, seeing salvation from his difficult situation. 'He has an official pass.'

'A Frelimo government pass?'

'*Sim*. It is signed by Brigadier Vaz.'

Branagh looked beyond the compound towards the rolling hills, their outline shimmering as the heat of the day rose. 'I'll take the Land-Rover and see if I can find them. Veronique can't realise what danger they might be in.'

Kathleen touched his arm. 'You're in no fit state.'

'A few bruises never hurt anyone.'

Maraika took his other arm and scowled across at Kathleen, her resentment plain. 'You stay, Mikey.'

But Branagh's mind was elsewhere. He shrugged himself free of the two women, and spoke to Francisco: 'You know the hills around here better than anyone. Fancy a ride?'

The village carpenter bared his large white teeth in one of his most infectious smiles. 'You bet, *bass*.'

Branagh took the road hard and fast. With the window down the warm slipstream was sucked inside to create a jinking vortex that tugged at their clothes and hair. Francisco was in his element, grinning fixedly as they bumped and rattled over the corrugated road. Like most Africans in remote areas the carpenter delighted in the

169

novel wonders of modern transport. And like most Mozambicans whom Branagh had met he had a total disregard for what damage the bad roads could do to a vehicle's suspension. Whilst Branagh would steer around or carefully negotiate the potholes, Francisco would career straight through them like an Arctic icebreaker. To the carpenter's chagrin he had long since been banned from driving Direct Action's vehicles, although he was always the first to volunteer as passenger on an unloading run whenever an aircraft came in.

Branagh guessed that today his joy was twofold: he was also returning to the hills where he had spent his childhood in the days before the monster of Renamo had been created.

There was no difficulty clearing the militia checkpoint as both men were well-known to the rag-tag group of villagers who manned it. Within minutes they were on the perimeter road which was nowadays rarely used by vehicles. Only once a year at harvest time would the big Embamo trucks come with their army of workers, while Frelimo lookouts stood guard against a surprise bandit attack from the hills.

There were no villagers here; no labourers on the plantation edge; no ox cart would dare venture beyond the checkpoint. It was a road that, to all intents and purposes, led to nowhere. A hundred and thirty miles of pitted track and blown bridges dotted with long-deserted settlements, that led eventually to the coast. And for its entire length was the ever present threat of ambush or hidden mine just waiting to detonate.

'Take road to lake,' Francisco called.

Branagh had heard of the lake, but in the years he had spent in Tumbo it had never been safe to visit. In the old days before the Portuguese pullout it had been a popular picnic spot for the da Grutas. And on one Sunday every year after harvest Jorge would organise trucks to take his plantation workers and their families to share in its delights. A shimmering silver-blue plate set in a high pass and fringed with weeping bean trees, gardenia and seringas. Many times on the verandah of the *cantina* Jorge had waxed lyrical over his nightly port. Remembering how a fish eagle would glide high over the lake on the thermals, looking down on the gathering flocks of jaçanas and crakes, plovers and waders. In those days elands, kudus and blue wildebeest would make their way to the waterside at dusk. Even the occasional elephant herd. But it was doubtful if many of these had survived fifteen years of Renamo poaching. No one knew what was left in the Mozambique wilderness, simply because no one had been able to go there except the bandits.

The lake road was now almost indistinguishable from the surrounding bush. Once it had been properly prepared, scraped by plantation bulldozers and surfaced with a layer of pounded stone. But the buffalo grass had encroached steadily over the years together with gorse and young thorns.

Those thorn branches now flailed noisily against the bodywork, whipping spitefully at the open windows as the Land-Rover growled manfully up the gradient. Branagh became steadily more conscious of the emptiness of the hillside with each mile of slow, bumping progress. Just vistas of grass-covered slopes, interspersed by stunted mopane trees and red bush-willow, for as far as the eye could see. And above, from an equally empty sky, the blinding white sun scorched mercilessly down on the vehicle's roof.

Francisco touched Branagh's arm. 'Ahead – my village.'

The Land-Rover slowed to a halt, brushing beneath an overhanging branch that offered some shade and cover from observation.

'How far?'

Francisco shrugged. 'Maybe five hundred paces.'

171

At this point the lake road had entered a gully which cut off the view from the rest of the hillside. From here they could see nothing, but then equally no one could observe them.

'We'll walk,' Branagh decided, and switched off the engine.

As they climbed out he was aware of the eerie silence suddenly pushing in on them from all sides. The utter quiet and stillness of the vast African bush was something that he still found awesome after all these years.

Each step sounded intrusively loud, rattling hidden loose stones underfoot. Sharp grass lashed its razor edge at their exposed flesh, drawing hairlines of blood, while opportunist thorns snatched viciously as though they had minds of their own.

By the time the bend was reached on the overgrown track, Branagh's shirt was adhering to his back like a second skin. Cautiously they rounded the corner.

Fifty metres ahead the gully opened up into a shallow depression where the remains of mud-brick buildings nestled on each side of the track.

'My village,' Francisco whispered hoarsely.

They stepped forward, and as they did Branagh realised that for the carpenter it was a walk back into his own tragic past. A few short miles and five long years. When he had been taken by the bandits to act as porter after watching his young wife gang-raped and then bayoneted to death.

It had been a year before Francisco managed to escape from a Renamo work camp miles to the north. But even the joy of his new-found freedom was soured by the certain knowledge that the bandits would butcher his cousins still in their custody. That was their way. An example to others who might have similar ideas.

For a year he walked the bush with no idea where he was. Surviving on brackish pondwater and grubs dug by hand from termite hills, he was finally found during a ground sweep by Frelimo troops. It was his lucky day; another twenty-four hours and he would have died of typhoid.

When he eventually recovered he tried to return to his village. But the government resettlement project around Gutala was as near as he could get.

'Thirty-four people died here,' he said softly, almost to himself.

Branagh became uncomfortably aware of an even more intense silence as they reached the first of the ruined huts. No birdsong, no cicadas, nothing. There was an atmosphere of desecration about the place. The air was heavy and sombre, and it smelled of death. Creepers now wound tentatively over the shattered remains of the mud bricks, scorched black by the fires that had burned off the rattan roofs.

There was nothing of any value or use left in the rubble. Five years before, the bandits would have taken everything, the spoils of their squalid war. Spoils that the villagers themselves were made to porter until they could walk no farther. Then the weak were shot; only the young and fit might live to see another day.

'My house,' Francisco said simply.

They stood, heads bowed, in a rough square of shattered brick, the acrid smell of charcoal still strong after all that time.

Branagh noticed the carpenter's hand go tentatively to the gnarled gristle that was all that remained of his ear. A tear broke away from his long lashes and hung glistening against the black sheen of his cheek. This was where it had all happened.

'One day,' Francisco said softly, 'I will rebuild this village. With my own hands.'

But Branagh knew he wouldn't. Because no one would ever want to live here again. It was no longer the place of Francisco's happy childhood memories. It was a place of evil. A place best left to the world of the spirits.

173

He left the carpenter alone with his thoughts and picked his way through the weed-infested rubble back to the road. He walked a few paces along the hot dusty track. Then he saw it, half-hidden behind a partially demolished wall.

Francisco rejoined him. 'What is it, Senhor Mike?'

Branagh pointed. 'The old Valiant that Armando came in.'

The carpenter's effervescent smile had returned. 'Ah good! I go see . . .'

'Wait!' Branagh warned, grabbing the man's arm. 'Let's not go rushing into something we might regret.'

Francisco followed Branagh across the overgrown track and behind some huts until they were able to scramble up the gully wall using bush-willows for cover. From this vantage point they were able to look directly down on the battered old limousine.

'One day I will have car like that,' Francisco enthused.

'There's someone in the front seat.' The driver was asleep.

'He is the one who drives Mr Armando. Maybe he is dead.'

Branagh strained to hear the indistinct sound. 'Dead men don't snore,' he said. And as he spoke the driver curled up into a more comfortable foetal position; the snoring stopped. Francisco relaxed. 'No problem, no *bandidos*. Senhora da Gruta and her friends are safe.'

'But where the hell are they and what are they doing?' Branagh tried to see farther up the lake road but the dense tangle of vegetation prevented him. 'Is there anything else on this road before one reaches the lake?'

'No, just the lake. About two miles. Not far in car.'

'We'll walk,' Branagh decided.

The carpenter followed the Irishman's stealthy advance along the top of the gully wall. It was a meandering route, avoiding angry clumps of thorn and overhanging trees. Away from the dead village, birds were again singing.

The sun was blistering but a light breeze cooled the hot air. It was almost pleasant. Branagh felt the temptation to relax his guard. They had found the car and no doubt would shortly stumble across the da Grutas and van der Walt enjoying sandwiches and coffee by the lake. Yet apprehension still stalked his mind. A nagging worry that refused to go away.

His eyes were distracted by the colourful flight of a white-fronted bee-eater.

The sudden impact of Francisco's palm on his back caught him off balance. He stumbled heavily onto his knees and the buffalo grass lashed at his face.

'Sorry, *bass!*' the carpenter breathed at his side. 'Look!'

Branagh parted the curtain of grass with his hands. Christ, had he forgotten everything he had ever been taught at Hereford? A child could have seen the sentry. Standing in the shade of an outcrop to avoid presenting a silhouette against the skyline.

'*Bandido,*' Francisco confirmed. 'See, he is not local. He has good uniform.'

'What does that mean?'

'A shock battalion, maybe from Gorongosa. Maybe one of Napoleão's men – like last time.'

'Napoleão?' Branagh echoed, remembering the events of the previous night. 'Oh yes. He's one of Napoleão's all right.'

Francisco blinked rapidly, his smile melting away. 'Yes. And it was Napoleão who destroys my village.'

Branagh turned his head at the sound of rasping steel. Sunlight flashed on the blade of the carpenter's panga.

'What do you think you're doing?'

'I will kill him.' Flatly.

'Put that bloody thing away. He's got an AK up there.'

Francisco felt for the juju charm at his throat. 'I will be fine. No problem.'

Branagh tapped at his own gold crucifix. 'I learned a

175

long time ago not to put too much trust in God. Mine or yours.' He glanced again at the sentry. 'There must be a camp nearby.'

The carpenter chewed on his lower lip. 'It is the Shangaan Queen.'

'What?'

'The Shangaan Queen,' Francisco repeated. 'The old mine.'

'You said there was nothing else here.'

'I forget. It is abandoned many, many years. When I am a boy we play there. Even then it is not used since my grandfather's generation.'

'What sort of mine is it?'

Francisco shrugged. 'It is before the time I work in South Africa and I do not go to the Shangaan Queen since.'

'We must try to find Senhora da Gruta and the others. They're in great danger—' But even as Branagh spoke, an uncomfortable thought occurred to him. Perhaps, just perhaps, the da Grutas and van der Walt hadn't stumbled into a bandit stronghold by accident. He said: 'Is there a way to get around that outcrop without being seen?'

'Sure, *bass*,' the carpenter replied, 'but it takes a little time.'

In fact it took ninety minutes to retrace their footsteps until they came across a dried-up streambed which fed out of the gully. The meandering ditch of water-smoothed pebbles ran downhill, then swept in a gentle arc half a mile below the outcrop. Its flanks of withered reed thickets offered excellent cover which allowed them to move swiftly if uncomfortably at a half-crouch. Once beyond the view of the outcrop Francisco picked up a game trail which climbed slowly back towards the gully and the lake road.

Approaching the crest, they began to move more warily between the basalt rocks that littered the area. Francisco led, worming between the larger formations

176

until he reached the edge of a large semicircular quarry which opened up immediately below them.

He moved to one side to allow Branagh to squeeze in beside him.

A hundred metres away the overgrown lake road could be seen continuing its upward path, partly obscured by the piles of mined slag that dotted the quarry floor like a range of tiny mountains. On the far side of the lake road a makeshift military camp had been erected using sheets of polythene to provide shelter for the small Renamo group. Branagh counted a dozen bandits, most of whom appeared to be sleeping or lounging idly.

Francisco nudged him and wriggled closer to the ledge to gain a better view.

The gaping mouth of the Shangaan Queen was clearly visible on the left side of the quarry wall. Crossed wooden spars barred the entrance and the message of the skull-and-crossbones sign was clear enough. *Perigo! Passagem probida!*

Between the slag piles on the quarry floor another small encampment had been made. There was a collection of rolled sleeping bags and dumped rucksacks. One African with distinctive Shona features was hunched over a naphtha stove and mess tin while two whites sat watching him boredly. All were dressed in casual civilian clothes. AK47s were stacked in a neat pyramid beside them.

Something triggered in Branagh's brain. A million years ago. A million miles away. Watching from the Armagh hedgerow. Cold water dripping from the leaves. The rubber eyepiece of a powerful 'scope to his eye. Alert on Dexedrine tabs. Observing the group of Provies, registering each minute detail. A full description, every nuance, every mannerism. Imprinted indelibly in his mind like a photograph.

It had been second nature then. Now he struggled.

One Shona tribesman with front teeth missing. Two

white men. One lank, sandy-haired individual in his forties: he took a hand-rolled cigarette from his mouth and
said something to the Shona. Even at that distance the
accent was unmistakably Rhodesian. The Shona laughed.
The second white man with a shaggy auburn moustache
didn't appear to share the joke. He returned to reading a
dog-eared paperback and seemed not to hear. The Shona
and the Rhodesian shrugged and laughed again between
themselves.

Francisco pointed a finger and Branagh manoeuvred to
change his angle of view.

There they were. Veronique da Gruta in an ample
culotted safari suit, and her son. Beside them Willem van
der Walt was in earnest conversation with another man.
Branagh guessed the bulky figure with the unkempt blond
hair was with the Shona's party. His denims were soiled
and stained and the deeply tanned face sported several
days' growth of beard.

Something was passed between them and a comment
made. Van der Walt laughed. 'Nico Dracht, you've a
wicked tongue!' the South African said loudly, and
Armando da Gruta shared the joke.

Veronique pulled a sour expression and snapped something that was clearly a rebuke.

Again it was van der Walt's distinctive accent that carried. 'Of course, the senhora is right. We must get back
before anyone comes looking for us.'

They broke up then, the group moving out of the
quarry enclave towards the lake road.

Branagh came to a sudden and impulsive decision.
'Francisco, I want to take a look in that mine.'

The carpenter stared at him. For once he was not smiling. In fact it was difficult for Branagh exactly to read the
expression in the Mozambican's eyes. Was it shock at
what he had just witnessed? Senhora da Gruta talking
with what appeared to be a team of white South African
mercenaries in a Renamo encampment. What sense of

betrayal must he feel? Europeans whom he believed he could trust in league with the very devils who had raped and murdered his wife? Those who had cut off his own ear and forced him to eat it.

Branagh said: 'We *must* find out what is going on – do you understand?'

There was no response. It was as though a mist had dulled the bright dark eyes.

'You *can* trust me, Francisco. We must look inside the mine.'

It was several moments before the carpenter eventually spoke. When he did his eyes were only inches from Branagh's. '*Can* I trust you, Senhor Mike? Can I trust any European? At this moment all I want to do is cut your throat.'

Branagh said slowly: 'I understand that. But I'm no part of this.'

'Senhora da Gruta is your friend.'

'Hardly, but that's not the point. I know nothing about this. Don't you want to know what is going on?'

'I know enough.'

Branagh said: 'Then I'll go alone.'

He began to wriggle back out of the narrow gap between the rocks when Francisco's hand restrained him. 'You do not understand mines. They are dangerous.'

'Then I need your help.'

The carpenter nodded grimly.

An access ledge had been deliberately cut in the quarry face. It led from the top down to the mouth of the Shangaan Queen, and was shielded by scrub that had miraculously taken root in what appeared to be solid rock. Only in the last few feet of the descent might they be observed by someone in the Renamo camp on the far side of the lake road.

But when Branagh peered cautiously from the cover of a stunted thorn he saw that the bandits had other things on their mind.

179

There was no sign of the da Grutas or the other Europeans. By the roadside a group of bandits had gathered around a mopane tree. From its branches a naked man hung by his feet.

'Carlos,' the carpenter breathed.

He made a sudden forward movement as the terrible scream reached their ears, but Branagh pulled him back. 'There's nothing we can do. I'm sorry.' He watched the sadness in Francisco's eyes. The carpenter had been there before. 'Let's get on.'

They scrambled over the cross spars barring the mouth of the Shangaan Queen to be swallowed up by the total darkness within. Branagh shuffled cautiously forward over the uneven rock floor.

'No problem,' came Francisco's whispered echo. 'You are safe for some fifty paces, I remember.'

A sudden wet-sounding noise began flapping above their heads. Branagh's heart skipped. Something fluttered against his face.

'Bats,' Francisco said flatly. 'Very small. Come on.' He took the lead and, a few metres farther down the rough-hewn tunnel, the frantic acrobatics of the disturbed creatures began to subside. Branagh followed the carpenter warily, ducking to avoid grazing his scalp on the uneven rocky ceiling. Ahead of him Francisco had come to a halt. 'We need to see now.'

Branagh took an old petrol lighter from his pocket and spun the wheel, the sudden flame harsh on his eyes.

'Yes,' Francisco murmured, 'as I remember.'

They were some fifty metres into the hillside, Branagh gauged, all the time progressing down a gradual decline. Now the narrow tunnel opened out into an antechamber of carved rock. Discarded tools of a bygone age were scattered about: broken picks, shovels and hammers, lengths of rotted rope and coils of rusting hawser.

'Nothing here,' Francisco observed. 'Just like when I was a boy.'

Branagh felt a mild disappointment. He had wanted to find something. A clue or some explanation as to what Jorge's wife was up to.

As he played the flickering light in one last arc, something caught his eye. A snake of heavy-duty electric cable ran away to a tunnel that veered off at right angles to the main passage. He stooped and ran a finger over it. Beneath the layer of dust the cable was glossy blue. New. With mounting curiosity he traced it back into the chamber where it disappeared under a mound of rotten hessian sacking. He pulled the stuff roughly away.

Francisco came to his side. There was no mistaking the bright yellow paintwork. 'A generator!'

Branagh kicked more hessian aside. White safety helmets lay in a neat row, complete with headlamps and battery pouches. 'Sure this mine's being used for something, Francisco.'

'Follow generator cable,' the carpenter suggested. 'It will be used to power lighting. Or drills.'

Branagh picked up a helmet. 'Try this for size.'

The batteries were newly charged, confirming Branagh's initial belief. Together they started to trace the generator cable down the right-angled tunnel. After a few metres the decline began to plunge so steeply that loose scree scattered away underfoot in a miniature avalanche. The ceiling was lower here, forcing them to bend double.

'Watch!' Francisco yelled.

Branagh froze, just in time. In the wavering beam of the head torch he had almost overlooked it and stepped straight into the shaft at his feet. It had been roughly concealed by cross bars of timber and more old sacking. The blue cable disappeared beneath it. Both a concealed entrance and a mantrap combined.

'You go too fast,' Francisco chided. 'Mines dangerous places. You let me go first.' He drew aside the sacking and peered into the void. Then he wrinkled his nose and sniffed the air.

'Cordite,' Branagh said.

'Someone use explosive down there.' He directed his head beam down the shaft. 'A ladder here. Not far.'

With the contraption missing half its rungs it made for a perilous descent to another horizontal passage that ran parallel beneath the tunnel above. Here the air was dense with the cloying bitter smell of explosive. Old railway sleepers had been sawn and jammed into position as roof supports, with bulb fittings attached to each and connected to the generator cable.

Francisco advanced carefully, playing his torch beam over the walls. He pointed his finger at various chalk markings and hieroglyphics drawn on the dark grey rock. 'See, the seams are marked and graded.'

'For what?'

The carpenter turned to face him. 'Platinum.'

'Platinum? Are you sure?'

'I worked on the Merensky Reef in Transvaal, Senhor Mike. To earn money so my wife and I can afford to marry. These are platinum workings.'

'Platinum,' Branagh echoed.

'The most valuable metal in the world.' Francisco stared up at the markings in wonder. 'So now you know what Senhora da Gruta does. She plans to plunder the wealth of our country.'

There was no answer to that. Branagh said: 'Let's get on.'

Only thirty metres farther along the tunnel came to an end, narrowing to the working edge, where two heavy-duty water-cooled pneumatic drills lay idly amidst the debris of extracted ore.

'Is this mine being fully worked?' Branagh asked.

Francisco gave a brittle laugh. 'No way, Senhor Mike. It takes ten tons of ore to extract one ounce of platinum. They will need tracks and wagons and winches to extract the ore. Then many lorries to take it to a special plant. There it is crushed and milled into a slurry. Then chemical

182

processes I do not understand. No such place exists in Mozambique.' He looked down at the pile of ore. 'This is a test drilling. To take for scientists in laboratory. See which seam is viable.'

'You can't tell by looking?'

He shook his head.

Branagh's head was reeling with the implications. Somehow he never had seen the mysterious van der Walt as an importer of Embamo bananas. That he had some plans for a secret platinum mine made much more sense. In the past year South African commercial investment money had been pouring into Mozambique with almost indecent haste. As though every businessman and entre-preneur in the region saw the opportunity of screwing advantageous co-operative deals out of a nation on its knees. The security threat of Renamo was still a major obstacle to those with cash to invest, but at least now there were talks about peace talks between the govern-ment and the bandits. Not that Branagh put any store by them. But then maybe Willem van der Walt knew more about that than he did.

By the time Branagh and Francisco emerged from the Shangaan Queen the sun was beginning its descent; the heat had gone from the air. To the Irishman's surprise the encampment had cleared. Vanished, as though it had never been. Renamo had taken to the coming night as they always did; Branagh just prayed that they weren't moving on Tumbo village and Gutala itself.

But he saw he had been wrong about one thing. The bandits had left just one macabre reminder of their earlier presence. The mutilated body of Carlos the farmer swung slowly to and fro from a branch of the mopane tree. Even if still alive he would never again have been the rake of Tumbo village.

7

'Veronique has gone,' Jorge da Gruta announced gloomily.

He was alone on the verandah of the Gutala *cantina* when Branagh arrived with Kathleen.

'I saw Hagan's plane take off on my way here,' the Irishman said.

'Flying to Harare with that smarmy Boer,' da Gruta confirmed. 'Taking her on a shopping trip, I ask you? Frelimo haven't got round to paying me for the past eight months – so it's our savings she's spending.' He snatched a fresh can of Castle from the table and tore off the pull-ring. 'At least she asked me to go with her.'

Branagh frowned. 'Isn't that unusual?' The da Grutas were not renowned for their shared marital bliss.

Da Gruta studied his fizzing glass ruefully. 'Yes, yes I suppose it is. Actually she seemed quite insistent on me joining them.'

'But you wouldn't?'

His brown eyes filled the spectacle lenses. 'Not with that Boer . . .'

'And Armando?'

Da Gruta sighed; he clearly considered his son to be a hopeless case. 'Apparently he dropped Veronique and van der Walt off after their trip to the lake. Then he drives back to Cuamba. The boy's got a death wish if you ask me. Crazy!'

'A picnic at the lake – is that what Veronique told you?'

Da Gruta nodded. 'Stupid idea of Armando's – could have got them all killed. And I wasted the whole day tearing around the plantations looking for them!'

Branagh studied the plantation manager for several moments. Over the years he'd grown fond of the man's taciturn manner and had learned to recognise the rare glimpses of bone dry humour. Beneath his matter-of-fact attitude he was deeply attached to the old family plantations. Why else should he work for seven days every week when the government was in such arrears with his miserly salary? And, although the manager would never have admitted it, Branagh had noticed the man's brusque affection for the estate workers. He went to unnecessary pains to provide welcome supplements to their routine diet of mealie; he would ensure that proper medical treatment was always available to them, and it was not unknown for him to donate some gift at weddings and other special occasions. In return his workers trusted and respected him like some Victorian father figure.

The last thing Branagh wished to do was to hurt him, but this was not a situation he could ignore. 'Jorge, I'm afraid Veronique did not go to the lake.'

Owl-like eyes blinked rapidly. 'What?'

Branagh told him about the day's events, the sighting of the bandits and the white mercenaries, about the mine. Kathleen listened with increasing incredulity as the story unfolded. Her step-cousin had mentioned nothing about it on their drive from Tumbo.

By the time Branagh had finished Jorge da Gruta had become quite pale. Without speaking he took time to unfurl the wrapping of one of the cigarillos he had imported from Oporto. He puckered his lips to wet the end. 'The Shangaan Queen,' he said at last, then paused to use his lighter. He exhaled pensively. 'It was started towards the end of the last century. Some Portuguese panners found gold grains in the silt in the streams up there. Asked our family if they could buy rights to open a mine.

185

In fine da Gruta tradition we booted them off and did it ourselves. Waste of time, though. A few viable seams, but not many. Too low-grade, you see. The family ran it as more of a hobby. I mean, labour was cheap enough. It finally closed during the last war.'

Branagh said: 'You know about the platinum?'

Da Gruta scratched at a wart on his cheek. 'That was down to my father, Dom Pedro. In the early seventies he was trying everything to hold our family business empire together. He was approached by some geologists involved in early American satellite surveys. They told him it was possible that there were platinum deposits in the hills hereabouts. An extension of the Merensky Reef in the north Transvaal. Nothing like that quantity, of course, more like the tail end of it. The leftovers.' He paused to watch his smoke drift across the square towards the hotel. 'Dom Pedro had some test drillings done discreetly. The analysis was good. There was little doubt it could have restored our family's fortunes. But then . . .'

'The Frelimo takeover?' Branagh guessed.

'Yes. But Veronique and I didn't know anything about it then. My father, the old bastard, kept it to himself. It was only when he died two years ago – you remember I was at the funeral in Portugal when Gutala was overrun and your woman's kid brothers disappeared?'

'I'll hardly forget it.'

'Even before the funeral reception was over, the lawyers pounced. The banks had finally foreclosed. Our *castelo* and the estate in the Serra do Caldeirão foothills was sold to become a golf course. An ignominious end to so many generations!' The big brown eyes were moist with the memory. 'Well, Dom Pedro left details of the Shangaan Queen surveys to young Armando. He'd always had such aspirations for his grandson. Saw a likeness to himself, I suppose. They say characteristics jump a generation, don't they? My father thought Armando might make more of it than I would. And I think he was right there.'

'What could Armando do?'

Da Gruta called for more beers. 'Until what you have just told me, I thought nothing. Veronique always had high hopes of doing something with the mine, but I told her it was ridiculous. This land is no longer ours, it belongs to Mozambique. It is as simple as that. But still she always talks about it.' He stopped while the *cantina* owner sullenly produced more cans from the bucket. His refrigerator was still broken. 'I hadn't counted on Willem van der Walt. He knew Dom Pedro from way back and promised to look after Armando in South Africa. He has come up with something, a crooked deal, I expect. But God knows what he hopes to achieve.'

'What about a deal with a corrupt minister?' Kathleen suggested.

Da Gruta looked at her with mild impatience; his view of pretty females was the same as his view of children and his black work force, that they should be seen and not heard. 'Young lady, Frelimo is not a particularly corrupt government. In fact, given the circumstances some might say it is remarkably uncorrupt. Clumsy and gullible perhaps. Inept some would say, but the one thing they've got going for them is basic honesty.' He shrugged. 'Maybe van der Walt is offering to mine the stuff for the government.'

'And the *bandidos*?' Branagh asked.

That was the conversation stopper. A full thirty seconds passed before da Gruta reflected. 'Veronique has always been a rash woman. Impulsive. It is what attracted me to her years ago. She always knew what we should do next. Full of ideas. Ambition . . . But the *bandidos,* I cannot explain that.'

Branagh said: 'It might be why she wanted you to go to Harare with her.'

Da Gruta's sombre expression hardly changed, but

187

Branagh sensed the shock that even the thought caused him. He murmured: 'She was very keen for me to go with her . . . Almost implored me.'

Kathleen leaned towards Branagh apprehensively. 'Do you think she might know about an attack?'

'It's possible.' Branagh's half-smile of attempted reassurance wasn't very convincing.

Both were caught off guard as da Gruta suddenly beat his fist on the table. 'Damn that Boer! He's behind all this.' He looked at Branagh. 'Of course, you know he was tied up with the Bureau, don't you? The Civil Cooperation Bureau.'

'I know.'

The plantation manager stared helplessly across the empty square. His words were thick with emotion. 'I love that woman, Branagh. Despite everything I still love her. You know, she was the driving force in getting this plantation up and running in the early days. A demon she was. Work, work, work. And since – well, it's been lonely for me. Always hoping she would accept what has happened. Come back here to stay, like in the old days. Stop tormenting herself with the likes of that Boer and her Portuguese cronies in Jo'burg – all craving for a past that will not return. And now – somehow she's got personally involved with *bandidos* – God!' The words of exasperation faded on his lips as a thought suddenly occurred to him. 'You won't tell Frelimo, will you? Not until I have a chance to talk to her – to find out the truth? If Brigadier Vaz was to find out, or the Administrator . . .'

'I'll say nothing,' Branagh promised. 'There's little to be gained by that.'

'Thanks, Branagh.' The taut features loosened for a moment in gratitude. Then: 'What about the carpenter boy?'

'I asked Francisco to trust me and keep it to himself until I had a chance to investigate. He wasn't happy, but he promised.'

188

'That's good—'

Branagh interrupted. 'But it can't be ignored, Jorge. I'll keep silent only until Veronique has a chance to explain what's going on. But in the meantime I think we have to anticipate another *bandido* attack.'

The plantation manager still wasn't thinking coherently. 'Oh yes, of course. Anything you say.'

'It could be tonight. That's a bit soon as the bastards only visited me last night, but we can't be sure. Francisco will put out the booby traps tonight, but we also need the militia down at Tumbo.'

Da Gruta grunted. 'You know what that baboon Vaz has said? Keep them in reserve here.'

Branagh nodded. 'I know. Any ideas? What about that chum of yours from the French tobacco station? He's got some troops in training.'

'Ask him yourself.' He glanced at his watch. 'He's supposed to be meeting me here for a drink. And he's late.'

It was another ten minutes before the rather smart Land-Rover of Robert D'Arcy entered the square and parked in front of the *cantina*. The driver was casually dressed but with a precision, from sharply pressed trouser creases to neatly rolled shirtsleeves, that suggested a strong military background. Again his strong dark features and the scarred right cheek struck Branagh as familiar.

D'Arcy didn't look too pleased. 'What a bastard of a day,' he announced and called for a brandy.

'What's the problem?' da Gruta asked.

'Remember I told you I've been sending patrols into the hills – trying to get some early warning of any bandit activity?' D'Arcy lit a small cigar. 'Well, one patrol got involved in a skirmish. No one was hurt, but I was rather obliged to pass the news on to Brigadier Vaz. So what happens? This morning I received a visit from the great man himself, pointing out in no uncertain terms that I'd no right to deploy our troops anywhere. Quite right, of

189

course, our role at the tobacco station is purely training. By the letter, only Vaz can deploy. I argued that the patrols were a form of advanced training – recce for intelligence, not recce to contact – but he'd have none of it. We've been officially confined to exercise only – and he's given me a new Mozambique officer of his choosing to ensure it – Moscow-trained.'

The brandy arrived, a local make which da Gruta advised had probably been watered down. When it refused to ignite to a match the *cantina* owner was summoned and, after a brief argument, a replacement glass was reluctantly produced.

'There were *bandidos* up on the lake road earlier today,' Branagh said.

D'Arcy savoured the fresh drink. 'That fits the pattern coming back from my boys – their own sightings plus reports from farmers and the survivors of recent attacks.'

'What exactly do you make of it?' da Gruta asked.

'I don't want to sound alarmist,' D'Arcy replied, 'but I'm getting the impression there's a large build-up developing.' He turned to Branagh. 'I heard about your trouble last night. If that *was* Napoleão, it means that the local Renamo yobos have been reinforced by at least one shock battalion from the Gorongosa. I think we could have big problems.'

'You told Vaz?' Branagh asked.

'Oh yes, but I got the usual reaction. Everything was under control. His.'

'I got the same answer when I asked for militia to be sent to Tumbo. We're the most vulnerable point, close to the hills and on the direct axis to Gutala.'

'And the airstrip,' D'Arcy pointed out.

'I'm seriously thinking of talking to the Administrator and asking him to evacuate the village. We can't rely on booby traps again.'

'Desert the village?' Kathleen interrupted. 'That's

terrible, so it is. Surely it would be ransacked. Isn't that playing into the bandits' hands?'

A ghost of a smile crossed Branagh's lips. She was learning fast. Almost beginning to sound like him. 'We might have no option, Kathy. I smell trouble and without protection . . .'

'But the harvest would be lost, your distribution centre and clinic—'

D'Arcy said: 'There might be a way. I could suggest to Vaz that some of my soldiers from the tobacco station conduct an exercise with the militia here in Gutala. He must agree to that. I won't be specific, but we could make sure they end up at Tumbo.'

Branagh grinned. He had taken an instinctive liking to the urbane Scot; it was as though their two minds thought as one. Almost as though to emphasise the point, D'Arcy said: 'We haven't met before have we, Mike? Northern Ireland perhaps?'

Branagh's smile was hesitant. 'The accent you mean? I don't think so.'

D'Arcy wasn't so sure. 'Ever been to Hereford?'

Momentarily Branagh felt his blood chill. It was Armyspeak for the élite Special Air Service Regiment based in the English county town. He felt suddenly exposed and vulnerable.

'No,' he lied, and the word seemed to stick in his gullet. It felt like a betrayal. Peter denying Christ three times before the cock crowed. Even now he could see Father McCabe reading the Bible passage from his pulpit in the rural Armagh chapel. Father McCabe who knew so much about betrayal.

Branagh was thankful for Jorge da Gruta's timely intervention. 'You can ask Vaz now – he's at the hotel tonight.'

They watched the khaki Soviet-built Gaz staff car with its tattered canvas roof as it rattled across the square. Almost before it came to a halt by the hotel entrance the passenger door opened and Brigadier Vaz stumbled out. He caught himself in time, swaggering and laughing with his colleagues. In one hand he held a beer can. The two other Mozambican officers fell out of the vehicle, one of them literally. Still laughing the three of them drained their beers and hurled the empty cans at an unfortunate mongrel dog which happened to be passing. It sped off, unscathed, as the three officers staggered into the hotel lobby. Their driver struggled after them carrying a crate of beer.

'Vaz said he had a staff meeting tonight,' D'Arcy mused.

'Wait until morning before you ask him,' Branagh advised.

Da Gruta watched in disgust. 'And you'd best not make it too early.'

Branagh and Kathleen left the *cantina* shortly after. The Irishman had no desire to be in the vicinity if Brigadier Vaz decided to join them in one of his more obnoxious and expansive moods. Drunk, and with sycophantic officers in his company, Branagh knew from past experience that Vaz would soon be on his usual political and racist hobby horse. Inevitably he would become more volatile and unpredictable with every can he consumed.

'What did Rob D'Arcy mean back there?' Kathleen asked as they approached Tumbo. 'About Hereford?'

Branagh glanced sideways at her. Cautiously he said: 'What did you think he meant?'

She stared ahead at the road. 'Did you know that my brothers believed you were with the SAS? Joseph was convinced you were working undercover to spy on them.'

A grunt. 'He must know Irishmen in the SAS aren't allowed to serve in Ulster. Think about it. Divided loyalties, relatives at risk. Joseph always was a prize idiot. Look where he ended up. In the Maze.'

Kathleen pulled a tight little smile. 'He never was too bright. Ma always said he was at the back of the queue when they handed out brains. She always spoke up for you. She'd never have any of it. Said their own kith and kin would never betray them.'

'Ma Coogan always took a shine to me – ever since I was a lad,' Branagh recalled absently.

'What D'Arcy said? You never were in the SAS, Mike?'

Branagh said brusquely, 'You heard what I told him.'

Before she could reply the Direct Action compound came into view. There was a gathering outside the hut. Branagh said: 'Looks like a welcoming committee.'

Fred Petkus and Leif Månson were in conversation with Francisco the carpenter and an older Mozambican with grizzled short hair. He carried an air of authority despite dust smears and patches on the well-worn dark suit.

'The Administrator,' Branagh explained as they climbed out.

Månson took the Irishman swiftly to one side. 'What the hell's going on, Michael? The Administrator is demanding to speak to you and he seems none too pleased about something. What have you been up to?'

Branagh could guess what it was about, but he said: 'I can't read minds, Leif. If he wants to talk to me that's my business. Nothing to do with you.'

The Swede's eyes narrowed. He didn't trust Branagh. The Irishman was an unorthodox rebel, happy to bend the rules without a moment's hesitation. How many times had he had to soothe the ruffled feathers of some autocratic official whom Branagh had upset? He had lost count. If he could he would have replaced Branagh, but he knew he'd get no one else to take on the front-line Gutala project. 'Just remember, Michael, everything you do here reflects on me and Direct Action – for good or ill.'

Branagh blew him a kiss and walked over to the Administrator. 'Senhor Conçalves, it's good to see you.'

He acknowledged Francisco who avoided looking at him directly. 'Come inside, Senhor, and have a good cup of coffee. Sure we might also run to a tot of whiskey.'

For a moment the Administrator forgot himself. His eyes lit up at the prospect of his favourite tipple, then he remembered the gravity of the purpose of his visit. 'Your hospitality is appreciated,' he said with uncharacteristic formality.

As Månson went to follow the Irishman, Francisco and Kathleen into the hut, Branagh barred his way. 'Sorry, Leif, this is by invitation only. Private. Sorry.'

'You'll overstep the mark one of these days,' the Swede blustered.

'I'll tell you about it in the morning,' Branagh replied amiably and shut the rough bib-and-brace door.

He called Maraika to make coffee and lit a hurricane lamp before producing a bottle of Jameson. Both Senhor Conçalves and Francisco looked ill-at-ease as he poured the measures.

'Senhor Branagh, I have the greatest respect for all you have done in Gutala and Tumbo,' the Administrator began. 'Therefore it saddens me all the more what I have heard from Francisco today.'

Branagh glanced reproachfully at the carpenter.

'I am sorry, Senhor Mike,' Francisco said. 'I know I promised, but my conscience would not allow me. I have only told Senhor the Administrator.'

The Irishman smiled. 'You're a good man, Francisco, a man of conscience. There should be more men like you. Of course you are right. I should have told Senhor Conçalves myself.'

'Then it is true?' the Administrator asked.

This unusually stern official face belied the man's normally genial disposition, the steady rheumy eyes reflecting a worldly wisdom not always found in the remoter corners of Mozambique.

Branagh said: 'I have always found Francisco an

194

honest man. I count him as a friend. He speaks the truth of what we found today.'

The old man pursed his lips thoughtfully. 'Including that you saw Senhora da Gruta talking with *bandidos* and South African mercenaries? You realise how serious this is? What it means? That the da Grutas are in league with the avowed enemy of the government.'

'Wait a moment, Alberto. I'm sure Jorge doesn't know what's going on. Any more than we do.'

'That may be for a court of law to decide. I am sure that is what Brigadier Vaz would say.'

Branagh considered for a long moment before saying: 'It is possible that Vaz himself is somehow involved. I understand he issued a pass to da Gruta's son, Armando. You know him?'

'I know Armando from a long time ago, Senhor Branagh.' It didn't sound like a pleasant memory. 'I believe he is now a soldier in the South African Army.'

'Certainly not someone to whom a pass should have been issued,' Branagh pointed out.

'You make this sound like some sort of conspiracy.'

'Perhaps that's exactly what it is. But there could be a more rational explanation to do with reopening the mine. Although that hardly excuses consorting with bandits. Nevertheless it may be better for us to sit on this knowledge for a while. If the government overreacts I can see the only result being Jorge languishing in jail – and who would run the plantation then?'

The Administrator nodded sagely. 'Wait until Senhora da Gruta returns to Gutala and confront her then?' He thought on his words as he sipped appreciatively at his whiskey. 'And the *bandidos,* Senhor Branagh, what of them? I am getting more reports that there is a massing in the hills. And I have heard of your unwelcome visitor last night. I am loath to recommend evacuation . . . of Gutala or even Tumbo. Now we have built so much, we have so much more to lose.'

'I intend to put out the booby traps here tonight and to place civilian sentries' He turned to the carpenter. 'If Francisco's friends will help? They'll not have guns, of course, but they can arm themselves with pangas and spears.'

'No militia?' the Administrator queried.

'Brigadier Vaz does not wish it.'

Senhor Conçalves shook his head wearily. 'Then perhaps you are right that Vaz is implicated. He does not act like a man with Gutala's best interests at heart. And I agree with you. Tomorrow morning I shall call a public meeting in Gutala. I shall exhort every man, woman and child in the district to stay and not flee from the threat of terror.'

Later, when their visitors had gone, Kathleen asked if the Administrator's decision had been a wise one.

Branagh poured himself another generous measure of whiskey. 'Nothing was ever gained by running away.'

'Is that so?' she asked softly.

But he appeared not to notice the irony in her voice. She watched in silence as he took his tumbler into the bedroom and drew the separating curtain.

Thoughtfully Kathleen rolled out her sleeping bag on the primitive sofa and removed her shirt and jeans. From the other side of the curtain she heard the mumble of conversation and the bright sound of Maraika laughing.

Just what sort of a man are you, Michael Branagh, Kathleen asked silently? Immediately she corrected herself. Cousin Seamus. Just what sort of a man are you? A man capable of such self-deceit. A man who could devote his life to the struggling dispossessed of the poorest country in Africa. A once good Catholic who could now live in sin and deceit with an innocent native girl. Telling her birth pills would prevent malaria while she yearned for marriage and a child. What bastard would do that to a woman he professed to love?

The fabric of the sleeping bag was cold against her

skin, and she shivered, drawing the thick material tight around her neck.

What a contradiction you are, Cousin Seamus. Still on the run. Hiding and drowning your memories in drink. But hiding from what? What does a man who doesn't flinch under the threat of murderous terrorists need to hide from? Alcohol had begun to cloud her own mind now. Who was Michael Branagh hiding from if it wasn't from himself? Had Ma been right? Was a man like Branagh incapable of betraying his own kith and kin? Of murdering in cold blood?

The sound of urgent body movement carried from behind the curtain on the sultry night air. Kathleen turned over, burying her head in the quilting of the sleeping bag. Yet the low masculine grunts and Maraika's breathless gasps seemed all the louder. Intrusive, haunting. Unreasonably she felt angry at such behaviour so close to her, unable to shake the mental image from her mind: Branagh's arched back, muscled, tanned and damp with exertion.

Damn you, Cousin Seamus, she cursed into the pillow, perversely aware of the stirrings between her own legs. Again and again she turned restlessly, seeking escape into sleep.

There came a brief ecstatic cry from Maraika, followed by a girlish giggle. Then silence.

An hour later Kathleen was still awake. Her loins were on fire, her head swimming with unbidden thoughts. At last she came to a decision, swung her legs off the sofa and began to dress. Then she lit the hurricane lamp, hanging it on the ceiling hook. After helping herself to a tumblerful of Branagh's whiskey she settled down with a pen and notepad.

He had to admit it was good. Bloody good.

Not that Branagh considered himself to be any judge of journalism, let alone literature. But the dozen sheets of neatly written prose seemed to capture the very essence of life in a remote front-line village in Mozambique. His life.

At dawn he'd found the embryonic manuscript on the floor beside the sofa where Kathleen had fallen awkwardly asleep, the pad on her lap and the pen still clutched between two fingers. His bottle of Jameson was empty on the table.

He read the article as he sat in the compound while Maraika prepared the maize porridge and coffee for breakfast. So this was it. The end result. His efforts all those years ago to prise a young mind from the claustrophobic bitterness and closed mind of a staunch Republican family of farmers. A small girl with winceyette pyjamas, pigtails and dark eyes bright with interest. A beauty even at that tender age. Unaware that she was at a crossroads in her young life. To follow blindly in her brothers' footsteps that stretched into history – back to the 1916 Rebellion and beyond – a self-perpetuating tribal war between the Taigs and the Orangemen that spanned the centuries. Or to open her eyes to another way, another world.

He ate his porridge in silence. His mind was suddenly full of the smells of Ireland. Damp lush grass and so many vibrant shades of green; fresh-baked soda bread cooling on the windowsill; the rich bitter taste of a smoky lunchtime Guinness. It was a long time since he'd allowed his mind to dwell on such thoughts.

'Mikey?' Maraika had been standing back, watching, concerned that something was wrong. She needed to talk to him, but was afraid that this wasn't the moment.

'Yes, sweetheart.'

She smiled uncomfortably. 'Last night was good?'

'Last night was very good. You were beautiful.'

A hesitation. 'My father wishes to speak to you.'

'Pascoal can always speak to me. He knows that.'

Maraika squatted by his side. 'My mother too.'

198

'Ah.' Ireland disintegrated in the sparkling African morning. Marta Matusi was a different matter. Now he knew what it was all about. He'd have been a fool if he thought he could stall for ever.

'You will speak with them?'

Time to bite the bullet, Branagh. 'Why not. Invite them over to eat with us tonight.'

Her face broke into a smile that almost made the prospect of meeting Senhora Matusi worthwhile. Maraika hugged him. 'I love you, Mikey Branagh.'

Fred Petkus appeared at the compound gate. 'Hey, Irish, what are you doing? There is an airplane come in, didn't you hear?'

Branagh laughed. 'Sorry, I was miles away.'

'Maybe the spares for my airplane are on board.'

The Irishman stood up. 'I'm meeting Rob D'Arcy in Gutala – so we can go to the airstrip on the way.'

'And little Irish?'

He waved the sheaf of paper he had been reading. 'She's had a hard night. She won't surface until noon.'

As they stepped out of the compound, Branagh became aware of people on the move. Not just women and children, but men who would normally have already left to work on the banana plantations. They were all walking in the same direction – towards Gutala.

'What on earth's happening?' Branagh asked. Immediately he feared the worst. Bandits had attacked in the night and no one had thought to tell him. This was the giant exodus.

He spotted Francisco with a group of friends who had been posted as overnight sentries. Branagh's fears were allayed as he saw them laughing and joking amongst themselves.

'The Administrator has called a public meeting,' the Russian explained.

It was with profound relief that Branagh recalled Senhor Conçalves's pledge to rally the people of this district. Feeling a distinct rise in his spirits, he began the ten-minute drive through the family cropfields to the plateau. The high-winged Caribou in Arbaerea livery had taxied from the strip and the crew were already unloading the sacks of fishmeal and rice from the rear ramp.

The cargo line boss, Ian Hagan, was examining the oil leaking from one of the engines. As he did so he was talking to a man who was evidently a passenger judging by the tailored business suit. A smart designer travel bag lay on the grass by his feet.

As Branagh approached, Hagan wiped his hands on his overalls. 'Hi, Mike. I've got tha' consignment of antibiotics tha' went missing. Turned up in a warehouse in Maputo. Customs red tape.'

'Månson will be pleased. He's been doing inventories all week to find it. I'm sure he suspects me of selling it on the black market.'

Hagan scratched his white hair. 'Talking of which – one crate of Jameson.'

'For me?'

Petkus stepped forward. 'For me. If you want a bottle you can buy it.'

Branagh laughed. 'And what about your precious spares?'

'Here too,' Hagan said. 'And another visitor for you, Mike. You are getting popular lately.'

Branagh had paid scant attention to the passenger; he'd naturally assumed the newcomer was a businessman with an appointment to see Jorge da Gruta. Now the man stepped out from beneath the shade of the aircraft's wing where he had been sheltering from the heat. Even when he removed his panama, it took Branagh several long seconds to recognise the rotund face. After all it had been a long time. A very long time.

'Hello, old stick. I've had a helluva job tracking you down. Took days to find someone to fly me.' But Vincent Mulholland hadn't changed. Fourteen years of good

200

lunches and sampling the best wines in London's club-land had added a few inches to his girth. The good life had also filled out the plump cheeks so that more than ever his face resembled a perfect circle like a football. He still had his hair, although it was thinner and more sil-vered than Branagh remembered. And the eyes still laughed within the deepening maze of crowsfeet.

'Helluva time tracking you down,' Mulholland repeated.

And he still had the knack of making any problem sound like it was Branagh's fault.

'That was the idea, Vincent.'

Mulholland wasn't that easily fazed. 'Well at least you learned something during your time with me.' His smile didn't waver.

Reluctantly Branagh accepted the offered hand. Say what you like about Vincent Mulholland, he was an absolute charmer and a gentleman. That was if you took things at their face value. Besides old habits died hard. Mulholland might be just a civil servant but in the old days to have refused Mulholland's hand was as unthink-able as refusing to salute a senior Army officer.

'How did you find me?'

Mulholland fanned himself with his panama. 'Through the gel, actually. Young Kathleen.'

Branagh had thought as much. 'And what do you want?'

The grin of satisfaction deepened and Mulholland drew in a deep lungful of air, inspecting the view from the plateau like a man released from solitary confinement. 'In good time, old stick, in good time.' He looked back at Branagh. 'And how's you? You're looking fitter and healthier than the last time I saw you.'

'The last time you saw me I had a bullet in my lung.'

The smile wouldn't go. 'Life here obviously suits you. Tell me, I gather there's an hotel of sorts in Gutala?'

Branagh's heart sank. 'You're staying?'

'I thought maybe a day or two.'

'Why?'

'So we can talk.'

'There's nothing to say.'

Mulholland replaced his hat, tilting it at a carefully rakish angle. 'Oh but there is – Michael, isn't it?'

Branagh said: 'The hotel's a cesspit and there's bandit activity in the hills. You won't like it here, Vincent. There's not a decent vintage bottle of plonk for a hundred miles.'

A soft, fruity laugh. 'I do believe you're teasing, Michael. Anyway I've a couple of bottles in the luggage and bandits don't worry me. Not after the real bandit country of Armagh, eh?'

It was meant to be a shared joke, but Branagh refused to play along.

'All unloaded,' Ian Hagan announced. 'I'd best be off while we've any oil left in Number Two.'

Mulholland said: 'Michael, old chap, I suppose you couldn't give an old chum a lift into town?'

The ride was as hard and bumpy as Branagh could make it. He'd had a mind to let Mulholland ride with the fishmeal sacks in the rear, but Fred Petkus considerately surrendered the passenger seat. Nevertheless the Englishman was pale and evidently bruised by the time they reached the town square. He grimaced at the bullet-pocked stucco façade of the hotel; there was an unmistakable smell of drains in the air.

'I did warn you,' Branagh said.

'So you did.' A bright smile. 'Join me for lunch, old stick. We can crack one of my bottles for old time's sake. I picked up a presentable Romeira '83 from the Polana Hotel in Maputo.'

'This place is a cesspit, I told you. Don't eat here unless you've got a stomach pump in with your bottles.'

'Don't be childish, Michael. I know you're not pleased to see me, but we do have to talk. Really.'

Branagh glanced around the square. Robert D'Arcy from the tobacco station was waving to him from the verandah of the *cantina* where they'd agreed to meet. Fred Petkus leaned against the Land-Rover bonnet, watching in a curious silence. Anything Vincent Mulholland had to say was certainly not for their ears.

'Get yourself unpacked,' Branagh said. 'I'll see you in the restaurant.'

Mulholland smiled; he was a man used to getting his way. 'Twelve noon, say?'

Branagh nodded and waited while the man entered the fly-blown hotel lobby.

'You are full of surprises, Irish. So many people from your past.'

'Stuff it, Fred.'

The Russian fell into step beside him as Branagh headed for the *cantina*. 'I begin to think, Irish, there is more to you than meets the eye, eh? That maybe it's not the poor hungry Africans that keep you in this stinkhole place. I think—'

'You don't think,' Branagh snapped. 'That's the trouble with you Russians.'

'Please, German now,' Petkus corrected amicably, and patted his pocket where he kept his new papers.

From the verandah of the *cantina* D'Arcy tossed down two beer cans as though they were hand-grenades.

Both were snatched in midair. 'You look cheerful,' Branagh observed.

'Something to celebrate,' D'Arcy replied. 'Vaz has agreed to my special force exercising with your local militia. Though I doubt he'll remember.' He waved a piece of paper.

As chairs were pulled up Branagh noticed that the former SAS officer was wearing military lightweight trousers and a khaki shirt. 'You're looking the part.'

'That's what I thought,' D'Arcy said, tapping the side of his nose. 'In view of what Jorge said last night I turned up at the hotel this morning with the orders I wanted already typed. Knocked on Vaz's door at precisely nine o'clock and reminded him we had a meeting. Hadn't, of course, but he didn't remember. Put him on the defensive.' He laughed. 'God, what a sight! Vaz and his two cronies sitting around in boxer shorts and singlets, already hitting the beer. Empty crates of the stuff everywhere. Enough to pay our recruits at the station for a month – not, of course, that they've been paid at all yet! Vaz was still pissed out of his brains from last night's session, trying to hide a couple of girls in his wardrobe in case I thought it conduct unbecoming. Anyway, I bum-rushed him through the plan, suggested it was really his brilliant idea, and got him to sign on the dotted line. In triplicate. I think he was glad to get rid of me.'

Petkus drained his beer. 'You, my English friend, should be in the Soviet Army.'

D'Arcy feigned hurt. 'Oh, I don't think so, Fred.'

'When does it all happen?' Branagh asked. 'Our sentries last night weren't even armed.'

'We've got two serviceable trucks at the tobacco station. I'll get a platoon of around thirty men down to Tumbo by mid-afternoon. Then you can use the vehicles to ferry the militia down from here. Can you deal with that?'

Branagh accepted a copy of Vaz's signed order. 'It will be a pleasure.'

'Maybe Vaz will change his mind?' Petkus suggested.

'I don't think so,' Branagh replied. 'He's got his real government soldiers to play with here in Gutala. He considers the militia beneath his dignity. We just won't mention our exercise ends at Tumbo.'

'I am thinking,' the Russian said. 'Maybe some more AK47s and ammunition would be useful.'

Branagh was incredulous. 'God, Fred, is this your idea of the free market? Turning arms dealer already?'

Petkus grimaced. 'You forget, Irish, this rubbish place

is also my home now, eh?' The serious granite face suddenly split as he guffawed heartily at his own joke.

In other circumstances Branagh would have shared the humour and celebrated D'Arcy's coup with enthusiasm, but the arrival of Vincent Mulholland was preying on his mind. He finished his beer quickly and then he sought out Rafael Costa, the captain of militia. At being shown the copy of Vaz's order the eyes in the crab-apple face widened and he pulled himself proudly up to his full five feet five inches. Apparently he had never actually received written orders before, possibly due to the fact that he couldn't read. But he appreciated Branagh's crisp delivery of the instructions. For the first time someone was treating the captain of militia as a proper soldier.

'Just the thing for a mobile reserve,' Branagh concluded. 'An exercise in being mobile. Transport will arrive around 1600 hours. Two trucks.'

Rafael couldn't believe his ears. Two trucks – his regular Frelimo soldier rivals would burn with envy. 'SAH!' He cracked the heels of his holed boots together and saluted with a panache of which a guardsman would have been proud.

'And, Rafael, do get your wife to sew patches on your knees,' Branagh said as he returned to his Land-Rover.

He drove speedily to another plantation village where Månson was planning to sink a new well with the help of Din Din Singh, the local Indian engineer. Work progressed slowly for the rest of the morning until it was time for Branagh to return to Gutala for his lunch appointment with Mulholland.

He found him in the hotel restaurant, the only customer in the sombre room with its faded vestiges of more prosperous days. Half the light fittings were without bulbs which was perhaps as well, because it served to disguise the peeling wallpaper and threadbare carpet. Even the pebbled mosaic columns failed to achieve the sense of

205

colonial Portuguese opulence that the architect had intended.

Branagh passed between the empty tables, each immaculately laid with heavy silver cutlery on snow-white cloths which had been scrubbed and bleached for twenty years until the linen had worn into holes. There was an atmosphere of hopeless optimism, as though a coach party of tourists were expected at any moment.

'I thought you might not come, old stick.' A bottle of Romeira was already opened on the table.

'You've hunted me this far, Vincent,' Branagh said. 'I can't see you giving up now.'

The smile smiled and the eyes twinkled. 'Too true, Seamus.'

Branagh took a seat opposite. 'Michael,' he corrected.

'Of course – Michael.' Mulholland peered at the menu. 'What do you recommend?'

'This isn't White's, Vincent. They cook in an open kitchen out the back. The fish soup's safe enough. Otherwise I should stick to an omelette and chips.'

Mulholland's face wrinkled in disdain. But the waiter was already hovering, anxious to please in his maroon tuxedo meant for a much smaller man and black trousers that were shiny at the knees. 'I don't speak Portuguese.'

'*Pode dar-nos à pescador e omelete, por favor,*' Branagh obliged.

Mulholland poured the wine. 'I thought you were dead, you know, Michael. I mean disappearing the way you did. Discharging yourself from hospital like that. I half expected you to be found in a ditch somewhere.'

'What did you expect me to do? Leave a pile of clothes on Brighton beach?' He sipped at his glass, his mind going back over the years. 'I just wanted out. I didn't even go back to my flat.'

He had wandered the London streets in a daze, still drugged with painkillers that failed to stop the searing sensation in his damaged lung. At the end of the day he found himself at Waterloo Station. He recalled looking at the destination board and seeing the legend Dover. Dover – France, Europe, the world, the universe. It was a word association game. The next morning he was in Calais. Marvellous thing plastic money. A credit card and a driving licence and they handed over a hired car. Without any particular place in mind he just drove.

'We traced you as far as Portugal,' Mulholland said. 'But the trail went cold in the Algarve after you handed back the car.'

'I took a room in a guest house. A little fishing village, Burgau. Spent six months there getting my mind back together.'

Mulholland smiled sympathetically over his glass. 'You'd been through a lot. And Portugal – hence this place?'

Branagh nodded. 'The woman who ran the guest house, she used to live in Mozambique and her son was a church missionary out here. The Portuguese had just pulled out and the place was a mess. He used to write and tell her how much they needed help. Then one day I thought hell, why not? Her son pulled a few strings to get me through the vetting procedure. It was close, but I've been here ever since.'

'Atoning for your sins, eh? The good Catholic.'

The arrival of the soup was timely.

'We gave up the search,' Mulholland said. 'I was sure you'd turn up in your own good time. Of course you never did.' He smacked his lips appreciatively. 'The soup's good.'

'So why now, Vincent?'

Mulholland dabbed at a trickle on his chin with a frayed napkin. 'It was through the gel – Kathleen. The family's still at it, you know! Well, two of the brothers anyway. They're either in the Maze, being released from it or hatching some plot that will get them sent back in. The beggars will never learn. So we keep the house under

207

constant surveillance. Bugged telephone and mail intercepts, you know.'

'And you intercepted my letter after Ma Coogan's funeral?' Branagh guessed.

'Quite so.' A smile of satisfaction. 'It was quite by chance I heard about it. I mean it was so long ago that it all happened, no one remembered you. The lads in Army Int. seem so young nowadays. Off duty they're all earrings and personal stereos—'

Branagh said: 'I recall we were all beards and psychedelic beads.'

The other man shoved away his plate. 'The point is, Michael, that I have continued to retain a personal interest in the family members. I soon learned that young Kathleen planned to come to Mozambique. I mean after your letter that can hardly have been a coincidence.'

'Don't tell me you've come all this way to bring my pension?'

Mulholland raised an eyebrow. 'I never thought of that.'

'You wouldn't, Vincent, you only ever thought about number one.'

A gentle chuckle. 'Not quite fair, old stick. But once I knew you were alive I had to come and see that you were all right.'

'Now you've seen.'

'And plans to return to the UK?' Casual. Too damn casual.

Branagh was driven by a sudden urge to be difficult. 'I've been thinking about it.'

It wasn't a lie, not entirely. He had no plans to go anywhere, but since Kathleen's arrival he had been thinking of life back home. Wondering what it would be like now, fourteen years on? Wondering whether he would still fit in, if indeed he ever really had?

Mulholland studied Branagh's face as the waiter removed the soup dishes and replaced them with plates of

208

anemic-looking omelette. For once the Englishman showed no interest in his food. 'Not a good idea, Michael.'

Branagh was intrigued. 'I don't recall having broken any laws before I left, Vincent. No warrants out for my arrest.'

'But it's possible there could be. I recall you were involved in Clockwork Orange.'

It was uncanny hearing those two words spoken. In an empty restaurant in a derelict hotel in upcountry Mozambique. Fourteen years and four thousand miles away from those dark days of intrigue and plotting in the corridors of Gower Street. When a Machiavellian plan had been hatched to discredit both the Provisional IRA and the Wilson government by MI5 and even some SIS 'ultras'. Secret Service 'ultras' like Vincent Mulholland. With their five-figure salaries and index-linked pensions and country houses in Gloucestershire. The untouchable fat cats who were beyond the law of the land.

'That was a long time ago,' Branagh said.

'Some people have long memories,' Mulholland replied tersely. The eyes weren't smiling now. 'People can't resist digging the shit, old stick. Picking over old bones. People we thought we'd shut up start to talk. The gutter press ferrets around waving cheque books. Investigations get promised. It can make life uncomfortable.'

'Are you being investigated, Vincent?'

The general clatter of cutlery against china stopped abruptly and the dining room became as painfully silent as a museum library. A waiter coughed.

Mulholland lowered his fork. 'This omelette's disgusting.'

Branagh said: 'That's why you're here, Vincent. You're being investigated and you're running scared.'

The smile returned, more ebullient than ever. 'Not at all, old stick, I've nothing to hide.'

And Branagh knew the man was right. Fat cats like Vincent Mulholland never had anything to hide. Total control and authority, but far removed from the dirty work. Files on Clockwork Orange – if any had ever existed – would have been sanitised long ago. Key pages missing from reports. Files mislaid. Witnesses discreetly paid off, or removed if they had nothing to lose by talking. Either discredited or framed on some bogus charge and put behind bars. Sometimes even worse.

Branagh said: 'Am I the one who got away, Vincent?'

'You've lost none of your perception, have you?'

There was a brief pause. 'It went too far.'

'Clockwork Orange?'

'Who the hell did you think you were? Trying to topple an elected government because you didn't like the company the Prime Minister kept.'

A grunt of dissension. 'It was the height of the Cold War, Michael, or have you forgotten? We had an untrustworthy socialist government – half the Cabinet were ex-Commies and couldn't even be trusted to see sensitive papers – we faced a massive Soviet military buildup, and the Provos were in our own back yard. Something had to be done.'

'Not a coup d'état.'

'Don't exaggerate, Michael. We just took a few precautionary steps. We had to, no one else could.'

Branagh's eyes blazed at him across the table. 'You forget I was in Aldershot when it was open talk in the mess. The Parachute Regiment was ready to seize key points in London, but they doubted the Regiments of Guards would go along with it. Luckily they were right. It was a damn close thing.'

'You said yourself, Michael, it was a long time ago.'

'I remember every damn detail. Every event and every date. I thought it was disgusting then, and I think it's disgusting now.'

In the brittle silence that followed, Mulholland helped himself to the last of the wine. 'So what do you want?'

'What?'

'Money? Enough to buy – I don't know – a yacht, or to build a bungalow some place?'

Branagh stared at him. 'You just don't understand, do you? I've left all that behind. I'm not interested. You sought me out, I didn't come running to you demanding a payoff for silence.' He shook his head more in sorrow than in anger. 'Go home, Vincent. Face your investigators. You'll be safe enough. I can't believe you haven't covered every contingency.'

Slowly Mulholland said: 'If I've found you, Seamus Gallagher, so can others. Your file has been reopened.'

'My file,' Branagh retorted. 'Your problem.' He stood up from the table. 'I'll send a vehicle for you next time an aircraft comes in.'

Mulholland glowered. Very carefully he said: 'Tell me, Michael, does Kathleen Coogan know you murdered her father?'

Branagh drove back towards the well site in a fury. Black storm clouds were pressing in on his mind, anger crackling in his skull like lightning. He scarcely noticed the villagers and goats scooting out of his path. His fist punched the horn, its bellicose squawk giving vent to his temper.

How the hell could he have been so stupid as to send that letter? Too much booze and one careless, mawkish moment.

It wasn't as though he had still retained any feelings of warmth for Ma Coogan, even when he had last seen her. Gone was the childish affection for a favourite step-aunt who spoiled him whenever he went to visit. In the harsh light of adulthood he had begun to see her differently. As a strict mother hen who had given birth to a brood of terrorist killers.

That hadn't, he knew, been her intention. She had the Bible and her own strict moral code to guide her.

Cleanliness was next to godliness, and godliness was saying grace and going to Mass once a week.

She believed it was right for the Irish people to run a united Ireland for themselves. That it was wrong for the Protestants to cream all the best jobs, and wrong for the Brits to be in occupation. That it was wrong to kill, but all right not to ask questions when her sons were sometimes out all night. Even on a night when a culvert bomb exploded under an Army patrol.

No, it hadn't been out of any sentimentality for Ma Coogan that he had, drunk and isolated in the African bush, put pen to paper. It had been to comfort a small girl in pigtails who called him Cousin Seamus.

Shit! He swerved violently to miss an overladen donkey, caught the edge of the pannier and sent a hundred corncobs flying in all directions.

He slowed down. This was crazy. Mulholland was buried with his past. If the man was being investigated back in London then that was his problem. He himself had merely been following military orders, seconded from 22 Special Air Service to the Secret Intelligence Service in Northern Ireland. Never in the full picture, just doing what Mulholland told him to. The dutiful undercover soldier. It had taken some time before he had realised the sort of man Mulholland was. As a young soldier he had been overwhelmed by the man's authority and immense influence. He could open doors in the corridors of power that no one else knew existed. Like everyone else Branagh had enjoyed his undeniable good company and irresistible charm. And he had appreciated the words of sympathy and understanding when times were bad.

Only when it was too late had he discovered the truth. That behind their backs Mulholland never had a good word for any of his operatives. It was his way of shifting blame, so that he could always say 'I told you so' to his superiors when things went wrong, as inevitably they sometimes did. The man had a magician's touch when it came to distancing himself from trouble.

Branagh was certain that Mulholland's enthusiasm for Clockwork Orange, essentially an M15 plot, had been because he saw it as the quickest way to the top had it succeeded.

By the time Branagh reached the well site his rage had subsided, yet his mind still wasn't on the job. Even Leif Månson politely mentioned the fact and received a sharp rebuff for his pains.

It was only at the end of the afternoon, when he drew up outside his compound, that Branagh remembered that Maraika's parents were coming to supper.

That's all I need, he bemoaned, and slammed the door.

The diminutive captain of militia waited for him by the compound gate. The holes in his camouflage trousers had been stitched and Branagh noted the red beret, recognising it as part of the uniform D'Arcy issued to his recruits. Rafael Costa saluted smartly, untroubled by the big tear in his newly acquired headwear.

'What's that, Captain? Shrapnel wound?'

The militiaman grinned, failing to understand. 'Major D'Arcy tells me to report all special force and militia deployed in Tumbo.'

'Well done, Captain.'

'And he says will you kindly inspect our positions.'

It was the only good news he had heard all day. 'It'll be my pleasure, Captain. I'll come around after supper.'

He couldn't resist a salute and Rafael responded instantly, his face glowing with pride. 'Carry on, Captain.'

'SAH!'

As he turned back to the compound he found Kathleen standing at the gate. 'Very impressive, Mike.'

'Rafael's a good man. They could do with more like him in the Frelimo Army.'

'And some good Brit training, you mean.'

When the Catholic Irish use the word 'Brit', it's rarely

meant as a term of endearment; Branagh didn't miss the barb, but he chose to ignore it.

Kathleen added: 'Your future in-laws have arrived.'

'What?'

'Marta and Pascoal Matusi.' She smiled mischievously. 'We've been having an interesting chat with Maraika as translator.'

The two parents were seated awkwardly on the sofa, each clutching a tumbler of sugarcane rum as though scared they might drop and break the precious glass. Both were dressed in Sunday best. Pascoal's wizened face was perspiring from the tight frayed collar and tie worn with a black Oxfam suit that was too big for him, and Marta was resplendent in a floral *capulana*.

Pascoal stood up formally to shake hands, evidently ill-at-ease away from the familiar austerity of his reed shanty home. Either that or he was unhappy with the diplomatic mission on which his wife had coerced him. For her part Marta stayed seated, merely offering a regal hand for Branagh to accept. All the time the eyes in her black walnut face exuded an expression of smug confidence. Meanwhile Maraika flitted and fussed in the background, casting uncertain glances in Branagh's direction.

In an aside to Kathleen he whispered: 'I think I detect a conspiracy afoot.' He threw open his hands expansively in an effort to break the underlying mood of tension. 'Let's eat!'

It was a special meal; Maraika had spent time and money in the market and had persuaded the butcher to provide roast pig to go with the mealie mash and dry beans. The Matusis ate it with relish, the main reason for their visit cheerfully postponed for as long as possible.

Not surprisingly it was Maraika's mother who, emboldened by several glasses of sugarcane rum, broached the subject of her daughter's marital status.

'It is four years now you live with our Maraika,' she

214

accused. 'For three years I am ashamed and have to listen to village gossip.'

Branagh winked at Maraika; she blushed prettily. 'And four happy years for us, Marta.'

'But not for me,' she retorted, the cutting edge of her words blunted by drink.

This wasn't strictly true, Branagh knew. In the early days she had positively boasted about her daughter's relationship with the white man whom most villagers regarded as little less than a saint. Before independence, Marta had known the White Order of Catholic Brothers who had resisted Portuguese oppression, and she had mistakenly believed Branagh to be one of them. That tolerance had evaporated after four years with no sign of a marriage in the offing.

'Haven't I looked after your daughter well?'

Marta looked down at the table of empty plates, she could hardly deny that. 'I lose my sons Benjamin and Jaime to the *bandidos*,' she croaked, 'and my other daughter Lisa is with child and no husband. She will not marry now. Am I to lose my oldest daughter to the devil for living in sin?'

Pascoal coughed pointedly. The usually subdued man, who thoroughly enjoyed Branagh's company, had clearly decided his wife was being far too antagonistic. 'Perhaps we understand why it is you do not pay *lobola*. We are human, too, Senhor Mike. No man wants to commit himself to marry a woman who is barren. What farmer wants to work a field that will not bear crops?'

'That is not a problem, Pascoal,' Branagh reassured. 'I love your daughter for your daughter's sake.'

The old man nodded in a way that suggested he knew better. 'You are a good man, Senhor Mike. You would not say such a thing to hurt our Maraika or to hurt Marta and me, but I know.'

Kathleen who had been leaning against the wall, observing in silence, said, 'Maraika has been visiting the village healer, Mike, did you know?'

Maraika shot off an angry glance.

'I didn't know that.'

'She's been absolutely heart-broken, so she has,' Kathleen persisted.

Branagh began to feel annoyed. '*Thank you*, Kathy.'

Now Maraika was starting to feel guilty at having gone behind his back. 'I am sorry, Mikey. I had to go.'

He smiled with understanding. 'And has it worked?'

Suddenly Maraika's face was transformed, lit up by a dazzling smile. 'Things will be all right now.'

Marta interceded: 'The spirits work in strange ways.' She had little trouble in reconciling Catholic teaching with the traditional African spirit world. 'We learn why our daughter has been infertile. The tablets you bring her to prevent malaria – they have another effect sometimes. A woman may not conceive.'

Damn that interfering, sanctimonious Swede! Leif Månson never had approved of his living with Maraika. It would be typical of the man. 'And let me guess who told you this?'

Maraika beamed. 'My friend. Your kissing cousin.'

Branagh turned his head. Kathleen still leaned against the wall, and was now absently watching a moth battering itself against the hurricane lamp. Miss Innocent. Butter wouldn't melt.

'So time will tell,' Pascoal was saying. 'And then you can make your decision. Marry our Maraika or let her go – while she is still young enough to find a husband.'

'I understand,' Branagh said, glancing around to see where he'd left the bottle of Jameson. He felt in need of a treble.

Kathleen produced it from behind her back. 'Are you looking for this, Mike?' There was an impish grin on her lips.

He snatched the bottle from her. 'I hope you realise what you've done,' he challenged angrily.

She lowered her voice to a whisper. 'It's no more than

216

you deserve. You're a wicked man, Cousin Seamus. You regard her like a whore – she deserves better than that.'

There was a sudden commotion outside in the compound. Voices were raised excitedly and heavy footsteps were heard pounding on the hard earth.

Fred Petkus appeared at the door. 'Hey, Irish, there is trouble!'

'What's happening, Fred? Renamo?'

'I don't know. There is talk that something is going on in Gutala. At the house of the Administrator.'

Branagh took a quick swig from the bottle and handed it back to Kathleen. 'Right, let's go. We'll take the Land-Rover.'

Petkus restrained him. In his other hand he held two Kalashnikov AK47s by their straps. 'I think we take these.'

'I don't use them, Fred, you know that.'

'I think tonight you may have to.'

8

The night was hot and sticky, and the road to Gutala was choked with people.

Some groups were walking away from the town, others walking towards it. Was it safer in the town or in the outlying villages? Everyone appeared to have a different opinion. Urgent discussions were taking place at the roadside, with much gesticulation and arm waving. No one seemed to know anything except that they didn't want to be where they were.

'Christ, something's spooked them,' Branagh observed, manoeuvring past another crowd of walkers.

Kathleen had insisted on going with them and now sat squashed between the two men. 'Do you think there's some kind of attack?'

'Look!' Petkus jabbed his forefinger towards the skyline.

A flickering bloom of light radiated from the outline shapes of the buildings as the town came into view. Palls of white smoke billowed out of the vibrant orange corona before being sucked up into the night sky. Glowing sparks of dry timber carried on the air like fireflies.

Branagh pressed down on the accelerator, taking the next turn in a four-wheel drift, locking back into a straight that ran between rows of mud-brick and tin-roof bungalows. The conflagration illuminated the scene in an eerie trembling light. At the roadside Mozambicans were gathering their few worldly possessions together, distributing bags of belongings among the family members. Those who had handcarts were piling them high. Branagh could sense the atmosphere of panic.

As they approached the small clutch of colonial Portuguese bungalows that were home to the town's few civil servants and wealthy merchants, armed government troops flagged them down.

'You go no farther,' an agitated young soldier told them.

'*Bandidos?*' Branagh asked.

But the soldier didn't seem sure and wandered off. Branagh parked the Land-Rover and they travelled the last hundred metres on foot, pushing their way through the nervous gathering of spectators. As they reached the front of the crowd Branagh could feel the intense heat from the raging pyre that had once been the home of the Administrator.

Petkus nudged him and indicated the ornamental cherry tree that stood in the garden. Its leaves were black and shrivelled, some blown sparking against the ultramarine sky. In places the bark had begun to smoulder and peel. One large bough strained to breaking under the weight of the three naked bodies that hung by the neck.

'Oh, sweet Mother of Jesus,' Branagh breathed. The new resettlement project at Gutala had largely been the creation of gentle and wise Alberto Conçalves. Gutala was his town, his inspiration. It had been his rallying speech of defiance to which the town and village dwellers had flocked earlier that day. Now he and his wife and their handicapped son hung like obscene rotten fruit in their own front garden.

'For God's sake!' Branagh was enraged. He called a nearby Frelimo soldier who stood gawping at the spectacle. 'Go and cut those bodies down this instant!'

The man slowly began to function, drawing a bayonet from the scabbard on his belt, and advanced uncertainly on the roasting corpses.

'Here you are, Branagh.' It was Jorge da Gruta. Behind him Vincent Mulholland looked on uneasily.

'When did it happen, Jorge?'

The taciturn face stared at the soldier at work. 'An hour ago. They must have broken into the place and butchered the family first. I was in the *cantina* when the explosion went off. Quite a fireball – a can of petrol, I expect. That was the first anyone knew. When everyone got here the bodies were already hanging on the tree. The fire was so fierce no one could get near.'

'What about the bandits – did they get away? Did anyone put up roadblocks?'

Da Gruta eyed him impassively. 'Come on, Branagh, you know this lot. Just ran around like scalded cats.'

'Have there been any other attacks?'

'Not to my knowledge.' He looked around. 'But *this* is enough. At lunch time Alberto was telling everyone they had nothing to fear – that they should stay and stick it out. Now this. They won't stay now.'

Branagh knew he was right. As the fire began to subside, the crowd was breaking up and drifting away. Everyone was talking, making decisions. Most of them had seen it all before. In Mozambique you could always try to run away from the terror, but one day you knew it would come stalking after you in its own good time. Fear was tangible in the very air itself.

'Where's Vaz?'

Da Gruta's face was inscrutable. 'Our heroic Brigadier Vaz took a flight to Cuamba this afternoon. A premonition, do you think, or did he just run out of beer?'

'Is the army doing *anything*?' Petkus asked.

The plantation manager smiled grimly. 'Shitting itself, I should think.'

'Who's in charge – Major da Silva?'

Da Gruta jerked his thumb in the direction of the square. 'He was getting pissed in the hotel bar when I last saw him, just before the explosion.'

'Let's find him,' Branagh decided. 'We need to have a council of war.'

Da Gruta agreed. 'It all fits the pattern. That visit to you and then this – it will not be long now.'

Vincent Mulholland spoke for the first time. 'So you are planning to take over as military commander now, are you, Michael?' He seemed to find it amusing.

Branagh turned on him. 'I suggest you go back to your hotel, Vincent, and stay in your room. It could be dangerous on the streets.'

'Vincent?' Kathleen hadn't recognised the man in the gyrating shadows of the fire. 'What are you doing here?'

'It's a long story, m'dear,' he replied easily.

She glanced at Branagh. 'You two know each other?'

The Irishman ignored her question. 'Let's move, we haven't much time. Jorge, come with us in the 'Rover.'

They left Mulholland standing amid the dispersing throng and returned to the vehicle. Branagh drove straight to the square where they found Major da Silva in heated debate on the hotel steps with two of his subalterns. If he had been drunk an hour earlier, then the explosion at the Administrator's house had achieved a remarkably sobering effect.

He was a tall man in his late twenties with a smart turnout which attested to his training at a Soviet military academy. That training had also given him a slightly misplaced confidence in his own battlefield prowess because it had also discouraged the taking of personal initiative. On a social level da Silva could be companionable enough when sober, but prickly if he thought his authority was being challenged.

'Major!' Branagh called.

Da Silva was apparently only too pleased to end his argument. He sauntered over to the Land-Rover with the air of a man who had everything under control. 'Good evening, Senhor Mike.' Despite the smile his eyes had a haunted look about them.

221

'We were looking for the brigadier,' Branagh lied.

'He is out of town.' The Frelimo major straightened his back. 'I am in charge. Can I help you?'

'The brigadier had promised to tell us about his defence plans for the district – obviously something urgent turned up.'

Da Silva looked worried. 'You need not concern yourself with military affairs.'

Branagh smiled. 'I'm sure we're safe in your capable hands, Major. But unofficially I am considered responsible for the safety of the European community here. That's why the brigadier takes me into his confidence. We're going up to the plantation house for a drink. Why don't you join us?'

The major had his cap off and was in the vehicle almost before Branagh had finished his sentence. Da Silva was obviously eager to be as far away from Gutala and his responsibilities as possible on this troublesome night.

It was only a ten-minute drive to the plantation house and just moments later they were all seated around the dining table while Jorge produced a bottle of Scotch.

As he poured the major a generous measure he remarked absently: 'It must be difficult planning a defence for Gutala district without radio communications.'

Da Silva looked miserable at the prospect.

It was a ploy that Branagh had suggested earlier as they were leaving the Administrator's house. Now he said: 'We were thinking we might be able to help, Major. Jorge has half a dozen short range walkie-talkie radios. He uses them to speak to his plantation supervisors. If an attack comes, they could prove invaluable to you.'

The major looked very interested.

'Actually, Branagh, it's four,' Jorge corrected. 'Two are broken.'

'What range?' da Silva asked.

222

The plantation manager shrugged. 'Only about ten miles or so.'

Da Silva's enthusiasm waned visibly. 'It will not cover all the villages in the district.'

Branagh said: 'It'll cover a couple – and Tumbo.' A sudden thought seemed to occur to him. 'Do you know what, Major? I do believe that the militia are on exercise in Tumbo at this moment. With some of those special forces from the tobacco station. That was a smart move – your idea I expect.'

The major opened his mouth, then shut it again. He smiled slyly. 'Tumbo is on the main axis of advance from the hills.' It sounded like Vaz talking.

Fred Petkus sat on the edge of the table. 'You could move your headquarters to this place – I expect that is what you are thinking. That is what a good Soviet officer would think. Safer than Gutala, communications with Tumbo. And my Portugeezer friend here has the only radio link with Maputo.'

The soldier began to look flustered but Branagh said soothingly: 'You've a good military brain there, Major. We know. Fred, you realise, used to be a Soviet pilot and I, too, was once a soldier. In the English SAS.'

Da Silva's eyes widened. Stories of the legendary commandos had even reached his ears via the military academy in Leningrad.

Across the table Branagh noticed that Kathleen had him fixed in a troubled gaze. When she saw him looking she smiled back uncertainly.

Petkus said: 'What is your plan for Gutala?'

'We will man our usual emplacements,' the major replied blandly.

'Including the observation posts?' the Russian asked pointedly.

'But of course.'

It was nonsense. Branagh knew as well as Petkus that the observation posts on top of the hotel, the Embamo building and other high points would go unmanned as usual. The concept had been that in the event of a bandit attack automatic fire from these OPs would keep the attackers off the main streets. This would deprive them of access to the town centre and buildings of importance, confining them to the outlying shanties until a counter-sweep could be organised to flush them out. But Branagh knew that Major da Silva and his men preferred to be in their ground trenches from which they could quickly run off into the bush if the going got tough.

Branagh said: 'I must return to Tumbo, Major. I'll take a couple of radios with me and act as your liaison with the militia there – if you wish.'

Da Silva pursed his lips. He knew liaison was a good thing, although it wasn't something of which he'd had much experience. He could see no objection. In fact the idea made him feel quite important.

'I will stay here with Senhor da Gruta at my new head-quarters,' he announced.

Branagh drained his glass and stood up. 'We'll get off to Tumbo, Major. I'll drop another radio to the Frelimo garrison at Gutala and get your headquarters staff sent up here.'

Jorge da Gruta said: 'I'll radio Rob D'Arcy at the tobacco station and see what's happening there.'

The major blinked. Everything was happening at once and his head was starting to swim after the Scotch. Nevertheless, everything did *appear* to be under control. He smiled contentedly then and relaxed back in his chair.

Branagh drove back through Gutala to Tumbo at breakneck speed. Time was running out. Only six hours were left before first light which was the ritual timing for Renamo attacks. And there was still much to do.

As they neared the village he was obliged to slow for the endless stream of pedestrians clogging the track. The earlier indecision had gone – now everyone wanted to be as far away from the foothills as possible. Gutala, with its military garrison, offered the nearest hope of sanctuary.

'What are you going to do?' Kathleen asked. 'What's the point of defending the village if everyone's gone?'

'There'll be plenty left,' Branagh answered. 'Besides if we desert Tumbo it'll be razed to the ground. If it's defended successfully the villagers will come back. They've nowhere else to go except the bush.'

'Hey, Irish!' Petkus shouted his sudden warning.

They were on a straight stretch of track, for once clear of refugees. A heavy tree branch had appeared in the headlight beam blocking their path. Branagh hit the brakes. He felt the wheels lock, sensed the vehicle start to slew as it skidded on the dust film. He was aware of dark figures at the roadside. Swiftly he released the brakes, then reapplied them, steering into the slide. Heard the crack of a carbine simultaneously with the sound of shattering glass.

Kathleen screamed.

The Land-Rover jolted to a halt. Branagh punched his fist through the frosted windscreen, ripping aside the crystals of safety glass. In the throw of the headlights he saw a scruffy group of armed men standing beyond the fallen branch. They watched in silence.

'God!' Kathleen breathed. 'Bandits?'

Then a familiar face appeared at the driver's side window, complete with torn red beret.

'Oh, Senhor Mike, I am sorry about this,' the captain of militia said.

'Rafael – what the hell do you think you're playing at?' Branagh demanded. But in truth he was too relieved to be angry.

'My man does not recognise your car. I am sorry. We are manning a roadblock. If Senhor Armando comes back I shall not let him through.'

'After this I believe you.' Branagh picked up a radio transceiver from the dashboard and held it out. 'You can keep in touch with me using this tonight. I've set the channel – just press this button and speak, right? Don't touch anything else.'

Rafael took the black plastic handset with both hands as though it were the Crown Jewels. 'Senhor Mike – oh, thank you,' he said in awe.

'It won't bite,' Branagh said unkindly. 'Now are all your men in position? No one's run off into the bush?'

The captain looked indignant. 'No, sah. They still await the inspection you promise.'

'Good. I'll speak to you later – on that thing.' He revved the engine impatiently as he waited for the militiamen to clear the branch.

When they arrived at the compound Maraika was waiting anxiously with Leif Månson.

'Mikey, is it true that the Administrator is killed?'

'I'm afraid so.'

Månson said: 'I was working back at the well site when I heard. I just can't believe it. Poor old Conçalves.'

'Was there any sign of trouble when you came back on the road?' Branagh asked.

'Only people fleeing the villages. They think something's up.'

Månson was undoubtedly right. Word of the Administrator's cruel death would have spread like wildfire and most villages of any size had a Renamo supporter or two, some of whom might act as agents. It only took one man to start a rumour.

At that moment Francisco appeared breathlessly at the compound gate, behind him his group of helpers. 'Senhor Mike, we have put out all booby traps now.'

'That's good,' Branagh said. 'Now we need volunteers to fight alongside the militia.'

Petkus stepped forward. 'I have two dozen Kalashnikovs. So I want men with good eyesight, eh? No blind men or one-eyed buggers.'

Francisco turned to his band of men. Someone had

226

already translated into Portuguese, and now the villagers were discussing the request earnestly, caught up in the urgency of the moment. There would be no shortage of volunteers.

'I take you to the river bank and give you instruction and target practice,' Petkus announced.

Branagh turned to Månson: 'Leif, could you drive up to Din Din Singh's place? Get him down to the river with his generator to light a target range.'

The Swede looked unhappy. 'We really shouldn't be involved in this sort of thing, Michael.'

'Leif, just do it. Look at it as safeguarding all the hard work you and I have put into this place.'

As Månson took the Land-Rover, Branagh set off on foot for his promised inspection of the village's defensive positions with Kathleen tagging along.

She said: 'You told that Frelimo major at the plantation house you *had* been with the SAS – so it is true?'

'I was with the Regiment for a time, but long before I came back to the farm,' he admitted as they walked. 'It's not something you put about.'

'I can understand if you were ashamed of it?'

She couldn't see his smile in the darkness of the village street lit only by the glow of cooking fires. 'No, Kathleen, I'm not ashamed of it. It's just that you have it drummed into you never to talk about it. Partly traditional secrecy and partly antiterrorist security.' He paused to light a cigarette. 'In your case I'm aware of the paranoia your family had about the SAS. I've heard your brothers mouthing off. I thought you might think the same way.'

Kathleen laughed softly. 'And you didn't want to upset my delicate sensibilities, is that it?'

'Something like that.'

She linked her arm through his as they started walking again. 'You needn't have worried, Mike. I'm my own woman – I make up my own mind about things. Since

227

working on the Belfast papers I've heard both sides of the argument.'

They had reached the outskirts of the village now and they could see where scrub had been cleared to provide a clear field of fire for the militia trenches. They had been expertly placed to cover the lines of approach, to provide a withering crossfire. Branagh suspected the man D'Arcy's hand in the plan; there was nothing to criticise.

A murmur of voices drifted on the velvet night air from the nearest trench and Branagh could see the red pin-pricks of lighted cigarettes. The maddening cacophony of cicadas rose from the surrounding bush but was no match for the deafening belch of the bullfrogs calling from the nearby river.

'It's the full moon,' Branagh explained. 'For some reason it always gets them going.'

'Magical,' she murmured. 'You wouldn't believe that such tiny creatures could make such a noise.' She stared out towards the dark mass of the hills. 'I think Tumbo is the most beautiful place I've ever seen. I find it hard to conceive that there might be bandits out there . . .'

'They've probably been watching us all day through binoculars.'

She shivered involuntarily and Branagh put a comforting arm around her shoulder. He could smell the freshness of her hair and the lingering traces of the light daytime scent she used. He was aware of the warmth of her flesh beneath his fingers. She suddenly realised that he was watching her intently, and looked up with a smile. He thought how like the little girl from Armagh she looked now in the pale moonglow. The fringe of hair blown into a soft muddle, her porcelain Irish complexion beginning to tan, eyes dark and clear and enquiring. She seemed very, very close. He felt the urgent pressure of her finger-tips on his arm, saw her eyes close and watched, fascinated by the arch of her throat, as her mouth reached up for his.

For several long seconds he was plunged into a kind of madness. The kiss wasn't casual or tentative, it was a driven force. Almost a devouring. Words of warning crowded in on him but he refused to listen. He was only aware of the sensation of her lips and tongue and teeth, exploring as fiercely as his own, urgent to make up for lost time. Her thigh pressed against his groin, telling him what he wished he didn't already know.

She pulled back, breathless. 'Can you believe I've wanted to do that since I was a little girl?'

Branagh looked at her, unsure about the conflicting emotions tumbling through his brain. It felt curiously like an act of betrayal. To Maraika and to the girl in the Armagh farmhouse. But mostly to himself.

'We'd better get back,' he said hoarsely.

The moonlight danced in her eyes. 'I'm glad, Mike. So glad it wasn't true.'

'True?'

'What my brothers always believed. That when you came to stay with us that time you were still with the SAS.'

'I'd left the Army before I came home,' he repeated. He said it easily almost without thinking. He'd said it so many times in the past he didn't even have to think about it. It wasn't exactly a lie. And anyway, if you lied to yourself long and consistently enough, he knew that you would come to believe it yourself.

She clutched his arm. 'I can't tell you what a relief that is.'

Senhora Veronique da Gruta had been in Harare for two days and nothing had happened to change her hatred of the place.

For her it was a sick vision of the future of all southern Africa. True, on the surface nothing much had changed since the Rhodesian whites had been obliged to hand over to the socialist government of Robert Mugabe. In the city there was electricity and drinking water, modern hotels, and plentiful food. But after ten years the system was starting to crack. For a decade the place had been stuck in a time warp. Small signs were everywhere. Service was surly. The economy was in a mess and Mugabe was edging steadily towards a one-party state. His. The health service was in decay and bureaucracy running riot as Africans took over management jobs that were once the prerogative of the minority whites. Black officers of the armed forces could be seen walking down the road holding hands, and it made her sick.

Thank God, she thought, for the vast Meikles Hotel as the taxi drove into the entrance portico on Third Street. Willem van der Walt paid off the driver and opened the door for her. From the outside the building might appear to be a charmless concrete monolith, but once inside the enormous carpeted lounge she felt instantly at ease with the atmosphere of order and quiet respectability. Uniformed waiters hovered to serve the coffee-lounge customers who comprised mostly businessmen and diehard white farmers in town to shop with their wives. At reception the Zimbabwean staff were smartly dressed, efficient and courteous.

This, thought Senhora da Gruta, was how things should be. How, one day, things would again be in Mozambique.

'Mr Ashton Smythe?' the clerk queried, consulting the guest list. 'Room 510. Shall I telephone to say you're here?'

'No need. He's expecting us.'

They took the lift, then walked the lushly carpeted corridor to 510. Van der Walt had scarcely knocked before the door was opened.

That Ashton Smythe had spent the previous night on the town was clearly evident from his bloodshot eyes. Unshaven whiskers showed on his neck above the open throat of his striped shirt. A cockscomb of hair stood defiantly on his head, having resisted all efforts to dampen it down.

'Veronique – good to see you.' He stepped solicitously aside to allow her in. 'And Willem. You look tired.'

'We've had a lot of people to see,' Senhora da Gruta answered.

'You're satisfied everything is ready?'

'Yes,' the South African replied, looking round the room.

It was sumptuously appointed in traditional English style with heavy carved furniture, floral drapes and seascape prints on the walls. The window looked directly onto Cecil Square with its sparkling fountains and avenues lined with conifers, palms and fever trees. A million miles removed from the decaying streets of Maputo.

At the window stood a man who had been admiring the view. He was black, tall and handsome and wore a beige safari suit which helped to make him look younger than his forty years. With watchful patience he waited to be introduced.

Ashton Smythe said: 'Of course, neither of you have met Colonel Montgomery Lantanga from Malawi.'

Van der Walt shook the African's hand. 'My pleasure, Colonel. That's a fine military-sounding name.'

Senhora da Gruta shook hands wearing a thinly disguised look of disdain as the Malawian officer said: 'I am from a family with an army tradition.' His voice was almost cut-crystal public school. 'I was named after Montgomery of Alamein.'

Smythe smiled politely. 'Of course, Colonel. Now I hope you don't think it's too early for a drink? We've something to celebrate as Senhora da Gruta and Mr van der Walt will explain.'

'I trust everything is running to plan?' Lantanga asked as Smythe fussed about at the mini-bar. 'We cannot make our move in Malawi until victory is certain. I'm sure you understand.'

Van der Walt understood perfectly. Beneath the small country's façade of a relaxed tourists' paradise, the vicious regime of its ageing dictator Dr Hastings Banda was not to be underestimated. Despite the president's aping of the trappings of British tradition and civilised behaviour, he had continually given succour to the Renamo movement and had long stated Malawi's claim to the northern provinces of Mozambique. Moreover his record on human rights was abysmal. If Colonel Montgomery Lantanga were to fail in his attempted coup d'état, he and his accomplices could expect no mercy.

'It will take no more than a week or two,' van der Walt assured. 'Our selected Renamo shock battalions are in position, poised throughout the provinces of Tete, Zambezia, Nampula, Niassa and Cabo Delgado.'

Lantanga nodded soberly. 'And the official Renamo leadership knows nothing of this plan?'

The South African smiled gently. 'Naturally Afonso Dhlakama knows of the movements – but not the plan. He believes them to be just a major offensive campaign. He is not aware that some of his most senior commanders are in our pay and that our orders to these local bandit chiefs go much further. Afonso is finished. His international reputation over Renamo atrocities is tarnished. And now, with the prospects of peace talks which Pretoria is anxious should be successful, he is being difficult. We have no further use for him. In the eyes of the world he'll be left with his followers in the south of Mozambique still fighting with Frelimo. Our Renamo battalions in the north will eventually be integrated into the state security force of the new country.'

Lantanga accepted the glass of lager that Smythe handed him. 'But Afonso's top commander working for us – Napoleão – he is nothing more than a thug.'

Van der Walt chuckled and sampled his whisky. 'But a buyable thug. Greedy, ambitious and ideally placed to do the job. After we seize power he will be replaced by a former Mozambican government general who will become defence minister of the new country.'

'Do I know this man?'

'Brigadier Vaz.'

Lantanga grunted; he was not impressed.

Ashton Smythe interrupted. 'The point is, Monty, that Vaz is Frelimo not Renamo. None of the new ministers of state must be seen as terrorists. They must be seen as Frelimo turncoats who are acting for the good of the people, cutting away from the rule of Maputo. Just good guys with a difference of opinion. An internal coup will not provoke the United Nations or antagonise world opinion.'

'Then you stage *your* coup in Malawi,' van der Walt continued enthusiastically, 'and declare your presigned federation with the new state.'

Lantanga stared deep into his beer; he might as well have been trying to read tea leaves. 'I am concerned about intervention from outside. We are a small country with only three battalions.'

'Federated to the new state,' Senhora da Gruta said testily, 'you will be quite a large country, Colonel.'

'Who is going to intervene?' van der Walt added. 'Britain has no love for Dr Banda.'

'But he has always supported South Africa,' Lantanga pointed out, 'and you are acting for military intelligence – not the South African government.'

'Exactly,' van der Walt laughed, 'and Pretoria can do nothing unless we in the military agree. No one will intervene. When the dust settles the world will see a new multiracial democracy emerge from one of the most troubled regions of Africa.'

Ashton Smythe nodded his vehement agreement. 'That is most important to my clients. The new country must be seen to be squeaky clean. Multinational conglomerates cannot be seen to get their hands dirty. The credentials of the new president must be impeccable.'

Lantanga drained his glass and stared out at the flower stalls on Cecil Square. 'You have such a man?'

'We do,' the South African confirmed. 'We have to for all the investment to pour in as soon as the independence of *Boeretursland* is declared.'

The Malawian officer raised an eyebrow. '*Boeretursland*? The last refuge of the Voortrekkers? What has happened to Rumbezia?'

Van der Walt made light of it. 'What is in a name, Colonel? It is still the South Africans and Portuguese who will flood into the new country with their expertise and investment to make it work. Only they have the experience to exploit its minerals and get the crops growing. When Inkatha Zulus and the ANC Xhosas are squabbling over who runs the new South Africa you'll find no shortage of good people to make sure your new country is successful. And it will be the last time that Malawi has to go to the International Monetary Fund with its begging bowl.'

Lantanga's eyes narrowed. 'I know that, Mr van der Walt. That is why I am doing this. And to free my country from a tyrant.'

Ashton Smythe watched the first sparks of antagonism with dismay. The Malawian officer was nobody's fool; he was acting for what he saw as the only hope for a prosperous future for his small, land-locked country. Not to mention his own political success. Van der Walt was seeking a new homeland for the Afrikaners where the black population would be more interested in stability, peace and prosperity than overall political power. And Veronique da Gruta? She just wanted her heritage back: the fertile Gutala plantations and the immense profits of the Shangaan Queen which would inject immediate wealth into the coffers of the new nation. To make it financially independent almost from the start. Other minerals would soon be exploited once the remote northern regions of Mozambique were opened up again. Gold, emeralds, cobalt, diamonds and copper, all were certain to exist.

But that was for the future. In the meantime Smythe had more pressing concerns. For the past two years, ever since the late Dom Pedro's plan had been hatched, he had been feverishly exploiting personal contacts he had made during his thirty years in Africa. Without his extensive commercial and political knowledge it would have been impossible: a disconsolate army officer here; an over-looked politician there; ambitious executives in international companies and powerful individuals like van der Walt and Veronique. Carefully he had worked out the delicate links like a spider's web, each strand dependent on the other.

Only he could have pinpointed a man like Lantanga with a vision and the guts, position and intelligence to make it happen. And a man like Brigadier Vaz who would do anything for a leather attaché case of dollars. Anything, including blowing up his own superior officer. And there were many, many others.

Smythe had nurtured a whole host of investors from the international marketplace, major corporations greedy to exploit an untapped region of Africa. Offshore sub-sidiaries had been set up and investment rights signed and left undated – just awaiting the inaugural speech by the new president of a new nation.

Then and only then would Smythe receive most of his just rewards. Hundreds upon hundreds of retainers, profit shares and percentages that would make him a billionaire within a year. No more seedy hotels and crooked deals; no more cheap flights and scratching to make ends meet.

And he certainly wasn't prepared to see it all put at risk because van der Walt couldn't resist patronising Lantanga with typical Afrikaner arrogance.

Smythe said: 'Monty, please understand that Willem here is as concerned for the future of Malawi and the new federation as yourself. That is why he is here. To explain to you personally *exactly* what is about to happen. He is in the unique position to know the details.'

Van der Walt's enigmatic smile deepened a fraction. He had read Smythe's signal as though it were a beacon. He despised the grubby little Englishman who conducted himself like a common street trader. Despised him and resented the fact that he had needed him at all.

Now the South African made himself comfortable in an armchair, cradling his Scotch with both hands. When he spoke it was so quietly that everyone had to strain to hear. 'Colonel Lantanga, at dawn this morning special battalions of Renamo under my indirect command began attacking throughout the northern provinces as far as the Rovuma River. As you know, bandits are mostly lightly armed. But South African military intelligence has established secret caches of antitank rockets throughout the territory. These will be distributed to defeat Frelimo armour where it exists. Strongholds like Lichinga and Cuamba. Teams of South African commandos under my personal supervision are overseeing the entire plan on the ground.

'All road links and bridges from the Zambezi River northwards will be severed. Instead of keeping to the countryside, Renamo will take towns and cities and hold them. In a crucial sector of the front Brigadier Vaz will ensure that Frelimo's military response is too little and too late. He will sow the seeds of confusion in Maputo. All diehard Frelimo politicos will be executed. As will any Frelimo military commanders who do not choose to change sides when they are given the choice between that and a firing squad. As each province and city falls, announcements will be made appointing our Administrators and the setting up of the new food, health and education programmes of the new regime. The people will see that there is something for everyone and there will be no mention of Renamo.

'When it is deemed appropriate the new president will

go on the air at a special high-powered transmitter station we have set up in the bush. We hope his speech will persuade any of those still holding out against us that this is the only chance of a new future – and an instant amnesty for the bandits in northern Mozambique.'

As he stopped speaking the sudden silence in the room was electric.

Slowly Lantanga inclined his head. 'It is a brilliant plan.'

Senhora da Gruta smirked. 'It cannot fail.'

He had scarcely slept that night. Maraika had been in an ebullient mood, happy and joking at the prospect of her long-awaited marriage. Worries about an impending attack did not appear to concern her; she had that African ability to live for the day, content to wait for what the dawn might bring. She was flirtatious and demanding and made love to Branagh with more than usual passion. He had put up a token resistance, still haunted by the encounter with Kathleen at the village edge. But Maraika was in no mood to be rejected, and he found himself responding with a physical desire that needed to be satisfied.

Yet in the final moments as Maraika gasped and twisted beneath him, visions of Kathleen's face floated tauntingly before his eyes. And when he lay back, perspiring and short of breath, he realised that mentally he had been making love to the Irish girl.

Turning his head to the separating curtain of the bedroom, he wondered if she had heard as she lay on the sofa beyond. As Maraika fell almost instantly asleep, a smile of quiet satisfaction on her face, he propped himself onto one elbow. Reaching for his cigarette pack he lit one of its contents. There were no doubts now. His past had well and truly caught up with him . . .

Maybe he'd dozed, but he hadn't been aware of it. Outside it was still dark, but through the open window he could see the tell-tale lightening of the sky.

Something had alerted him.

He was out of bed and had pulled on his trousers before Maraika stirred.

'Mikey, what is it?' She rubbed the sleep from her eyes. 'I am dreaming that I hear the whistles.'

Branagh stared at her, wondering, then crossed to the window. Nothing moved in the direction of the hills. The cicadas still threw up their wall of noise as though in defiance of the approaching dawn. He cocked his head to one side, straining to hear.

He didn't, but Maraika did. 'Mikey!' Her face paled. 'I hear the whistle!'

'Are you sure?'

Even as he asked he knew she was. That was one sound she would never mistake. Her mind was attuned to it, even in her subconscious. Awake or asleep her antennae ceaselessly scanned the airwaves for the warning of the terror that was to come.

'Up!' he snapped. 'Up and dressed!'

Struggling into his shirt, he brushed aside the curtain and stepped into the living area. He fumbled in the dark for the hurricane lamp, lit it and hung it on the ceiling hook. The sudden flux of light caused movement in the sleeping bag on the sofa. Another pile of notepad sheets on the floor suggested she too had not been asleep for long.

'Kathy, wake up!' he hissed.

She sat up, startled. As she did, the top of the sleeping bag slipped free and Branagh found himself looking at her small round breasts. For a moment he stared at the dark studs of her nipples, then turned away abruptly.

'What's happening, Mike?'

'Bandits,' he said, moving towards the door.

He heard her light chuckle. 'There's no need to be embarrassed.'

'Stop clowning!' he ordered, and pushed open the door.

A sudden crackle of distant small-arms fire broke the spell. It was no mistake. The sound was drifting from the far side of the village. He extended the short aerial of Jorge's pocket transceiver. 'Rafael, this is Branagh. Can you hear me?' There was no response. 'Rafael, can you hear me?'

The set crackled with static. '*Senhor Mike?*' He sounded sleepy.

'Are your lot awake, Rafael? What's happening?'

'*I don't know, Senhor Mike. There is shooting from the eucalyptus woods. Maybe* bandidos *shoot into the air.*'

'They're just making a noise, Rafael, to frighten you. To make you think there are more of them. Stay in your defensive trenches. I'll get straight down there.'

'*Yes,* bass. *We stay here.*'

There was a flurry of activity now from the surrounding huts and rondavels, lamps were being lit and voices raised. Fred Petkus appeared at the compound gate, tucking in his shirt. Behind him an anxious Leif Månson had dressed hurriedly, combining lavender safari suit trousers with a striped pyjama top.

The sound of gunfire was growing, nearing.

Petkus said: 'This is our moment, Irish. You were right, I think.'

Francisco the carpenter came rushing up out of the darkness with half a dozen other villagers following.

'Your new fire team?' Branagh asked.

The Russian grinned. 'I give them two hours' intensive training last night. We shoot across the river. I choose fifteen who are good.'

'I hope it's not a mistake. They could turn out to be more of a liability.'

Petkus was affronted. 'I am not a fool, Irish. These are the boys who handle the guns well. They don't hit shit, but they will not shoot themselves either.' He turned to Francisco. 'The guns are in the compound. You make sure all are properly loaded and safety catches on.

Remember last night's training. I hold you responsible for your boys.'

Francisco smiled broadly. 'I am sergeant major.'

Petkus grimaced. 'Sure you are.'

Branagh watched the carpenter lead the way. 'He's a grand man, so he is, Fred.'

The Russian grunted sceptically. 'What you want I do with these guys? Go and join the militia?'

'No, keep them back here. After the bandits' last experience with our booby traps, they may try a different approach. I want to be ready for them, so keep your men here in reserve. I'm going down to the militia trenches now.' He handed Petkus the radio transceiver.

'What shall I do?' Månson asked.

'Take one of Fred's guns and stay in the compound with the girls. Should any of the bastards break through, don't hesitate to shoot. They can do nasty things to men as well as women, Leif. Remember that.'

Leaving Månson to examine nervously his first Kalashnikov close to, Branagh took the Land-Rover the short distance to the militia positions. A couple of times he stopped to tell lingering villagers to go back inside their compounds.

He pulled up short, parking behind the gigantic trunk of a baobab tree. Ahead of him in the clearing he could see the bobbing heads of the militia and D'Arcy's special force. They offered no returning fire as they peered at the muzzle flashes winking from the edge of a mealie field some thousand metres distant.

Exhausted rounds fell in a haphazard pattern around the defending emplacements, kicking up small fountains of red dust.

Branagh watched with silent approval. Rafael was keeping his powder dry, refusing to waste precious ammunition on targets that were hidden at maximum range.

The moment of truth had come. Branagh looked down at the AK47 propped against the passenger seat. It took an almost determined effort to reach out and grasp it, the polished wooden butt cool to his fingers. Fourteen years and the memory flooded back. Handling a firearm was like riding a bicycle – something you never forgot even if you wanted to. The familiar smell of graphite oil, the impassive cold feel of gunmetal, the routine. Checking that the safety was on, removing the magazine, checking the breech was clear, replacing the magazine. The reassuring click as it went home.

Then he was out of the Land-Rover, running at a low crouch towards the designated command trench. A zigzag wake of machine-gun rounds sang wishfully at his heels as he dropped into the emplacement behind a low wall of sandbags.

'They not come on, *bass*,' Rafael said, recovering from the surprise of Branagh's unexpected appearance.

The man knelt grim-faced with his torn red beret pulled down almost to his ears; he clutched his rifle so tightly that his knuckles were almost white.

'No problem,' Branagh assured. 'They're not going to come rushing madly in here after their last experience of the booby traps. It'll slow them down while they locate and disarm them. You've done right to hold your fire.'

Rafael's eyes clouded with concern. 'I talk to special forces commander from tobacco station. He say D'Arcy fellow teach them—' He struggled with the word – 'acoustic warfare. He says make big noise together but don't hit nothin'!'

Branagh smiled. 'I see his point. Putting down an intimidating barrage of suppressive fire can be more effective than hitting targets . . .' The captain of militia looked confused. 'But I'm sure we can do better than that. Put the word out. Tell your best marksmen to take their time – concentrate on one target at a time. The rest of you can concentrate on acoustics.'

The Mozambican appeared to see the sense in this and excitedly passed on revised orders down the line.

As it turned out there were another twenty minutes to wait. The misty dawn had clearly broken when the first Renamo bandit appeared at the edge of the mealie field. He was dressed in what looked like new camouflaged tiger fatigues and a khaki forage cap. The bandit made no attempt to conceal himself as he viewed the approaches to Tumbo village. Branagh guessed that because no one had fired from the trenches, the bandits were uncertain as to what they contained. Perhaps they suspected that they were shelter emplacements for civilians.

The man raised his right hand. For a moment nothing happened. Then another bandit appeared at his side, and another. All along the edge of the mealie field bandits emerged tentatively. There were scores of them, and more kept appearing until the entire field edge was lined with armed men. A whistle blasted from their leader and the first rank began to move forward. As they did so, more stood up between the bobbing corn stalks behind them.

Branagh felt a flutter of panic. He had no idea how many he had expected. A couple of dozen perhaps, even fifty. But now even without counting he could see that there were at least two hundred, possibly as many as three hundred. This was no rag-tag bandit group. This had to be a full battalion, if not more. Undoubtedly a dreaded *Grupos Limpa*, a clean-up squad of shock troops from the Gorongosa.

Beside him Rafael swallowed anxiously, his eyes fixed and staring at the awesome sight offered from the sand-bag revetment.

As the first two waves advanced steadily into the cleared area of scrub, yet another rank followed from the mealie field. Branagh realised then that the village was paying the price for the previous successful defence of Tumbo. This time Renamo was taking no chances.

Leaning against the wall of the trench, Branagh cranked the Kalashnikov's cocking handle and fed the first round into the breech. He moved forward, edging the weapon's snout out through a gap between two sandbags. Rafael saw his movement and, with deep concentration, copied him. All along the trench Tumbo's amateur militia followed suit.

Branagh thumbed off the safety. The barrel shifted to the left. He settled down, consciously relaxed his muscles and steadied his breathing. Lined up the pip. Waited until he'd drawn a full breath . . . Hold. His finger closed around the trigger in a gentle squeeze.

Beside him Rafael jumped at the sudden snap of Branagh's rifle. In the centre of the scrub the leader of the advancing bandits stiffened suddenly as though he'd received an electric shock. Without bending at the knees he fell backwards like a toppled tree.

Rafael recovered, found a target, and fired. As he did so the entire trench erupted with the sharp crack of outgoing rounds. It was a ragged volley, as in their excitement half the militiamen forgot to release their safety catches.

Even so half a dozen bandits pitched forward into the red dust and the neat line of advance broke in confusion seeking whatever meagre cover they could find.

More volleys came from the militia trenches, each more coordinated than the last, as they began to establish an uneasy rhythm.

Clouds of choking blue cordite wafted across the slit trench, stinging the eyes and making it difficult to see the enemy as they ran.

Branagh felt a sudden surge of adrenalin. He swung the barrel to a new target, this time double-tapping with two rounds in rapid succession to make more certain of a hit. Those bandits nearest the edge of the field began crawling ignominiously back towards the corn. Others caught in the open returned shots in near desperation, their aim wild as they were seized by panic.

The radio transceiver began to squawk and Rafael

reluctantly stopped shooting to answer it. 'It for you, *bass.*'

Fred Petkus was at the other end. *'Hey, Irish, you better get up here. The bastards are comin' across the river. Dozens of them*!'

Branagh thought for a moment. He had totally under-estimated the number of bandits that might be in the area. Around Tumbo alone there must be at least two battal-ions. Taking no chances, a second force was coming in on their flank. The river was quite fast-flowing, but fordable in several places. He thanked God he'd kept a reserve.

'Are Francisco and his men still there?' he asked.

'Sure. They can't wait to go, Irish. Some with my rifles and the rest with sticks and pangas.'

'Then get them to the river – don't let the bandits get established. But for Christ's sake keep back those without firearms; we don't want them massacred.'

He handed back the transceiver to the captain of mili-tia. 'Rafael, leave the radio with your deputy. Then get six of your best men to come with us. My Land-Rover's up at the big tree.'

Again he glanced through the gap in the sandbags. The bandits were in full retreat. With no concern for the dozen or so of their fallen comrades, they were scrambling into the mealie field with spouts of earth bursting all around them.

Cries of triumph broke from the rows of militia and special forces as the more bold among them sprang up to go in hot pursuit – strictly against orders.

Branagh reached the tree and looked back to see that a dozen soldiers had taken up the chase as the bandits took to their heels. As he started the engine, Rafael arrived with his motley collection of heroes. Eyes and smiles were bright in the sweating black faces that were flushed with success. Rafael climbed in beside him while the others scrambled into the open cargo hold as Branagh accelerated hard back into the village.

Mothers and children waved and cheered from the compounds as they roared through, Rafael's men grinning and giving clenched-fist salutes of triumph. In the village centre, Branagh swung the vehicle onto the track that led to the river with its fringe of weeping bean trees.

He pulled up at the edge of the embankment which fell away to the swirling silver eddies of the river. On the far bank there was movement in the buffalo grass that had grown up between the rice paddics. Flashes blinked at intervals, delivering probing fire into Francisco's group of newly trained riflemen who were scattered amongst the trees. Branagh could already see the bodies of two stricken villagers.

Fred Petkus was down at the front line, his bulky frame easily distinguishable as he tried to instil some order into his nervous fire team. Meanwhile at the top of the slope a group of village men milled anxiously out of the line of fire. They were armed with a mixture of pangas, home-made assegais, knobkerties, axes and pitchforks.

Branagh called to Petkus who waved back then started to make his way back up the slope, zig-zagging from tree to tree to throw off anyone aiming from the opposite bank.

He arrived breathless at the Land-Rover. 'You arrive just in time, Irish. Those bastards are crossing upstream – see!'

To their left, through the riverside ferns, the first group had reached the bank, struggling through the dense reed thickets for dry land.

Rafael was on his feet. 'We wipe *bandidos* out, *bass*,' he declared.

Branagh found the Mozambican's smile irresistible. The villagers' pride and self-confidence had returned. That was the real victory after years of subjugation and oppression by the terrorists. 'Get your men lined on the top of the embankment and fire together. Full magazines, then hold fire. And *stay* in position.'

'Sah!'

Rafael set off at a trot with his line of militiamen following.

Branagh called over the leader of the gathered villagers who approached timidly despite the enormous knobkerrie he brandished. 'Follow me,' the Irishman told him.

They set off in Rafael's footsteps, reaching the top of the embankment just as the militia opened up to their captain's order. A dozen AK47s released a tirade of rapid fire which rained down on the bandits as they splashed about in the reeds. It was a short but awesome display as full magazines were emptied, loosing off nearly four hundred rounds in little over thirty seconds.

Beside him the leader of the villagers gulped in surprise, his mouth open in disbelief.

'Sure,' Branagh said, 'it's all yours.'

The villagers exchanged glances and a couple of words, and then the battle cry went up. They swarmed out through the ferns and down the slope, shouting and yelling, pangas and axe heads glinting in the strengthening sun.

Branagh turned away and walked slowly back to the Land-Rover.

He found Petkus watching the last stages of the retreating attack as Francisco's new riflemen found their aim. On the far side of the river dark figures were seen scurrying towards the cover of the distant eucalyptus woods.

'The battle of Tumbo will go down in legend,' the Russian quipped.

Branagh tossed his Kalashnikov towards his friend, who snatched it from the air with a practised hand. 'So you remember how to use this?'

'I remembered.'

They took the Land-Rover back to the compound where Leif Månson appeared uncertainly at the gate brandishing his assault rifle.

'It's all over, Swedish,' Petkus greeted.

'Won't they come back?'

'Not before they've had a hard think about it,' Branagh replied. 'I hope they'll be off to find an easier target.'

Maraika and Kathleen emerged from the hut, smiling with relief. Kathleen held a bottle of Branagh's prized whiskey. 'Expect our heroes could do with some of this.'

Branagh grinned at her then took a swig straight from the bottle, gasping as it burned the dust from his throat. Then Petkus took three enormous mouthfuls, just as the transceiver in his jacket pocket began to crackle. He handed the radio to Branagh.

It was Jorge da Gruta. *'We've got trouble, Branagh, big trouble.'*

Gutala had been hit. It appeared that a massive Renamo force had bypassed Tumbo and swept on to the town, encircling it. At the same time reports had been coming in of virtually simultaneous attacks all over the district. Villages everywhere had been put to the torch and the tracks and the bush were filled with fleeing inhabitants. The plantation manager had never known anything quite like it. He had been on the radio to Robert D'Arcy at the tobacco station, but even his force was starting to buckle under the weight of the onslaught in their sector.

'What are the government troops doing?' Branagh asked.

'Holding out in the centre, it's all they can do. They've got the square and the hotel – that's about it. I'm worried about your friend.'

'What?'

'The Englishman, Mulholland. He's the only European in town. If Frelimo collapses he'll be in danger.'

Branagh felt like saying that it was no more than the man deserved; in truth he was more concerned with Jorge himself, who was only five miles the other side of town. He said: 'What's the Frelimo major doing?'

'At this precise moment da Silva is sitting under my dining-room table rocking back and forth with a bottle of

247

*my best brandy and muttering how it isn't his fault!
There's a handful of his men here and they're shaking in
their boots.'*

'Did da Silva man the OPs in Gutala like he promised?'

'*Did he hell! That's why they're in this mess.*' De
Gruta's usual taciturn tone had reached a pitch of controlled hysteria. '*Look, Branagh, you must help. D'Arcy
says he can't hold out at the station – he's pulling his men
back into Gutala. They will sweep in from the east to
drive the* bandidos *out of town if your men could come in
from the south to meet them. D'Arcy reckons with a
bigger force he'll be able to retake his tobacco station
later.*'

Branagh listened intently. D'Arcy's plan made sense.
A two-pronged attack on Gutala to flush out the bandits
followed by a regroup in strength. Jorge da Gruta's own
life was also paramount and, despite himself, Branagh
could not consider leaving even Vincent Mulholland to
Renamo's tender mercies.

He said: 'Radio D'Arcy, Jorge. Tell him we are sending two truckloads as a flying relief column from here.'

'*When, Branagh, when?*'

'*Now.*'

Branagh led the convoy of two of D'Arcy's Berliet
trucks in his Land-Rover. Fred Petkus rode shotgun in
the rear; Kathleen was by his side having persuaded him,
against his better judgement, that it was her decision as a
journalist to go with them. Typically it had been Månson
and his Swedish 'rights of the individual' approach that
had swung the matter. Branagh would have preferred her
to stay with Maraika and Månson in Tumbo where the
immediate danger had passed.

The trucks were loaded with Rafael Costa's militia and
members of D'Arcy's special force. All the men were on
full alert, gun barrels bristling on both sides of the vehicles so that they resembled two men-o'-war under full

sail. They left behind Francisco's riflemen at the village to guard against any unexpected trouble.

As they sped through the tall green swathes of the banana groves there was no sign of life. Any bandit movement would take place well clear of the road and by this time all civilians would have taken to the bush. However the danger of mines was ever present.

The convoy crested the last hill before the town and the entire vista of destruction was revealed before them. A patchwork of compounds and rondavels, dissected by red dust tracks, spread out towards the buildings of the town centre. At intervals the shanties had been put to the torch, the blazing thatch sending columns of white smoke billowing into the cobalt sky. In the distance antlike figures could be seen running – probably villagers seizing an opportunity to escape. Other figures moved stealthily along the tracks, working their way inexorably towards the square. The bandits were closing in.

Branagh pulled off the road a hundred metres short of the first outlying shanties.

He put a radio call through to da Gruta. 'Jorge, are you still all right?'

'*As far as I know no* bandidos *have approached the house yet.*' The deadpan voice was resigned. '*They'll want to take Cutala first.*'

'We'll get through to you at the house with some more militia as soon as possible,' Branagh assured. 'What's happening in town?'

'*How the hell should I know – the Frelimo garrison has stopped using the walkie-talkie. Probably some idiot stepped on it!*' His hidden fear was starting to show.

'What about D'Arcy's force?'

'*They left the tobacco station half an hour ago, but they're not ready to start their sweep. I'm waiting to hear.*'

Branagh grimaced. They were probably having to fight their way into town. He said: 'We're starting now from the south. Tell D'Arcy when he calls in.'

As soon as the convoy had debussed, Branagh selected four militiamen to ride in the back of the Land-Rover with Petkus. Rafael's militia was given the job of sweeping through the shanties on the left of the road, coming up behind the advancing bandits. D'Arcy's special force was given the right-hand sweep. They were, he observed, a well-disciplined bunch, given to much saluting and sharply turned out considering the second-hand uniforms they wore. Their general manner was far more businesslike than most government troops and showed an unmistakable British influence. Branagh prayed it was a good omen.

He returned to the Land-Rover and waited for the two sweeping columns to disappear into the first of the outlying compounds. Then he hit the accelerator, thundering towards the town centre in a choking cloud of dust.

9

It was a nightmare drive.

Branagh had no option but to rely on speed and surprise to get him through. The five weapons in the cargo hold could provide all-round fire, but it was unlikely they would hit anything as they bounced over the rutted track.

He swept into the first bend only to be confronted by a Renamo roadblock of planks and oil barrels. He had no time to count, but judged there to be some half a dozen heavily armed bandits. They must have been as surprised to see the vehicle as he was to see them. He pressed the accelerator to the floor. After a moment of stunned paralysis the bandits threw themselves aside. Kathleen squealed. The Land-Rover hit the central barrel of the row, spinning it high into the air.

Gunfire cracked like a bullwhip. Branagh spun the wheel, zig-zagging to throw their aim. A lucky strike sang gleefully off the rear panel as he veered in the opposite direction. Ochre dust spewed from the rear wheels, churning a dense cloud in their wake.

Now the run was straight and clear to the centre square. But the bandits at the receding roadblock still had them in open sights. Ahead bandits at the trackside turned at the sound of the vehicle's approach.

Branagh had no alternative. He took the next right-hand turning at speed, the wheels sliding over loose gravel before they gained purchase. The rear fishtailed violently, straightening up abruptly as he accelerated out of the turn.

They were in a narrow alley he didn't know. Tall wicker compound walls enclosed them on both sides. Hens scattered noisily from their path, feathers flying.

Ahead lay a T-junction with the next main street that led up to the square. Without pausing, Branagh turned left. Ahead at the top of the street he could see the square and the white facade of the hotel. But between him and it was a line of bandits moving towards its objective.

At the rear of the column, heads began to turn. A cry of alarm was raised and almost instantly a volley of small-arms fire was unleashed in the Land-Rover's direction. Branagh heard the headlamp shatter and distinctly felt the rush of displaced air as another high-velocity round whistled past his ear.

Two loud reports answered from above his head, as he realised that Petkus was shooting over the cab roof. They were now dangerously exposed. Something had to be done. Branagh threw the wheel again, crashing the vehicle into the nearest compound wall, and carrying the entire section of interwoven wicker before it like a 'dozer blade. Blindly they ploughed into a rondavel to the ugly accompaniment of rending timber. A cooking pot bounced heavily onto the bonnet. They hit something solid and stopped dead. The wicker section fell away in tatters to reveal a large wooden upright. Beyond it a young woman cowered, trembling, in a corner with a feeding baby clutched to her breast.

Petkus's angry upside-down face appeared at Branagh's window. 'Irish, what the fuck you doing?'

Branagh restarted and threw the lever into reverse gear.

'You can't leave that woman and her child!' Kathleen protested.

'They're safer here than with us,' Branagh retorted as the vehicle pulled itself free.

'Please,' Kathleen pleaded, then before he could reply she was out, rushing towards the terrified woman. As understanding dawned, the mother smiled with enormous

252

white teeth and hastily clambered into the unfamiliar cab, crushing Branagh up against the driver's door. The baby began to bawl.

With difficulty Branagh manoeuvred his way back through the debris of his own creation and began to pick a way through the interlinking compounds, unavoidably collapsing hut walls and fences as he went. He had no idea where he was. This was deep in the shanties, a haphazard maze of compound fences and narrow walkways. At each opportunity he turned to the north, working up blindly towards the square.

Suddenly he was confronted by double timber-framed gates of corrugated tin. Above them was the rear wall of the Embamo building, Jorge da Gruta's administrative headquarters in the square. The gates led under an arch and out the other side, past a loading bay which served the warehouse.

'We're in luck,' he murmured, and edged the LandRover's fenders into the gates. Grudgingly the tin began to buckle, the supporting frames groaning and splintering until the gates fell away, still hanging by the ripped hinges.

It was dark under the arch formed by the overhead offices, another pair of tin gates shutting out the light at the far end.

Branagh opened his door and approached on foot. The gap between the gates offered a clear view of the town square and the hotel opposite. To his right he could see the *cantina*. Its verandah was filled with bandits who were sheltering behind the upturned metal tables. On the left-hand side of the square blue cordite drifted from the row of deserted shops that had become the Frelimo billet. He could also see the sandbagged observation post on the corner rooftop position of the hotel. It was unmanned.

Across the square a sudden movement caught his eye. Half a dozen bandits were making a dash from the *cantina* to the front of the hotel opposite. With their backs

253

pressed hard against the front of the building they edged cautiously along the raised sidewalk towards the closed lobby doors.

'We must do something, Irish,' Petkus said, joining him at the gates. 'Your friend is in the hotel.'

Branagh didn't answer. He glanced up again at the observation post. If they could get to it, they could clear the square of bandits as well as part of the main road. He said: 'Fred, get our men lined up behind these gates.'

After he'd outlined his plan, the four militiamen went down on one knee and raised their assault rifles to the firing position. Hurriedly Branagh searched in his tool box for the small pair of military-style bolt cutters and handed them to Petkus. As the Russian quietly snipped the padlock chain, Branagh returned to the Land-Rover.

Under gentle pressure from Petkus the gates yawned slowly open under their own weight. Sunlight flooded into the dark archway.

Across the square the bandits edging towards the hotel stared in amazement at the sight revealed by the suddenly opened gates. The militiamen fired in unison. Before the bandits had a chance to react they were cut down in the hail of bullets. It sent them spinning and reeling in all directions, onto the sidewalk and into the street, where they lay in the extravagant postures of men killed by surprise.

'NOW!' Petkus yelled.

Branagh drove out into the square and braked. He waited anxiously for Petkus and the militiamen to scramble into the cargo hold, then accelerated diagonally across the square.

Shots sang above their heads, some from the Frelimo billet where in their panic the soldiers had failed to recognise the Direct Action Land-Rover.

The moment of exposure was scarcely thirty seconds but it felt like as many minutes before Branagh was able to swing onto the corner road then turn sharply into the kitchen compound behind the hotel.

'Get inside,' Branagh ordered as he leapt from the vehicle and raced past the smouldering cooking fires to the hotel's restaurant serving area. Two waiters sat beneath a table, shaking with fear. Smiles of relief broke on their faces as they recognised the familiar figure of the Irishman.

He ran on through to the lobby where he found more hotel staff hiding behind the reception desk.

'Where's Senhor Mulholland?' he demanded.

'The *Britânico*?' Taken aback. 'Room 14.'

Branagh mounted the stairs with Petkus and the militiamen hard on his heels. He took the steps three at a time until he reached the unlit passageway on the top floor.

He turned to Petkus. 'Take the boys up to the observation post, Fred, and get shooting.'

The militiamen exchanged glances uneasily, but the Russian was in no mood for dissension. He hustled them towards the ladder that led to the roof.

Branagh continued swiftly down the corridor, mindful that bandits might have already infiltrated the building. At the door of Room 14 he hesitated, listened, then reached for the handle and pushed.

The door creaked open to reveal Vincent Mulholland sitting propped up on his bed. There was a bottle of local brandy on the cabinet and a glass in his left hand. His right held a Browning automatic aimed directly at Branagh's stomach. He was smiling.

'It's your lucky day, old stick,' Mulholland said. 'I thought you were Renamo. The gunfire has been pretty close. Thought I'd take at least one of the bastards with me.'

Kathleen turned up behind Branagh. 'Is he all right?'

'His sort always are.'

Mulholland lowered the automatic. 'Almost like the old days, eh?'

Kathleen was astonished. 'Aren't you frightened?'

'Dear child, when you get to my age you don't let a

bunch of mindless black thugs worry you.' He levered himself from the bed and peered carefully out of the window. 'I've seen it all before. Eoka, Mau Mau, the IRA . . .'

The crackling voice of Jorge da Gruta burst suddenly into the room. '*Branagh, Branagh, are you there?*'

He lifted the radio set to his ear. 'Receiving you, Jorge.'

'*D'Arcy's called in. He's starting his sweep from the east. But listen – we've got problems at the house here. My boys have been watching from the rooftop. There's movement out in the groves about a mile away.*' He was talking rapidly. '*It's just a guess, Branagh, but I think a Renamo column has bypassed the holdup at Cutala and is making for us here. That will encircle the town. The bastards are all over the district. I've spoken to Maputo on the main radio – they reckon it could be the start of a major offensive up here. Attacks are happening all over north of the Zambezi River!*'

Branagh considered the implications. The situation was changing swiftly. If Renamo forces in the district were as large as they seemed he could hardly spare more militia to protect the plantation house five miles away. D'Arcy had already discovered that at his isolated tobacco station. Yet to lose the plantation house was also to lose da Gruta's main radio – their only link with the outside world. It was a hard decision to make.

He said: 'Jorge, I think you'd better come back into town with da Silva – concentrate what forces we have.'

There was a mirthless chuckle at the other end. '*Would that I could, Branagh! Ten minutes ago da Silva took my Toyota and set off with his soldiers. Last saw them taking the road to Cuamba like bats out of hell!*'

'Christ,' Branagh muttered. There was no choice now. 'I'll get over and pick you up. Give me fifteen minutes.'

He started for the door. 'You can't go alone,' Kathleen protested. 'It's too dangerous.'

'I've got to leave Fred here, otherwise the militia are likely to head off for the bush. And you're certainly not coming.'

Mulholland picked up the automatic from the bedside cabinet and tucked it into his waistband. With a smile he said: 'Ah well, when the going gets tough . . . As I said, old stick, just like old times.'

'You, Vincent?' Kathleen asked. 'You're . . .'

'Too old, dear child? Nonsense. C'mon then, Michael Branagh, let's get on with it.'

When they went outside they found the square clear of bandits. Steady gunfire from the newly manned observation post on the hotel roof had effectively driven the attackers back. The Frelimo garrison had emerged nervously from their billet in the row of shops; now they stood discussing what to do next. Branagh informed them of the two-pronged sweep being jointly conducted by the militia and D'Arcy's force from the tobacco station. Smiles of disbelief replaced the expressions of dire anxiety. Sporadic shots were heard from the shanties, getting ever closer as the bandits were flushed from their hiding places.

Before leaving in the Land-Rover he suggested they organised two sweeps of their own to join up with the advancing friendly forces – to crush the bandits between a rock and a hard place.

The Cuamba road that led past the plantation house was empty. Just mile upon mile of whispering banana groves stretching for as far as the eye could see. But while the plantations could have been as deserted as they appeared, they could equally well be providing cover for an entire division of Renamo infantry. It was an eerie sensation.

But Mulholland appeared untroubled, staring absently at the passing scenery as he hummed a tuneless tune. After a mile or so he said: 'I could kill you, Seamus. Now, before you can reach that AK47.'

'What?' Branagh glanced tersely at his passenger.

'No one would ever know. Shot dead by bandits.'

'Is that a threat, Vincent?'

A dry chuckle. 'Just food for thought. The Service has a long arm and people have long memories.'

'I told you, Vincent. I've no interest in your being investigated, no interest at all.'

'And should the investigators find you here – as well they may?'

'I can hardly deny I know you, can I? All I can do is tell the truth as I know it. You're the one who said you had nothing to hide, remember?'

Mulholland lit a cigarette and watched the smoke being whipped away by the slipstream. 'One man's truth is another man's lies, old stick, remember that.'

'What *do you* want, Vincent? A bloody vow of silence?'

'Got it in one, old chum. But we can hardly corroborate our stories – too much happened and too long ago.' He again stared out at the banana groves. The track was climbing now as they neared the plantation house perched on its commanding plateau. 'What I need is insurance.'

Branagh knew what he meant. He saw now that Mulholland's earlier offer of money had been a crude attempt at entrapment. Had he accepted, it would have looked to any investigator like hush money. Guilt by association. It would have been in Branagh's own interests to keep his mouth firmly shut.

'Insurance, Vincent?'

'I've offered you money which you turned down in the heat of the moment. I haven't come all this way to take no for an answer. The Service can be a good friend but it also makes a bad enemy. It can set you up with a new identity that the investigators won't be able to trace.'

'You don't mean the Service, Vincent, you mean you,' Branagh answered sharply. 'The investigators don't worry me. It's you I've been avoiding all these years.'

258

'Think on it, old stick,' Mulholland persisted. 'I'm a reasonable man, but I know where you are now. You won't be able to disappear again, that I promise you.'

'You mean I'll never know when to expect a knock on the door.'

'You know the form.'

Branagh shook his head. 'Crawl back into the woodwork, Vincent. As far as I'm concerned you'll deserve everything you get.'

The Land-Rover crested the slope, sweeping through the gardens of mimosa and umbrella pines and onto the gravel forecourt. A houseboy saw them from the steps and ran inside to tell his master.

Moments later Jorge da Gruta appeared at the door with a small handgrip. Three other houseboys followed him, each clutching a pathetic plastic bag of possessions.

'No trouble on the road, Branagh?' he asked, squeezing into the front seat while his boys clambered into the rear.

'We've seen nothing.' Branagh replied, beginning the return journey.

Da Gruta grunted as he watched the house disappear from view. Branagh knew how the man must be feeling beneath his impassive exterior – wondering if he'd ever see his family home again. 'I spoke to Maputo just before you arrived. The Defence Ministry is in a right state of panic, and I can't say I blame them. They say reports of attacks in the north started a week ago. Patchy at first but now a pattern is emerging. Because of poor communications they first thought they were isolated incidents. In fact they now say it's over the whole of northern Mozambique. It appears to be fully coordinated. God, I hope we can get out of this alive.'

Branagh shook his head sadly. It occurred to him that van der Walt's recent presence in the area with Jorge's wife might well be connected with this sudden turn of events. But the plantation manager was miserable enough without reminding him of the possibility.

Da Gruta added: 'And there's something very strange going on. Renamo aren't just hitting and running. They're taking villages and towns and holding territory. Apparently they are even appointing their own Administrators and announcing their own social and political programme. They never bothered to do that before.'

'What's the significance?' Mulholland asked.

'It's putting the fear of God into the Defence Ministry, that's what!'

Mulholland was none the wiser. 'I still don't understand.'

'It's the one thing the government have always dreaded,' Branagh explained. 'The Rumbezia syndrome. That northern Mozambique between the Rovuma and Zambezi rivers might be cut off and annexed. The country's two thousand kilometres long with the capital in the far south – the farther from Maputo, the less control the government has, especially as there are no usable road links. It's a nightmare scenario.'

Mulholland gave a light whistle of understanding. 'I see the problem, but is it feasible?'

'It's feasible,' da Gruta confirmed. 'Renamo is quite capable of it. But it would depend on the political will of the people pulling Renamo's strings. And those bastards are capable of anything.'

'Malawi has laid claim to the Zambezi and Nampula provinces for years,' Branagh added, 'and in the past they've allowed the bandits to use Malawi as a springboard for their attacks. It's all too feasible, yet with the current noises of conciliation coming from South Africa I don't think anyone was expecting it just now.'

They slowed on their approach to Gutala, unsure how the situation had developed in their absence. It was a relief therefore to see a group of D'Arcy's special forces manning a roadblock just behind the hotel. The confident smiles told the story.

Branagh drove into the square and parked in front of the hotel. A number of government troops were milling around talking to militiamen and special force soldiers. A row of dejected Renamo prisoners sat in the dust with their hands on their heads. Guarding them was Rafael Costa, the captain of militia. He waved triumphantly when he saw Branagh.

They found Robert D'Arcy in the restaurant. He had already commandeered the place, drawing together several tables on which to spread out a large-scale map of the district. A dozen Mozambican officers of both his special force and Frelimo pored over the layout of napkin rings which served as improvised unit markers. There were two Europeans dressed in British-style drill shirts and DPM trousers whom D'Arcy introduced: a large, moustached Englishman named Dave Forbes who walked with a pronounced limp and an unsavoury-looking Corsican called Saint-Julien.

'I've taken command of Gutala,' D'Arcy announced matter-of-factly. 'I know I'm going to get a bollocking from Brigadier Vaz, but it can't be helped. Lives have got to come before niceties about my company's remit.'

'How did the sweep go?' Branagh asked.

D'Arcy smiled. 'First-rate. It really caught the bandits napping when our forces came up their rear. A couple of own goals, I'm afraid, but it's confusing fighting in the shanties. Still a few pockets of resistance, but I'm confident we'll clear them out. You'll be pleased to know that all the OPs are manned at last – mind you, we had to send our boys up at gunpoint.'

'According to Maputo the whole area is in Renamo hands,' da Gruta pointed out gloomily.

D'Arcy nodded. 'I can believe it. The tobacco station was overrun. My clients won't be too pleased, but then we never expected anything on this scale. Another couple of months' training and our force might have been able to see them off. As it was we had to fight our way out to get here. We passed two villages burned to the ground on the way here, bodies everywhere. Bloody tragic.'

'How can we help?' Branagh asked.

D'Arcy looked at him for a moment. 'Fred tells me the Direct Action aircraft is still on the strip at Tumbo. Apparently only another half-hour's work is needed to get it airworthy. I'd like to get all foreign nationals out.'

'I'll get down to Tumbo with Fred and take a look.'

D'Arcy hesitated. 'Mike, this won't come easy – but I'm not sure Tumbo will be tenable for much longer. This Renamo offensive is massive and widespread and your village is out on a limb. This afternoon I'd like to bus any remaining inhabitants up here to the town centre for safety, I'm sorry.'

Branagh knew it made sense. He tried not to think of the likely consequences of abandoning the place to the bandits, all the hard work that would count for nothing. 'If you can watch the things you gave your life to, broken . . .'

D'Arcy smiled sympathetically. 'Kipling – And stoop and build 'em up with worn out tools.'

'That is the story of Mozambique,' da Gruta added gruffly.

Branagh said: 'Let's go, Fred, while there's still day-light.'

They took four militiamen with them in the rear of the Land-Rover in case of trouble, but no one was encountered on the road to Tumbo.

'Will you leave Gutala with the others?' Petkus asked.

Branagh shook his head. 'Not while there's a chance of holding out. I'll stay while D'Arcy's force is here, but I'd like to get Maraika out. And you?'

'Someone's got to fly the airplane,' he mused. 'But I'll be back to get you and the others out.'

Branagh started to smile, but it froze into an expression

of abject horror. Angry white smoke stained the sky ahead. 'Sweet Mother of Jesus . . .'

Instinctively Petkus raised the AK47 from his lap. The vehicle surged forward as Branagh squeezed the last reserves of power from the pounding engine.

They streaked through the spot where the militia had set up a roadblock earlier. It was deserted. A boot with a hole in the sole lay discarded. Some hundred metres from the road two king vultures soared on massive outspread wings above the banana grove. They had found something, or someone.

'Steady!' Petkus cautioned, and Branagh slowed. The Russian was right; they didn't want to drive straight into a village full of Renamo.

The smell of the burning thatch came out to greet them, eddies of smoke drifting under the light breeze that fanned the flames. And another smell, sickly sweet.

Petkus wrinkled his nose. He'd smelled that smell in Afghanistan after the napalm raids. Smelled it in burned-out helicopter gunships and ambushed armoured vehicles. He knew Branagh would know it too, but neither man said a word.

At the village edge they stopped, killing the engine. The silence was uncanny: no baying dogs, no chattering voices or children laughing, no cocks crowing or bleating goats. Just utter silence, and that smell.

Branagh took one side of the track with a couple of jittery militiamen while Petkus advanced on the opposite side with the other two. They edged forward, Kalashnikovs at the ready, safeties off. At the first compound Branagh's worst fears were confirmed. Two bodies lay in the dust; one had been decapitated.

He swallowed hard and moved on. Each compound had its own story to tell. Some were deserted, cooking pots missing where the occupants had ignored advice to stay and had taken all their portable belongings. Others showed signs of instant evacuation with charcoal fires left smouldering, food left half-eaten. They would have fled in time or have been abducted. In other compounds it was as though a mad artist had created his own private vision of hell. Putrefying bodies and sometimes their separated limbs lay on the hot earth, the spilled blood dried by the sun.

Branagh felt a sharp prickling sensation behind his eyes. The swelling knot tightened at the back of his throat. This was *his* fault. *He'd* assured them it was safe to stay. It had been his misplaced self-confidence. Christ, what a mess!

There was a sudden movement across the street, some distance ahead of Petkus. A voice called.

The crack of a rifle shot came from behind Branagh.

He spun on his heel, deflecting the militiaman's next shot. It spent itself harmlessly in the thatch of a roof.

'Senhor Mike!' the woman cried, stumbling from her compound gate to cross the track and fall at his feet. It was the wife of Carlos, the farmer abducted a few days earlier and then murdered at the mine.

'They come, they kill, they take prisoners!' she wept.

He looked down at her. Like Mary Magdalene at the feet of her Saviour. How wrong could she be.

Branagh knelt. 'When did this happen?'

But she couldn't answer; she was inconsolable. He passed her back to the militiaman who had almost killed her.

He broke into a run now, oblivious of the dangers. He just ran blindly towards the Direct Action compound, jumping over corpses, waving aside the wafts of woodsmoke. Tears flowed freely down his cheeks, his heart pounding and his lungs searing with exertion and the acrid smoke. From the corner of his eye he saw the slowly twisting bodies of the executed militia guards hanging from the baobab tree.

At the compound gate he stopped, chest heaving, and raised the Kalashnikov. His mind was numb, a blank void

264

of despair He took one step. The sudden flapping of the great bird's wings took him by surprise. Feathers flew as the king vulture struggled to get airborne in the confined space. The assault rifle jerked in his hand. Once, twice. Cordite stung his eyes, adding to the tears. The creature fell into the road, screeching like a lost soul, its huge talons trying to grip in the dust, dragging its shattered wing.

Its half-naked victim lay inside the kitchen lean-to. The pregnant body of Lisa Matusi was on its back, hands clasped to its swollen belly in a last attempt to protect the unborn child. Raped and then bayoneted to death.

He felt the vomit rise and he fell back against the gatepost to steady himself. Breathing rapidly he managed to regain a measure of self-control. Preparing himself for whatever else he was about to see.

Then he plunged into the entrance of the hut. It was still and dim after the bright sunshine. This hut was normally never quiet, always filled with the sound of chattering women and visiting villagers' laughter, or sometimes angry words as Maraika threw one of her tantrums or his own voice telling jokes to Pascoal Matusi.

The sofa that Francisco had so proudly built was shattered, its cushions flung in all directions; the coffee table was upturned.

He didn't see Leif Månson at first. The Swede sat in the corner, legs outstretched, propped against the wall. He held the Kalashnikov in an uncertain grip on his lap. His eyes stared accusingly at Branagh.

'Leif?'

Branagh rushed forward, reaching out for the man's shoulder. As he did so, the body slid sideways, the exit wound in his back smearing a vermilion arc on the wall.

Branagh staggered to his feet and looked around. 'Maraika! Maraika!'

He flung aside the curtain to the bedroom. It was empty. Without waiting he ran back to the compound, through the kitchen area to the vegetable plot at the back. Nothing.

Then he returned to the compound gate. The wife of Carlos stood there, Petkus by her side.

Her eyes were filled with pain. 'They have taken her.'

Branagh bowed his head, fists clenched at his side to stop the rising explosion of fury within him.

'B-A-S-T-A-R-D-S!!'

His voice thundered through the village towards the hills, and the words seemed to echo back at him in a cruel mocking laugh.

They buried Leif Månson and Lisa Matusi in shallow graves at the end of the vegetable plot. Petkus watched in grim silence as Branagh lashed sticks together to form two memorial crosses.

Leaving the militiamen to gather together the few surviving and injured villagers in readiness for the promised convoy from Gutala, Branagh and Petkus took Carlos's widow with them in the Land-Rover. Their detour to the airstrip did nothing to raise their spirits. The Direct Action Twin Otter lay like a crippled bird on the cropped grass. Someone had taken the trouble to shear some of the undercarriage bolts so that one of the aircraft's wheels had buckled under. An axe had been used on the body and wing surfaces. Scorched grass was a testament to someone's half-hearted attempt to set it alight. Perhaps the bandits had been interrupted in their work; or else a passing villager had doused the flames. Either way no one would be flying out that day.

It was a sombre drive back to Gutala. On the way they passed D'Arcy's convoy heading out to pick up the survivors of Tumbo.

At least the fires were out in the shanties of the town. Disconsolate Mozambicans could be seen picking through the charred remains of their homes, looking for anything to salvage.

Their news of the second Tumbo attack was met with a mixture of shock and sad acceptance by everyone at the hotel. All had believed that the village was safe, but the events of the day had gradually persuaded each one that it might be a false hope.

Kathleen had listened with horror. 'Leif and Lisa, no! And Maraika . . .' Memories of the nocturnal visit by Renamo to their hut flooded back. Haunted images filled her head and she was helpless to prevent the welling tears.

Even dour Jorge da Gruta commiserated, his enlarged eyes moist behind their pebble lenses. 'Sorry about the girl, Branagh – I know how much she means to you. And your boss – we owe him a lot.'

Kathleen managed to find her voice. 'What about Maraika's parents, Marta and Pascoal?'

Branagh shrugged. 'There was no one at their compound. They may have been taken or be hiding in the bush. I hope they'll be on the convoy when it gets back.'

Only Robert D'Arcy and his men took the news with cool detachment; like Branagh they had been professional soldiers and for them the tragedy was not so personal.

D'Arcy said: 'Mike, we had a long discussion while you were away. Our assessment is that we might be able to hold Gutala – if we're spared an overwhelming attack and our ammunition holds out. Two big ifs. It's possible that if Renamo are attacking the whole of the north, they'll go on to easier targets and attend to us later. I was hoping to fly out Europeans today and to start evacuating locals tomorrow.'

'Evacuate to where?' Branagh asked. He could think of nowhere that offered sanctuary.

D'Arcy looked uncomfortable. 'It's not an ideal solution, Mike, but there's a halt on the Malawi-Nampula railway about fifty miles to the north. Jorge tells me there's an armoured train due through at midday tomorrow.'

Branagh glanced at da Gruta for confirmation. 'That's

267

correct. Only yesterday I sent two trucks of bananas up there with some of my armed boys. We have two reserved wagons.'

'We'll dump the bananas,' D'Arcy said, 'and fill the wagons with our refugees. They can get off at Cuamba.'

'Isn't Cuamba under attack?' Branagh asked.

'It wasn't,' da Gruta replied. 'At least not when I spoke to them before I left the house.'

'It's the headquarters of Frelimo's 7 Brigade,' D'Arcy pointed out. 'The hangars at the airfield there are filled with light Soviet armour. It'll be a tough nut for the bandits to crack. Certainly it's the safest place around here. We might be able to organise a train shuttle between Cuamba and the halt to get more evacuees out.'

'The road to the halt is through open bandit country,' Branagh reminded.

D'Arcy nodded. 'It's still better odds than us holding out here, Mike, and we can't feed the civilian population. If Cuamba can't get a relief column to us in the next few days, we're snookered anyway. I need you to organise the first convoy by dawn tomorrow – you can take the Europeans and as many locals as you can find trucks for. You and Jorge are the most likely ones to be able to influence the army commanders at Cuamba.'

Kathleen said: 'What if all the refugees can't get on the train?'

'Africans will always find a way to get on a train,' da Gruta retorted testily.

D'Arcy said: 'If they can't, the trucks can drive alongside the train. They don't travel fast. At least they'll have protection from the soldiers on the train.'

And so the die was cast. It was going to be a long, hard night preparing the mixed collection of available trucks for the journey to the railway halt. Branagh found that, not surprisingly, the resident mechanical genius Din Din Singh had already made a start at his workshop.

With his crew of half a dozen Mozambican engineers,

who he had trained himself, the Indian had begun canni-
balising wrecked vehicles for spares. Working under
generator-fed arc lamps he aimed to have a total of six
usable trucks by the morning, in addition to the two of
D'Arcy's Berliets which returned from Tumbo in the late
afternoon. Marta and Pascoal Matusi were not on board.

By the time the first fingers of dawn spread into the
eastern sky a Spanish Barreiras and a couple of Polish
Star trucks were deemed roadworthy after some ingen-
ious improvisation. The sixth vehicle would take another
day's work. Then the triumphant little convoy rumbled
into the town square to join the Berliets of the special
force as the civilians, mostly women, children and old
folk mustered with their meagre parcels of belongings.

Some seventy of them managed to squeeze aboard the
five trucks along with the Europeans and a section of
D'Arcy's troops. The refugees who were left gathered
tearfully around the line of trucks, passing up last minute
family treasures, bananas and corncakes to eat on the
journey, blankets and a couple of live chickens.

The more reliable Berliets were placed at the fore and
rear of the convoy, each with a contingent of soldiers.
Branagh decided to take Kathleen and da Gruta with him
in the cab of the lead Berliet and sent Vincent Mulholland
to join Fred Petkus in the rearguard vehicle.

D'Arcy came out of the hotel and crossed to the lead
Berliet. 'Good luck, Mike.'

Branagh lit a cigarette and settled behind the wheel.
'Let's just hope the train's still running to schedule.'

'And don't be tempted to come back, Mike. I know it's
difficult, but it's better you get everyone safely to
Cuamba.'

'If you hear anything . . .' Branagh began.

'About Maraika? Of course, I'll make certain you get a
message.'

Branagh turned the key to bring the Berliet coughing
and spluttering into life amid belching clouds of diesel

exhaust. He put his hand out of the window and gave the thumbs-up sign. In his rearview mirror he saw his fellow drivers respond likewise. He engaged gear and released the clutch, the truck jolted forward, bouncing the over-crowded passengers as it rounded the first crater of the journey and rattled out of the square onto the northward road.

After half a mile the convoy passed through the special force checkpoint and exchanged subdued waves with the soldiers staying behind. As the soldiers receded from view there was no other sign of life in the regimented acres of banana plants. Even above the noisy pounding of the engine the uneasy quietness of the countryside was noticeable. In normal times a safe district like this might have been bustling with activity: the workers cutting down the crop and loading it aboard Embamo trucks, women on the road with gourds of water balanced on their heads or carrying produce for sale in Gutala market. But this day it was like most of Mozambique, abandoned to the birds and wildlife – and the bandits.

Kathleen pointed to a cluster of umbrella pines on the skyline. 'Isn't that the plantation house?'

Da Gruta stared at the black smoke rising lazily from behind the trees. 'Yes,' he replied flatly.

'Then we got you out just in time,' Branagh observed.

The plantation manager said nothing. The Irishman wondered if the unequal fight for survival had become too much for his friend: perhaps da Gruta was thinking that he should have stayed and died at the house that had been his home for most of his life. But as usual the man wasn't giving anything away.

It was a tense moment as they passed the track that led off to the house. No doubt the bandits had sentries posted, but there were none visible to the convoy.

There was a tangible relaxation in the atmosphere of the cramped cab. They were clear of Gutala and its troubles, and the solid ranks of banana at last gave way to

270

the open bushveld with its high buffalo grass and ubiquitous thorn trees. In their wake the billowing dust
enveloped the rest of the convoy so that from a distance it
appeared as though one lone vehicle had created the
monstrous red cloud.

The going became slower, the rains from the last wet
season having left the earthen road to bake into rock-hard
ruts and ridges. Engaging lower gears they were bumped
and jostled as each pothole was negotiated, the entire
convoy weaving drunkenly after the lead vehicle.

At a flat-topped kopje the road divided, the right-hand
fork taking the long and tortuous route to Cuamba.
Branagh swung left on the much shorter road to the
railway halt. After a few miles they picked up the meandering river that passed through Tumbo farther upstream.
They caught a small herd of impala unawares. As the deer
scattered from the cover of bush willow and seringas, the
sudden movement disturbed a flock of saddlebill storks.
They rose on the wing together, creating a vast black and
white cloud which filled the sky above the river.

Da Gruta said suddenly: 'You should have seen this
place in the old days.' His gruff words failed to hide the
emotion of the memory. 'It was a paradise of wildlife –
and not spoiled and modernised like South Africa . . .'

'What's happened to the wildlife now, Jorge?'
Kathleen asked.

Da Gruta shrugged. 'Who knows? The *bandidos* have
to eat. But they've systematically slaughtered elephant
and rhino for cash. No one knows what's left.'

'Perhaps some breeds will have benefited,' she suggested. 'You know, with the countryside abandoned?'

'Perhaps.' He didn't sound convinced.

The road reached the river. An old stone bridge
sprawled, flattened, across the water; it had been detonated years before. Beside it burnt staves were all that
remained of a replacement timber bridge which the bandits had set alight. At this time of year, before the start of

the seasonal rains, the river was still fordable. Branagh changed down and nosed the truck into the water, the huge vehicle waddling ungainly over the uneven bottom for several minutes before it reached a low shingle slope on the far side. The next two trucks followed success-fully, but the driver of the fourth approached too fast, spraying two vast wings of water which brought squeals of excitement from the passengers. Halfway across the engine cut out.

An anxious fifteen-minute wait followed until the spark plugs dried out and it was able to restart.

As the journey continued, the convoy passed several burnt-out villages, deserted years earlier. Now the buffalo grass was reclaiming the land for itself and thorn saplings were already growing inside the mud-brick ruins. A pen-sive silence came over the passengers as they bypassed the rusting charred hulks of trucks and cars, ugly memorials to previous Renamo ambushes. Now the wrecks had become home to nesting red-winged starlings and oxpeckers.

The track wound remorselessly on through the undulating bush broken only by occasional basalt out-crops. A copse of tall mlala palms appeared ahead as they rounded the lower slope of a hill; the road led directly into the dappled shade provided by the fringed canopy of leaves. High above a vulture hovered unerr-ingly on a thermal.

Branagh slowed. Da Gruta sensed it too. He picked up his ancient Soviet rifle and rested the barrel on the sill of the open side window.

Hardly had their eyes adjusted to the gold-flecked shadows of the copse than they saw the blackened shape of the first lorry. It had toppled to one side, a front wheel lost to the mine which had cratered the track. Its load of bananas had spilled out into the dust. A second lorry stood upright, both cab doors left open. The faded Embamo lettering on its tailgate was riddled with bullet holes.

272

Da Gruta said: 'It's the consignment that left Gutala yesterday. Some of my best boys were with it.' He swung open his door.

'Careful, Jorge,' Branagh warned.

The plantation manager dropped to the track; two soldiers from the rear cargo body joined him. They advanced tentatively, checking the hard-packed earth for a sign of more buried mines. Vervet monkeys shrieked from their vantage points in the copse, sudden flurries of movement visible in its darker recesses. No doubt the animals had been attracted by the unexpected abundance of bananas.

Da Gruta raised his rifle. The sharp shock of the report shook the copse. There were more excited shrieks from the monkeys and Branagh glimpsed the shaggy pelt of a hyena as the creature scurried into the undergrowth.

'For God's sake, Jorge,' Branagh remonstrated under his breath.

'What is it?' Kathleen asked.

'He'll bring every bandit within miles,' Branagh replied, as he began to edge the Berliet forward.

The bodies of the banana truck crews were scattered around the wrecks having been shot and then attacked with pangas. Nature's scavengers had then taken an interest.

Da Gruta was pale and visibly shaken when he rejoined them in the cab. He didn't or couldn't speak, but he managed a grim smile when Kathleen touched his arm in a gesture of sympathy.

There was no time to bury the dead; the little convoy rolled on. Apprehension was even stronger now, nervous eyes scanning the roadside and the track ahead for any sign of bandits or their mines. The relief was tangible as they cleared the copse and entered open bushveld once more.

Half an hour later memories of the incident had been replaced by anticipation of their arrival at the railway halt. No one knew for sure exactly how long the journey should take. It was impossible to gauge an average speed as they crawled around potholes and occasional fallen trees or slowed for numerous false alarms over planted mines.

Heat from the late morning sun beat down on the cab roofs and outside the air was still. Perspiration saturated the back of Branagh's shirt and drowsiness dragged at his eyes after the hard night without sleep.

All he could think about was Maraika. He kept seeing her face in the fly-smeared windscreen, floating before his eyes like a hallucination. Laughing, pouting, sulking, laughing again. The vision went through her entire repertoire of expressions, interspersed by unwanted flashbacks of them making love together.

The explosion rocked the cab.

At the same moment the vehicle lurched to the right so that the combined weight of da Gruta and Kathleen crushed Branagh against the door. Screams filled the air from the passengers in the back. Steam hissed and billowed from the radiator.

'Mine!' da Gruta gasped.

Frantically Branagh tried to change gear, but the lever jammed at the gate. He declutched and tried again, and again. All the time he glanced around, trying to evaluate the seriousness of their predicament. The convoy had just entered a steep defile surrounded on both sides by embankments of acacia scrub. Then he heard the drumming of small-arms fire on the bodywork. Branagh's side-screen shattered as a bullet punched into the cab and exited through the front windscreen. Kathleen yelped as glass crystals whipped at her face. Da Gruta pulled away handfuls of the frosted glass so that Branagh could see. His palms dripped with blood.

The second vehicle in the line hooted urgently for the Berliet to move.

Branagh at last managed to engage the gear and the truck wobbled forward on one front wheel, the cab swaying precariously. Steam was now rising in a geyser from its snub nose. Through the wafts Branagh could just distinguish the bandits on the road ahead and a mopane trunk blocking their path.

In an ambush it goes against all natural instincts to drive on, seemingly straight into the face of enemy fire. But Branagh knew it was the only ploy that could work – to break right out of the trap before it closed.

'Shoot ahead,' Branagh ordered da Gruta as he struggled to keep the vehicle moving. 'Kathy, take my gun and use it.'

She looked hesitant.

'USE IT!' he repeated.

Their truck had almost reached the roadblock. She picked up the weapon, cocked it and released the safety. Her thumb pressed the catch onto Full Auto. Poking the snout through the shattered windscreen, she took aim and pulled the trigger.

The noise was ear-shattering as the AK47 stammered out its full magazine, the barrel jerking skyward in her grasp. Bandits scattered left and right in the face of the looming cab. Branagh braced himself as the remaining front wheel crunched into the fallen tree. It shifted half a metre then held fast, locked under the cab. The truck jerked to a halt as the rear wheels spun in the powder-dry earth. The stench of burning rubber and the disintegrating clutch plate mingled with the smell of cordite. The screech of rending timber sounded like a living thing. There was some grudging movement. The tyre treads bit, spewing stones and dust, and the Berliet wobbled unsteadily forward. With a final groan of protest the tree trunk split – they were through.

Then catastrophe. A lucky shot hit the remaining front tyre. The cab rocked again, the truck dropping down onto its axle with a sickening crunch of collapsing metal. Branagh tried to steer to one side, to clear a path for the following vehicles. But it was hopeless. The Berliet was a dead dinosaur.

'Get out and take cover!' Branagh yelled. 'Use Jorge's door!'

Startled, Kathleen followed da Gruta out, now able to step straight down into the trackside grass where the shot tyre lay like a snake that had shed its skin. They cowered behind the buckled metal of the bonnet as Branagh crawled across the seats to join them. Behind the cab the refugees were scrambling over the sides, mothers screaming as they handed their children down to other women on the ground. Wailing babies added to the tumult.

The troop escort tried to find targets at which to shoot, but the situation was one of total confusion. The main gunfire appeared to come from the right where muzzle flashes blinked amid the thorn scrub.

Back down the track, the passengers were now abandoning the other trapped trucks. Through the smoke Branagh could just discern Fred Petkus's Berliet reversing frantically in a shroud of dust.

'We're not going to get out of this,' da Gruta forecast gloomily.

Branagh took the Kalashnikov from Kathleen. 'Sure your man's not finished yet,' he snarled. 'Stay put and shoot back.' He snapped in a fresh magazine.

Kathleen's face was ashen. 'What are you going to do?'

'This is only an ambush party – we've probably got as much fire power as they have . . .'

Without further explanation he turned to the mass of women, children and old people trying to shelter beneath the rear cargo hold. 'Don't run away,' he warned them in Portuguese. He jabbed a finger to the embankment behind them which appeared to be free of bandits. 'Mines.'

He reached his contingent of special force soldiers. They were understandably confused by the speed of events, but they were standing their ground and shooting

276

back. And it wasn't wild fire; they appeared to be seeking out individual targets. Thank God for D'Arcy's training, Branagh thought, and beckoned them to follow him.

At a running crouch he crossed the gap to the next truck which was in the throes of similar pandemonium. Again he warned the passengers not to run away up the embankment, and again he called the soldiers to follow him. He repeated the process with the third truck.

Petkus's Berliet had successfully reversed out of sight. Branagh was relieved: either the bandits had been too incompetent to put out a rear stop-group to close the trap or else they were short of manpower.

Only the fourth truck, the dilapidated Spanish Barreiras, remained. As Branagh braced himself for a sprint across the final gap, he saw the woman run. She sprang without warning from the lee of the Barreiras, a baby strapped to her back by her *capulana* shawl, and started up the embankment on all fours.

Branagh yelled at her to come back, but she seemed not to hear. He watched transfixed, hoping she'd get lucky, hoping he was wrong.

It came as a crack and a dull thud accompanied by just a small whiff of smoke. It hardly seemed powerful enough to cause injury. But the woman's ear-piercing scream told otherwise. Two soldiers left the Barreiras and ran after her, dragging her body unceremoniously back down to the shelter of the truck.

When Branagh got there one soldier had already put a field-dressing on the stump of her right hand and the other was bandaging her eyes. Miraculously the child had survived unscathed. It was only then that he recognised the woman as the widow of Carlos the farmer.

Time was running short. They had already sustained two dead and several injuries from the bandits' poorly aimed gunfire. Now Branagh had his entire force gathered behind the last truck of the convoy.

In Portuguese he said: 'When I give the word we will

attack together. We will run up the opposite embankment. Run and keep running. Fire everything you've got. And shout at the top of your voices.'

He was mad. Every wide-eyed expression said so. Then he remembered. 'Acoustic warfare!' he said.

That they understood. Much grinning and nodding followed as Branagh lined them up.

It was a strange moment. Never since his basic infantry training had he ever had to do anything quite like this. To lead from the front, to crash pell-mell into the brunt of enemy fire. In his youth he'd have been terrified, but now knowledge helped to conquer his fear. He knew how to break out of an ambush, knew the bandits would buckle. Knew he could die. But *certain* he would if they stayed where they were, picked off one by one. He locked on the bayonet.

'GO!'

His thumping heart suddenly went unnoticed as he leapt from behind the Barreiras, firing from the hip in short bursts as he ran. The scream of rage that bellowed from his lungs was not his; the fearsome vocal power was the release of pent-up anger and desire for revenge. It echoed up and down the narrow cutting, joined by the warrior yells of the Mozambican soldiers.

Breath came in hard, painful gasps as he pounded up the steep incline, in the heat of the moment the agony of straining muscles forgotten. Sweat stung his eyes; his teeth clamped into a fierce grimace of determination. Up and up, one leg driven remorselessly after the other like pistons.

He saw someone break and run ahead of him. His Kalashnikov spat as though it had decided by itself that the man would die. Its rounds hosed him down, scything him behind the knees, studding the offered back. Others broke, their hidden presence only revealed as the camouflaged bandits detached themselves from the landscape before the screaming horde fell on them. Their shooting stopped. It was a rout. All around him bandits were running, some throwing away their rifles and others attempting to surrender. Still Branagh ran and fired, overwhelmed by the exhilaration of released tension.

'*Atencão!*' one of the soldiers shouted in warning.

He spun round. The bandit was a mere fifteen feet away, half-hidden beneath a thorn bush. Branagh had a split second to register the polished black skin of the young face, the fear and hatred in the wide open eyes, the levelled rifle.

Branagh fired. Nothing. The hammer bit onto an empty breech. A cardinal sin – failing to count the rounds. He lunged blindly, dazzled by the muzzle flash at point-blank range and choked by the sudden discharge of gunsmoke.

He was aware of the overwhelming strength of his own muscles as they powered the bayonet point into the man's belly as he tried to twist away. In and turn, hard, driven by a compulsion to destroy. To kill this bastard who had taken Maraika, had killed Lisa and Leif Månson, had destroyed this land. He pulled the bayonet free. Saw the man's hand jerk in spasm, fingers twitching. Stabbed the blade in again. Just to be sure.

Branagh fell exhausted on his victim. He felt his all-consuming anger fall away, like water draining from a beach at low tide. His pulse slowed, his breath came more easily.

Slowly he climbed to his feet, trembling, feeling suddenly old. The face that looked up at him belonged to a boy who could have been no more than fifteen years old. Little older than Benjy Matusi would be now if he were still alive. The eyes stared at him in blank incomprehension. As though waiting for a question to be answered.

The truck hooted its horn. Branagh turned to see Petkus's Berliet bouncing through the rough bush; the Russian had swept round in a circle to attack the bandits from behind. Those who had not been killed stood with their hands in the air, watching dolefully as the special force soldiers cheered and waved their rifles in the air.

Branagh looked again at the corpse by his feet, and then at the palms of his own hands. They were moist with blood from the dead boy.

Fourteen years. Fourteen long years and it had come to this.

Petkus leaned, grinning, from his cab window. 'Hey, Irish, let's get on! We have a train to catch.'

Maraika sat on the earth in the middle of a long row of prisoners taken from Gutala district. There were men and women, young and old, and many children. The lines of seated figures filled the hillside quarry which someone told her had once been the entrance to a mine called the Shangaan Queen.

She had counted almost two hundred people and still they came. Sad silent columns trudging up the track, heads bowed. Behind them strutted the bandit escorts in their camouflage suits, lashing freely with seringa whips or rifle butts. Those too frail to walk she had seen being bayoneted in order to save precious ammunition, then left by the wayside to die.

In the past six hours she had witnessed horrors she would not have imagined possible. The treatment had been arbitrary: a man chosen at random, then mutilated or killed, or both. A child given a rifle and told to shoot its mother if it wanted to live. A father shot because his daughter refused to submit herself to a group of bandits.

She kept her eyes averted, gazing at the pale undersides of her feet as she sat cross-legged. Her fear was that she would catch some bandit's eye. Already she cursed because her dress was tight and red. Surreptitiously she had smeared it with dust whenever she had the chance. Her hair, too. She had grabbed a handful of earth and worked it into the strands until they were matted and dirty.

Her parents were there. Marta and Pascoal were in another line, mixed up with prisoners from Gutala town and other villages. But she avoided letting them see her. The fewer relations or friends the bandits knew you had the better; then they had no God-given lever to use.

Francisco the carpenter was in her line, but she had ignored him too. He had seen her and looked hurt as she turned her head away. She did not know why the bandits had not hanged him with the other riflemen who had tried to protect Tumbo. Some were hanged, some were taken. There was no cause or reason. When death called you went. It was as simple as that.

She thought of Lisa and of the bandits who had stood laughing as she died. And of Leif Månson who had tried to protect her. She had stared at him in horrified disbelief when he was shot. He was a white man. He was very important and even had his own aeroplane. How could he be shot like that by a teenage *bandido*? It wasn't possible, such things couldn't happen. Only Mozambicans were shot and massacred.

Not white men. Not men like Mikey Branagh who had left her in Tumbo. She could not forgive him for that. Why did he leave her? Why did he leave her and go to Gutala with his cousin? His kissing cousin. Kathleen would have his protection now, while she was in the hands of Renamo. So much had changed since his cousin had arrived. Tears began to roll down Maraika's face.

A big man moved forward in front of the line, surrounded by bandit officers. He shuffled under the weight of his huge belly and dabbed at his heavily jowled face with a grubby handkerchief. She thought he looked familiar, and then a chill finger of fear ran down her spine. The night of the visit to her hut . . . the Renamo commander called Napoleão.

He turned to address his dejected audience, a fat smile on his face. 'You, fellow Mozambicans, are the lucky

281

ones! You have allowed yourselves to be used by Frelimo scum – to be resettled in a show town so they can boast to the world what a good government they are . . .' The smile had gone, but now returned: 'But we in Renamo are forgiving. You are to be moved to new controlled areas where you will build new villages and start new lives and pay your taxes to us. We will invest those taxes in new schools and clinics for you and your children.

'It will be a long march, but you will show your support and enthusiasm for Renamo by doing your bit and carrying supplies. We have no time for malingerers and anyone trying to run away will be shot or handed over to the *mujiba* – our own police – for special punishment. Now you all know. Long live Renamo!'

He turned away and the long lines of seated prisoners began climbing to their feet as the *bandido* guards shouted at them and lashed out with their whips.

Maraika's line formed into a queue before a huge pile of looted goods. Mostly it was food – sacks of stolen aid rice, flour and fishmeal. But there was also bedding, electric fans, portable radios, medicine boxes, beer crates, tools – anything that was usable.

Her turn came in the line.

The bandit pointed to a pile of fishmeal sacks. 'You look strong enough, take one of those.'

She saw the stencilled legend on the hessian – *Direct Action. Not for resale* – and straightened her back. 'I will not carry that.'

The man stared at her. 'Come on, I haven't got all day.'

But she was defiant. 'I will not carry that. I will not steal from my own people in Tumbo.'

She didn't see it coming, just heard the angry swish of the seringa cane and felt its tip lacerate the skin of her cheek. As her hands instinctively flew to protect her face, another blow stung the backs of her thighs. She stumbled forward into the dust, squealing under the wicked thrash of the whip across her buttocks and back.

Someone grabbed her hair and forced back her head. She found herself looking into the face of the bandit.

Very slowly he said: 'Did I hear you say something, woman?'

She struggled painfully to her feet and reached out for the sack of fishmeal. Tears streamed from her eyes, mingling with the blood on her cheek as she strained to lift the load onto her head. With misted eyes she followed the man in front of her as he followed the man in front of him.

The long pitiful snake of humanity wound out of the quarry on the long march north.

10

A derelict tin-roofed warehouse marked the railway halt. Its sun-bleached rotted timbers merged with the buffalo grass, almost lost within the dry golden ocean of savannah that stretched to the horizon. Only the thorn trees and marulas broke up the scorched monotony of the landscape, providing occasional islands of greenery. A herd of zebra grazed its way across the far skyline.

The Berliet rumbled over the crossing where the steel tracks were rusting and dulled through lack of use, bindweed threatening to obscure them completely. As handbrakes were applied, drivers and passengers climbed down onto the hot earth, thankful for the opportunity to stretch their cramped limbs. Since the loss of Branagh's truck in the ambush, the refugees had been redistributed amongst the remaining vehicles. The rest of the journey had been suffocatingly squashed and sweaty.

Branagh sent soldiers out to form a wide defensive cordon around the warehouse where the refugees flopped exhausted in its shade.

'No train, Irish,' Petkus observed.

'This is Mozambique,' Branagh reminded. 'It'll come. Today, tomorrow, next week.'

'What will we do if it doesn't turn up?' Kathleen asked. 'We've virtually no food or water, and a lot of those women have children and babies.'

Branagh scanned the horizon. 'They'll survive. They'll survive because they have to. If the worst comes to the worst we'll drive alongside the track in the direction of Cuamba until the diesel runs out.'

'And then?'

'We'll walk.'

She looked at him angrily, irritated by his seeming indifference. Not for the first time she thought there were two men in Mike Branagh, two very different men. The laughing, easy-going Irishman with a heart of gold who would do anything for anyone. And then another, darker and more sinister character, as hard as steel and just as cold. A loner.

Vincent Mulholland interrupted her thoughts. 'Come in the shade, m'dear, this heat's a killer.'

She smiled. 'You're right. It could be a long wait.'

They found a space beside the warehouse. Kathleen removed her Tilley sunhat and using its floppy brim to fan her face, leaned back against the desiccated timbers of the building.

Mulholland searched in his pocket. 'Cigarette?'

'Thanks.' She waited as he offered a light and inhaled deeply, closing her eyes. 'That's good. And there's me trying to give it up.'

'You might have to – I'm down to my last pack. The bandits managed to loot the whole stock from the *cantina* in Gutala as they retreated. Never thought I'd find myself in a place on this earth where you couldn't get a packet of fags.'

She opened her eyes. 'Sure I don't understand why you're here, Vincent. Your man there refuses to talk about you and, well, for some reason you didn't tell me you knew him back in Maputo.'

Mulholland's eyes crinkled. 'Nothing sinister, m'dear. I just didn't think we were looking for the same person. Typical civil servant's caution.'

'And that line about you checking for the British Government – how its aid is being used?'

He didn't even blink. 'Perfectly true. That's the reason

285

I came to Gutala. Like for you, meeting Mike was a bonus And like you I thought I'd combine my aims.'

'But you never even went to the Direct Action compound.'

'Ah!' He smiled awkwardly. 'As you probably noticed, Mike Branagh didn't welcome me with open arms. A bit difficult to impose oneself.'

Kathleen exhaled and watched the smoke linger in the still air. 'Besides, Direct Action doesn't use British Government aid. It's an independent charity based in Geneva.'

A flicker of irritation showed in Mulholland's eyes. 'I expect you are a very good journalist, Kathy. Very perceptive. Perhaps intrigue at the prospect of meeting Mike overcame my reason.'

'Why should you be so intrigued to see him? I mean when did you last see him?'

Mulholland brushed away a persistent blowfly from his face. 'Oh, our paths crossed years ago,' he replied dismissively.

'Did you meet him in Ireland?'

For once the smile left Mulholland's face; she could sense that he was choosing his words carefully. 'I believe it was. I think he was unemployed at the time.'

Kathleen flicked the ash from her cigarette and stared towards the railway track where Branagh stood talking to Fred Petkus.

'Cousin Seamus is coming home.' She could hear Ma's voice as distinctly as if it were yesterday. It was a Sunday morning in spring and there was no work to do on the farm. The early milking over, the family gathered for the one breakfast in the week at which everyone was present. It was a ritual. The crisply starched red gingham tablecloth spread over the refectory table; the smell of a loaf cooling by the open kitchen window; the frantic sizzling of bacon rashers and farmyard eggs. That day there had been a milk jug of daffodils on the table. She could even remember that. All those years ago. How old was she? Of course, thirteen.

She had sat at the table in the sullen mood of early adolescence There had been a junior disco the previous night at the village hall, but Ma had said no. All her school friends had gone, wearing their mother's lipsticks, tottering in their first high-heeled shoes. All gathered, giggling and whispering, at one end of the hall while all the boys stood at the bar ordering soft drinks. A pattern of mutual stand-off that wouldn't change in later years when the drink would be porter followed by whiskey chasers. Dutch courage to ask for the last and only dance. But for the young Kathleen there had been no dance at all.

Pa had taken his place at the head of the table, tousle-haired and unshaven because it was Sunday, but wearing a clean white shirt in deference to Ma. He had told his daughter not to sulk and then lost interest in her, turning instead to his sons, each seated clockwise in order of age. Another ritual of the Sunday breakfast.

Matty was the eldest at twenty-eight then, quiet and taciturn with dark fiery eyes; one who kept his own wary counsel. Then Nial, two years younger, who had wanted to be a priest when he was a child, but who as a teenager had learned to play the guitar and had developed an insatiable desire to bed as many women as would have him. He had always held Matty in great awe and respect; probably more respect than his older brother deserved.

Following Nial came Padraig, the studious one. Born a year to the day after his brother, he appeared to be the complete antithesis. A collector of stamps and builder of Meccano; later a student of chemistry and engineering. All qualities that eventually led him to become one of the Provie bomb-makers most wanted by the Brits. It was typical of the quiet, innocent-looking Padraig that he should evade the dragnet without fuss and successfully disappear abroad.

And then there was Joseph. The curly-haired youngster

of the four boys at nineteen. Always a problem from the moment he could walk. Restless and tormented; argumentative and disobedient. 'A troubled little soul' had been Father McCabe's verdict when Ma had confided in him. Aping his older brothers who found him tiresome tagging along on their grown-up games. Ignored by his father who preferred to go fishing alone and tolerated by Ma who had been drained after bringing up her three eldest.

Not surprisingly at that Sunday breakfast table it had been Joseph who had reacted first to the news that Cousin Seamus was coming back from England. 'What does he want?'

'To see us again,' Ma replied easily, returning to the pan. 'To be sure it's been a long time, so it has. He needs a place to stay. There was no house left after the bombing.'

'Here?' Joseph was disgusted. 'That Brit-lover in our home? A bloody traitor. If it *was* a Proddie bomb that killed his parents, then it was rough justice.'

'Mouth!' Ma scolded. 'That's my sister you are talking about. And on the Lord's Day.' She deftly distributed the eggs and rashers to the row of plates on the worktop. 'Your step-cousin Seamus has left the British Army. He needs a roof over his head while he looks for a job. I at least owe that to my sister.'

'You hated her,' Joseph retorted. 'Sure wasn't it you who called her a stuck-up cow?'

Huffily Ma Coogan said: 'Kathleen – here and help pass the plates.'

Kathleen had obeyed instantly. Even at thirteen she was deeply conscious that she had been an 'unwanted accident'. The result of Pa returning home drunk one Saturday night. She was for ever trying to make amends.

'There are no jobs here,' Nial said. 'And no one would give a job to Cousin Seamus, anyway.'

'And why should that be?'

288

Matty glowered at the plate Kathleen put before him. For once he voiced his opinion. 'You know why, Ma. Because he's a soldier in the Brit Army.' He almost spat out the words.

'*Was*,' Ma corrected. 'And you should be thankful to the Holy Mother that he's seen the error of his ways. A man should always be given a second chance.'

'That's not what the Provies will say,' Joseph sneered.

Ma sat at her meal. 'And since when have those thugs ever opened and read the Good Book?'

Joseph was undeterred. 'The Provies say Cousin Seamus is a SASman.'

'And what do they know about it? Cousin Seamus was in the Royal Engineers.' She said it with a certain pride.

Matty stopped eating. 'They don't tell people what they do, Ma. Cousin Seamus joined the Engineers, but it doesn't mean he stayed with them. He's not going to tell us he was a SASman.'

A brittle silence had fallen over the table, emphasised by the clatter of cutlery on china. After a few moments Ma said: 'Well, it's settled, anyway. Your father and I have decided.'

Pa looked up from spreading a layer of butter on a doorstep slice of bread; he moved his mouth, but as usual didn't actually say anything. Matty caught his eye and for a moment they stared at each other. Then Pa's attention returned to his bread.

'Cousin Seamus arrives next week,' Ma said decisively. 'He'll have to share your room, Matty.'

Matty scowled, suddenly pushing his meal away, and stood up, kicking back his chair. 'I'll not share my room with a Brit soldier. No way, Ma. It's not as if he's even your sister's own child. He's an outsider.'

'Then you can sleep on the couch,' she replied unmoved.

Matty leaned across the table, his fists planted firmly on its surface. 'And what if he hasn't really left the Brit

Army? What if he's coming here to spy on us and our friends?'

Ma picked delicately at her bacon. 'Such a notion! Anyway, it's not as though this family has anything to hide. Is it?'

The four brothers looked at each other and at Pa. Pa was adding a thick layer of marmalade to the butter. Oblivious.

Afterwards when helping Ma with the washing up Kathleen had asked: 'Do I know Cousin Seamus?'

'You wouldn't remember, child. No, you don't know him.'

And now, fourteen years later and sitting in the shade in the bushveld of Mozambique, she still didn't know him.

Mulholland was saying: 'I met him when I was looking for a job. Through a friend of a friend as I recall.'

'In Armagh?'

'I think it was Belfast.'

She had liked Mulholland almost from the moment he had introduced himself at the Polana Hotel in Maputo; now she began to have doubts. 'There is no British rice sent to Northern Ireland, Vincent.'

The man would have been an excellent poker player; there was no change of expression, no sign of concern in the eyes. 'I am a civil servant now, Kathy, as I was then. A different department, that's all.'

'The Ministry of Defence?' she challenged.

'Not exactly.'

She stubbed out her cigarette in the earth. So that was it. She turned to face him. 'Until we met in Maputo, I didn't know you, Vincent. But you knew me, didn't you? Me and my family. You followed me here.'

He didn't answer her question directly. 'You're a charming young lady, Kathleen, but believe me I have absolutely no interest in you or your family. None at all.'

As a rule she was slow to anger, but Mulholland's

smooth fencing of her questions was beginning to irk. 'But Mike *is* part of my family. So why was it so important that you saw him?'

He shrugged nonchalantly. 'If you really want to know that, m'dear, then you must ask your cousin.'

A small shout of excitement came from a boy seated in the crowded shade of the warehouse. He sprang to his feet, pointing and gabbling in Portuguese.

'What's happening?' Kathleen asked.

All the refugees began looking in the direction from which the convoy had just come. Some people climbed expectantly to their feet, craning their necks to see over the shoulders of their neighbours.

Then Kathleen saw them. They emerged on the track from Gutala where it disappeared into a bush willow thicket that was scattered with knobthorn and marula trees. She counted five at first glance. Five great titans of the bushveld, ghost-white with dust, their giant ears fanning easily at each powerful, ponderous step.

Kathleen stood and moved forward to join Branagh.

He glanced sideways at her. 'This is a privileged sight in Mozambique, Kathy. A breeding herd.'

'God, they're magnificent.'

The first five elephants had just been the vanguard, behind them trudged some twenty more of all shapes and sizes, an old queen and several nursing cows with calves trotting at their heels. Among them they raised an immense cloud of dust that hung in the air like smoke blotting out the immediate landscape.

But it was the lead beast that caught her eye. The old bull was enormous with vast grey flanks like the sides of a battleship. Probably weighing some seven tons he moved with heavy ease, his huge head swaying from side to side as his trunk inspected each passing tree. He had just one tusk, she noticed, a massive curling six-foot spike of yellowing ivory; the other had snapped halfway. The animal shuffled to a halt beneath a marula tree, attracted

291

by the yeasty smell of its ripening yellow fruit. The trunk unrolled and stretched, the tip quivering with anticipation as he delicately plucked the luscious berries and carried them down to his mouth.

Branagh said: 'They get intoxicated on marula berries.'

When the old tusker had eaten his fill he meandered into the centre of the track, then scooped up a helping of dust in his trunk and tossed it over his back to scatter an annoying swarm of flies. Then as the trunk arched forward, it stiffened suddenly, alerted, sniffing the air.

'He's got us,' Branagh said. 'Watch, he'll take the air sample to his mouth. It has some gland in the lower lip, the sense of smell.'

As the bull threw back his head, the ragged ears wide like wings, the trumpeted warning carried across the bush. Its power was awe-inspiring. Within moments the other adult elephants were jostling alongside the old tusker, trunks raised, sampling the air, assessing the danger for themselves.

They began to move on with calm, plodding determination as though confident of their own strength, refusing to be intimidated by the near presence of so many humans. Trailing their wake of dust, they stalked slowly around the defensive perimeter of the warehouse. Only the majestic old tusker came closer, like a huge grey man-o'-war protecting the flank of his fleet. He was near enough now for Kathleen to see the heavy folds in his hide and to have the rank smell of the great beast in her nostrils. So close that she could see that he was half-blind, a small puckered crater of wrinkled flesh marking the spot where an eye had once been. The surviving eye had a wild look to it, the look of a crazy man.

'It's been shot,' Branagh said. 'It could have brain damage.'

'Bandits?' Kathleen asked.

'Who else? He must be a tough old bastard.'

The huge gnarled head was thrown back, the trunk

curled as he stood in defiance before the audience of refugees. An awesome screech of warning shattered the stillness of the bushveld, sending the Mozambican toddlers rushing back to their mothers in terror. Lifting his huge stumped foot the tusker pawed the earth as though in anger, then turned suddenly, bowed his great skull and pushed it against the trunk of a lone cassia tree. Powering legs, wider than the tree itself, drove his deadweight bulk remorselessly forward. With a creaking and groaning of timber, the twenty-foot tree was uprooted and contemptuously tossed aside. The message was clear. Another trumpeting; another celebration of strength; another earth-shattering venting of hatred. In the gathering of speechless refugees, a baby began to cry.

'I do not think he likes the human species,' Petkus observed.

The old tusker turned, his baggy shanks shifting like a pair of enormous armour-plated trousers. It was almost possible to feel the ground quake beneath the mighty footsteps as the beast strode slowly and purposefully after the herd. It was travelling north. Deeper into the uninhabited vastness of the bushveld.

Branagh said: 'It looks like everyone's leaving Gutala district.'

They watched while the dust cloud diminished, finally disappearing over the horizon. Still the sun beat down unhindered by even a trace of cloud. There was not a breath of wind to stir the tinder-dry grass. The heat could actually be felt reflecting back off the rock-hard earth. There was no escaping its energy-sapping power. In the shade the air was still oven-hot; the slightest listless movement was enough for sweat to break out of every pore. The afternoon was seeming to last for ever.

'*Trem!*' someone shouted.

Branagh stirred. He must have fallen asleep beside Kathleen. It was four o'clock now and still the sun blazed remorselessly. There was a sudden ripple of activity amongst the huddle of refugees as the word uttered by the sharp-eyed youngster was repeated. People stood and stretched, babies were lifted into arms, toddlers wakened. The tide of humanity ebbed towards the track, all eyes anxiously seeking the distant hope of salvation.

The train advanced with maddening slowness. It was rolling on old, unmaintained track, distorted by the heat and overgrown with bindweed. A massive tail of wagons was being hauled. At any moment the driver could expect to have his lead carriages derailed by mines or deliberately removed track. Slow speed was the only precaution available. In fact the line had just recently been reopened, running across Mozambique from landlocked Malawi to the deep-water port of Nacala and the freedom of the Indian Ocean.

It was the throaty grumble of two twenty-two foot Brazilian-made locomotives, travelling back-to-back in the centre of the train, that they heard first. Only later was the asthmatic noise of the diesels joined by the discordant clank of the rolling stock. Already passengers could be seen standing in the open wagons, peering ahead nervously at the gathering of refugees by the wayside halt.

An angry blast of the air-horns sent pairs of red-crested korhaans fluttering in panic from a nearby copse of thorn trees.

Branagh said to Kathleen: 'Keep well back. They're not expecting all these people to be here and some of the troops on the train might be a bit trigger-happy.'

He stepped forward, deliberately standing between the lines and raising both hands in a friendly wave that was also a gesture for the train to stop.

A rifle shot cracked in warning from one of the forward troop wagons; it was followed by another vibrant burst on the air-horns. Branagh stood his ground.

The train trundled noisily on, unheeding. Then, suddenly, the locomotives began grunting in complaint as the driver applied the brakes. The wagons groaned reluctantly, jostling and nudging at the slowing momentum. It was followed by a final exasperated jolt, the train coming to a stop just feet from where Branagh was standing.

Sand filled the empty first wagon for the purpose of triggering any mines placed on the track without causing casualties. The second open wagon had been rigged with eucalyptus frames to which a reed thatch sunshade had been fitted. From beneath it a dishevelled group of Frelimo government troops peered out warily.

But it was from the third wagon that someone actually climbed down. Branagh recognised the neat olive drab uniform of the Malawian Army complete with black beret. He saw then that the wagon from which the officer descended was bristling with Malawi troops. The difference between them and the shambling Frelimo soldiers was profound. While the untidy Mozambicans were sitting or standing, some with weapons and some without, the British-trained Malawi troops were neatly lined along the sides of the wagon, weapons gleaming and ready, the men smart and alert.

Branagh smiled and extended his hand as the officer approached. 'We're pleased to see you, Major. I'm Mike Branagh representing Embamo from Gutala.'

The man was wary; he looked towards the throng of refugees. 'Who are these people?' he asked in perfect English.

'Citizens from Gutala.'

'We're to take on a banana shipment here, Mr Branagh. I'm not authorised to carry civilians from this place.'

'I understand, Major. I don't expect you've heard. There's been a massive Renamo offensive over the whole of northern Mozambique. Gutala district has been overrun. Only the town itself is holding out. I need to get these people to Cuamba.'

The officer regarded the crowd pensively. 'I have heard rumours of these attacks . . .'

'You've had no trouble on your journey?'

'There was an incident. A rocket-propelled grenade was fired at one of our locomotives about ten miles back. But armour has just been fitted, so there was no problem.'

'I'm pleased to hear it.' He offered the soldier a cigarette which was graciously accepted. 'I must get these people to safety and then come back for more. I'll clear it with Brigadier Vaz at Cuamba.'

'You know Brigadier Vaz?' Surprise.

'I know him, Major.'

A sly smile; the innuendo was not missed. 'Then I wish you luck.'

Branagh said: 'The banana shipment was ambushed, so my people can travel in the wagons reserved for that. Besides, we have special force soldiers with us. They may prove useful between here and Cuamba.'

The officer made a snap decision. 'Get your refugees aboard, Mr Branagh. I want to cover as many miles as we can before nightfall. I'll have my soldiers provide fresh water and some food. Do you have injuries?'

'One woman has lost a hand and we had minor gunshot wounds in an attempted bandit ambush.'

'You were ambushed on your way here?' Incredulous.

'We counterattacked,' Branagh explained simply.

The officer appeared to have a suspicion confirmed. 'I think that perhaps you are – or were – a soldier, Mr Branagh?'

The Irishman smiled.

'I'll have my medical orderly attend your injured immediately.' Then, on impulse, the officer snapped his heels and threw an immaculate Sandhurst salute.

As Branagh began to walk the length of the train, the line of refugees fell happily into step behind him. Beyond the two troop wagons came a seemingly endless chain of flat cars, freight vans and fuel tankers. Mozambican

296

passengers filled every available space not taken by the main cargo of cotton bales and tea chests that was making the four-hundred-mile journey to the coast. A journey that would take fifteen days to complete.

In the centre of the train the two giant armoured locos stood back-to-back, hissing and grumbling, with orange paint peeling from the quarter-inch manganese steel plating and its protective grill shield. The 'Kremlin Mesh', Branagh knew, had proved effective on British Army Land-Rovers in Ulster, the idea being to detonate prematurely any rocket-propelled grenade before it could damage the main body of the engine.

The driver grinned down from the cab and pointed proudly to a blackened dent in the mesh shield – evidently the result of the unsuccessful attack.

More wagons followed and more passengers; many smiled and waved as he passed. He located the two vans reserved for Embamo produce, and beckoned back to the traipsing column of refugees. Between the vans and the end of the train were a further two troop wagons and a third on which an old Ferret armoured car had been mounted, complete with a businesslike 7.62 mm machine gun.

Overall an impressive effort had been made to protect the unprotectable. For even with armoured locos, troop wagons and a forerunning sand wagon to detonate mines, the rest of the train was pitifully exposed.

It took ten minutes for the refugees to settle aboard their allocated vans and for the overspill to squeeze in with the existing cram of passengers. Branagh bade farewell to the few special force soldiers who would attempt the perilous return journey to Gutala to fetch more refugees.

The Malawian officer approached. 'Mr Branagh, would you and your European friends care to travel in my troop wagon? It is less crowded, probably safer – and I am about to brew a cup of tea.'

It was not an offer to be lightly refused. Being amongst the cheerful and professional English-speaking Malawian troops gave Branagh a vaguely familiar feeling. Apart from the black lustre of the soldiers' skin it was almost like old times with former comrades. The train had hardly begun again on its noisy, clanking, creaking way before the officer's mess tin was bubbling on the stove beneath the sunshade.

It was with an immense sense of relief that they sat beside the soldiers while tin mugs of tea were dispensed. The hot liquid was like nectar to their parched throats. Each mouthful was savoured as they watched the deserted landscape inch by.

'No Butter Osbornes, I'm afraid,' the major apologised. 'But we have army biscuits if you have strong teeth.'

'When will we reach Cuamba?' Kathleen asked.

'Sometime tomorrow afternoon,' the Malawian officer replied.

Branagh explained: 'It's too dangerous to travel at night.'

'We will stop and put all lights out,' the major added. 'My troops will spread out and form a defensive circle around the train. Ahead there is a spot where the track goes through a depression, a saucer of land. That is a place I like to stop.' He glanced at his wristwatch. 'I hope we will make there before nightfall.'

Kathleen turned to Branagh. 'And what after Cuamba?'

'We'll wait for an available flight back down to Maputo for you and Vincent. It could be several days but I've friends who'll put you up.'

'And you?'

'I expect Jorge and I will see what develops at Gutala. We'll both want to return if we can.'

'I don't feel my own work is finished there. And I certainly don't want to travel south with Vincent.'

Branagh frowned. 'What's he been saying to you?'

She smiled sheepishly and glanced quickly across the wagon to where both Mulholland and da Gruta had fallen asleep side by side, like two small boys. 'Nothing much. It's just that I don't feel I can trust him. He never let on that he knew you, and now he won't tell me how he was involved with you.'

'You're wise not to trust him.' Branagh didn't want to say too much, but then he had to tell her something. Before Mulholland did. 'I worked with him when I was in the SAS. He was my controller on some undercover assignments.' He added pointedly: 'But not in Ulster.'

'Vincent was with the intelligence people?'

'Probably still is.'

She stared out at the horizon. 'I thought it must be something like that. Then he has been lying. He said he met you after you'd left the Army. Then I'm certain he *does* know me and my family. He must have followed me out here.' She turned to look at him, her face flushed with anger. 'Holy Mother, why can't they just leave us alone!'

'Vincent was the main reason why I left the Army.'

'Are you going to explain?'

She was very close now. He could smell the animal scent of her, the day's sweat and dust. He could see the startling clarity of her eyes, the coffee-coloured irises against the flawless whites. He could feel the soft strands of her hair blowing against his cheek and had a sudden urge to reach out and stroke it. To hold her. To make love to her.

He said: 'The past is buried. Vincent is in trouble with his masters and I'm one of the skeletons in his cupboard. He came here to make sure I wasn't going to rattle any bones – he just used you as a means of finding me. It's nothing for you to worry about.'

She smiled. 'Thank you.' And kissed him quickly on the mouth.

The explosion rocked the wagon. A geyser of sand and

gravel spurted skyward at the head of the train. Simultaneously the sound of the detonating mine shattered the early evening air. Branagh's head turned just in time to see the front sand wagon being tossed contemptuously aside like a toy. Metal bogies were spun into the bush, glittering spent coins amid the buffalo grass. The second wagon, filled with government soldiers, crunched noisily into the side of the sand wagon which was now askew across the track. Driven on by the pounding locos the second wagon began to climb remorselessly onto the first as though in a bizarre attempt at mating. Screams of terror came from the soldiers as they found themselves sliding helplessly back down the sloping floor.

Branagh saw what was about to happen, but was helpless to do anything about it. The front of the Frelimo wagon rose into the air and he realised it would be their turn next He watched in total horror as the Frelimo wagon hovered uncertainly. It seemed an eternity while he willed it to stop. Then in hideous slow motion it toppled almost lazily to the resounding percussion of crumpling metal. Uniformed bodies spilled from the wagon, some thrown, some leaping for their lives – only to be crushed between the growing layers of the steel mountain.

He heard the screech as the brakes went on, friction sparks showering in the effort to halt the irresistible slide of hundreds of tons on the move. He felt the crunching impact as their own wagon hit the obstruction, the wheels torn clear of the track. The floor canted violently as it tried to mount the pile of debris. At the front the wagon veered, finding the way of least resistance to one side of the peak.

Branagh grabbed Kathleen as she screamed. He didn't know what he intended to do in the desperation of the moment. It had all happened too quickly. All he knew was that he had to protect her. But his arms were hardly around her before he found himself spinning through space, blinded by dust and smoke.

The impact of his landing blew the breath from his lungs. He had landed catlike on all fours, instinctively rolling with the momentum of his fall, and finally coming to rest on his back. He opened his eyes in panic, expecting to see the steel side of the wagon crashing down from above, filling his vision. But the locos had finally dug in their heels, dragging back the forward momentum to leave the wagon clinging precariously to the side of the wreckage.

All around him stunned Malawi troops were lying, gasping for breath or staggering like drunkards as they tried to orientate themselves. Weapons lay everywhere, even the upturned tripods of heavy machine guns and mortar tubes. Soldiers who had not been thrown clear were gingerly clambering down through the twisted tangle of debris.

Kathleen sat, dazed, just a few feet from him. Blood trickled from a cut on her forehead. Branagh scrambled across to her.

'I'm all right, Mike. But I think Jorge has hurt his shoulder.'

The plantation manager was wincing as Fred Petkus knelt beside him, tearing a makeshift sling from his shirt. Before Branagh could offer help he was interrupted by the stuttering chatter of a heavy machine gun. It came from somewhere in the surrounding bush. Tracer fire glowed in the twilight and he watched in fascinated horror as the rounds hosed along the length of the train. They chewed effortlessly into the sides of the freight vans where passengers huddled for protection. He could see bodies toppling out of open doors onto the trackside and hear the screams. Some victims lay still where they had fallen, but others attempted to crawl for cover only to be caught by another rake of fire.

Towards the rear of the train the turret of the Ferret armoured car swung into action, its own machine gun spitting out its response. Some of the Malawian troops had retrieved their weapons and were providing covering fire while their colleagues began reassembling machine guns and mortars lost in the crash. The few Frelimo soldiers who had survived from the first wagon began to copy the Malawians' example. Meanwhile the air was alive with incoming rounds, ricocheting madly around the wreckage.

'Cover, quick!' Branagh urged, lifting Kathleen to her feet and bustling her towards the shelter offered by the steel bogies of the next wagon.

As Petkus and da Gruta followed, they were joined by Vincent Mulholland. An automatic pistol smoked in his hand. 'Christ, what a way to be woken up,' he complained. In his other hand he carried an FN rifle dropped by one of the soldiers. 'I seem to recall you were good with these, old stick.'

Branagh glared at him, but then another welter of bullets began digging up the trackside earth and he took the weapon from Mulholland without a word.

'This does not look good, Irish,' Petkus decided. 'They take out half our soldiers in the first few moments.'

He examined the Kalashnikov he had found and wrinkled his nose at the condition in which the previous owner had kept it.

Branagh realised that the bandits had chosen the ambush site well. Looking around he could see that at this point the track ran into a depression of land. He guessed it was the very 'saucer' to which the Malawian major had referred. The major had intended to make it a sound defensive position for the train, but having arrived first the bandits had turned it into a deathtrap. The attackers knew exactly where the train was, whilst the defenders were shooting at phantom targets in the dimming landscape.

He heard the abrupt thud and flash of a rocket-propelled grenade as it streaked out of the gloom. It was an inaccurate weapon, so either the firer was lucky or else he

302

was extremely skilled. Either way the first shot found its mark and in the flash of the impact the Ferret was seen to lurch at a peculiar angle. Its turret gun fell silent.

After frenzied minutes of activity the Malawian troops had one of their mortars readied and began feeding bomblets into the tube. The soldiers made hurried adjustments between rounds, listening and watching for the dull crump of each explosion as they tried to locate the rocket launcher's position.

But it was now almost dark and they failed. Instead, no doubt using the light of the fires that now raged along the length of the train, the rocket launcher found them. The round burst in the middle of the group, blasting the bodies apart like rag dolls. Shrapnel scythed through the air, pinging noisily on the bogies from which Branagh and the others were shooting at anything that moved.

The problem was that in their huddled position beneath the wagon there was very little that they could actually see. Although they were fighting blind, it was becoming perfectly obvious that they were being overwhelmed.

Yet the end when it came was as quick as it was unexpected.

A voice behind them yelled: '*Parada! Rendiçao! Rápido!*'

Branagh swung round, rifle poised, to find himself looking into the muzzles of three weapons. The black faces of the bandits were slick with perspiration from the heat of battle. Their eyes oscillated wildly between each member of the crouching group beneath the wagon. Hesitation, stand-off. From the corner of his eye he saw Petkus's finger edge towards the trigger of his Kalashnikov.

'Don't, Fred!' he hissed in warning. They wouldn't have stood a chance.

'*Rendiçao!*' one of the bandits repeated tersely.

Branagh threw down his gun. Slowly the others followed his example with growing apprehension. The

303

bandits stood back to allow their prisoners to wriggle out from the confines of their shelter.

It was a scene from hell. The entire train was now ablaze; bandits were frantically stuffing piles of cut brushwood beneath the locos to create an inferno that ensured they could never be used again. The leaping flames lit the surrounding bushveld with a quivering intensity that resembled daylight. Wafts of oily smoke hung in the air to obliterate the scene of carnage. The gunfire had almost ceased, only to be replaced by sickening screams as the bandits swept through the wreckage with their pangas. It seemed that no one was spared. Civilian men and soldiers, women and children and old people were butchered on the spot. Even those already dead were attacked again and again. For ten minutes the holocaust continued until not one body stirred. Branagh doubted that anyone feigning death had survived.

'Their blood is up,' Petkus murmured as they looked on beneath the uneasy gaze of their captors.

'High on ganja,' Branagh said. It was well-known that the bandits were given hash to smoke before a major attack.

'*Silêcio!*' demanded one of the guards.

Branagh glanced down at Kathleen by his side. She was ashen, her body visibly shivering with shock. Waiting for their turn to come. Slowly, so as not to provoke their guards, he slid a comforting arm around her waist. Let her feel the tenuous hug of reassurance. Her eyes looked up at him, beseeching, and the tears began to run.

As officers blew whistles at last the Renamo bandits started gathering into organised groups. Many of their number were no more than children. Some wore haunted, vacuous expressions; others laughed and giggled as they recounted their exploits. Branagh felt a sudden sharp jab in his back as the guard urged him forward with the muzzle of an AK47. '*Avançado, rapido!*'

He began to walk, the others falling in warily behind

him. Then they were lined in front of a thin, pinch-faced Mozambican officer who eyed them contemptuously before saying: 'Do you all understand English, yes?' He had a heavy Portuguese accent. 'Renamo has no argument with the white man, only our Marxist brothers in Frelimo who do not see the error of their ways. You are to be our guests until I receive orders to release you.'

Branagh couldn't believe their good fortune. But even as his spirits began to rise they were to be dashed again. This time he could not believe his ears: Fred Petkus had begun a mocking slow handclap in response to the officer's speech.

'You!' the soldier snapped. 'Stop that. Who are you?'

'Fredrik Petkus,' came the brusque reply.

Branagh cringed. The accent was so thick you could cut it with a knife. And to be a Russian in the hands of Renamo was to be so much dead meat.

'Get his papers,' the officer ordered.

Two bandits rushed to search him, found the documents and handed them to their commander.

The man read them ponderously. 'Fredrik Petkus. A citizen of the Federal Republic of West Germany.'

A conceited smile broke across the Russian's face. It remained while their hands were tied behind their backs and, linked together with rope, they began the long march into the night.

11

Dawn had never been a more welcome sight.

The night had seemed endless. Hot and humid air had pressed in on the weary line of prisoners until they were sweating profusely and clothes were sticking like a second skin. Mile had followed weary mile across the bushveld through chest-high buffalo grass, the procession frequently whipped by sadistic thorn branches that sprang out of the darkness.

As light stole across the landscape Branagh could see the column of Renamo bandits stretched out ahead of him. They had been walking now for eight hours without a break. From the stars he had assessed their direction of travel was west towards the Malawi border. As though in confirmation of this the purple outline of distant hills showed tantalisingly on the horizon, shrouded in dawn mist. These hills were an extension of the range in the south of Gutala district which swung round in a vast crescent.

His feet had long ago begun to blister and he wondered how the others were faring. Kathleen appeared to be wincing at every step, but he was unable to speak to her. His last attempt had met with the butt of a Kalashnikov in his kidneys. Now he noticed her expression was one of grim acceptance.

Each step was a private agony and with each passing hour his throat became more parched until he doubted that he could speak even if he had needed to. For the first few kilometres of the march he had worked at the ropes binding his wrists behind his back, but all he achieved was chafed flesh. He knew it was an instinctive throwback to his SAS training years before, but all he could think about was how to escape.

As the first tentative sunrays of the day warmed his back, he began to think more rationally. Escape may have been an answer if he were alone; however he also had Kathleen to consider. If he ran with her he must be certain of success – the guards had made it unpleasantly clear what retribution failure would bring. And anyone left behind would pay a terrible price for any attempted heroics.

To his surprise he realised that not all the train passengers had been slaughtered. A dozen younger, fitter men had been spared and had now been coerced into acting as porters.

The Renamo contingent itself appeared to be made up of two distinct types. There was a hard core of officers who wore fairly new camouflage fatigues and good boots. They gave their orders in Portuguese, but when talking amongst themselves they reverted to Shona. Branagh guessed they were members of Renamo's South African-trained elite, press-ganged from the organisation's heartland of Gorongosa, adjacent to the Zimbabwe border, when they would have been forced to carry out atrocities to secure their allegiance. The others were less well-dressed in a mix of tattered issue uniforms and civilian clothes; some even wore Frelimo forage caps or blood-stained fatigues taken from corpses. Few had proper boots or showed any sign of proper military training. Some were only boys. maybe as young as ten. They were both the saddest and the worst. With lacklustre eyes, they would strut about with AK47s that were as long as they were tall. The only time their eyes lit up was when they were taunting and prodding the prisoners.

By the time the column reached the foothills the sun was starting to burn. The final climb over rough ground covered in tall grass sapped all remaining strength.

Branagh had to reach deep inside himself just to find the determination to put one foot in front of the other. The old tricks. The mind games. Delving into the imagination to divert concentration from his screaming muscles and feet that were on fire.

In his mind he conjured the cooling rain. Leaking out of a Welsh leaden sky, trickling down his face. His feet deep in the waterlogged turf of the Brecon Beacons. How many years before? Training with the Regiment, a young man, eager to learn and untainted by bitter experience. Determined to succeed. Fresh-faced and without a spare inch of flesh around his waist. A powerhouse of muscle and sinew, revelling in his own strength as he bounded up the gradient with an eighty-pound pack. No easy routes following the contours. Up and straight over the top. SAS style. The shortest distance between two points.

Kathleen stumbled and fell, right in front of him.

He was obliged to stand and watch as the boy-soldier screamed at her. His face was ugly with hatred, a gargoyle gnome. Again he screamed and this time Kathleen struggled to her feet. The boy raised the butt of his AK47.

'*NAÕ!*' Branagh shouted.

The child stopped in mid-strike. He blinked in disbelief at this European who had yelled at him. His eyes met Branagh's.

It was a strange moment. Branagh's rage was a boiling cauldron about to burst its confines. He felt the surging strength of a madman, knowing that if his hands had not been bound he would have torn the boy's head from his neck. In an instant he would have snuffed out the young life without a moment's hesitation. Stamped him into oblivion.

Kathleen swayed on her feet. The boy remained staring at Branagh, butt still poised, eyes uncertain. The eyes of a man who sees a tethered bull pawing the ground, knowing that he *should* be safe, but nevertheless unwilling to take that chance. In Branagh's mind the boy was already dead, and the boy knew it.

An older, weary-looking bandit pushed the child away, then shouted at Kathleen and at Branagh. He waved his arm, telling them to move on. The incident passed and they trudged on.

Nothing has changed, a voice said in Branagh's head. Fourteen years after renouncing violence, and nothing's changed. Fourteen years convincing yourself and forgiving yourself. Then yesterday you killed a teenager and you actually enjoyed it. Today it could have been a child.

Just when it seemed that the ground would never flatten out, it did. They had entered a shallow high pass between two basalt peaks. A clear stream giggled its way through the languid shade of coral trees and nyalas, under which dozens of reed shelters had been built. Everywhere, there were bandits: sleeping, cooking, washing or just standing around. There must have been hundreds of them.

The column halted and the soldiers dispersed, leaving the guards to take the prisoners to the stream. Roughly their bindings were removed. Branagh could hardly believe it. He held back, half-suspecting it to be a mirage as the other prisoners threw themselves on their bellies to scoop up handfuls of water. But it was no illusion. The guards selected boulders to sit on, and watched while their charges drank their fill and wiped the grime from their faces.

He joined the others, shameless in his greed for the crystal, sweet liquid. Cupping handfuls into his mouth, he felt the parched membrane slowly soften and his saliva run again. Felt the water coursing down his throat, radiating out its coolness like a breeze through his burning body.

'God, Mike, I thought I was going to die,' Kathleen breathed.

He splashed water on his face and wiped it with his shirt tail. 'You and me both.'

The night's march had taken its toll. Her eyes were sunken with exhaustion and her hair was matted. The tight denim jeans were dust red and her blouse ripped into holes by thorns. She looked small and vulnerable, almost the child he once knew.

He said: 'Get some sleep while you can. You never know when they might move us on.'

She smiled wearily and curled up in a patch of soft grass, and was asleep the moment her head touched the ground. But Branagh was unable to follow his own advice. He found himself endlessly scanning the encampment for signs of other prisoner groups, hoping to catch sight of Maraika. However, all he could see were the Mozambicans abducted from the train.

'You look for her, too, eh, Irish?'

Petkus dropped heavily by his side. 'I think maybe the *matsangas* will bring her here, too. This is a big, important camp. I think the main one for this district.'

Branagh pulled a battered pack of cigarettes from his shirt pocket and offered one to the Russian. 'It's uncanny. To think this camp has probably been here for months. Just a few miles from Gutala and we never even knew. I imagine they'll bring prisoners here from all the villages. Yes, she might turn up.'

Petkus drew heavily on the cigarette and closed his eyes. Bliss. 'And if she does, Irish, what can you do? These bastards could just kill her to spite you.'

'Sure, I know that. But it seems that it's "be nice to Europeans" week, so they might put her in with us if I ask politely.'

'I would not count on that, my friend.'

Mulholland saw the rising cloud of blue smoke and walked across from the stream. 'Can you spare a gasper old stick? The bastard guard found mine.'

The Irishman tossed up the pack. 'Be my guest, and offer the last one to Jorge. I always did intend to give it up one day.'

310

'Jorge has crashed out – like the sleeping beauty here,' Mulholland replied. 'His shoulder's been giving him gyp. Didn't say much, but you could see it in his eyes. Really needs a doctor. Maybe these bastards have got a medical orderly, or captive doctor.'

Branagh smiled bitterly. 'I doubt it, Vincent. First aid isn't their priority or they wouldn't make a point of killing every doctor or nurse they come across.'

'Really?'

'And teachers.'

'Christ, what a place,' Mulholland muttered with feeling and lit the cigarette. For a man of his weight and age he'd survived the forced march remarkably well. At the time, his breathing had been hard, his eyes bulging from the exertion, but now he seemed in the bloom of health. 'What d'you think we should do, old stick?'

'Do?'

'Well, do we sit on our butts or do we plan something?'

'This isn't an escape and evasion exercise on Exmoor, Vincent,' Branagh pointed out acidly. 'The whole district is crawling with gun-happy Renamo kids, high on ganja. It's three hundred miles to the nearest city on the coast.'

'What about the other way? West towards Malawi.'

Petkus grinned. 'Minefields and more bandits, my friend.'

Mulholland's enthusiasm visibly drained. 'Jesus . . . So we just sit here?'

'While we're not in immediate danger, yes,' Branagh replied. 'Hopefully, they intend to keep us alive and feed us. And don't forget, if we do try an escape we've got to take all five of us, including Kathleen and Jorge. It's *got* to succeed or we're dead, and we can't leave anyone behind.'

As the morning drew on and the sun gathered strength, sleep finally overcame the three men. For several hours

311

each surrendered the horrors of the real world for the confused and bizarre terrors of their disturbed dreams.

To Branagh it seemed that he had only just lost consciousness when he was suddenly wide awake again. He was lying on his back, staring at the sun-whitened sky through the rustling green canopy of a nyala tree. Again he shut his eyes. He must sleep – then he sensed the presence of someone nearby. Someone watching. His eyes opened in alarm.

'So, Irishman, you do not take my advice.' The deep phlegmy voice was eerily familiar. God, Napoleão! Branagh drew up his legs instinctively to protect himself from the blow. Arching his back, he rolled to the left and came up on both feet, braced in a defensive crouch.

The mocking laugh rang in his ears as he tried to orientate himself. Napoleão's enormous bulk stood just a few paces in front of him, surrounded by a group of sneering Renamo officers. At Branagh's feet, his companions stirred from their troubled sleep.

'If you had done what I told you, Irishman, you would not be in this trouble,' Napoleão said. 'I told you to leave Gutala, not to stay and fight. For that I should cut off your testicles . . .'

Branagh made no move; the officers tittered and the seated prisoners looked up anxiously at their abrupt awakening.

'Careful, Branagh,' Jorge da Gruta warned.

'You are still lucky,' Napoleão continued. 'My orders are not to kill you – unless you try to escape. Remember that, because it can be arranged. As it is, you will have to stay with us here until it is decided to return you.'

'How long will that be?' Kathleen asked.

He looked down at the girl, his eyes focusing on the gaping cleavage of her blouse. 'That is not for you to know.' He smiled, moving his gaze to her face. 'It is pleasant here. Fresh water and the guards will see that you are fed.'

Branagh pointed to Jorge. 'This man needs medical attention. Can you do anything about it?'

Napoleão peered at the unfortunate plantation manager. 'What's wrong with him?'

'A dislocated shoulder.'

'Who is he? I think I recognise his face.'

'Jorge da Gruta, the manager of Embamo.'

The flesh folded beneath Napoleão's chin as his mouth dropped. Initial surprise overcome, the man rounded on Branagh. 'Why do you lie to me, Irishman? Senhor da Gruta flew out to Harare.'

'Veronique da Gruta flew out, but not her husband. You have been misinformed. But he does need treatment.'

The bandit commander regarded da Gruta with consternation before turning to his men. 'Very well, bring this da Gruta fellow.'

As they stepped forward, Jorge squealed: 'Don't let them take me, Branagh! I don't trust them.'

Napoleão became irritable. 'Bring the Irishman as well. It won't matter now.'

Before he could reply, Branagh was hustled forward at gunpoint by two Renamo officers. With da Gruta following, he was marched deeper into the encampment. After several hundred metres, they emerged at the other side of the trees which gave way to flattish, open grassland between hilltop peaks on either side. A herd of impala grazed unperturbed on a landing strip marked by lines of neat reed beacon piles ready to be put to the torch.

To Branagh's left, well-hidden from the rest of the camp, a khaki tent had been erected beneath a fat and burgeoning baobab tree. It took several seconds before he realised that four of the men who sat outside on canvas chairs were blacked up with cam cream. The Afrikaner accent amid their muted conversation was unmistakable.

A big man, with boxlike shoulders like those of an American footballer, rose to his feet. Sun-blond hair peeped incongruously from beneath the scrim scarf tied round his head. 'What the fuck do you think you're doing?'

Napoleão raised his hand in protest. 'Wait, Senhor Dracht. There is a mistake.'

Now a second white man was on his feet. Black-haired and handsome with flashing teeth. Branagh choked. It was none other than Armando da Gruta. And these were the other men he had seen at the Shangaan Queen.

'*Pai!* What in the name of God are you doing here, *Pai*?'

Jorge da Gruta just stood, transfixed. His mouth opened and closed like a fish, the liquid eyes blinking behind the pebble spectacles. 'Armando? I don't understand . . .' The voice tailed away. Then his mouth snapped shut like a portcullis coming down. His eyes hardened. 'Or perhaps I do understand. Is this part of your mother's crazy scheme?'

Nico Dracht intervened. 'This is your father, Armando? He was supposed to have left for Harare with your mother.'

The younger man shook his head and laughed. 'The stubborn old bugger probably refused to go. I warned my mother she'd have trouble with him.'

Dracht gave a snort of disgust. 'He's lucky he didn't get himself killed.' He turned to the Renamo commander. 'Anyway, you shouldn't have brought him to us. You know the rules.'

'He is injured,' Napoleão explained lamely. 'I think his son will want to look at him. You people have medical knowledge.'

'Yeah,' Armando drawled, 'I guess you did the right thing for once.'

'Where did you find these people?' Dracht asked the Renamo commander.

'They were on the train to Cuamba.'

'How many Europeans?'

Branagh answered: 'Five of us.'

Dracht said: 'And who asked you?'

'The Irishman from Gutala,' Armando interrupted 'Mike Branagh. The one the kids at Sunday school call the Jesus Man.' He snickered. 'I met him over supper at the plantation house. Likes to get on his high horse about Mozambique and South Africa.'

'Any *kaffir* lovers are wasting their time here,' Dracht snapped at Branagh. 'So keep the lip buttoned, right?'

'Maybe we should keep the Europeans with us now,' Armando suggested. 'The blacks are working up a helluva bloodlust right now, Nico. You can't trust the bastards – we're likely to find these people with their throats slit in the morning.'

Dracht rubbed at the lengthy stubble on his chin. 'You could be right. It'll be all over in a couple of days.'

'What will be over?' Jorge da Gruta demanded testily.

His son laughed. 'We're liberating Mozambique, *Pai*! Well, the north anyhow. We're liberating Gutala.'

'Enough!' Dracht ordered.

Jorge stared. 'Rumbezia? This is your mother's madness. She and that Boer boyfriend of hers.'

'At least van der Walt has had the balls to do something about it,' Armando retorted. 'He doesn't just whinge and let the *kaffirs* walk all over him.'

'He recruits Renamo thugs to do his dirty work,' Jorge growled. 'What sort of country will that be?'

'One where we can live without worrying about the fucking *kaffirs*, *Pai*! Without our family's heritage being nationalised by some tinpot dictator!'

'You've said enough, Armando,' Dracht warned darkly.

Jorge da Gruta shook his head in sorrow. 'You are no son of mine, Armando. And your grandfather, Dom Pedro would turn in his grave if he knew what you were doing.'

Armando's teeth gleamed against the dark cam cream on his face. 'It was Dom Pedro's idea. I may not be your son, thank God, but I am *his* grandson.'

Finally, Dracht stepped between the pair of them like a

man breaking up a dogfight. Too much had been said already. He ordered Armando to tend his father's shoulder and this was duly done in mutual and bitter silence.

Branagh was told to sit beside the tent under the watchful eye of an armed bandit while Kathleen, Petkus and Mulholland were sent for. As he waited, one of the South African commandos gave him some biscuits and a welcome tin mug of sweet tea.

Everything made sense to Branagh now. The mysterious arrival of van der Walt at Gutala and his visit to the Renamo unit at the Shangaan Queen mine with Veronique da Gruta. Her wish to regain control of her family's land was no secret. That wish had become an obsession. And that obsession had become Rumbezia – the ultimate nightmare for the Mozambique government. To see their country ruptured in two, with the fertile and mineral-rich north breaking away.

In fact Branagh knew that, had Renamo truly been the resistance movement it claimed to be, then such a thing might well have happened years before. The bandits fielded a guerrilla force of twenty thousand fast-moving men who could strike anywhere of their choosing.

Against them were pitched a mere thirty thousand ill-equipped conscript troops. It was an unequal task.

He had no doubt why Renamo made no serious attempt to take over the country. No one did. The organisation was run by van der Walt and his cohorts in the Civil Co-operation Bureau. And their objective was only to destabilise and dominate their neighbour whilst creaming profits from the landlocked states forced to use South African ports.

So why change now? Branagh asked himself. Had van der Walt and his diehards seen the writing on the wall? Mandela had been freed and all the talk was of the new South Africa. Pretoria had reputedly shut down the Bureau. There was to be no place for the likes of van der Walt in the new order. And in Mozambique? Deserted by

Pretoria, the bandit warlords would break up into rival factions. With the arms they already had they could survive for years, well used to living by terrorism and with youngsters too brutalised to comprehend any other way of life.

Was this van der Walt's last desperate gamble? To seize a virtually vacant country and to make a fat profit in the process? And if it was, who was going to stop him? The answer was depressing. No one.

Kathleen arrived with Petkus and Mulholland under armed escort.

'Little Irish is worried they shoot you,' Petkus said later. 'I tell her this man has nine lives.'

'I think we're safe enough,' Branagh assured.

The Russian jerked his thumb contemptuously at the tent. 'And you say these are the South African commandos you see at the mine?'

'Yes, including Jorge's son.'

Kathleen said: 'God, I didn't recognise him under all that warpaint. Have you found out what's going on?'

Branagh told them. The plot to seize the northern provinces appeared to hit a chord with Mulholland. It was almost as though he could recognise the scheme as one of his own.

'I like it, old stick. Can't see how it can fail.'

The Irishman gave him a withering glance. 'If you want it, grab it – is that it? God, Vincent, you've not changed.'

'But if it'll mean an end to the fighting—' Kathleen suggested.

Branagh shook his head. 'In the north perhaps, but what about the south of the country? And, anyway, can you imagine the sort of country that Veronique da Gruta and van der Walt would want. It'll just store up trouble for the future.'

Petkus shrugged. 'It would depend who ran such a country.'

317

Branagh smiled grimly. 'Who indeed.'

A new voice joined them. 'I should keep your voices down if I were you.'

The commando with the shaggy auburn moustache towered above the seated prisoners with two mugs of tea. 'I've been given the job of looking after you.' He handed the drinks to Kathleen and Mulholland. 'And if you want to stay alive, I suggest you stop speculating. This is a sensitive mission and Nico likes to keep things to himself.'

'Nico?' Branagh asked. 'The one Napoleão called Dracht?'

'The boss – Nico Dracht – with the blond hair.' The man spoke in a quiet, measured tone. 'Don't cross him. He and the others are quite capable of cutting your throats if it suits them.'

'And you?' Kathleen provoked.

A lazy smile spread across his face. 'I am not one of them. I am a last-minute replacement on the team. That is why I get the job of looking after you.'

Petkus said: 'Then do I get tea – or do you have something a little stronger?'

The eyes hardened. 'This is not a holiday camp. Do not push your luck.'

'Do you have a name?' Kathleen asked.

'Enough questions.'

'We have to call you something,' she said.

Again the lazy smile. 'Anton will do.' Boyd rose to his full height and fetched another mug of tea for Petkus.

'Who are the others?' Kathleen asked when he returned.

'You've asked enough, lady.'

'I'm a journalist. Kathy Coogan.'

'Then you'll have some story to tell when you get out of here.' He glanced towards the tent. 'But I shouldn't mention your occupation to Nico or the others. They don't like publicity.'

318

'And the others? Are their names all secret? We already know Armando.'

Boyd thought carefully. Then: 'I guess there's no harm. The lanky Rhodesian with the ginger hair, that's Wenwee Drummond.'

'Selous Scouts?' Branagh asked.

'Ex-Rhodesian Light Infantry,' Boyd corrected. 'And the black. He's Shona and calls himself Moses Chipoko.'

'Anton,' Kathleen said coolly, 'would I be right to assume you don't care too much for your comrades-in-arms?'

The South African's posture stiffened. 'Your tongue could get you in hot water, lady. I've warned you, don't cross them. Or me.'

'Anton!' Nico Dracht called suddenly from the tent.

The commando walked nonchalantly across to the flap, stepping aside as Jorge da Gruta emerged with his arm in a sling. He sat down beside Branagh. 'You should see it inside there! Bloody American satellite communications equipment. No wonder the *bandidos* have tied Frelimo's lot in knots. They're still communicating by jungle drum.' He shook his head in disbelief. 'Anyway, I gather not *everything* is going their way. Apparently the Frelimo garrison at Lichinga is proving a tough nut to crack.'

'Where's Lichinga?' Kathleen asked.

'The provincial capital to the north of here,' Branagh explained.

Da Gruta added: 'It seems essential to their plan that Lichinga falls quickly, especially now, because 7 Brigade in Cuamba has sent a column of armoured cars to reinforce them.'

Branagh was surprised. 'Cuamba is still in government hands?'

'So it seems. Putting up one hell of a fight, I gather. They're doing well enough to be able to send the armoured column to Lichinga. Our friends are having to fly up some heavy antitank weapons to stop them.'

'Any news of Gutala?'

Da Gruta shrugged. 'I am afraid not. That bastard son of mine kicks me out in case I hear any more. He has betrayed me, Branagh. He and Veronique have betrayed everything I've worked for. Betrayed this country that once they called their own.'

The Irishman shared his friend's sense of outrage, but there were no words of comfort he could offer. Instead he asked: 'How is the arm?'

'Do you send a sick animal to a vet or a butcher? I will survive.'

Just before dark, large numbers of bandits left the encampment, the long column stretching away in the direction of Cuamba.

The South African commandos seemed more relaxed, and confident enough to light a fire. Strips of impala meat were laid out on a makeshift grill of chicken wire.

'Fancy a *braai*?' Boyd asked. 'The wife and I have one every Sunday back in Durban during summer. This takes me back.'

Kathleen shuffled closer on her knees until she could feel the warmth of the crackling brushwood. 'God, that smells delicious. I'm starving.'

'Pity I don't have my favourite – cheese-flavoured sausages – still it's better than the mealie Napoleão's mob lives on.'

Kathleen glanced towards Branagh and laughed. 'I'm not sure Mike would agree.'

Boyd looked at the Irishman. 'Gone native, eh? A lot do.'

Branagh said: 'Why all the jollity; has Lichinga fallen?'

The South African looked reproachful. 'It's dangerous to eavesdrop, friend.'

'Jorge overheard, that's all. Sure we can't do anything about it; we're just interested. We understood a relief column had set out from Cuamba.'

320

'It didn't get far,' Boyd replied flatly. 'Renamo stopped it about five miles out. We'll have some antitank stuff there by tomorrow and then we'll take the lot out.'

'You seem confident,' Branagh pressed.

'The boss is happy, that's what counts. And the sooner this is over the sooner I can get back home.'

He stopped then and looked up from his cooking as Napoleão and his reed-thin second-in-command João Chande stepped into the dancing firelight.

'Senhor Dracht wanted me,' Napoleão announced.

Boyd didn't bother to hide his contempt for the huge African. 'Wait there. I'll fetch him.'

As Boyd went to the tent, Napoleão turned to the group seated around the fire. He sniffed at the aroma of barbecued meat. 'I see the whites look after their own as usual. Personally, I should like to see you all hung up and quartered like that impala.' His gaze hovered on Kathleen. 'Except perhaps the woman.'

'Colonel!' Chande hissed in warning as Dracht came out of the tent.

The South African didn't bother with niceties as he addressed Napoleão. 'An aircraft is coming into the strip in twenty minutes. It's got the antitank weapons on board and we will be going on with it, flying to another strip up north.'

'To stop the column?' Napoleão asked.

Dracht almost smiled. 'Long before it reaches Lichinga. We can't leave it to your bunch of wankers, can we – Mr President?'

Branagh couldn't believe his ears.

The Renamo commander rounded angrily on the South African. 'And you will not talk to me this way when that time comes!'

'Cool it, Jumbo,' Dracht retorted evenly. 'Just get your men to light the beacons in fifteen minutes. And try to get it right.'

Christ, Branagh thought savagely, it's bloody-well

true. The bastards were going to make Napoleão the head of the new state in northern Mozambique. A puppet leader who would do anything for a bag of gold and the trappings of power.

Jorge de Gruta had heard it too. 'Some promised land my son has in mind,' he muttered beneath his breath.

It was a quarter of an hour later when they all heard the distant hum of the aero engines coming in. Almost simultaneously the intermittent lines of beacons began spluttering into life along the edges of the strip. Soon they were all ablaze, crackling fitfully in the velvet night. The aircraft noise began to swell as it fixed course for the run-in, an inky batlike shadow against the night sky. It grew in size by the second, the noise fast rising to drown out the sounds of the bushveld.

And then the all-black DC3 was down, bouncing over the rough ground, its brakes squealing as the momentum slowed. Then it taxied off the strip towards the tent. The engines died abruptly and the nocturnal noises of the bush rushed in to fill the sudden silence.

The pilot who climbed down was wearing khaki fatigues. He wiped his hands down the front of them as he walked forward.

'Which one's Captain Dracht?' he addressed the commandos.

'I am. We're all ready.'

The pilot gave a thin smile. 'To go where?'

'North as arranged,' Dracht snapped.

'Not in this aircraft you won't,' the man replied easily and sniffed the air. 'A *braai*? Smells wonderful. Any spare?'

'For fuck's sake,' Dracht cursed, grabbing the man's lapels, 'what are you talking about?'

Napoleão stepped forward, expecting to see a fight.

The pilot smiled sweetly and plucked away Dracht's fingers. 'I mean that I'm on one engine and one magneto. We nearly hit a peak on the way in.'

'Is this a joke?' Dracht demanded.

'Are sanctions a joke? Don't blame me if we have to fly granny's bedsteads.'

'I don't believe this,' Dracht said. 'How long to get it repaired?'

'It's not a question of repairs. Each engine has two magnetos. A primary and a backup. No one's bothered to check the backups. They're both duds. Now I've lost a primary. Get it? I'm not taking off against mountains on one engine and no backup. The aircraft will have to be destroyed. The chiefs won't want any evidence of our involvement.'

Armando stepped forward, 'Say, Nico, there is still an aircraft at Tumbo village – the one the Russian flies.'

Dracht turned to Napoleão. 'Did your apes destroy it in the attack?'

The Renamo commander looked sheepish. 'It got broken, yes.'

'I'm no flight mechanic,' the pilot said.

Armando da Gruta pointed at Petkus. 'But he is. And the Irishman is an engineer. My father's told me how they fix anything between them. Cars and trucks, generators. Them and the Indian in Gutala.'

'Aircraft are different,' Branagh began.

'Don't bullshit me,' Dracht retorted. 'If I say you repair it, that's what you do. Unless you'd like to see a bullet between your girlfriend's eyes.'

Kathleen flinched at his words.

'And the Russian can fly it,' Armando added in triumph.

The pilot said: 'He'll have to. I've strict orders not to get involved in what you're up to. I've a safe-route out to Malawi.'

'Then get the fuck walking,' Dracht snarled.

'It won't work,' Branagh protested.

Vincent Mulholland grabbed his arm. 'Think on, old stick. Play your cards right and you can get us all out of this place.'

323

Branagh turned to face him. 'And help their plan? Get stuffed, Vincent!'

'Think of Kathleen,' Mulholland insisted. He looked at Dracht. 'Listen, if we helped you, would you let us fly out of here? Say, to Harare?'

The South African appeared suddenly calmer. 'I might consider it.' He walked across to Petkus. 'You, Russian, what aircraft is it you have?'

'It's a Twin Otter.'

Dracht considered. 'And it will take, say, ten people, each carrying a rocket launcher?'

The Russian nodded slowly. It was pointless to deny it. The machine had been purchased specifically to carry cargo and to land on short unprepared strips.

Dracht said to Mulholland: 'Then that's what we'll do. A night's march to the airstrip at Tumbo, and you'll all have to carry your share of our equipment. We'll be able to take much less than I intended, but it'll have to do.'

'And if we refuse?' Branagh asked.

The South African regarded him coldly, then with slow deliberation unholstered the Spanish-made 9mm Star automatic strapped to his hip. Cocked it and put the snub muzzle to Kathleen's temple. The girl froze, closed her eyes and swallowed. 'I told you, Irishman. Don't even think about refusing to co-operate.'

Branagh raised his palms defensively. 'Okay, I believe you. There's no need for the dramatics.'

Nico Dracht lowered the gun. 'Right, we've no time to lose. First we'll unload the equipment and tell our special guest of the change of plan. Armando, please.'

'What special guest is this?' Napoleão demanded as the Portuguese commando strode towards the aircraft. 'I have been told nothing.'

Dracht suddenly smiled with genuine amusement. 'No, I do believe we may have forgotten to mention it to you.'

At the aircraft, Armando da Gruta helped the passenger down. He was a tall, well-built and handsome

Mozambican, dressed in smart chino trousers and bush shirt. It took Kathleen several seconds to place where she had seen the friendly, intelligent eyes before. The man at the Sheik disco in Maputo who said that he was too old to dance. The same man who had assisted her from the hotel pool. The friend of the late Brigadier Santos. The man who had told her he could not trace her cousin Seamus.

'Ngoça,' she gasped.

Branagh frowned. 'The deputy minister?'

'I met him in Maputo.'

Napoleão turned to Dracht. 'What is the meaning of this?'

'Meet the real president of the new state,' Dracht sneered.

They had walked all night and through the drumming heat of the day. Many had fallen by the wayside. Their loads were redistributed to others by the bandits, and their bodies left for hyenas and vultures to fight over.

Maraika walked on, upright, her eyes fixed straight ahead at some point in the middle distance. She did not allow her gaze to stray to the sick and frail who lay beside the game trail. Yet she couldn't help but cringe at the occasional report of a gun as the fallen were finally despatched by a bullet through the head.

Mikey had told her once that with determination, the human body could endure any suffering, any pain. The mind could take care of such things, survive on another mental level. And that the brain could blot out the worst horrors from the memory.

But Mikey was wrong. Wrong, wrong, wrong.

Her mind had wandered. She had allowed herself a fatal lapse in concentration. She no longer walked on a carpet of duck down. Her bare feet were torn and bleeding and the muscles in her thighs were begging her to rest. There was no longer a cool breeze but the throbbing furnace of the mid-afternoon sun. The imagined child she carried, a joyous burden. Hers and Mikey's. There was no child. It was the deadweight of a sack of fishmeal.

No, Mikey, you *were* right. I am such a fool. Why don't I believe you? You are always right.

And then she looked to the wayside. Just a dozen paces farther along the track. Her mother, Marta Matusi sat in the long grass, legs crossed, her head buried in her hands as she wept. At her side Pascoal knelt, a comforting arm around the old woman's shoulders.

Maraika glanced up and down the remorselessly grinding column of porters. There were no guards immediately in sight.

She broke from the line, dropping down on her knees beside her parents, the sack of fishmeal cast aside.

'*Mamãe*, what is wrong?'

The black walnut face lifted from the hands to behold her daughter. There was despair in the tear-filled eyes, her mouth contorted with anguish as she tried to speak. She could not find the words and contented herself by clutching her daughter's wrists. A lifeline, a forlorn last hope.

'She cannot go on,' Pascoal said. Below his tufty white head of hair, the anthracite features shared his wife's grief. 'Your mother is old and her legs are bad. She is afraid she'll be left behind. She does not want to die.'

Marta found her voice. 'My daughter, it is good to see you.'

'We did not know if you were alive or dead,' Pascoal added. 'The Lord is merciful.'

'Can you help us?' Marta begged.

A shadow fell across them. The Renamo officer was tall and in his thirties. He had a pronounced scar on his left cheek. 'What is going on here?' he demanded.

Maraika climbed wearily to her feet. 'My mother is sick. She cannot walk.'

The officer appeared not to hear. 'We cannot wait. Our men are advancing rapidly. They will need their food and ammunition.'

326

'Please don't kill her,' Maraika pleaded. 'She is a good woman.'

He looked into the girl's beseeching eyes for a moment then turned to the pathetic couple. 'What does the old woman carry?'

Pascoal pointed to the discarded sack of rice. 'That is what she carries, sir.'

'Can she walk if she does not carry?'

'If I cut her a stick,' Pascoal answered. 'But I have no knife.'

The officer stepped forward, the blade of the panga rasping as he drew it from its scabbard.

Maraika's eyes widened with horror.

The steel glittered in the sun as it fell, slicing through the straight young branch of the trailside knobthorn. He held out the stick to Pascoal. 'This will do.' As the old man accepted it thankfully with both hands, the Renamo officer placed a shiny boot on the rice sack. It rolled over and disappeared into the grass. 'Our men will not miss one sack of rice. Now – get moving!'

'Thank you, sir,' Pascoal cried.

The officer turned to Maraika. 'Your parents are lucky to have such a beautiful daughter. But don't be stupid enough to tell another guard that you are related. You know what can happen.'

She bowed her head. 'Yes, sir.'

Then she felt his hands in her hair, a tentative touch. 'There is water at the next camp. You must wash out this dirt when we stop.' His fingers withdrew and he straightened his back. 'Now, get marching!'

Obediently, she lifted the sack of fishmeal onto her head and rejoined the passing procession. She turned her head to see Pascoal help Marta uncertainly to her feet. The officer had gone.

'What happened?' asked a voice.

Maraika turned. For a moment she did not recognise the tall, elegant woman walking by her side. Even though the serene expression on her face and the finely arched eyebrows were familiar, she found it difficult to place her without the starched white nun's wimple and habit. Now she wore a turban and *capulana* like all the other women.

'Sister Graca!'

'Sssh,' the nun warned. 'Do not call me Sister. If they find out I am a nurse, they will kill me. Luckily, I have seen no one here who will recognise me. You are the first. When they attacked Gutala, I was able to run away and steal these clothes.'

'But you were caught.'

Graca smiled pensively. 'No more than I deserved. Perhaps it was punishment for running. For denying my faith.'

'No,' Maraika protested.

'Perhaps not, but I feel that I have betrayed His trust.'

'God would not want you to die. You have done so much for the children of Gutala.'

The woman blushed; her skin was lighter than Maraika's and it showed distinctly. 'What happened back there? Was that your mother?'

Maraika recounted the incident.

'There is some goodness in all men,' Graca said. 'Even amongst the ranks of Satan's sinners. We must remember that. I will pray for your parents and for that officer.'

'*Mamãe* needs more than prayers. She is weary and her feet are badly cut. As ours are, but she is old.'

'I will help her. I am told I will work in the camp kitchen tonight. I will bring her proper food.'

'God bless you – dear Graca.'

It was then that they heard the strange noise. A high-pitched roaring whine that echoed across the bushveld. With every passing second it became louder and harsher, causing heads to turn.

And then it had flashed by them in a deafening crescendo. A huge black motorcycle that belched clouds of exhaust into the wake of dust it created. A boy bandit sat astride it as though he were taming a wild bull, throttling up on its horns, a Kalashnikov rifle strapped across his back.

'Beware of that one,' said the porter behind Maraika. His words were hushed with fear. 'He is from one of the *Grupos Limpa*. To see him at work is to see the very devil himself.'

Maraika walked on in silence. Meeting Sister Graca had revived her, given her new strength. And by then the sun had lost its hammerlike heat, waning until the endless bush was drenched in a mellow amber glow.

They reached the transit camp at twilight. It was just an area of flattened grass between a group of ironwood trees where the bandits laid out their bedrolls. A stream ran nearby and the porters were allowed to drink. But the water was a mere trickle and contaminated with insect larvae.

Maraika remembered the Renamo officer's words and sat where she could watch her parents from a distance. Her father held the old woman in his arms as they both slept, propped against an ironwood trunk. For years she had not see them so caring. So close to each other in their hour of need.

A big fire had been lit in the cooking area around which the bandits gathered. Smells drifted, mouth-watering on the night air.

'We will not be fed tonight,' a male voice said.

Maraika turned her head. The man sitting beside her was hidden in shadow. 'Francisco?'

The carpenter's white teeth glistened in the darkness.

'I think that you ignore me, Maraika.'

She averted her head quickly. From the corner of her mouth, she said: 'It is best. If they know you have relatives or friends, they can use it against you. Look away, Francisco, please. I am sorry.'

'And that is why you watch your parents from this place?'

'It is safer. For me and for them.'

'What are these people doing to us, Maraika?' he murmured.

After a moment's silence, she said: 'You say there is no food.'

'A guard told me. The food we carry is for the *bandidos* at the front of the battle. If they feed us, there will be nothing left for them when we get there.' He looked towards the fire. 'Only the *bandidos* will eat tonight.'

'I am so hungry.'

'Here.'

She looked aghast at the fat white beetle grubs, wriggling in his open palm.

'Go on,' he urged, 'they will not hurt you. I survived many years in the bush. Go on, eat.'

With a shiver of revulsion, she picked one with her thumb and forefinger and carried it gingerly to her mouth. Then quickly in. A hurried gulp and another shiver as she felt it slide down her throat. She gagged involuntarily, felt the bile rise.

Francisco laughed. 'You will get used to it. Maybe you like this better. Baobab seeds that I pick on the march. You must learn these things if you are to survive.'

But, she decided, eating and survival would have to take second place to her body's more pressing demand for rest. She declined the carpenter's offer of more food and lay back on the crushed grass. Instantly she was asleep.

In her dream she was in the plantation house. A vast banqueting hall like Branagh had told her existed in old Irish country mansions. A wooden table of glittering silver cutlery, dazzling candles and overhead chandeliers of cut glass. She and Mikey and Fred were there with Veronique and Jorge da Gruta. She was so happy as they all laughed together and drank wine. Then Senhora da Gruta announced the main course and lifted the silver tureen lid. A writhing mound of maggots. Everyone laughed, everyone except her.

'She has stolen food from the camp kitchen.'

330

The words permeated her sleep, prising her away from her dream. Suddenly she was wide awake, her head pounding and her body in a sweat.

'What's happening?'

Francisco said: 'There is trouble.'

'What?'

Her eyes adjusted to the bright beam of the motorcycle headlamp. The machine had been propped on its stand so that the circle of light shone directly at the woman who cowered on the ground. For a moment she thought it was her mother, then realised it was the wrong place. The sense of relief was replaced by a dread realisation.

'It's Sister Graca.'

Francisco was astounded. 'The holy sister? They are accusing her of stealing food.'

'To take to my mother,' Maraika remembered. 'What will happen?'

But she did not have to wait for the answer. The boy bandit was in his teens, she guessed, but it was difficult to tell because it was so dark. He stood over Sister Graca and swung the assault rifle from his shoulder.

'You steal our food, woman! Why do you do this?' he demanded. 'You steal from the *bandidos* who give their lives to free your country.'

The solid wooden butt of the rifle thudded into the prone body. There was no scream or cry, just a painful dignified silence.

Francisco sprang to his feet. 'Get away, Maraika,' he ordered. 'Do not be involved in this.'

On all fours, she scurried into the shadows, turned and peered back through the fern leaves to see Francisco striding towards the young bandit.

'Please, please, sir!' the carpenter called. 'Spare the woman. She is Sister Graca, a nun of Gutala.'

The boy froze in mid-action, rifle poised above the stricken woman. At his feet, Graca fingered the blood that ran from the gash on her forehead.

'Seize him!' snarled the boy. He hardly needed to raise his voice in order to bring his comrades running. They were young like him, and it took several of them to overcome the strength of the carpenter.

'You say this woman is a holy sister?' the boy asked darkly.

'A holy sister.' He did not mention nurse. 'A good woman who serves the Church. A woman of God.'

There was a fire in the young boy's eyes. 'Did you say God?' He almost spat the word, as if it had a bitter taste. 'She does not look like a woman of God. What nun wears such clothes?'

'But she is,' Francisco protested.

The boy spoke very quietly: 'A woman who steals food is not very holy.'

Another young bandit stepped forward. He picked up something from the ground beside the woman. He held it up. 'It is true,' he said. It was a small wooden crucifix.

Something seemed to trigger in the boy motorcyclist's mind; he trembled as though attempting to control some inner rage. Francisco could sense it and it filled him with sudden fear.

Yet when the boy spoke, his voice was restrained and calm, almost a whisper. 'Then she must be punished as an example to others. A nun must lead by example.' He turned to the carpenter. 'You can have the privilege of killing her.'

Francisco's eyes widened. His mouth dropped open but no words came out.

'Give him a rifle,' ordered the boy. Another youthful bandit stepped obligingly forward.

The carpenter took a backward step. 'No!'

'Take it,' the boy snapped, 'or I will kill you and—' He swung his finger to point to the nearest group of seated, horrified men and women – 'these people here.'

Even before the words left his mouth, the other bandits stepped forward, raising their weapons in unison and taking aim.

'Do it,' said the boy.

Francisco took the gun. 'I cannot.'

'Do it,' the boy repeated.

The carpenter slowly raised the weapon, then lowered it again.

Turning to the other bandits, the boy said brusquely: 'Shoot them.'

'No!' Graca called. In the tense silence that followed all eyes turned to the nun lying in the grass. She looked only at Francisco. In a small voice, she said: 'Dear Francisco, I forgive you for what you have to do.'

Francisco swallowed hard. His heart was pounding and his sweating palms made the rifle slippery in his hands. He was shaking as he lifted the butt to his shoulder. Two single tears escaped his eyes and rolled slowly down his cheeks. His eyes stung; his vision was a blur. He squeezed them shut, tight. Opened them again. Clear. A deep breath, steady. She must not suffer. Two rapid shots as Branagh had once taught. To be certain.

A double whipcrack shattered the motionless silence. Sister Graca fell back on the grass. Her body twitched once, twice. Then lay still.

The carpenter dropped the gun and fell by the dead woman's feet, hunched in prayer, his body wracked with sobs.

Abruptly the boy bandit turned, crossing the headlamp beam, and mounted the black motorcycle.

Maraika stared open-mouthed from the ferns. She had seen his face in the light.

The roar of the motorcycle filled the air as the boy rode away with the arrogant air of a conqueror. In total disbelief she whispered one word.

'Benjamin.'

12

Once he had made his decision Nico Dracht acted swiftly.

Napoleão was confined to his tent under guard and stripped to his underpants to deter any escape attempt. But he was so stunned at having been used and manipulated that he put up only token resistance, he appeared to have no will to cause trouble.

His second-in-command João Chande did not hesitate to accept Dracht's offer to him to take over control of the bandits. Perhaps he was just sick of Napoleão greedily taking the glory for the work he had done. Or perhaps it was just the bill rolls of rand that Dracht handed him.

The South African insisted that Jorge da Gruta stay at the camp as insurance. Apart from which he was in no fit state to carry anything on the march back to Tumbo, no doubt Dracht regarded him as a liability. Nevertheless Jorge seemed happy with the decision after his son's reassurance he would be safe in Chande's hands provided the others continued to co-operate.

Ten Soviet-made RPG-7 antitank rocket launchers were unloaded from the aircraft, each member of Dracht's team shouldering two of them. The small Shona soldier had the additional burden of a radio set.

The HEAT grenade rounds, each weighing five pounds, were carefully stowed in rucksacks. Branagh, Petkus and Mulholland were each given a load; even Deputy Minister Ngoça was not exempt. To his credit he did not complain at carrying his share. Kathleen was handed a lighter load of provisions, enough to keep them alive for several days. Everybody was given a webbing belt with two canteens of water and a stern warning to use it sparingly. It was not known when they would next be able to refill them.

At ten they set out under a waning moon, crossing the encampment to pick up a game trail that would eventually lead them to Tumbo. Leaving the shelter of the trees, they passed a forlorn column of porters coming in. In the poor light Branagh did not see the hand waving frantically, nor did he hear Maraika's distant call above the sound of his own boots crunching on the stony ground.

It was a gruelling eight hours. They trudged remorselessly, negotiating the contours of the foothills, stumbling over the uneven rocky terrain. Blisters that had been pricked, drained of fluid and bandaged now just burned dully as though their feet were walking on red hot embers. Following the previous night's march, stiffened leg muscles began to flex with less complaint, but the heavy loads of grenades brought new discomfort.

For Branagh it was easier to accept. Past training, his own physical fitness and his mental attitude allowed him to adjust to the punishing progress. But Mulholland and Ngoça were clearly struggling as the rucksack straps bit deep into their shoulders. If Petkus was suffering he showed no outward sign; his huge bulk powered on with never a pause.

Dracht permitted a standard five-minute respite in every hour's travel. It enabled them to regain strength and stretch straining muscles, but did nothing to ease the pain when the loads were taken up again. If anything the weight seemed even heavier.

Branagh did not know the hills. During all his time in Gutala district it had never been safe to wander, even with military protection. He tried to assess their general position by estimating their speed and direction of progress, but he got it wrong. It came as quite a surprise, although not an unpleasant one, when they heard the distant sound of rushing water. The river could mean only one thing; they had reached Tumbo village.

It was a strange sensation, wading through the swirling green flow in the first steely light of day. Climbing out through the familiar reeds of the embankment and hearing again the rustling of the weeping bean trees. Approaching the village that for so long had been his home. But approaching this time with real apprehension. Three of Dracht's men had fanned out ahead, not sure whether the place was occupied or not. And if so, by whom.

Despite the recognisable features, it was a different place to Branagh now: many of the huts were charred ruins, others had simply been vandalised, and there was no sign of human, or even animal, presence. It sounded different. Just an eerie silence. It even smelled different. Alien, hostile.

'Wait,' Dracht ordered, and they welcomed the opportunity to stop while the Rhodesian Drummond, his Shona sidekick Chipoko and Anton Boyd scouted ahead.

After fifteen minutes Boyd reappeared farther up the track and gave the thumbs-up. Dracht motioned everybody forward.

As they drew level, Boyd said: 'There's no Renamo here. Just the odd family of villagers who've crept back in from the bush. They'll be no trouble.'

'We'll find somewhere to hole up,' Dracht announced, 'while the aircraft is being fixed. Any ideas, Branagh?'

'Use my place. If it's still standing.'

In fact it was exactly as he had last seen it.

'How can they do this?' Kathleen asked, standing amid the wreckage of the furniture that Francisco had so lovingly made. 'Such wanton destruction.'

Branagh looked at the wall; Leif Månson's blood had dried into a brown stain on the limewash. 'Let's get it cleared up.'

Dracht's men brewed coffee and opened ration packs

while Kathleen and Petkus helped Branagh throw the debris out into the compound that Maraika had always kept so spotless. Then they all sat together around the room to eat and drink in an awkward silence.

'You and the Russian get some sleep in, Branagh,' Dracht said. 'It's seven-thirty now. At ten we'll go up and inspect the aircraft.'

Branagh's head had hardly seemed to touch the rucksack which served as his pillow before he was being shaken awake. It was time to go. Dracht and Armando da Gruta led the way along the track, up through the deserted cropfields to the grass plateau and the airstrip.

The crippled Twin Otter lay as he had last seen it: undercarriage sabotaged and scorch marks on the bottom of the fuselage.

'We'll need the welding gear for the bodywork, and replacement bolts,' Petkus decided. He strode across to the wooden store-shed where the door half hung off its hinges. Inside the neat row of nail pegs that usually held the tools was empty. The lot had been taken. He grunted, then began rummaging beneath some old tyres and a dirty tarpaulin until he located a rotting timber chest. The ancient, rusted set of tools had accumulated over several decades.

'Some of these date back to the last century,' Branagh observed.

Dracht said flatly: 'Then they'll have to do.'

The looting bandits had no use for welding equipment, assuming that they even knew what it was. Petkus found it thrown aside with a half-empty gas cylinder. A miscellany of self-tapping metal screws and assorted bolts had to be retrieved on hands and knees from amid the rubbish on the floor. The mobile hoist was discovered in the small scrapyard of discarded aircraft parts behind the shed and wheeled across to the Otter. Once harnessed with old ropes to a padded support spar, the wing on the ground was hand-cranked back up to its correct height. Then the two men got to work under the watchful eyes of Dracht and da Gruta.

They tackled the buckled wheel first, cutting down and filing rusted bolts to fit. Then the damaged control and body surfaces were repaired using a mix of welding and improvised reinforcement with strips of tin and self-tapping screws.

'Will it hold?' Dracht asked.

Branagh shrugged. 'God knows, but it's the best we can do with what's available.'

The South African commando looked up at the sky. 'We'll get everyone up here before nightfall and take off at first light tomorrow.'

As the strength seeped from the wavering sun, they began the long walk back to Tumbo. On the way they saw only one other human. Probably a farmer, the Mozambican stood amid a crop of mealie that had been crushed by the bandits during their rampage. When he saw the approaching four he immediately took flight towards the nearest stand of eucalyptus.

The only sound in the village came from the Direct Action compound. Moses Chipoko was crouched by the gate, his AK47 cradled in his lap. Inside, the incongruous air of normality jarred Branagh's senses. Where Maraika and Lisa might usually have been in the kitchen lean-to, Anton Boyd was boiling up a pot of vegetables. Petkus's favourite chair in the shade of an overhanging bean bush was occupied by the Rhodesian Drummond. Mulholland and Ngoça dozed in the sunshine beside him.

Branagh was suddenly overwhelmed with anger by this occupation of his home. He almost expected Maraika to come to the door of the hut as she heard his approach. She didn't, of course, but Kathleen did, looking clean and fresh as she towelled her hair dry.

'How did it go, Mike?' She appeared relieved to see him.

'So-so, but it wouldn't get a certificate of air-worthiness.'

'We'll eat now,' Dracht announced, 'then carry everything up to the strip.'

Little was said over the meal. It was the first decent food any of them had eaten in days and it was devoured with unseemly relish. Each had fears and concerns to consider, but in the presence of the commando team no one cared to share them. Only Armando da Gruta had anything to say, directing his comments mostly to Kathleen who did her best to ignore him.

'Maybe your *mamãe* never tells you it is rude not to answer a question,' he complained at last.

'She told me it is rude to talk with your mouth full, so it is.'

Armando grinned at her; he liked a woman with spirit.

With the meal complete the launchers and grenades were once again distributed and the journey back to the strip began. As twilight fell the distant clamour of small-arms fire echoed from the direction of Gutala. As they gained high ground the bright light of fires could be seen far away against the dimming landscape.

'There is still fighting going on,' Petkus said to Branagh. 'I hope our friend D'Arcy and his troops will hold out.'

Dracht overheard. 'That Englishman from the tobacco station? He is wasting his time. Gutala will fall, along with Cuamba and Lichinga. It's going to be different this time.'

'You mean Renamo won't murder and rape?' Branagh asked sarcastically.

The South African chuckled drily. 'Your sort make me laugh. Bloody do-gooders. Should be thankful we're doing this country a favour, kicking out those Frelimo bastards once and for all. Incompetent monkeys.'

'Forgive me if I don't see a bunch of Renamo thugs as the salvation of Mozambique,' Branagh replied evenly.

For the first time, Deputy Minister Ngoça spoke. Treated with indifference by Dracht's team and with hostility by Branagh and the others, he had kept very much to himself.

'It will be different when we take power. All this violence will stop.'

Branagh viewed him with contempt. 'Oh yes? You saw Tumbo. You haven't got off to a good start, have you? They murdered my boss, Månson and raped and murdered a pregnant woman in my house. And for good measure, my woman—' he corrected himself '—my *wife*-to-be has been abducted. So what's new?'

Ngoça was sweating heavily under his load. 'I am sorry about that, Senhor Branagh, truly sorry. As soon as we have control I shall see that your fiancée is returned safely to you.'

'It may be too late for that.' Acidly.

The Mozambican's eyes were clouded with concern. But whether it was concern over Maraika's fate or concern that his motives might be misunderstood, Branagh was uncertain. 'You must realise that the situation cannot be changed overnight. The *bandidos* do not even know yet that they are fighting for liberation this time. Only a few commanders like Napoleão know the true purpose of this particular campaign. Even Renamo's high command do not appreciate that we have hijacked their foot soldiers.'

'You mean their murdering terrorists,' Branagh needled.

'I tell you it *will* stop.' Ngoça was emphatic. 'But I cannot stop their methods until I have control. Not while they are fighting in the bush. When they discover what has happened, they will realise that they have won. There will be no more fighting in this land.'

'And you really believe that?' Branagh asked.

'Every Mozambican wants peace.'

Branagh was incredulous, but realised he shouldn't be. Politicians greedy for power always thought they knew

340

best. He said: 'And you believe that these terrorist war-lords will meekly return to the cropfields and agree with everything you tell them. Surrender their own power to work for South African and Portuguese bosses.'

'Some may even become politicians themselves,' Ngoça said earnestly.

'Killing and looting are not very good credentials for a politician,' Branagh retorted. 'And what about southern Mozambique? Don't you think the government might have something to say about your seizing half their country? I understood you were always greatly respected in Maputo, Senhor Ngoça. Now I think they might just consider you to be a traitor.'

Ngoça's eyes were filled with anger. 'Respect without the power to change things is useless.'

So that was it. Always a mere deputy minister and never his hands on the reins. Brooding resentment and unfulfilled ambition had finally led him into the clutches of Willem van der Walt.

Dracht laughed aloud. 'You're wasting your time talking to his sort, Ngoça. He'll change his tune once we've taken this province.'

'But Gutala isn't proving so easy is it?' Branagh provoked.

It must have touched a raw nerve because Dracht sneered. 'What are you, some military expert? Shut the rap and keep walking.'

Petkus grinned at the Irishman and winked; they continued in silence, each wondering how D'Arcy was surviving in the beleaguered township.

The next morning Branagh awoke shivering in the early dawn light, The simple blankets brought from Napoleão's camp were inadequate against the cold air on the plateau. Only Dracht's team with their lightweight down sleeping bags had a comfortable night.

'Tea?' Anton Boyd offered. Branagh took the steaming tin mug gratefully.

'Bloody freezing,' Mulholland moaned, cupping his mug with both hands for warmth. 'I'm too old for this sort of caper.'

They had slept in the lee of the store-shed. From where they sat they could see the Twin Otter's ghostly outline amid the coils of rising mist. Dracht and Armando da Gruta were loading aboard the launchers and rucksacks of grenades.

Petkus yawned loudly and stretched his arms, 'It is so long since I fly, I hope I do not forget.'

'So do I,' Kathleen agreed with feeling. She was sitting huddled in her blanket like an Indian squaw.

Boyd gave a wry smile. 'I never thought I'd live to see the day I'd be flown by a Russian pilot.'

'German,' Petkus corrected darkly. 'And you may not live to see that day, Afrikaner. Not if your boss insists on flying a full load. This could be the last day any of us see.'

The sandy-haired Drummond overheard. 'Don't waste your time, Ivan. That plane's designed to carry twice this load. And when the boss makes up his mind, it stays made.'

'You *want* to die?' Petkus said.

'You won't put the wind up us,' the Rhodesian sneered. 'You pilots are a breed of whingeing willies, all of you. I've seen crates like that fly for years in the bush. Held together with string and sticking plaster, some of them. You'll get us there all right if your own life depends on it.'

Dracht and da Gruta returned, the South African going straight to the portable MEL PRC 319 burst-transmission radio. Using separate frequencies for transmit and receive, it provided secure communications with his masters in South Africa via the Silvermine listening station on the Cape. He spent ten minutes exchanging signals, punching messages into the electronic message unit for automatic encrypting and squeeze transmission.

At last he appeared satisfied. 'The airstrip is confirmed in our control,' he announced.

'And where is this place exactly?' Petkus asked impatiently. 'It might not be suitable for my airplane.'

'It's suitable. Midway between Cuamba and Lichinga, near the village of Torrola.'

'I know of no airfield there.'

'You wouldn't,' Dracht said. 'It was built by South African special forces for clandestine supplies.'

Petkus shook his head. 'The airplane will not take a rough landing.'

'I am not a fool,' Dracht snapped. 'It's grass, but it's as smooth as a baby's bum. It has been checked out overnight and the grass has been scythed. So stop fretting and let's get this crate fuelled up.'

By the time the Twin Otter's tanks had been filled from the underground avgas tank and Petkus was satisfied with his instrument checks, the sun had cleared the horizon, shedding welcome warmth and dispersing the night mist. Once the load of weaponry had been lashed down and the passengers settled into their seats, Dracht took his place beside Petkus. The Russian primed the engines in turn. One of them coughed, spluttered and cleared again.

'What's that?' Dracht asked.

'Maybe dirt in the fuel lines. It's clear now.'

'Then let's get on.'

Engine sound filled the cockpit as the flaps were checked and set to takeoff position. The aircraft bumped its way across to the short grass of the strip, where Petkus turned the white nose into the eddying breeze and halted, cranking up the power.

'Rpm is still unstable on Number Two,' he intoned, his eyes scanning the instrument panel, 'but they are inside the safety limit. Really, I should check it.'

'What would that involve?' Dracht demanded.

'Stripping the engine,' Petkus returned, 'blowing the fuel lines.'

'Forget it,' the South African decided.

Petkus shrugged and eased on the power levers, holding against the brakes. Gradually the pressure built until the aircraft shell began to tremble under the strain, anxious to be set free. The perspex rattled irritably in one of the ports. The engine whine reached an ear-piercing crescendo until everything started to shake, then the Russian released the brakes. The Otter surged forward eagerly like an unleashed hound. Bouncing and jolting, it gained momentum with every passing second. Buffalo grass flashed by the window in a blur of burnished orange. In the back, Branagh found himself willing the machine forward, sensing the effort of the spinning props as they dug for power, struggling to defy gravity.

'We're not going to make it,' Kathleen whispered anxiously.

The end of the strip rushed to meet them. Beyond the plateau, eucalyptus tops waved threateningly. Branagh heard the girl's sharp intake of breath as Petkus eased back the column. The wheels lifted and the bumping stopped. Inches from the ground, the Otter swept off the plateau edge, skimming the treetops below.

Petkus exhaled in a low whistle and rubbed a hand over his sweating brow. He turned to Dracht. 'Next time, crazy man, you fly it yourself.'

They climbed slowly up over the foothill peaks, banking gradually and circling round to establish a northward course. Through the perspex film of the port, the reed shanties of Tumbo stood like a child's model village. Nothing moved. The aircraft levelled out over the banana groves, an undulating sea of glossy green leaves that stretched towards the horizon. Petkus followed the line of the red dust road that meandered towards Gutala.

'Don't get too low,' Dracht warned. Petkus ignored him.

Branagh shared the Russian's desire to see what was

344

happening in the town. Anxiously he leaned forward for a better view as the outlying huts of the suburbs appeared. A large contingent of men stood in the road ahead. Renamo on the way to Gutala, waiting to join the onslaught.

Petkus eased the controls forward, pushed up the throttle; the nose began to dip.

'What the fuck are you doing?' Dracht demanded.

The aircraft plunged into its dive like a mad thing, engines screaming and the fuselage vibrating. Petkus lined up the road, gently flattening out his descent, settling into a level course just feet above the pockmarked red earth. Ahead startled bandits turned and stared. Transfixed. Like rabbits in a car's headlights. Faces open-mouthed with horror. They seemed to fill the windshield, suddenly scattering right and left as the Otter rocketed through their midst.

'YEAH!' Petkus roared gleefully, sweeping skyward. 'I enjoy that!'

Dracht gulped, his face drained of blood. 'Christ, you Russian bastard, don't *ever* pull a stunt like that again.'

Petkus eyed him squarely. 'So what you going to do, my Boer friend? Shoot me?'

As they flew low over the centre of the town, there was little to indicate how the siege was going. At least most of the observation posts appeared to be manned and all four roads to the central square had been barricaded. Fires raged in various isolated places and men were glimpsed dashing across streets for cover. It was impossible to tell whether the bandits or D'Arcy's men had the upper hand.

Shanties again gave way to swathes of banana groves, the plantation house glimpsed momentarily amongst its surrounding umbrella pines off the port wing. Eventually they passed the perimeter road and were flying over open bushveld. There may well have been hundreds of bandits on the move, but there were none to be seen from the air.

345

Only occasional herds of buffalo, zebra and impala were spotted through the gathering heat haze.

Petkus jabbed his thumb at the horizon. With morbid fascination the passengers found themselves straining to see the Nacala railway line as it appeared ahead, the tracks glinting like a snail's trail amid the yellowing grass. Then the ugly black worm of burned-out train came into view surrounded by scorched bush. The aircraft dipped gently over the wreckage, disturbing vultures which had been picking over the corpses that still lay bloated in the sun.

Branagh turned to Ngoça. 'That's the price of your sort of peace. I just hope you can live with yourself.'

The deputy minister looked uncomfortable.

'Stow it, Branagh,' Dracht warned. 'You make omelettes, you break eggs. Period.'

The aircraft droned on, Cuamba miles to the east beyond the horizon. More acres of bushveld, unending.

They all felt it. The sudden stutter of the engine made the entire aircraft tremble. It dipped momentarily, then the engine picked up again, and the Otter levelled off. Another splutter, this time continuing like a persistent cough. Phlegm that wouldn't clear.

'Rpm on Number Two,' Petkus announced brusquely. 'It's dropped below the limit.'

Kathleen was closest to the port. 'Oil is pouring out.'

The Russian said: 'I'll feather Number Two.'

There was a noticeable slackening in momentum. Now they were effectively driven by one engine and Petkus was struggling to hold course. The passengers shifted uneasily; no one spoke. In the confined, sun-heated fuse-lage the atmosphere was becoming distinctly claustrophobic.

'Number One,' Petkus reported suddenly. 'Rpm down.'

'What does it mean?' Dracht demanded.

Petkus hunched his shoulders. 'I reckon contaminated fuel. Condensation. Or maybe your *matsanga* friends sabotaged the avgas tank.'

'Is this some sort of game you're playing?' Dracht snarled, suddenly suspicious.

The Russian tapped the rev counter. The white needle wavered back and forth across the red line. 'See for yourself.' He reached one-handed for his map, spreading it out.

'What are you doing?' Dracht asked.

'Looking for the nearest strip. The engines must be checked and the fuel lines cleaned. Then fresh avgas or we have to siphon off and filter out the impurities.'

'We go on,' Dracht said.

'We go on, we die.'

The South African hesitated. 'Where's the nearest strip?'

'Cuamba.'

Armando gave a dry laugh.

'Don't get funny with me, you Russian bastard,' Dracht said. 'Cuamba's a government stronghold.'

'You want to put down in the bush,' Petkus retorted, 'with a damaged undercarriage?'

As if to add emphasis to his words, the aircraft shuddered again as Number One engine missed.

'We are *not* going to Cuamba,' Dracht said emphatically.

The Russian shook his head sadly. 'Then you are a fool.'

Without waiting for a reply, he banked the aircraft, canting into a shallow descent, levelling out low over the bushveld. He looked right and left as the terrain flashed past, his eyes seeking an area flat enough and long enough to take the aircraft. But it was impossible to be certain from the air. Even if there were a stretch free of trees, rocks or branches, other obstacles could be lurking beneath the grass.

Again the engine spluttered, jerking the occupants violently. Petkus made his decision. He eased on the controls to bring the aircraft around in a gentle circle, lining up on the stretch of bush he had selected. It was a long, narrow area of flattish land, well grazed by a nearby herd of wildebeest. Its perimeter marked by knobthorns and jackal berries.

Another cough from the engine, violent this time.

'Strap yourselves in,' Petkus ordered. 'Put your heads between your knees. Do it!'

As the occupants hurried to obey, the engine noise stopped abruptly. The sudden silence was shocking. They were floating, gliding, powerless.

Petkus struggled with the controls. The only sound was the hissing rush of air beneath the spread wings. He eased back on the yoke. Telling himself to concentrate and not to panic, over and over again. It took an age for the nose to respond as the flaps went down. Slowly, slowly, grudgingly. The nose raised, the buffalo grass hurtling beneath it in dazzling confusion. More height, he willed, more height.

Branches scratched briskly at the undercarriage as the aircraft cleared a knobthorn, leaves swirling away like green confetti. He breathed again, eyes watering as they strained to see the impossible. This is it. Clear down now. Drop, drop, drop. Shit! The termite hill loomed, the compacted column of orange earth hidden amid the tinder-dry grass. Up, up. He heard the dull thud as a wheel clipped the top of the insect castle, soil exploding in their wake.

Do it! Down! The big hands edged the column forward, coaxing the wheels down to the ground. Inch by inch by inch. His mind was filled with the mental picture of their improvised repair; he could see it straining, sense its fragility. Another inch. Another . . . The main undercarriage gingerly sought out the ground. Contact! The sudden jolt made him wince. Expecting the sound of ruptured metal. Nothing. He breathed again. Now they were bouncing hard over the hidden imprints of countless impala, baked rock-hard by the African sun.

Then he saw it. The deep green scar across his path

amid the yellowing grass. Small reeds. The meaning flashed in his brain like a red light. A stream. And then they were on it.

The nose wheel plummeted down into the deep trench no wider than a man's stride. It jammed fast and the forward momentum of the aircraft lifted the tail skyward, rolling over in an attempt to overtake the nose. Cries of terror filled his ears. Rocket launchers began to slip their lashings, rasping on the deck. He could do nothing as the aircraft stopped dead, the tail pointing to the heavens, hovering as though undecided which way to fall.

Crackling metal. Rivets popping. The starboard wing crumpled under the weight of the fuselage, rolling over onto it like a shot beast. It died to the resounding percussion of tearing metal and cracking perspex. The red dust of the bushveld rose up all around.

Something jammed into the Russian's leg with the force of a crossbow bolt. As he threw back his head in a silent scream, the side of the cockpit came forward to meet him. The lights went out.

Moments later, he found himself staring at the shattered windshield through which buffalo grass had started to grow. He shook his head. He could have been unconscious for seconds or even hours. His nostrils were filled with the stench of avgas. He reached out his hands; they were dripping blood, but he could see no cut.

Branagh's face appeared beside his own. 'Are you okay, Fred?'

'I don't know,' the Russian gasped. 'I cannot move one of my legs.'

'How is Dracht?'

Petkus glanced sideways at the South African. The man was groggy, trying to orientate himself. 'He lives.'

Branagh was contemptuous. 'More than he deserves. And more than can be said for the Rhodesian. He's alive but only just. I think he's broken his neck.'

'Young Irish?' Petkus asked.

'Everyone else is all right – just cuts and bruises.'

'I am thankful for that. This is my fault.'

'You did your best, Fred. Now let's get out in case this whole thing goes up in a ball of flame.'

The fuselage had cracked in half like an eggshell. It was through this twelve-inch gap that the survivors had to climb. Unfortunately for Drummond he had been sitting next to it on impact and had somehow been thrown clear, only to be half-strangled by his seatbelt. Chipoko had laid the Rhodesian out on the grass. The man was totally paralysed, lying as still as a corpse on his back. Only his pleading eyes gave any indication that he was still alive. Chipoko pressed a canteen to his lips but Drummond was unable even to swallow. The water trickled uselessly down his chin and dribbled into the parched earth.

Ngoça and Anton Boyd helped Branagh release Petkus from his seat and drag him out through the shattered side window in the cockpit. It was impossible now to tell what had caused it, but something had broken his left femur. Probably the control panel as it caved in on impact. He was in severe pain but was at least conscious.

Neither had Dracht escaped unscathed. But despite the obvious discomfort of his fractured left elbow, he did not forget to retrieve his AK47.

Branagh did his best to reset Petkus's leg. It had been years since he'd undergone the SAS bush doctor training course, but it was not something easily forgotten. And he'd had plenty of occasions to practise during his time in Mozambique. Now he splinted the thigh, using stout stems cut from a nearby thicket, tying them with bandages from Armando da Gruta's medical kit. Meanwhile, the Portuguese commando attended to Dracht, setting the damaged arm in a sling.

Anton Boyd meanwhile lit his stove to brew up some much appreciated mugs of tea.

When they had finished, Dracht climbed to his feet.

'Right, we've wasted enough time. Start getting those rocket launchers unloaded.'

Branagh stared at him. 'They're no use to you here.'

'We'll walk,' Dracht replied evenly.

'Your chum and Fred aren't walking anywhere.'

'They will have to wait here. We'll just take as much kit as we can.'

'You can't leave them to die,' Kathleen protested.

'They will have food and water,' Dracht answered impatiently. 'And I'll leave Drummond's gun with the Russian. He won't see out the night anyhow. I'll arrange to have 'em picked up by friendly ground units when I make my next transmission tonight.'

'Why not now?' Branagh pressed. 'It could take days to get a foot patrol here.'

Dracht was unmoved. 'Anyone could have seen that plane come down. We need to get away.'

Branagh's anger flared. 'If you leave an injured man alone here, it's a death sentence.'

For once Mulholland backed him up. He'd been sitting nursing a cut forehead, but now he stood. 'Listen, Nico old stick, this is all very well, but Branagh's right. You cannot leave a man who can't walk alone in the bush. Lions, bandits, hyenas – I mean it's just not on.'

To Branagh's surprise, Boyd added quietly: 'Leave Chipoko with him, boss. He's pretty cut up about his buddy anyway. Him and Drummond go back a long way.'

Dracht rounded on his second-in-command. 'What is this, Anton? Are you going soft? If we leave the Shona behind, that's another two launchers we have to ditch.'

Boyd wasn't deterred. 'We can manage with what we've got.' He did a quick head count. 'Six launchers and three sacks of rockets. It's enough.'

The South African hesitated. 'All right Chipoko stays. The rest of us leave for Torrola in ten minutes.'

*

Her sighting of Branagh had lifted Maraika's spirits.

It had been nightfall as she was marched into the new camp situated in a high pass amid coral trees and nyalas. She could not believe her eyes when she saw the column of white men coming the other way, loaded with rocket launchers and rucksacks. Branagh's fair hair and beard had marked him out. She was not mistaken. He had even been looking in her direction, but had not seen her amid the crocodile of Mozambican prisoners. At first she had been irrationally angry that he did not recognise her. Only later she realised that from a distance she would appear like any other dust-covered black woman. Her ploy to avoid unwelcome attention had worked all too well. Then Branagh had looked away as she started to wave.

At least she knew he was alive. And might not be far away. It was a consolation. He could still rescue her.

Their column joined other refugees camped by a stream, and she collapsed thankfully amongst them. This night they were fed. Just basic mealie but it tasted like the best dish she had ever eaten.

Eagerly she asked those refugees who had been at the camp for some days about the white men. Speculation was rife. Yes, the fair bearded one had been there for one day. With him was a big man with a bullet head and wild moustache who spoke with a strange accent. It must be Fredrik Petkus, she thought. And a rather fat European whom Maraika assumed to be the man called Mulholland from England. But it was the presence of the white woman that had really started tongues wagging. Who was she and why was she there? Why were any of them there? Had they been abducted or were they conspirators?

While she talked her father approached. He looked tired and emaciated and walked with a stoop.

'*Pai*,' she greeted as he sat beside her. 'How are you and *Mamãe*?'

'Dear daughter.' His bony hand clutched her wrist. 'Your *mamãe* dies today on the road.'

Maraika's heart sank. 'No, it's not true.'

Pascoal's rheumy eyes were moist. 'With no food and little drink she was just too weak to go on. She just sat by the wayside, closed her eyes and died.'

She put her arms around her father's neck and hugged him closely, giving comfort, needing comfort herself. His tears were warm against her skin. 'I am so sorry, *Pai.*'

'They did not even let me bury her.' His words were mumbled against her cheek.

A tremble of rage ran through her. That her mother should be left for the jackals. Marta Matusi who had always read to her as a small girl from the faded Children's Bible that was her prized possession. 'One day, *Pai*, the men of such evil will be punished.' And even as she spoke she thought of Benjamin and knew that one day he, too, would be punished.

Maraika was suddenly aware of someone standing over her. 'Who talks of men of evil?' said a voice.

It was the scar-faced Renamo officer who had befriended her on the trail.

'I meant nothing by it, sir,' she said quickly. 'I am just told my mother dies today.'

The man smiled sympathetically. 'I am sorry. And sorry that Mozambicans must make such sacrifices for their freedom. I understand you are very upset. Nevertheless you should guard your tongue. Others would not take kindly to your words.'

'Yes, sir.'

The officer sniffed airily and looked out at the camp site. 'Perhaps I can bring you a little cheer. I am asked to find a detail of women who cook well to serve at the kitchen. I thought of you.'

'You remembered me?'

'Do you cook well?'

'My mother taught me.'

'Then her death won't be in vain – if her daughter cooks for Renamo officers.'

Maraika was becoming increasingly alarmed. 'I would prefer to stay here.'

The officer appeared surprised. 'You would prefer to stay with the porters and march for days, sometimes without food and drink? To be beaten if you fall and probably die out there in the bush? In the kitchen you will be safe. You will have as much food as you want and warm blankets against the night air.'

Pascoal touched his daughter's arm. 'Go, child. It is important that you survive.'

She looked into his eyes and saw his sadness. He nodded his head in confirmation. Uncertainly she climbed to her feet. 'I shall come.'

'But first,' the officer said, 'wash your hair and your clothes in the stream. You cannot serve Renamo *solados* while you stink like a bushpig.'

He waited while she found a secluded spot by the stream, hidden from view by tall reeds. In ten minutes she returned with her hair as black and glossy as a raven's wing, her face scrubbed and her wet dress clinging to her like a second skin.

The officer's eyes lingered on her. 'I always knew there was beauty beneath all that dirt. Come, follow me.'

He led her through the trees to a clearing where several cooking fires burned and women prepared vegetables that had been taken from villages attacked earlier that day. She joined the workers and began to shell beans as she was instructed.

The fat woman next to her gave a playful nudge. 'He is a fine specimen, that officer of yours. All the women like him.'

'He is nothing to me,' Maraika replied haughtily.

'He has taken a shine to you. I can tell. Don't tell me our Sergio means nothing to you. I don't believe it.'

'Believe what you want,' Maraika said. 'He is Renamo.'

The woman laughed. 'Renamo he may be. But he is a Mozambican and a man first.'

354

Maraika ignored her until the woman became bored with talking to herself. When the stolen chickens and the vegetables were cooked, she took them with the other women to where the officers sat. It was an area screened off by reed partitions to form a compound lit by two hurricane lamps. The men sat around, laughing and drinking.

They greeted the women with much joking and lewd suggestions, pulling down the willing ones to sit with them and share their food. Maraika drew back into the corner shadows.

But before anyone had a chance to notice her, the gathering was interrupted by a commotion outside. The officers were alarmed. They abandoned their food and their women, and left the compound to find out what was happening. The women followed, curious and speculating amongst themselves.

Maraika went after them, keeping her distance. A furious row was taking place between some Renamo officers whom she recognised and a group of newcomers. These bandits were also in uniform, but they looked very smart, as though they had stepped straight from a parade ground. Their whole manner and bearing was different and they spoke with great authority.

Their leader was a tall, well-built man in his fifties. He wore tortoiseshell spectacles and sported a hairline moustache above his thick top lip.

'That's General Alberto,' whispered a voice at her side. It was the fat woman again. 'I saw him once before, last year. He came to inspect the *bandidos* in the camp where we were then.'

'Who is General Alberto?' The name meant nothing to her.

'You do not know? You have only recently been abducted?'

'Yes, from Tumbo.'

The woman seemed proud to have knowledge of such

an important man. It was obvious in the way she spoke. 'He is the Renamo commander of the entire North Sector of Mozambique. Only Afonso Dhlakama himself is more important than General Alberto. If he has come here, it must be a very serious matter.'

'He seems very angry.'

'He has heard that Napoleão has been relieved of his command and that João Chande has taken over. He wants to know why.'

At that point the argument began to peter out and the newcomers were left standing alone while the junior officers returned to their compound.

The scar-faced Renamo officer called Sergio caught Maraika's eye. 'You, come here.' Reluctantly she took a step forward. 'You have a great honour. You will serve our great General Alberto with his meal. I am sure you will be pleasing on his eye.'

A new khaki tent was erected, away from the other bandits; a trestle table and some collapsible chairs were set up. A hamper was produced as though from nowhere, and a white well-laundered linen tablecloth taken from it. Then bundles of proper silver cutlery. Maraika had not seen such things since Branagh had once taken her to eat at the hotel in Gutala. Many times since she had crept into the restaurant, fascinated by the snow-white tables, the glittering knives and forks and spoons, and the uniformed waiters.

'I will lay the table,' she offered.

Sergio looked at her. 'Do you know how?' It was clear he did not. 'The general is very particular.'

'I know,' she answered.

It was a curious sensation handling the cutlery. Magical. Each in its special place. Neat squares, perfectly balanced. She wasn't too sure which way round the knives and forks were supposed to go, but she didn't mind. It *looked so* good.

When she had finished, she stood back and watched as

the general and his staff officers gathered around the table. They were joined by Sergio and João Chande.

'Sit,' the general invited brusquely and began cleaning his spectacles on the edge of the tablecloth. He seemed to be deliberately taking his time. Sergio and Chande looked distinctly uncomfortable. At last the commander of North Sector replaced his spectacles. 'Firstly, Sergio, you are to be congratulated on advising headquarters of events here. You are correct that something is not right. Explanations are indeed wanted.'

Sergio beckoned Maraika and she rushed to bring the first course of melon and some bottles of Portuguese wine.

Chande was saying: 'All I know, sir, is that the plan is to attack northern Mozambique and to form a government. That's what the South African, Dracht, was saying.'

The general looked worried. 'Of course headquarters knows about the attacks, but this idea of a government of the northern provinces is totally new. We have simply made no provision to govern yet. You know our method. To control the rural areas and confine Frelimo to the towns.'

'I understood it was a change of policy,' Chande said lamely. 'That is what Colonel Napoleão led me to believe.'

'He was obeying orders directly from Dracht?'

'Yes, as were several others of the strike battalion commanders up here. Dracht had direct radio communications with them.'

The general plucked a slice of melon from his plate and sucked noisily at the juicy flesh. With his mouth full, he said: 'You suggest that Napoleão and others of my key *chefes de grupo* are in league with Dracht?'

Chande averted his eyes, fiddled with his knife. 'I would not say that.'

Impatiently the general said: 'I appreciate your loyalty to Napoleão, but you *must* tell *me* the truth.'

Chande took a deep breath. 'It seemed to me that Napoleão knew all about Dracht's plans, that is all I can say. I – all of us – assumed it was on the orders from headquarters.'

The general's eyes became dark with menace. 'Yet Dracht put Napoleão under arrest, and you in charge?'

'That was when Deputy Minister Ngoça arrived by aircraft.'

'What? Ngoça? He's involved in this?'

'I gathered he is to be the new president of the north. Napoleão had thought he was going to be head of state.'

General Alberto pushed away his plate of melon. 'This is outrageous! I can see now what has been happening.' He turned to Sergio. 'Go and bring Napoleão to this table. Instantly.'

The Renamo officer rose promptly to his feet with a nervous little bow of respect, spilling his wine in his haste. While he was away Maraika served the stew of goat meat and vegetables. The general looked at her and smiled, but he was too preoccupied to take any more notice of her.

Sergio returned with Napoleão lumbering after him. The genial face with its heavy folds of perspiring black flesh seemed thinner than Maraika remembered. His smile was ingratiating, but there was no humour in his eyes.

'General Alberto, thank goodness you have come.'

'Really?' The general looked sceptical.

'You can put an end to this injustice.'

'What injustice, Napoleão? That you are not to be president of a new state in northern Mozambique?'

Napoleão glanced angrily in Chande's direction. 'I thought it was your reward to me for my service to Renamo over all these years. That's what Dracht told me.'

'And you believed him?'

'Yes.' Embarrassed.

'You never thought to check it with me or head-quarters?'

'You know what Dracht is like.' His voice was imploring. 'Everything is secret with him. He knows everyone in South Africa and at headquarters. He just tells us what he wants us to know.'

'And there was no bag of gold?'

Napoleão looked guilty. 'There was payment, yes. Again, I naturally assumed it had your authorisation.'

Thoughtfully the general picked at his stew, but in truth he had lost his appetite. At last he said: 'Napoleão, I think you are a treacherous dog. But as it is, you too have been betrayed. Along with all of us at headquarters.'

'I don't understand,' Napoleão protested.

'Do you not?' General Alberto said and once more removed his spectacles for ritual cleaning. 'Then I shall tell you. This is all some plan that has been cooked up by the South Africans. Probably by the Directorate of Military Intelligence or the old boys from the Civil Cooperation Bureau. I cannot believe that the present government in Pretoria would sanction such a move. Dracht's people have bought off our key commanders – perhaps unwittingly – and are using our Renamo *bandidos* to drive Frelimo from power.'

'It is incredible,' Sergio thought aloud.

'It's audacious,' the general agreed, 'but quite practical. It is something our high command has seriously recommended in the past. Only then it was vetoed by the South Africans. Now they are doing it *without* the Renamo high command. By planning to install Ngoça, I can see that they are clearly out to win over moderate world opinion. No doubt *bandidos* taking part in the fighting will be offered an amnesty and some reward, probably land.'

Sergio raised an eyebrow; he could understand the appeal of such an offer. If it were made to him, would he reject it in favour of a continued life of uncertainty in the bush?

General Alberto read his expression. 'It must not be allowed to happen.'

'What would become of Renamo?' Sergio asked.

'Realistically, all we could do would be to continue to fight against Frelimo in the south. But already aid from Pretoria is reduced to a trickle – our allies there are obliged now to be extremely careful. And meanwhile, Frelimo has renounced Marxism and is offering free elections – elections we cannot be certain of winning.'

Sergio noticed Maraika hovering with a fresh bottle of wine. 'Sir, should we be talking in front of the girl?'

General Alberto looked up, smiled half-heartedly and said: 'A village peasant girl – I doubt she understands a word we are talking about.'

Maraika smiled demurely as she poured the wine. Inside, she was fuming with indignation. Peasant girl indeed! And she understood almost everything that had been said. Living with Branagh had opened her eyes to the political issues that were above the heads of most inhabitants in Gutala district.

'The key to all this is Ngoça,' the general decided. 'Without him it will be seen by the outside world as a pure Renamo action. He gives it credibility and is the one man who could unite both sides.' The general hesitated. 'Where is he now?'

'He has already left for Tumbo with Dracht,' Chande said. 'They are taking the European prisoners with them to carry antitank weapons. They plan to fly north to Torrola to stop Frelimo from relieving the district capital, Lichinga.'

'How long do we have?' the general demanded.

Chande looked to Sergio for inspiration, but the officer just shrugged. 'They will not reach Tumbo until tomorrow morning. Then they have to repair the aircraft. So perhaps the following day they will take off. In forty-two or forty-eight hours they may be in Torrola.'

'How far is Torrola?'

'About a hundred and twenty miles.'

The general suddenly pounded the table with his fist so

hard that the plates jumped, startling his staff officers. To their amazement, their chief was actually smiling. 'This is what we do – tell me, your radio network is fully operational?'

'Sir,' Chande confirmed.

'Then we signal all Renamo units fighting in the north to disengage. No explanation, just orders from headquarters. They will be none the wiser. Meanwhile all will be put on alert to look out for Dracht and Ngoça. And the *bandidos* in Torrola will arrange a welcoming committee for the plane when it lands from Tumbo.'

Napoleão coughed in deference before he spoke: 'General Alberto, it is possible such orders will not be obeyed. We do not know how many local commanders Dracht has in his pocket.'

The general's eyes were fierce slits. 'Like you, you mean?'

'That is a monstrous suggestion!' Napoleão protested.

'Then this can be your chance to redeem yourself.' The general appeared amused by a sudden thought. 'And to save yourself from the execution our leader Afonso Dhlakama has asked me to carry out. Prepare a column of your most trusted and experienced men to travel overland to be in Torrola when Dracht's aircraft lands. I want Dracht, Ngoça and his whole party wiped from the face of Africa.'

Napoleão's smile burst forth. 'I shall lead it myself.'

'You will not!' General Alberto retorted. 'You will be here so that I can personally shoot you if they fail.' He glanced round the table. 'I suggest Chande here leads the column and this other officer.' Sergio nodded graciously; it was a tall order to cover such a distance in the time, but it was nevertheless a most unexpected honour.

Chande said: 'It will be my pleasure, General. And I have in mind one particular person to go ahead of us as scout. It may fall upon him to reach Dracht first, so we must be sure he will do the job.'

'Who is this man?'

A slow, lopsided grin crossed Chande's face. 'He is little more than a boy, General. But he is the most efficient killing machine I have ever witnessed. He carries out all orders without question. He shows no mercy and no remorse.'

'His name?'

'Benjamin Matusi.'

Maraika dropped the plates she was carrying.

13

'Just look at that old bastard.' Nico Dracht's tone suggested something close to awe. It sounded incongruous coming from the lips of such a man.

The ancient tusker stood knee-deep in the shallows of the water hole, lazily swinging his heavy trunk, showering away the coating of dried mud. Droplets glittered like jewels on the wrinkled grey hide. He was apart from the main herd where the nursing cows tolerated the exuberant play of the frolicking calves. It was as though he had no time for the innocence of youth. He was king. Leader and protector. Standing, watching over his charges. Ever alert to the lurking dangers that the wisdom of the years had taught him to expect.

Dracht let the branch go and the brushwood closed on the scene. He turned to Armando da Gruta: 'A hundred metres. I could fell him in one.'

That's more like the Nico Dracht we know and love, Branagh thought.

'You can't—' Kathleen began.

The South African looked at her and laughed at the concern on her face. 'You're right, I can't. Not without alerting every Frelimo or bandit within miles. But I'd like to, believe me.'

'I believe you,' Kathleen replied coldly.

'A proper little conservationist,' Armando da Gruta sneered.

Dracht said: 'I reckon that one's had his three score years and ten. I'd be doing him a favour. Did you see the bullet hole in his eye-socket? Half-blind. Probably in constant pain.' He stared wistfully at the sky. 'It's years since I've been on a cull. Me and the old man together, stalking in the bush. I was just a lad then. Things were different. Now it's rules and regulations for everything.'

Kathleen glared defiance. 'Since when have you worried about the law?'

Dracht's memories dissolved before his eyes. 'You've a sharp tongue on you, girlie. I should keep it still unless you want it cut out.'

She took an involuntary step back into Branagh's arms. The Irishman said: 'There's no need for threats.'

'It's not a threat. It's a promise.'

Mulholland interrupted. 'Look, Nico old stick, are we staying here for the night? My feet are blistered to buggery. I can hardly stand.'

Dracht shook his head. 'Your feet aren't my concern. Blisters won't kill you – you numb to the pain if you keep going. We'll just top up the canteens here, then press on.'

'Won't there be lions around?' Mulholland asked suddenly. 'I mean, they stake out for a kill at dusk, don't they?'

The South African smiled. 'One golden rule of the bush when it comes to lions. You only have to run faster than the man next to you.' He pushed aside the brushwood and began walking towards the water.

Da Gruta thought the expression on Mulholland's face was a huge joke as he beckoned the others to follow the South African.

A pair of duikers broke first. In a series of short, bouncing leaps the diminutive antelopes scattered in a haphazard fashion, seeking the nearest cover. They were followed by a scampering family of bushbucks. Then a herd of some twenty zebra took fright as Dracht approached the reedbed.

A powerful, urgent trumpeting reverberated across the

dark green water as the old tusker threw his head in the air to bellow the alarm.

'It's the same one,' Kathleen whispered to Branagh. 'I'm sure of it. The elephant we saw at the railway halt.'

'You could well be right,' he conceded. 'We're only some thirty miles north of the Nacala line now. Let's just hope it's a better omen this time . . . Give me your canteens.'

He waded into the reeds behind Dracht, clear of the cloudy sediment at the edge, and scooped water into the containers. On the far bank, the elephant herd had begun a lumbering retreat while the old bull stood his ground, the ears opening to a ten-foot width like ragged calico sails. Again he trumpeted. Then in a series of quick high-stepping trots of incredible agility for such an aged and massive beast, it closed on Dracht. It stopped again suddenly, the displaced water sending circles eddying to the bank. The ears fanned out once more and another ear-splitting screech shook the quiet of the water hole.

The message to the South African was clear. He was an intruder and was not wanted.

'You old bugger,' Dracht said quietly and chuckling to himself, backed away towards Branagh.

'You're not popular,' the Irishman said.

Dracht grinned at him. 'I nearly had to shoot him after all.' He turned and looked back. 'Looks like they're going our way. Maybe I'll get another chance later.'

The old tusker seemed satisfied. With a huge effort, his sinews rippling like tree roots beneath his hide, he slowly turned and trundled after the retreating herd.

Branagh added purification tablets to Kathleen's canteens before handing them back to her. 'It's still best to boil it before you drink it,' he advised.

'Thanks, Mike.' She strapped on her webbing belt, adjusted the balance of the bottles on her hips. 'I just hope Fred has enough water to last until he's found.'

'The Shona will see he's all right. They'll be able to

survive for months in the bush. Chipoko will know where to find water and food. He'll stay there out of loyalty to Dracht and to Drummond.'

'I can't help feeling sorry for that Rhodesian.'

Dracht overheard. 'Save your sympathies, girlie, he'll be dead by now. And no one will shed any tears apart from the Shona perhaps.'

Kathleen was puzzled. 'But he was one of your team.'

The South African hoisted the rocket launchers onto his bulky shoulders. 'He knew what to expect. We all do. If you live by the sword . . .' He left the sentence unfinished. 'Right, let's move it.'

Dracht and Armando da Gruta set the pace, but by the time dusk fell the small column had spread out farther and farther apart as the fatigue began to bite. Branagh and Kathleen dropped back to give encouragement to Ngoça and Mulholland who were struggling visibly with their loads.

'C'mon,' Anton Boyd chided from behind. 'Where's this British grit we're always hearing about?'

'I lost it with my fiftieth birthday,' Mulholland retorted. 'I'm used to pushing a pen nowadays, not hacking across the bloody wilds.'

'I have to stop soon,' Ngoça complained. 'I am feeling dizzy.'

Boyd said: 'From what I hear, you've most to gain from all this.'

'It'll go down in Mozambique's history,' Branagh added sarcastically. 'Like Mao Tse-tung's Great March.'

'Leave him alone, Mike,' Kathleen chided. 'This is Dracht's idea, not his. Can't you see he's not well?'

Respite came as they crested the next low hill. Dracht and da Gruta were waiting on the other side. Moonlight cast its pale purple glow over a series of gently undulating hills and valleys.

'Tea country,' Dracht announced. 'These plantations have been abandoned for years since the Renamo attacks.'

'We're going to have to stop for some of these guys, Nico,' Boyd said.

Dracht looked at Mulholland and Ngoça with undisguised disdain. 'You'll find the going easier when we pick up a road. Now move on.'

In fact, the road when they came across it was no more than a hard earthen track, studded with clumps of seeded grass and encroached on by vegetation on both sides. The straight ranks of small leafed tea bushes were neglected and overgrown. Inexorably the bush was reclaiming the cultivated land as its own.

For another hour they marched until they stumbled on the huge deserted warehouse. Its towering stucco walls and tin roof loomed unexpectedly out of the darkness. A giant eagle owl was disturbed as Dracht and da Gruta scouted ahead, its sudden soft flapping and eerie call adding to the uncanny sense of desolation. The others followed at a distance, beckoned on as each section of the complex was found to be clear. Apart from the enormous slab-sided warehouse itself, there was a low accommodation block with a rusting water tower and an administration annexe. All the windows were broken and inside the desks and floors were scattered with papers that had turned yellow with age. The last date ringed on the wall calendar was June 6th, 1987.

The burned-out hulks of half a dozen trucks filled the loading bay, all with shattered windscreens, some with tyres missing. Dracht shone his flashlight inside the warehouse and, as the others ventured in behind him, they were assailed by the pungent and overpowering smell of tea. Huge mountains of the stuff were piled to the rafters, still awaiting a collection that never came. In the torch beam, bats gyrated madly high above their heads.

'This will do,' Dracht announced. 'We'll stay here till morning.'

The accommodation block had been wrecked, furniture overturned and handbasins wrenched from their pipes. Mildewed mattresses were extracted from the debris and placed in one room which they made a half-hearted attempt to clear.

The radio was set up and a request sent for a friendly Renamo unit to locate Petkus and the Shona and escort them to a safe zone. That done, Dracht and da Gruta went outside to keep watch while Boyd got the stoves working. Kathleen helped prepare a concoction from the assorted rations available as the rich aroma of coffee filled the room.

'God, that smells good,' Mulholland said. 'I don't know what I need most, coffee, food or sleep.'

'I could sleep for a week,' Ngoça added.

Mulholland eased off his shoes. 'Surely Dracht doesn't think we can go on much longer.' He peered distastefully as his bloodied feet. 'What an awful sight.'

Branagh said: 'He'll push on for as long as it takes.'

'Recognise the type, do you, Mike?' Mulholland asked with an air of innocence.

'What do you mean by that?'

Mulholland leaned back against the mud-brick wall and shut his eyes. 'Oh, nothing. It's just that when I look at Dracht, I see you as you were back then. Ruthless and determined. Stop for nothing and nobody.'

Kathleen looked up from the stove.

'It was nothing to be proud of,' Branagh's voice was low. 'I lived to regret it. In the end, there was just no point.'

Mulholland opened his eyes again. 'Dracht sees the point. He's got something to aim for. Something to live for. I don't see him turning into some kind of born-again Christian.'

Branagh ignored the taunt as Boyd began handing around mess tins filled with a curious type of stew. 'Dracht is a born-again killer,' the South African said quietly. 'You meet his sort a lot in these parts. They've spent years in the bush behind enemy lines. Seen it all and done it all, used to having it all their own way. Answerable to no one. In the end they go bush-crazy. Lose sight of right and wrong.'

'You're not like that,' Kathleen said.

Boyd smiled as he settled down with his food. 'I've had my moments. But I've got a kid now. It changes your outlook. Brings you back to reality. This dream of a new *Boertursland* is reality for Dracht, not for me. You can't stand like Canute and try to change the tide of history. Leastways not without drowning in the attempt.'

'So why are you with him?' Kathleen asked.

'Because I'm ordered to and it's my job.'

'Couldn't you get out?'

Boyd toyed at his food with a fork. 'The wife and I are thinking of emigrating to New Zealand. After this business, we'll think even harder.'

Ngoça appeared to have at last been revived by the hot meal. 'I am sorry this has inconvenienced you all so much,' he apologised with a politeness that seemed inappropriate in that setting. 'Believe me, I had no idea it would all work out like this. On paper, it seemed so simple.'

'It always does,' Branagh said acidly. 'That's the trouble with politicians. They rarely see the results of their grand schemes, the sacrifices that the common people have to make.'

Ngoça turned to him. 'I am sorry you feel this way, Senhor Branagh. I am aware of the work that you have done, and I wish that you wouldn't consider me to be your enemy. We are both working for the good of the people in our different ways.'

'But as a politician, you know best,' Branagh provoked. 'Frelimo might not be the most efficient government in the world, but they are trying. They've renounced Marxism and are planning to introduce multiparty politics.'

369

'I do not think the people can wait any longer,' Ngoça returned sharply.

'Or do you mean you can't wait any longer?'

Ngoça scowled. 'Yes, Senhor Branagh, that too. You will be aware that the government has some very good ministers, but others who are corrupt. But all stay because they were heroes of Mozambique's so-called revolution. It is their reward for fighting the bush war against the Portuguese. Only I have never been forgiven for not playing a part in that. At the time I was at university in America, learning the political skills and making international political friends that my country would one day need.' His eyes blazed with intensity. 'You can see how much my country has need of them. Needs them now. Yet I am condemned endlessly to serve Mozambicans who have no idea how to run a country. Senhor Branagh, I weep when I see the state we are in and with no sign of any improvement.'

It was an impassioned statement and to a large extent Branagh could understand Ngoça's frustration. But not quite. 'And our mutual friend – the late Brigadier Santos – did he share your vision?'

In the confines of the small room, the tension in the air was almost tangible. Ngoça's eyes widened as though the Irishman's words had prised open some inner secret. He recovered his composure slowly. 'Santos did not share that vision, you are right.'

Branagh nodded. 'So his aircraft was blown out of the sky so that Vaz could take command of this sector for the government and let Renamo run all over them.'

'I had no hand in that,' Ngoça protested.

'You had your friend killed,' Branagh pressed, 'just because he couldn't be bought, but Vaz could—'

'No!' Ngoça shouted. 'I have no military experience. Everything like that was worked out by the others. By Willem van der Walt. It is his strategy . . .' There were tears in the man's eyes as his words trailed off. He

370

swallowed hard. 'Santos is of the greatest personal loss to me. His death was a tragic mistake.'

'Watch it, Branagh,' Boyd warned. 'And you, Mr Ngoça. If Dracht was here he'd have you both pistol-whipped. These events aren't for public discussion.'

Branagh rounded on the South African. 'But Dracht's not here, Anton, is he? It's you sitting with an AK by your side, forcing three innocent people to go along with this madness.'

Boyd was unmoved. 'I recall it was your choice to come.'

'Under duress. It wasn't much of a choice.'

The man considered for a moment. 'Besides, you're safe enough with us. Once we've got to Torrola, Dracht will get you over the border to Malawi.'

'You told Fred he'd be safe with you, too,' Kathleen pointed out icily.

'The Russian? That was an accident – they happen. For Christ's sake, what do you expect me to do about it? I'm just following orders.'

Branagh said: 'Those orders are illegal, Anton, and you know it. It may be set up to look like an internal coup to the outside world, but we know different, don't we? I doubt it's even got the sanction of your own government, just some squalid little group of Boer diehards who think they're above the law.'

Boyd eyed Branagh suspiciously. 'Perhaps they are.'

'But are you, Anton?' Branagh challenged. 'If things go wrong, it'll be no excuse that you were just following orders. You'll be executed by Frelimo before anyone can even get you to a court.'

Perhaps Branagh had hit a nerve. Perhaps Boyd had been harbouring just the smallest feeling of guilt; or he may have wondered how his wife and child would cope without him. Either way he became uncharacteristically angry and defensive: 'Listen, Branagh, I've served for thirteen years in this bush war. In Namibia and here in

371

Mozambique. We've never once been near to being caught. That's not going to change now. We're professionals. You might not like Dracht any more than I do, but can you imagine a bunch of black Frelimo dodos getting the upper hand over him? It's just not going to happen.'

Branagh said very slowly: 'Why take that risk, Anton? Why be part of this? Dracht and Armando are outside – you've got an AK. They wouldn't know what hit them.'

'How dare you!' Ngoça cried. He turned to Boyd. 'Don't listen to him.'

The South African smiled uneasily. 'Don't worry, I won't. Lucky for him I'm deaf. If I'd heard what he'd just said, Dracht would put a bullet between his eyes.'

'If you plan to say nothing, then I will,' Ngoça warned angrily.

Mulholland intervened. 'You're a fool, Branagh. Do you want to get us all killed? You know what sort Dracht is. What would you have done in the old days in his position? You wouldn't even have hesitated if it meant getting the job done.' He glanced at Ngoça before turning back to Branagh. 'Forget any airy-fairy notions about the morality of what these people are up to. Let's just concentrate on staying alive – and that means keeping on the right side of Dracht.'

'Sensible man,' Boyd murmured.

'Dracht's sort don't lose,' Mulholland continued. 'I told you earlier he was ruthless and determined. Just how you *used* to be before you filled your head with all this woolly liberal thinking. And he's backed by military intelligence in South Africa. You can't fight those sorts of people.'

Branagh glared. 'You mean the fat cats, Vincent? The untouchables. To be sure, you'd know all about that.'

Before Mulholland could answer, they heard the sound of running feet outside.

Dracht burst into the room with Armando da Gruta

close on his heels. 'Quick, put those lights out! And the stoves! There's a Frelimo patrol coming!'

'God Almighty,' da Gruta groaned. 'This place stinks of coffee.'

The speed of the march left Maraika stunned.

All the bandits and their porters had been chosen for their youth or fitness. She was amongst a dozen women selected by the scar-faced officer called Sergio. He had refused her pleas to be allowed to stay with her father, but had generously permitted him to join the special column because, although old, he still had strength and stamina developed over years of working in the fields.

'Remember this favour I have done you, pretty one,' Sergio said with a lopsided smile. 'Even Renamo can have compassion.'

She wanted to spit. Compassion! How she loathed the *bandidos* and everything they stood for. Her burning anger fuelled her aching muscles as she trudged on like an automaton. There were a hundred people in the column, half of them porters carrying food and ammunition. Because they had to travel fast, each load was unusually and thankfully light. At the head of the crocodile João Chande, Napoleão's former second-in-command, set a blistering pace along the game trail.

On the morning of the second day they were already more than halfway to Torrola. It was then that one of the bandits spotted an aircraft on the distant horizon behind them. At his cry the column shuffled to a halt; the glazed eyes of the porters turned to follow the distant speck. The faltering sound of its engines was distinct but grew fainter as the aircraft dipped from view. Abruptly the noise stopped.

The Renamo officers gathered in a huddle. Rumours and speculation passed up and down the line in whispers.

'They say it is the plane from Tumbo,' Maraika's father said. 'The one with the South Africans on board.'

A knot of apprehension began to coil in her stomach. 'And Mikey will be on it, too.'

Pascoal wrinkled his face. 'They cannot be certain. But it is the only aircraft we have seen. I hear a *bandido* say that it is the time it might be flying.'

Oh, God, no. Only Fred Petkus could fly the aircraft, she knew that. And Branagh would not let him go alone. Branagh must have been on board. Mikey Branagh and his kissing cousin. If it had crashed they would all be dead.

Orders were given for the porters and bandits to rest. Maraika did not understand. She wanted to ask the officers what was happening but did not dare. Sitting disconsolately beside the trail with her head in her hands, she wept quietly.

It was some hours before she discovered the reason for their stop. The buzzing roar of a motorcycle alerted the dozing porters and bandits; the Renamo officers climbed to their feet, anxious for news.

Maraika hid her face as Benjamin Matusi rode past astride his black motorcycle. She was thankful for her father's poor eyesight, and thankful that her brother paid scant attention to individual prisoners. If Pascoal had met his son, known what he had become, then that knowledge would surely have killed him.

The boy pulled up in a cloud of dust a few paces away. As she peered over the shoulder of the man in front of her, she saw that her brother was talking to Chande himself. Then, for the first time, she noticed that a body hung over the pillion seat.

She strained to hear snatches of the conversation.

'It is the Direct Action aircraft . . .' Benjamin was saying. He lifted the head of the body by its ginger hair. Maraika looked aghast at the neat black hole in the forehead and the trickle of congealed blood. The eyes were still open and seemed to stare straight at her. 'This is the only thing I find.'

'The Rhodesian,' Chande observed. 'And did you shoot him?'

The boy shook his head. 'No, sir. This is as I find him. The others had gone away. There are two spoors. One of two, maybe three people. One of them is injured – there is blood. It goes south. The other spoor goes north several peoples carrying much weight. There were rocket launchers on the aircraft.'

Maraika was astounded at Benjamin's knowledge – to understand so much from footprints in the dust and crushed grass. Then she recalled the many hours that Mikey Branagh had spent with him in the bush, teaching the boy how to track and hunt.

Chande said: 'So what do you think has happened, Matusi?'

Benjamin pointed a finger in the direction that the aircraft had been last seen. 'I think there are some injured people. They hide from me. They kill this man when I come, so he is not caught alive. They do not know if I am friend or foe . . . Maybe . . . But I am sure others take weapons and walk north. Maybe they walk now to Torrola.'

'Towards us here?'

The boy shook his head. 'To the west of us. Through tea country.'

Chande's face lit up at the news. 'How far from us would they be?'

Benjamin frowned. 'We lose some time now . . . but not long. Maybe half a day's march. Not more.'

The Renamo commander made his decision. He issued brisk orders to his officers who immediately began shouting at the bandits and their porters to get in line. The whips came out and there was much use of rifle butts to persuade the exhausted ones to move. But move they did as whistles blew and Chande set off on a new course. They left the game trail, veering at a north-westerly angle that would eventually cross the path of their quarry.

Maraika didn't know what to make of Benjamin's findings. At least she could be fairly certain that Mikey hadn't died in the crash. But was he hiding somewhere in the bush, dying slowly of his injuries? Or was he ahead of them now? The very thought of seeing him again filled her with excitement, until she remembered the orders that General Alberto had given Chande. She searched her memory for the exact words. She could see his face now the fleshy lips framing around each syllable. *Wiped from the face of Africa.* She shuddered.

Dusk found them at a water hole. Strangely, there were no animals present.

As they approached, she saw that Benjamin Matusi had arrived ahead of them. His motorcycle was propped by the water's edge and he was kneeling to examine the damp earth by the reeds.

'What do you find?' Chande asked anxiously. She sensed his excitement, a hunter with the scent of the prey in his nostrils.

The boy stood up. 'They were here. Very recent.' He looked out across the deep green water. 'Something disturbed the wildlife. Nothing drinks. Maybe two hours. See the prints – just as at the aircraft. They have not yet been disturbed by animals coming to drink. One is of a woman. Small and light, but she carries a heavy load.' He ran a finger carefully over a patch of shiny, compressed grass. 'See, it is still flat.'

'Do you know how quickly they move?'

'Not fast. Some are tired. The placement of the feet is uneven.'

Chande said: 'Then we must go on now and catch them.'

'That is difficult, sir,' the boy said. 'To track at night needs much experience which I do not have. I may lose them or they may ambush us in the dark. It would be best to wait until morning when the sun is low.'

The commander was clearly irritated by the enforced

delay, but reluctantly he had to agree that it made sense. Benjamin Matusi was a quite remarkable tracker, especially for one so young.

Chande gave orders for the column of bandits and porters to make camp beneath a stand of mopane trees on the far side of the water hole. Maraika was ordered to work in the camp kitchen along with the other women, lighting a cooking fire and preparing maize porridge.

When she had completed her chores she stole quietly away into the undergrowth where she found her father sleeping, curled into the foetal position like a small child. She smiled to herself and sat down by his side and reached to stroke the head of greying curls. How good to see him at peace. Over the years he had endured so much, yet never with a word of complaint. From a boy he had worked the Portuguese cotton plantations for a pittance to provide food and shelter for his wife and children. Then had come the uncertainty and abject poverty of independence, followed swiftly by the terror years of the bandits. Months at a time hiding in the bush. Then eventually finding sanctuary in the Gutala district – only to have his two sons taken from him. It had been a bitter blow to both his heart and his pride, but still he had managed to keep cheerful. To do otherwise, he had once told her, was to let the *bandidos* win. And it would show a disrespectful lack of faith in Our Lady.

Now this. His youngest daughter butchered with child, and his wife cruelly taken from him on the march.

What more could a man be expected to endure, she wondered as she looked out over the water hole? Lances of light from the fire played on its silken black surface, breaking up the reflection of the high lemon moon. The rustle of the reeds provided a soothing background to the urgent percussion of cicadas and frogs. From somewhere distant the echoing thunder of a lion's roar carried across the miles. She shivered, glad of the closeness of her father. Glad, too, that Branagh was near, but apprehensive of what might happen when the *bandidos* caught up with him and his kissing cousin and the South African commandos.

Her father stirred, sensing her presence. 'Daughter?'

'I am here, *Pai*.'

He rubbed his eyes. 'You are not sleeping.'

'I cannot sleep.'

'It will be another hard day tomorrow. You must try.'

'I will try, *Pai*,' she promised and watched as he lay down his head again and was instantly asleep.

It was then that she saw the flashlight beam and heard the snap of twigs behind her. The movement triggered some inner alarm and she was quickly on her feet, turning to face the direction of the sudden intrusion. Her eyes darted back and forth, straining to see beyond the dazzle of light amongst the mopane trunks. She heard the harsh boyish laughter and the careless trampling of undergrowth. Sweat gathered in the small of her back.

'What have we here?' an amused young voice asked. Then hiccuped.

The bandits were barely in their teens. All three had been drinking, no doubt from beer cans looted from village shops. She could smell it from several paces, mixed with the cloying sweet aroma of ganja. Blue smoke wafted through the torch beams, making it difficult for her to distinguish their grinning black faces. The one who had spoken wore a tatty camouflage jacket that was several sizes too large for him; the dried bloodstain over the breast pocket suggested he had taken it from a dead comrade. His even younger companions were dressed in fatigue trousers and the smaller of the two had on a holed yellow T-shirt. Each carried a Kalashnikov assault rifle that was almost as tall as himself.

'What have we here?' repeated the oldest boy.

'Runaways,' said the next. The youngest giggled.

Maraika felt a rising panic. 'No!' she protested. She

378

knew that the penalty for attempting to escape could be amputation or death.

'Then what are you doing here?' the oldest boy demanded.

The question was so stupid that for a second she was tempted to answer back. With difficulty she controlled her anger. 'I am resting, of course. With my father here.'

A beam played over the body of the old man as he uncurled, suddenly awake and alarmed at the disturbance. He lifted a hand to shield his eyes.

'You should be with the others,' their spokesman said.

Despite his arrogance, Maraika's fear subsided. They really were just children; in the torchlight she could see their youthful faces now, their skin beaded with the sweat of alcohol. In other circumstances they might have been three mischievous lads at the school in Gutala, testing their new-found pubescent confidence against the teacher, only for it to end in tears when they were reported to their parents.

'What is happening, daughter?' Pascoal asked, confused.

'Shut up, old man,' ordered one of the bandits.

The oldest boy looked hard at Maraika. There was something strangely cold about his eyes. Again she felt a creeping sensation of apprehension at the back of her neck. The boy's pink pointed tongue appeared in a short flickering motion as he moistened his lips. 'So you do not run away, woman?'

'No.'

'So you support Renamo?'

She hesitated. 'Of course.' The words stuck in her throat.

The boy bandit gave a mirthless smile. 'Then you will not object to giving comfort to Renamo soldiers?'

Her heart filled with dread. 'What do you mean?'

'It is the Renamo tradition, you know that.' Icy. 'A woman is expected to give comfort to the soldiers.'

She could hardly believe her ears. 'You? You are children.' It was laughable.

Indignation coloured the boy's cheeks; his eyes glittered in the torchlight. 'We are men, soldiers. You insult us. I have killed over fifty peoples.' He turned to the second boy and laughed harshly. 'The question is – is she woman enough for us?' The second boy grinned, a hand-rolled ganja cigarette hanging from his mouth like a white dribble.

'She is *old*,' the smallest boy said, wrinkling his nose in disdain.

The older boy laughed. 'Little José is scared! He has never made *coito* with a woman before. He is not scared to slit a man's throat, but he is frightened to make *coito*.'

'I am not!' the twelve-year-old protested lamely. 'She is too *old*, I tell you!'

'How old are you, woman?' demanded the leader.

Maraika swallowed hard. 'I am nineteen,' she answered defiantly.

The bandit turned to the smallest again. 'That is a good age. She has experience – perhaps she will be gentle with you.' The boy with the cigarette tittered; the youngest looked nervous. But their leader was undeterred. 'I admit she is a bit skinny, but she has a pretty face. And look at those firm round breasts.'

Somehow she wasn't expecting him to step forward like that. To reach and squeeze her body through her dress as though he were testing a mango fruit for ripeness in the market. 'Stop that!' she snapped, startled.

Pascoal was on his feet. 'Leave my daughter alone, you *bandido* scum!' He grabbed the leader round the throat with both bony hands.

The barrel of the second boy's assault rifle jabbed hard into the old man's lean belly. It knocked the wind from his lungs and loosened his grip. He fell back, shocked, his eyes watering.

Rubbing at his neck, the boy leader recovered quickly

from the unexpected attack. 'So, old man, you are not a Renamo supporter, I see. You know what the punishment is for a husband or father who tries to stop a woman giving comfort. Tie him!'

Maraika watched, horrified, as the second bandit bound her father to the nearest mopane trunk with a length of sisal. Her step forward was halted by the muzzle of the same gun that had stopped Pascoal.

'Your *pai* can watch how well his daughter makes *coito*,' the leader smirked. 'Now lie down, unless you want to watch him hacked before your eyes.'

Trembling, she fell to her knees. This wasn't happening, God, it wasn't happening!

'Put your hands together in front of you.'

She closed her palms together as if in prayer. Prayer? This was a time to pray. She shut her eyes. But there were no words in her head. Her mind was swimming in confusion, blank with terror. Aware of the small hard fingers on her wrist, the tightening of rough sisal against her flesh, biting into her skin. Then a faint outline vision came into focus on the blackness of her closed eyelids. It sharpened, lighter, a drifting image of a child at her parents' side. Mikey Branagh was reading from a book.

Rough hands pushed her so that she fell onto her back. She gasped but fought to concentrate, to hear the Irishman's words as he read.

Her wrists were wrenched above her head, the sisal binding secured to the stump of a bush, holding her spine hard against the ground. She heard the words at last. Held onto them. Her lips moving imperceptibly as she spoke them in her mind.

Our Father which art in Heaven, Hallowed be Thy name.

She was distantly aware of her red dress being peeled ignominiously up over her body, left in a rumpled tangle above her breasts before the same hands tore eagerly at her pants.

She squeezed her eyes tight shut until they hurt. Concentrate!

Thy Kingdom come, Thy will be done, in earth as it is in Heaven.

Small hands were cool on her exposed body, tentatively caressing, enquiring, probing. Then harder. Stiff, angry little fingers.

Give us this day our daily bread. And forgive us our trespasses . . .

The boot prised itself between her knees, forcing her thighs apart. 'There you are, little José. Be a man. In you go!' Giggles of mirth.

She made a mistake and opened her eyes. The three of them stood before her and above her, looking down. Their trousers had been discarded but they hadn't bothered to remove their shirts. Against their pathetic childish legs, the organs of the older boys looked out of all proportion, pumped and primed for manhood, for her. Next to them, the thin pencil of the youngest's penis was laughable more than threatening. And yet, as the others urged him onto her, she knew it was the greater humiliation.

Mesmerised, she watched his troubled little face, just inches from her own, as he struggled to make his entrance. Her eyes focused mistily on the yellow T-shirt. Its faded slogan – Save the Dolphin. If it hadn't been so pitiable, she could even have laughed. She felt the wet, sticklike tip of him touch the soft flesh of her labia.

As we forgive those who trespass against us!

She was aware of the involuntary jerk as he came the second that their bodies touched, and felt the sudden warm dash of premature fluid on her thighs.

And then heard the squeals of mocking hilarity as the older boys laughed. In a moment of madness she had an inexplicable urge to reach out and comfort the shamed child.

But then the second boy was on her, forcing himself into her, his teeth grinning in her face as he panted for breath. God, it hurt!

382

She shut her eyes again. *And lead us not into temptation, but deliver us from evil.*

He was spent. A function over. Manhood proved. Then it was the leader and he was different. Different and indifferent to her comfort, he pushed her legs wide until she thought she would split. And he stared at her face, watching her eyes as he drove himself in, watching her pain. Enjoying it. Deep, hard, unrelenting. His eyes had a maniacal gleam as though he were consumed with an inner anger. All the hatred and confusion of his tragic life were concentrated on this one act. The bloodshed and the terror he had both suffered and perpetrated culminated here. Revenge or failed contrition? She saw it all in those haunted eyes, but did not understand it.

For Thine is the Kingdom, the power and the glory.

'You are the devil's children!' Pascoal shouted, his voice trembling. His words echoed chillingly through the mopanes.

The boy leader hunched his back in a final spasm and fell onto her. She felt the coarse woolly hair of his head scratch against her breast.

Her lips parted. In a dry whisper she said: 'I forgive you.'

He jolted suddenly. Pulled himself from her as though he couldn't wait to get away. He stared down at her, eyes blazing. 'How dare you say that to me? Who do you think you are? A priest?'

Snatching his assault rifle from the second bandit, he raised it at Pascoal and fired. One shot. It shook the stillness of the water hole, the sound reverberating round and round, rippling away to die somewhere out in the vastness of the bushveld.

Maraika's father slumped forward, held in place by the bonds of sisal. A single drip of blood escaped the neat round hole in his forehead and splashed onto the chest of his white singlet to form a moist red starburst.

Now the leader stood over her again, looking both absurd and menacing at the same time with his flaccid genitals hanging below his shirt. He lowered the smoking muzzle of the gun until it pointed at her face. The acrid stench of burned cordite filled her nostrils.

Suddenly she heard running feet, the crackle of undergrowth being brushed aside.

'What is going on here? Who fired that shot?'

It was a new voice, oddly familiar.

Bejamin Matusi stood, legs astride, behind the young bandits. They turned awkwardly, trying to pull on their fatigue trousers. Nervous eyes watched the new arrival as he stepped forward and looked around him. His face was an emotionless mask as his eyes took in the corpse of his own father, strung against the tree. Then his sister, pinioned to the ground with a young *bandido* standing over her naked body.

'Go,' he said. His voice was hoarse. The youngsters shuffled uneasily. Their leader retrieved his trousers. He glared malevolently at Benjamin Matusi, resentful at being cowed by someone no older than himself. Resentful of the fear he felt in the presence of the bandit whom their commander affectionately called Boy-Killer.

There was more commotion as other, older bandits came to see what had happened. They stood pensively, watching, curious to see what Boy-Killer would do. Among them was the Renamo officer called Sergio; even he knew better than to interfere.

The youths slunk away into the shadows and all eyes were on Boy-Killer as he knelt at the girl's side. She looked up at him, remembering the once familiar features. But now those same plump cheeks were emaciated and drawn, rings of exhaustion around his eyes. His eyes flat and empty like the young *bandido* who had raped her. Devoid of expression; no hint of emotion.

Her throat was parched. She moistened her lips. 'My brother.'

Boy-Killer looked away, indifferent, as he unsheathed the panga from his side. Momentarily their eyes met

384

again and she shuddered. Shuddered at the sudden realisation that he was no different from the others. That he
may even be worse. That he may prefer to kill her than to
face his own sister with the admission of what he had
become.

The panga rose above his head and fell. Air displaced
with a hiss as the blade chopped the sisal bonds at a single
stroke.

As she struggled onto her elbows, he pulled roughly at
the red dress, unfurling it to cover her exposed body.
Around them the gathered bandits stayed silent.
Expectant.

Maraika looked into his face. 'Thank you, my brother,
you have saved my life.'

His eyes were averted. 'Do not thank me. I am not
your brother.' He found himself staring at the corpse of
his father. 'Renamo is my family now.'

She suddenly saw that there were tears in his eyes, but
they would not flow. He stood abruptly and walked
towards the watching crowd. They parted respectfully to
let the small figure pass.

Maraika was on her feet, brushing down her dress,
running after him. This was crazy! Her sister, her mother
and now her father. She could not let her brother go.

She pushed aside the standing men, racing to catch up
with Boy-Killer, reaching for his arm.

He turned on her. 'Leave me alone,' he hissed.

'Benjy, it is *me*. Maraika, your sister. In the name of
God, what has happened to you?'

He looked beyond her at the moon above the water
hole. 'I told you, I am not your brother . . .'

'I am your family, Benjy,' she said, desperately trying
to get through to him. 'And your young brother, Jaime –
wherever he is. *We* are still your family.'

His features froze. There was a curiously glazed
expression in his eyes as he regarded her. She could have
sworn he was in a trance. 'Jaime is dead. He died two

385

years ago. Just after they shot Dog and took us from Gutala.'

An ache began to swell in the pit of her stomach. 'What happened, Benjy?'

He stood and stared morosely at the ground.

Her voice was low. 'What happened?' she repeated.

Benjamin Matusi looked up at the rustling canopy of the mopanes, chewed his bottom lip. Trying to stop the tears and trying to find the words. 'I killed him. The *bandidos* put a gun in my hand and told me to shoot him. A sign of allegiance to them . . .' He looked down at his feet once more. 'And I would be spared.'

She frowned. 'And you killed him?'

'I killed him.' He swallowed hard and took a deep breath. The eyes that looked at her now were misted and full of despair. 'A brother does not kill a brother. No family forgives that. I cannot forgive myself that. So – this is my life now. There is no other place for me.'

Her hand reached out. 'My poor, poor Benjamin—'

He pulled away as though scalded. 'Leave me! I must go now – tomorrow—'

This time her hand closed on his wrist. 'Tomorrow? Benjamin, those people you are hunting . . . You must know, one of them is Mikey. He has always loved you as I have loved you. You belong with us, not here. We forgive you as God forgives you, little brother.'

Roughly, he broke her grip. 'Him?' His face contorted with hatred like some stone gargoyle. 'Him? He is the worst of all. I *believed* him, everything he said. But he *lied* to me. Lied, lied, lied!'

Maraika's jaw dropped. 'I don't understand.'

He mouthed the words with slow deliberation. 'If I am to burn in hell, I shall take him with me.'

Dracht pressed the snout of the automatic under Branagh's chin. 'Don't get any bright ideas, Irishman. One false move and I'll see that you're the first to get it.'

They were crouched beneath the flyblown panes of the window. Outside, the first open-topped Gaz jeep drove into the loading bay of the tea warehouse. The crew of five government troops were smarter than most, their camouflage fatigues recently washed and their forage caps properly centred. They looked wary but confident as they climbed out to stretch their legs.

'Shall we start a search?' one of the soldiers asked.

The NCO viewed the ramshackle hulk of mud brick. 'Wait for the others. It's a big place.'

For several minutes the soldiers shuffled their feet impatiently; one cupped his hands to light a cigarette. Then the second Gaz appeared, spluttering noisily as one of the cylinders misfired. It had just rumbled alongside the first vehicle when the engine finally expired in an acrid kickback of exhaust. The second NCO got out and thumped his fist on the bonnet.

'What a way to fight a war,' he complained.

'You'll have to repair it yourself,' observed the first NCO, scarcely hiding his amusement, 'or stay here. You'll be all right for tea.'

The second Mozambican sniffed the air. 'Or coffee. Can you smell it?'

'No.'

'Have you searched the place?' Apprehension crept into the man's voice.

'It's a big area. I was waiting for you.'

'Let's do it now.' He beckoned his men.

The sudden burst of violence in the stillness of the night was shocking in its intensity.

It began as agreed with a single shot from Dracht, fired from behind the torn gauze of the mosquito shutter. The bullet took the lead NCO full in the chest, blowing him back and over the bonnet of the Gaz like an unseen wind.

The stunned pause that followed can only have lasted a split second, but it seemed like several while the astonished Frelimo troops gawped. Mannequins frozen in horror. Then Armando da Gruta opened up with his favourite M48 sub-machine gun from his vantage point on the water tower. A hail of lead hosed down into the yard in a noisy stammer. Boyd closed the square, adding to the deafening cacophony as he began shooting from the yawning mouth of the loading bay. Dust rose like theatrical ice-fog as the hapless victims began a macabre dance to avoid the shower of death. One by one they were cut down. Blasted into the shadows or just dropped where they stood, vanishing into the swirling miasma of dust and gunsmoke.

Not one shot was returned in defence, so swift had been the onslaught. Only one man dared to defy the odds. The second NCO – driven by fear or remarkable courage – dived across the bay and launched himself at the window. Straight into the blazing muzzle of Dracht's assault rifle.

The remaining panes shattered, sending shards of glass bursting into the room like shrapnel. Dracht drew back and Branagh covered Kathleen with his body as the human torpedo blasted through the window – and stopped dead. The tattered mosquito netting had halted his momentum and now he hung, half in and half out, struggling like a drowning fish to free himself.

Dracht moved without hesitation. In one deft movement, his left hand grabbed the man's hair through the tangled netting. Then with his right he sliced the blade of his combat knife across the offered throat. The scream died before it began. Blood frothed out of the severed windpipe. Specks of vermilion showered into the room, blown out as the soldier's lungs exhaled. Kathleen shrieked as the warm stuff splattered over her face and hair.

Satisfied that the man was dead, Dracht tore aside the net and hauled the body in, dumping it unceremoniously on the floor. Then Ngoça and Mulholland watched with Branagh and Kathleen in shocked fascination as the South

African sliced off the dead man's ear and added it to a leather pouch in his belt.

'Christ, you're a barbarian,' Kathleen breathed, hardly believing the evidence of her own eyes.

'Shut it, girlie,' Dracht ordered.

Armando da Gruta arrived at the door just in time to witness the girl's outrage. He grinned, showing a lot of polished teeth. 'This is Africa, sweetheart. This is how it is. Just the boss's souvenir. If it had been the other way around, that black bastard would have hacked off our balls.'

'No more than you deserve,' Kathleen muttered in disgust.

Da Gruta smiled even more widely. She had spirit all right. 'You wouldn't say that if you'd seen 'em, sweetheart.' He made an obscene gesture with his left hand. 'You'd love 'em, believe me.'

Anton Boyd entered the room and looked down at the corpse. 'He was a surprise. I thought I'd hit him.'

Dracht said: 'You thought wrong. What about the others?'

'They're not going no place,' Boyd confirmed casually.

'And the vehicles?'

'Picked up a couple of stray rounds. Nothing serious. They're usable.'

Branagh's heart sank. He'd been hoping that Dracht's schedule had been blown by the aircraft crash. That by the time they reached Torrola, the Frelimo armoured column would have passed through and been well on the way to relieving the district capital of Lichinga.

'Good,' Dracht said, then looked hard at Branagh. It was as though he had been reading his thoughts. 'We'll leave as soon as the second truck is fixed. You can start work at sunup.'

Branagh looked uncertain. 'The engine didn't sound good. It might well be beyond repair.'

Dracht bared his teeth like an angry dog. 'You're an

engineer, Irishman. You'll fix it if that girl's life depends on it.' As an afterthought, he added: 'Not to mention your own.'

It was then that Ngoça stepped forward. 'You should not trust him, Senhor Dracht. While you were outside earlier, he tried to persuade your colleague to turn his gun on you.'

The South African turned to Boyd. 'Is that right, Anton?'

An uneasy grin. 'I think it was a joke, boss.'

Ngoça scowled at the denial.

Dracht regarded Branagh carefully before speaking. The Afrikaans drawl was slow and deliberate. 'I don't have that kinda sense of humour, got it? I'll play along with you while you do exactly what I say. But, remember, when my use for you and your friends is over, you'll be relying purely on my goodwill to get you out of this alive.' He paused. 'And goodwill is not something I'm well known for.'

Da Gruta interrupted. 'Boss, there's a signal coming through on the MEL.'

An awkward silence fell while the Portuguese commando crossed the room to the portable set and sat down as the alphanumeric crypto unit unscrambled the message. For several moments he sat staring at the printout.

'Well?' Dracht asked impatiently.

'I don't understand,' da Gruta murmured. 'Silvermine listening station has been picking up signals from Renamo HQ in Canxixe. Telling all units to withdraw.'

'Christ!' breathed Dracht.

'Van der Walt wants to know what's happening.'

'He's not the only one!' Dracht snarled. 'But I can guess. Somehow we've been rumbled. Renamo HQ have got wind of what's happening up here.'

Da Gruta climbed to his feet. 'You could be right. The orders were issued on behalf of General Alberto.'

'That bloody snake.'

'There's more,' da Gruta said. 'All Renamo units have been put on alert to hunt us down. They've actually given out our names.' He looked up at Boyd and Dracht; he did not feel comfortable. 'With a declaration that we are to be – I quote – wiped from the face of Africa.'

For a moment, Dracht stared at the radio in disbelief then slowly his face cracked into a smile and he began to laugh. To laugh until his eyes began to water. At last he managed to overcome the outburst of mirth. 'First Frelimo and now Renamo . . . I don't think we have a friend left in the world!'

14

The two Gaz jeeps roared out of the tea warehouse compound at ten the next morning, heading at speed along the overgrown road that would eventually lead them to Torrola.

Branagh drove the first vehicle with Kathleen by his side; Dracht and Boyd rode shotgun in the open back. The second Gaz was driven by Mulholland who had Ngoça as his passenger and Armando da Gruta in the curious role of both feared guard and welcome guardian.

In fact it had been with a real sense of urgency that Branagh had begun work on the repairs at first light that morning. The prospect of being deliberately hunted by Renamo in the middle of wild country was daunting. For the first time they actually *needed* the armed protection that the South African commandos provided.

During the long night Dracht himself had explained how he was convinced that he could regain control of the situation if they reached Torrola soon enough. After all, he argued, the bandit leader there knew Dracht personally and was on his payroll. The man must have been thrown into confusion by the contradictory instructions now coming from Renamo headquarters. But once Dracht was there on the spot with some sort of cobbled explanation and the antitank rockets the bandits needed, the local commander could be swiftly persuaded to continue. Another bag of American dollars would take care of any lingering doubts that might remain.

'It's the other bastards that concern me,' Dracht had confessed later in the night. Da Gruta had produced a bottle of brandy from his rucksack and, after such a long period of abstinence, the strong liquor had a swiftly mellowing effect. 'Since we loosened control of Renamo they've been splitting up into regional groups. Local warlords with their own little empires and axes to grind. My bet is that half of them ignore their own HQ anyway. But if they've put a price on our heads—' he stared gloomily at the mug of amber liquid clutched in his hands '—those bandit groups could be out there now. Anywhere.'

It was the first time Branagh had ever witnessed a hint of self-doubt in the man. Not that Dracht appeared in any way defeated. In fact he looked totally at home, his massive shoulders hunched, his sleeves rolled to reveal an ingrained African tan on heavily muscled forearms. His wild hair and new stubble were bleached white by the sun. Even his eyelashes were so fair as to seem non-existent, emphasising the pale ice blue of the irises. Eyes born of the bushveld.

'Why?' Kathleen had asked suddenly.

'What?'

'Why are you doing this?'

Boyd shifted uncomfortably, anticipating a hostile reaction from his boss. But Branagh could see that the South African was momentarily beguiled by the curiosity and innocence in those large brown eyes. The same curiosity and innocence that had bewitched him in Armagh all those years before.

'Why am I doing this?' Dracht echoed. 'Because I am an African. I am fighting for my country like any man would.'

'Mozambique is not your country,' Kathleen pointed out gently.

Dracht smiled slowly. 'They are giving my country away, girlie. Everything the Boertrekkers fought for.

Generations of lives sacrificed to make South Africa great. Toil and sweat and blood. Name one other country on this great continent that is prosperous and well-run and not ruled by a tinpot dictator with blood on his hands? I want to tell you. Nowhere. Now they're throwing it all away to the Zulus and Mandela's Marxist brotherhood. Can you imagine what South Africa will be like after ten years of black majority rule?'

'It's their country too,' Kathleen said defiantly.

Dracht swigged at his mug. 'If you said that in some places I know, they'd be the last words you ever spoke. Me – I'd just ignore you. You can't argue against that sort of ignorance. You see, girlie, it was the Dutch who settled the Cape, not the bloody *kaffirs*. Only the Hottentots and Bushmen were there first – their descendants became the Cape coloureds today. There wasn't a bloody *kaffir* to be seen.'

'Nico's right,' Boyd added suddenly. 'We've as much claim to the land as anyone. More so. It was years later before the blacks migrated completely south.'

Dracht snorted. 'And in droves when they wanted to earn a living after we had developed the land. Saw us as their bloody saviours against drought and starvation.' He looked at Kathleen directly. 'Well, they want it, and now they are going to get it. So I and many others are looking for someplace else. And *this* is it.'

Boyd said: 'I can't say I think it's right though, Nico.'

'Can't you, Anton?' Dracht sneered. 'That does surprise me. Look, man, this is Africa. You have to fight for what you want. That's how it's always been. Go out there and grab it.'

Boyd shrugged. 'Things might not be so bad under the blacks . . .'

Da Gruta laughed. 'You mean you'd plan to stay?'

The other man looked sheepish. 'If I was single, I'd give it a try. But with a wife and kid – well, we'd been thinking of emigrating. Maybe New Zealand.'

Dracht grunted. 'If your wife's still waiting for you after you've survived this operation.'

Da Gruta grinned; Branagh gathered it was some sort of private joke.

Boyd sensed it too. 'What exactly do you mean by that?'

Dracht glanced up at his Portuguese companion and winked. 'Shall I tell him?'

'Put him in the picture, Nico. Why not? The facts of life never hurt anyone.'

Dracht turned to Boyd. 'You've been posted as missing in action. We all have.'

'What?' Boyd was incredulous.

'You knew this was a highly sensitive mission,' Dracht continued without sympathy. 'A totally deniable operation. So several days ago your wife will have received a visit from your commanding officer with the sad news that you are missing in action behind enemy lines.'

'Christ!'

Dracht was unmoved. 'Depending on the circumstances she'll be encouraged to move to a new country, all expenses paid. She'll accept the offer, it'll be too good to turn down.'

Boyd still could not believe what he was hearing. 'What in God's name is the reason for that charade?' he demanded.

'Why do you think?' Dracht replied irritably. 'So there's no evidence this operation ever took place. When it succeeds – or even if it fails – no one will want people blabbing to the media to earn a quick buck. You'll agree to the terms if you want to be with your wife again. But it won't be in South Africa. You've left it for good – we all have.'

No doubt Dracht's unwelcome revelation explained why Boyd had been morose and self-absorbed all morning. In the back of the Gaz a strained silence hung between him and his boss as they scoured the passing acres of tea plantation.

It was high country, the air refreshing and breezy after their previous days in the bushveld. They picked up an old laterite road that zigzagged down to a meandering river some half-mile wide. According to Dracht's map there was a bridge, but when they reached the spot all that remained were the burnt-out piles. Blackened timber fingers gestured at them in obscene mockery.

Branagh eased the vehicle to a halt; the brake shoes were down to the rivets and slowing was a precarious process. Mulholland drove alongside. 'What now?' he asked.

Dracht studied his map. 'We either go west into the hills – that could mean Renamo. Or east towards government territory.'

'Will there be somewhere to get fuel in the hills?' Mulholland asked. 'This one's on the red, and there's nothing in the spare can.'

'That's crazy,' Dracht said. 'Is it the gauge that's faulty? Even Frelimo troops wouldn't stray as far as that warehouse without fuel to get back.'

Branagh climbed out and went down on his back beneath the other vehicle.

'Well?' Dracht asked impatiently.

'This is your answer. The fuel tank's rusting through. A slow leak.'

'You were supposed to check everything,' Dracht accused.

'Get stuffed. I had enough problems with the bloody engines.'

Da Gruta intervened. 'There's no point arguing, boss. If the tank leaks, it leaks. We'll need more fuel anyway. What's in yours?'

'Under a quarter tank,' Branagh said.

Da Gruta scrutinised Dracht's map for a few moments. 'There'll be no fuel in the hills, Nico. But there's a Frelimo garrison about ten miles to the east. A new safe-zone development around two villages. I remember getting a briefing about it some three months back.'

Dracht scowled. 'You suggesting we go ask Frelimo for fuel?'

The Portuguese commando showed his teeth. 'Not quite what I had in mind, Nico. As it's reckoned to be a safe zone there's probably some traffic on the road between the two villages. Shouldn't be too difficult to stop something and syphon off their fuel. Maybe even hijack the vehicle if it's better than these crates.'

'Better than these? In Mozambique?' Dracht taunted. 'Okay, let's try it.'

They left the bridge, running with the laterite track until it parted company with the river and headed once again into open bushveld.

After five miles a dirt trail spurred off to the left. 'Take that!' Dracht shouted down from the rear. 'It'll bring us out on the road between the villages.'

Branagh swung the wheel, the old springs of the Gaz complaining noisily as they bumped over rocks and clumps of coarse grass. Thorn branches rattled at the sidescreens, clawing spitefully for a victim. Red dust tumbled out behind them, blotting out the arid landscape. A flat-topped basalt kopje rose from the vegetation clustered at its base. At Dracht's instruction Branagh pulled into its lee shadow and stopped.

Moments later the second Gaz pulled up behind them, the engine beginning to stutter as it sucked at dry fuel lines. Then it cut out completely.

'That's it,' Mulholland declared. He looked around. 'What a place to finish up. Miles from anywhere.'

But Dracht ignored him. 'The road between the villages runs by on the other side of this rock. Anton, get up there and keep a lookout. Give us a whistle if you see a likely looking vehicle.'

Sullenly Boyd began to climb the wind-smoothed side of the kopje. He finally settled himself in the shadow of a lower peak.

The rest followed Dracht down into the steep gully through which the road ran. It was a natural collecting place for any rain that fell and the resultant lush vegetation had grown up to form a natural archway of interlinking branches overhead. The shade was refreshingly cool after the sun-baked air of the open bush.

'What happens now?' Ngoça asked.

'We wait,' Dracht replied, 'and hope something comes along. Go and sit down out of sight of the road.'

They waited for three long and tedious hours. The only bonus was a chance for the noncombatants to catch up on much needed sleep. It was a piercing blast from Boyd's whistle that jolted Branagh back to reality. He climbed to his feet and peered through the wild shrubs that hid him from the road. Dracht was already in place at one end of the gully, Armando da Gruta at the other.

'What is it?' Kathleen asked, waking beside him.

Branagh could hear the uneven beat of an engine. 'There's something on the road.'

Mulholland scrambled up to join them. 'Thank God for that, old stick. I know plenty of places I'd like these bones to be buried, and here isn't one of them.'

'It's a bus,' Branagh said. Through the screen of undergrowth and tree trunks he caught the sun reflecting off the cracked windshield. Light flashed in rapid succession on the row of windows.

'Let us hope this will answer our prayers,' Ngoça said anxiously.

Branagh looked at him curiously but said nothing.

It was ancient and noisy, belching noxious plumes of exhaust. A petrol-driven Bedford SB with a locally built body. The chrome on its snub nose had long been pitted to extinction and the peeling orange paintwork hung in tatters. Sacks of aid rice were stashed on the roof rack along with a chicken cage and a lone government soldier who appeared to be enjoying the view.

The bus rattled and bumped down into the gully, its spent suspension failing to keep its overloaded bodypan from scraping in the ruts. The driver changed down a gear and the bus sighed wearily, groaning in the attempt to drag itself back up the incline.

There was no warning.

A single shot took out the soldier on the bus roof. One moment he was there, smiling contentedly as the vehicle wobbled into the delicious cool of the gully. The next the force of the 9 mm round blew him backwards off his perch. He slid helplessly over the side, one foot snagging on the roof rail so that he swung limply like a carcass in a butcher's shop.

Armando da Gruta stepped out into the vehicle's path, feet planted firmly apart, hunched low over his M48 sub-machine-gun. His fixed grin was a mask as he opened up in full view of the driver. The frozen image of the man's horrified expression shattered to smithereens as a full magazine spat into the windshield and down the fly-clogged radiator to the front tyres. The black rubber shredded instantly, ripping round like a ragged catherine wheel until the front of the bus dropped. Its chrome fender gouged into the track, spraying stones and dust. The engine groaned its last as steam expired from the radiator with a long and mournful sigh.

Cries of panic were clearly heard as the passengers were pitched forward out of their seats. The chicken cage had fallen from the roof and smashed; its occupants looked around in a daze at their unexpected freedom. Anxious Mozambican faces peered out of the windows.

Da Gruta ran to the front passenger door and slid it open. '*Fora!*' he ordered.

No one moved. He repeated the command, pointing his gun at the nearest passenger. Reluctantly the woman gathered her young son to her side and climbed down the steps to the road. One by one the others followed.

They were a sorry sight. Some twenty people in all: men and women, young and old; babies and toddlers. Almost everyone clutched a bag of provisions. Branagh guessed that they had been returning from a village market. Bewildered and apprehensive they formed a line alongside the bus under the guns of Dracht and da Gruta. At their feet the newly freed chickens began to peck and claw around for something to eat, unconcerned.

Da Gruta's eyes flickered sideways at his boss. 'Nico?'

Dracht's voice was low. 'It has to be done.'

The two weapons exploded into action simultaneously in a stuttering outburst of fire. Branagh was stunned, his head ringing from the closeness of the awful sound; he stared, helpless, witness to the withering hail of bullets that cut through the standing row like a scythe through flowers. Only one woman managed to let out an ear-splitting scream of pure terror before it was abruptly snuffed out. She appeared to implode, collapsing in on herself in a crumpled heap. Yet, even as she lay twitching in her death throes, her cry continued to echo across the distant bushveld.

Branagh felt Kathleen's hand on his arm. He looked down to see her eyes, silently begging him for an explanation.

Ngoça recovered first from the shock. 'W-What in God's name have you done?' He broke into a run, racing to the nearest victim. It was a young girl of maybe seven years. He hugged her to him, oblivious of the fresh blood soaking into his shirt. Cradling the lifeless head against his chest he turned on Dracht. Tears carved lines through the dust on his cheeks as he tried to find the words. 'Why, why did you do this thing?'

Dracht snapped a fresh magazine into his AK. 'We don't want witnesses. If there are rumours of white men around, Frelimo will start pointing fingers at South Africa.' He looked at the carnage by his feet without emotion. 'They'll put this down to the bandits.'

Branagh said: 'Why not – you're no better than they are.' His initial disbelief had given way to a boiling anger. 'Are you going to add their ears to your trophy bag, too?'

Kathleen clutched his arm; she was still trembling with the shock of what she had seen. 'Leave it, Mike. He's quite capable of turning his gun on us.'

Armando da Gruta chuckled. 'Believe it,' he said, and pulled the hapless Frelimo soldier down from the roofrack.

The hunched figure of Ngoça rose from where he had laid the child in her mother's outstretched arms. Slowly he backed away and crossed himself. He looked at Dracht. 'Senhor Branagh is right. You are no better than Renamo.' His eyes bored into Dracht's. 'No, you are worse. Most of the *bandidos* are illiterate farmers, driven on by those they fear. Not you.'

'Spare me the crocodile tears,' Dracht said.

'I have a daughter the same age as that child. It could have been her.'

'But it wasn't,' da Gruta interrupted cheerfully.

Ngoça transferred his angry stare; he did not begin to understand these men. 'This was not meant to be how it was. I want no part of this.'

It was Dracht's turn to stare. 'You're goin' to have to grow a thicker skin than that if you're goin' to run a country.'

Ngoça frowned. He appeared to be in a trance, confused by his own emotions. 'Country? Whose country? I can see that such a country would not be mine. I was naïve to believe van der Walt's promises. Yes, I see that now.'

At the harsh rasp of the cocking handle, Ngoça looked up. He found himself staring into the business end of

401

Dracht's Kalashnikov. 'It's your country, Ngoça, whether you want it or not. Don't tell me you're willing to die for it already?'

Ngoça hung his head in shame. He knew the South African's words were true. He was not willing to die for his country, any country.

'Give him a chance,' Branagh said, placing a consoling arm around the Mozambican's shoulders. 'Can't you see he's cut up? Sure he's just realised what scum he's got himself involved with!'

Dracht's anger was on a hair-trigger. 'I won't tell you again, Irishman! Keep that blarney trap of yours buttoned. And be thankful that I need an engineer to keep those motors running. Otherwise you'd end up with the bus passengers!'

Anton Boyd appeared out of the vegetation. 'What's happening, Nico?' He stopped dead in his tracks. 'Kerist! I don't believe this.' His mouth fell open as he took in the bloody scene. His eyes moved quickly from corpse to corpse. He looked at Dracht. 'Only one soldier?'

'Don't you start,' his commander warned.

It was then that they all heard the faint crackle of static. A small disembodied voice squawked in Portuguese from the direction of the dead soldier.

'Damnation!' da Gruta cursed and dropped to his knee beside the corpse. He found the radio transceiver clasped in the rigid fingers of the man's right hand.

'Come in, Atansio, come in! Are you there? What's happened?'

The tinny voice died under the crunch of da Gruta's boot. 'The bastard must have been talking to the local garrison when we attacked.'

Dracht needed no spurring on. 'Right, we're against the clock now. They'll maybe send out a patrol to find out what's going on. Armando, get back to the jeeps. Bring the plastic tubing and the spare jerry cans. Take this fucking Irishman with you. Maybe some work will

402

take his mind off making trouble. Anton, you go too – keep the bastard covered at all times. I don't trust him.'

Any dissent Boyd might have felt about the massacre was overshadowed by the urgent need for survival. Once that bus was found by a government patrol, they could expect no mercy. He prodded Branagh into a run and the three of them set off for the jeeps.

It took twenty minutes to drain the bus of its fuel. The stuff didn't look good, contaminated by a sediment of dirt and rust particles. But it would have to do. As they waited in the lee of the kopje for the last jerry can to be loaded, the sound of an approaching vehicle was heard on the road.

'Time we weren't here,' Dracht said laconically, and swung himself into the back of the first Gaz alongside Boyd. Branagh gave Kathleen an unconvincing smile of reassurance before turning the ignition key. The engine fired half-heartedly, spluttered for a moment then fell into an uneasy rhythm. The tension evaporated noticeably. Now it was Mulholland's turn. He tried three times before giving the thumbs-up sign.

Dracht nudged Branagh in the back and the two vehicles headed off, side by side, across the bushveld in the direction from which they had come that morning.

They rejoined the laterite road towards the burnt-out river bridge, making good time. Soon they would be out of the government-held zone and heading for the sanctuary of the remote hills and a route to Torrola. Branagh's Gaz edged into the lead, Dracht standing in the rear, his shaggy blond mane whipped by the slipstream. He grasped the rollover bar with both hands like a tank commander as he scanned the horizon for signs of trouble.

A few minutes later he found it. Two truckloads of government troops and a command car were parked in zigzag formation across the road to create a checkpoint.

'SLOW!' Dracht yelled.

Branagh waited for the brakes to bind. 'What is it?'

'Roadblock,' Dracht replied tersely, crouching down in the rear. 'Don't stop or they'll come to us. Just continue forward nice and slow.'

Kathleen turned back to him. 'What are you going to do?'

He picked up one of the rocket launchers and grinned across at Boyd. 'We've brought these beauties all this way. Shame not to use them, eh?'

Boyd's returned smile was half-hearted. He'd seen enough slaughter for one day. But this was different. This was kill or be killed. He selected a bulbous high-explosive antitank warhead and screwed it into the rocket and sustainer motor before loading it into the second launcher. The four-pound warhead was capable of penetrating some fifteen inches of conventional steel.

The huge dust trail thrown up by the Gaz jeeps had already alerted those manning the roadblock. Frelimo troops stood expectantly in their trucks or spread out in an arc across the road. Fingers moved itchily onto safety catches, checking that their weapons were ready to fire. All had heard of the bus massacre; some had had relatives or friends on board. They were taking no chances. And were taking no prisoners.

Dracht and Boyd edged forward until the front-heavy warhead nose of the launchers rested on the rollover bar. Officially the effective maximum range was five hundred metres, but the weapons were notoriously inaccurate. Vulnerable to crosswinds. They must get closer. Against such odds there would be no second chance.

'Wave!' Dracht ordered. 'They'll see you're white – they'll wait. They'll be expecting bandits.'

Kathleen looked at Branagh. 'Surely we can't . . .?'

'Do it,' Branagh said quietly. 'There's enough of them to riddle our jeeps like colanders.'

Reluctantly she followed his example and waved amiably. The lead troops relaxed, lowering their weapons.

They were anxious to vent their anger on the *bandidos*, not some European technicians or aid workers.

Two hundred metres.

Dracht flicked up the optical iron-sight and grasped the two handgrips.

One hundred metres.

'NOW!' As Dracht shouted, both he and Boyd rose to their knees, the launchers on the rollover bar, zeroing in on the two trucks. The double detonation was deafening, jets of flame back-blasting from the rear venturi funnels as the rockets hurtled towards their respective targets.

The trucks went up simultaneously. Two massive fireballs ignited in unison, great tongues of fire spewing skyward, flaming bodies tossed into the air like human shrapnel. Secondary explosions shook the very earth as fuel tanks and ammunition blew, the shockwave of displaced air radiating out towards the approaching jeeps.

'HIT THE GAS!' Dracht screamed.

Branagh's foot went down on the pedal. The vehicle surged forward towards the scattered arc of foot soldiers who had been blown aside like ninepins by the shockwave. Dazed and reeling, they stumbled to their feet. Some saw the jeep bearing down on them, others didn't. Branagh pressed the horn. It didn't work. The soft thud and crunch of human flesh was heard from the blinding swirl of dust and oily smoke as the Gaz burst through the line. A soldier bounced onto the bonnet. For a moment the body stuck fast, a black face in a frozen deathmask staring at them through the fly-smeared screen. Then it was gone, whipped aside by some obstruction.

The smokescreen parted suddenly and they were through to the other side; the open laterite road stretched invitingly ahead. From behind them they could hear the urgent *ratatat* of da Gruta's M48 as he fired from the hip as the second Gaz followed through the roadblock, sweeping any remaining resistance aside.

As they sped on past the burnt-out bridge and continued west towards the hills, Branagh noticed that Kathleen's face had become quite ashen. She sat upright and immobile beside him, staring ahead into the middle distance. He understood. She had witnessed so much slaughter and horror in the short time she had been with him. Shock upon shock, giving her no time to recover. No time to adjust. A mental pounding that left the brain dazed and the senses numb. He wanted to reach out to her. Comfort her. But he knew there was nothing he could say that could make things better. She would have to come round in her own good time.

As they began the climb, the state of the road gradually deteriorated. Years of rains had washed away the surface gravel so painstakingly laid by previous generations of Mozambicans labouring for their Portuguese overseers. Now it was down to bedrock and the two Gaz jeeps were reduced to a crawl as they negotiated the deep ruts and dried-up rain channels. Steam began creeping from beneath the bonnet of the first vehicle as it struggled uphill.

Branagh pulled over and climbed out to inspect the engine. He was immediately engulfed in a hissing white cloud.

'What is it?' Dracht demanded.

'A hole in the radiator. Someone must have got a round off when we crashed the roadblock.'

'What can you do about it?'

Branagh shook his head. 'Not a lot without equipment. It needs replacing.'

'We can't stop here,' Dracht said, staring over the roadside precipice to the river valley far below.

'I can keep topping it up with whatever water we have. We might struggle on a few more miles.'

Dracht came to a decision. 'Do it.'

Branagh attempted a makeshift repair, stuffing the bullet hole with a piece of oily rag, while the commandos assembled their remaining fresh water supply. The

406

radiator drank it all greedily until they were down to one canteen among all of them.

Then they limped on. The track followed a tortuous course, winding steeply up into the rugged hills where only coarse grass and knobthorn trees survived. No sign of human habitation had been seen for miles when, as they negotiated another precipitous bend, the villa came into view.

'Villa' was an exaggeration, but despite its miniscule size there was no other appropriate description. Clinging to the steep mountainside, its rotted clapboard shape showed all the old Portuguese colonial style with paint-peeled balconies and archways. It was clearly one man's folly, an eccentric architectural statement in the middle of nowhere.

Dracht took Boyd and went on ahead, checking it out before beckoning the two jeeps to park by the shaded verandah. The engine of Branagh's vehicle died with a final asthmatic wheeze. As he climbed out a lizard scampered along the balustrade and disappeared into a festoon of overgrown bougainvillaea.

'A strange place,' Kathleen whispered, half-expecting the owner to appear at the door.

Branagh ventured inside. Apart from the accumulation of cobwebs and dust that had blown in through the shattered window panes, it could have been just as the occupants left it. A large living room, a bedroom and a kitchen, all fully furnished. There was a sun-starched yellow newspaper on the table and cutlery laid out for a meal. At the windows the fancy curtains disintegrated to the touch.

There were documents in the rolltop desk in one corner. They related to a diamond mining company.

'That's your answer,' Branagh said. 'A prospector whose wife insisted on all the home comforts. These documents are dated 1976. That's how it was then. Here one day, gone the next. The big Portuguese pullout.'

407

Da Gruta overheard them. 'We should never have done it. We should have stayed to fight those Communist bastards. My grandfather would have done it if he could. If anyone else had. So would I had I been in the position.'

'I thought you had been fighting them all these years,' Branagh said pointedly.

Da Gruta slumped in an armchair; dust billowed from the upholstery. 'Not from outside. We should have stayed on and fought instead of caving in. Lisbon betrayed us. They betrayed all this—' He waved his hand at the room. 'Some Portuguese miner went to all this trouble bringing civilisation to the interior, and what did he get for his pains? Most fled, except those like my father. Kowtowing and arse-licking.'

'Jorge was a realist,' Branagh said.

There was a burning anger in the Portuguese commando's eyes. 'My father was a coward. He had his chance and gave it all away. Not a thought for me and my inheritance. It was my birthright he gave away. *My* future.'

Kathleen said: 'But now you intend getting it back – your way.'

Da Gruta considered her words for a moment; he liked the sound of them. 'Yeah, my way. Like the song.' The strong white teeth flashed. 'It's the second time I've seen you in a civilised setting. You look good. This place suits you. You could do worse than throw in your lot with me.'

Kathleen gave a dry laugh. 'Is that a proposition, Armando?'

He puckered his mouth thoughtfully. 'Yeah, I guess it is. A life in the new *Boeretursland* would suit you. All the wealth you could want, a handsome husband . . .' Another smile.

She said sharply: 'You haven't *got* your land yet, Armando. All you've got is a dream, and I don't like what I've seen of it so far.'

Before he could respond Anton Boyd and Dracht

walked into the room followed by Mulholland and Ngoça.

'I've found a freshwater spring outside,' Boyd announced. 'Presumably that's why the house was built here. It solves one of our problems.'

'But not the other one,' Branagh interrupted. 'The vehicle I'm driving isn't going any further. It's had it.'

'Okay, okay,' Dracht said irritably, 'we'll work something out. Meanwhile I've got to talk to van der Walt. I haven't a bloody clue what's going on out there. Armando, get the MEL rigged, will you? We'll discuss everything else later.'

It was half an hour before Dracht and da Gruta returned from the verandah where they had been exchanging signals with Silvermine. Both men were grim-faced.

Boyd looked up anxiously. 'What is it? What's happened?'

'I don't believe it,' Dracht said. 'I just don't believe it.'

'Tell me,' Boyd implored.

But his commander wasn't in the mood to talk. He rooted in his rucksack until he found his brandy flask. He sat disconsolately in an armchair and helped himself to several swigs.

Da Gruta was left to explain. 'It looks like we're too late. That Frelimo flying column has reached Lichinga district capital from Cuamba. Apparently they had some British-trained Mozambicans who put up a helluva show.'

'You mean we've been carrying those blasted anti-tank weapons for nothing?' Mulholland complained.

'We'll still have use for them,' da Gruta assured. 'They say that the impetus of the *bandido* attacks has slackened off all over. Apparently there's confusion about the conflicting orders from the Renamo HQ.'

Dracht spoke at last. 'The bandit hierarchy are on to us – doing their best to stop the operation.'

Branagh almost smiled. It was somewhat satisfying to see the arrogant bastard cut down to size. But da Gruta's next words took the gloss off it: 'Our people have intercepted signals – there's a *bandido* search party closing on us.'

'Bollocks!' Dracht snorted in derision. 'It's a mistake. Those apes are the least of our worries. They haven't even got transport.'

Boyd looked at him, his concern deepening. He recalled the poker session on the *Jan Smuts* during the run-in. The claustrophobic atmosphere in the mess, his early assessment of Dracht's team. And remembered his words of warning to Armando da Gruta.

He repeated them quietly now: 'It doesn't do to get complacent, Nico. We haven't been making such fast progress ourselves.'

Da Gruta sneered. 'I told you he is bad juju, Nico.'

Dracht took another swallow of brandy. 'No, Armando, he's right. We mustn't get careless just because we're up against it. We've still got a lot to fight for. Van der Walt's afraid his international backers are going to get cold feet unless we make some progress fast. And that bloody Malawi colonel is refusing to launch his coup until he sees us installed over here.'

'So what are you going to do?' Mulholland asked.

Dracht rubbed thoughtfully at the blond stubble on his chin. 'Van der Walt wants us to get Ngoça to Lake Malawi where he can be picked up by motorlaunch. They'll arrange for him to make a radio broadcast, tell the Frelimo troops that he's ending the war and that they will be granted an amnesty if they surrender to advancing Renamo units.'

Boyd said: 'Isn't the problem that Renamo has stopped advancing?'

Dracht spared him a withering glance. 'We'll soon change that once we've delivered Ngoça. We've got key men like Brigadier Vaz who'll lead the way in surrendering

410

to the nearest bandits. They'll soon get the idea as the word spreads.'

Ngoça had been standing by the window, staring out across the valley as the sun sank rapidly into the orange furnace of the western sky. He had been morose and uncommunicative since the bus massacre; even now he appeared not to be listening. But it was a false impression. Suddenly he turned to face into the room. 'I will have no part of this.'

Dracht looked up. 'I beg your pardon?'

'I am finished with you. You and van der Walt. The whole thing. I will have no part of it.'

The South African's face hardened. 'We have a deal, Ngoça. And it was made perfectly plain to you – there's no get-out clause.'

Ngoça smiled gently. 'So what will you do – force me at gunpoint?'

'If necessary.'

Da Gruta stepped in. 'Look, things today got a bit out of hand. We were all on edge. Nothing like it will happen again.'

'It has already happened,' Ngoça said flatly. 'And what has been done cannot be undone. You cannot breathe life back into that child I held.'

Dracht rose to his feet. 'Don't waste your time Armando. We're taking him to Lake Malawi whether he likes it or not. He can argue the toss with van der Walt. We'll eat here, then we'll go.'

'We've only got the one vehicle now,' Boyd reminded.

'I've been thinking about that,' Dracht said. 'I think it's time to leave our passengers behind.'

It was then that Mulholland made his move. 'You can't trust Branagh and the girl. You know what he's like – he hates everything you stand for. That Frelimo safe zone is barely ten miles away. If you leave now he'll be there by morning. Telling them all about your plans.'

411

'Vincent, what are you saying?' Kathleen protested.

Branagh said evenly: 'He's just running true to form.'

The South African was bemused. 'Well, well, what have we here? Just what are you saying, Vincent? I told you, we've only the one vehicle now. We can't take the three of you any farther, even if we wanted to.'

Mulholland said brusquely: 'Get rid of them.'

Dracht was incredulous. 'What?'

'Negotiate them. Terminate – whatever your damn expression is. Kill them. I tell you they cannot be trusted.'

'You're probably right.' Dracht smiled uncertainly. 'So what makes you so sure I can trust you to keep your mouth shut?'

'Because I want to help you.'

'I don't need help from any aid worker, Vincent.'

Mulholland blinked. 'Aid worker? Whatever gave you that idea, old stick? I'm with the British intelligence service.'

Da Gruta laughed harshly. 'Pull the other one – old stick.'

Mulholland fished his wallet from the back pocket of his trousers and extracted a plastic identity card. 'Branagh and Kathleen Coogan are both wanted for terrorist activities connected with the Provisional IRA.'

'Christ!' Branagh protested. 'You've pulled some stunts before, Vincent—'

Kathleen paled, her mouth dropping open in amazement.

'I'd just caught up with them,' Mulholland went on rapidly, ignoring the Irishman's outburst, 'when the attack on Gutala began.'

Dracht stared down at the identity card with its sealed photograph in his hand; it looked authentic enough. 'And you want us to kill them? What's the idea?'

Mulholland said: 'You've heard how difficult it is to extradite these people and get a conviction. Especially as Branagh's crimes were committed some fourteen years ago. It would save my government a lot of trouble if they were to disappear. Permanently.'

412

Armando da Gruta chuckled. 'So little Miss Prim and Proper is a 'terr' – well, what d'ya know!'

Dracht's curiosity was getting the better of him. 'And what can you do for me?'

Mulholland's butter-wouldn't-melt smile returned. 'I can promise you a swift recognition of your new regime by the British government – as soon as Ngoça makes his broadcast. I'm not without influence in our Foreign and Commonwealth Office. There are those who would jump at any likely peace deal in Mozambique – especially with a respected man like Ngoça as president.'

A lazy smile broke on Dracht's face. 'That's some proposition you're putting down, Vincent.'

Mulholland raised his hand. 'There's more, Nico. If things don't work out as you plan, my people can offer asylum to you and everyone involved in this operation. You've said yourself you wouldn't be able to go back home. This way you'd get a new life. All paid for and guaranteed. You couldn't lose.'

Branagh read it in the South African commander's eyes. He'd swallowed it. Hook, line and bloody sinker. Mulholland knew who he was dealing with. Knew Dracht's type. He'd been working with Dracht's type all his life. Men like Branagh himself had once been; but he hadn't run true to form. Mulholland knew how to manipulate such men. He was a past master at it. Knew which nerves to touch, which hidden fears to play on. Branagh doubted Mulholland had any such plans to assist Dracht's scheme. He doubted his former controller any longer had the influence he once enjoyed. Not now that he was under investigation. Mulholland was fighting for his very survival. And now he had the opportunity to achieve it. And the means. A willing executioner. The evidence buried on the barren hillside in a remote corner of Africa where it would never be found.

It was now or never, Branagh decided. A moment's hesitation and it would be too late.

'An intriguing prospect . . .' Dracht was saying, warming to the notion.

But Branagh wasn't listening. His eyes darted surreptitiously round the room. Ngoça by the window, out of harm's way. Dracht standing and talking to Mulholland. His AK propped against an armchair, inches from his hand. Boyd sat in another chair, listening in silence as usual, an assault rifle cradled across his lap.

Mulholland said: 'You can get me in the jeep. One more won't make a difference.'

Da Gruta stood by the door on the other side of the room, his beloved M48 hanging in a loose grip by his side. That's it, Branagh decided.

'You've got yourself a deal,' Dracht said. 'I must have been soft even to think of letting the Irishman go.'

Branagh dived. He launched himself into the centre of the room in a forward roll. Head down, taking the weight on his hunched shoulders, legs up and flying to overtake his body. He landed on his feet in a crouched stance immediately in front of da Gruta. He straightened up like a rocket, his skull driving up under the commando's chin. He felt the jawbone against his head, felt it snap shut and saw the man stagger back. Branagh's hand was out, wrenching the M48 from his grasp, spinning around to face back into the room.

Dracht had moved with the speed of a leopard, recovering fast. Already he had his fingers around the trigger guard of the AK, pulling the weapon towards him.

Branagh swung up the M48, fumbling to find the unfamiliar safety-catch as he did so.

'FREEZE!' Boyd shouted.

Both men stopped in mid-movement, the two barrels pointing, fingers just millimetres from dispatching their deadly loads.

'Both of you – drop the weapons!' Boyd ordered, his AK wavering between the two of them.

'What is this, Anton?' Dracht demanded angrily.

'Shut it!' Boyd commanded. 'And put the AK down or you're dead meat.'

Dracht threw the weapon down in disgust. 'I had my doubts about you from the start.'

Boyd swung his assault rifle toward Branagh, careful to kick Dracht's weapon into a corner as he inched around it. 'And you, Branagh. Don't piss me about.'

The M48 clattered to the floor.

Armando da Gruta had recovered somewhat, gingerly testing his jaw with his fingertips. 'I told you the bastard was bad juju. Christ, I've got a loose tooth.'

'This is a mistake,' Mulholland said. 'No one's going to thank you for saving a couple of terrorists.'

'Shut up,' Boyd demanded. 'I don't give a toss who or what you say they are. I'm doing this for me as much as them. I want no part of this. No part in massacres like that bus this afternoon. And no cold-blooded executions.'

'You're a traitor,' Dracht snarled. 'Van der Walt will see that you pay for this. Interfering with a government mission.'

Boyd shook his head. 'A military intelligence mission, Nico. Nothing to do with government.' He paused. 'Anyway, what you do is up to you. I'm out, that's all.'

Dracht's eyes narrowed. 'You mean you're not going to stop us?'

Boyd sounded tired. 'No, Nico. You can take Armando and the jeep now. Get out of here. If you want to play silly buggers it's your lookout.'

'And Ngoça?'

The Mozambican was still dazed by the speed of events. 'I-I do not want to go with these men.'

'There's no point without him,' Dracht warned. 'Let him come and I'll make sure you get reunited with your wife and kid.'

Boyd waved his gun towards Ngoça. 'You go,' he said wearily. 'You're in no danger – too many people want you alive. If you want out, you tell van der Walt when you see him.'

Dracht smiled. 'You won't regret it, Anton.' He turned to Mulholland. 'What about you, Vincent, does your offer still hold good?'

'Of course, old stick.' But he looked angrily in Branagh's direction. 'If you can get me out of this place alive it'll be something.'

'No problem.'

Twenty minutes later Dracht started up the working Gaz, a sullen Ngoça sitting by his side. Da Gruta and Mulholland dumped their rucksacks in the cargo hold and climbed in after them. Boyd handed up a hessian sack.

'What's this?' da Gruta asked.

'Your weapons. Stripped down and the parts mixed up. Empty magazines and loose rounds,' Boyd said. 'Just in case you decided to change your mind and come looking for us. It should take you a while to sort that lot out.'

'Thanks a bunch.'

Boyd smiled. 'It was Branagh's idea. I don't think he trusts your new-found pal Mulholland.'

Da Gruta sneered and the Gaz jerked into motion, rocking through the potholes on its way up the hill towards Lake Malawi.

As it was swallowed up by the night Branagh said: 'Thanks, Anton. I'm glad you saw sense.'

Boyd grunted and looked at Kathleen. 'I didn't want to see the girl killed. Or you. I've got to know Dracht – he'd have done it. And I'm not sure I believed what Mulholland said about you.'

Kathleen smiled with relief. 'But did Dracht really believe we were terrorists?'

The commando turned back to the verandah. 'It wouldn't worry him one way or the other. Mulholland sounded pretty convincing. But it was his offer that appealed to Dracht. He'd believe it just because it suited him.'

Kathleen said: 'Well, just for the record it *isn't* true.'

'What happens now?' Branagh asked.

Boyd closed the door behind him. 'It's up to you. Despite what Mulholland said you had in mind, I wouldn't recommend returning to that government safe zone. Not after the bus and that roadblock we carved up. Personally I'll take my chances with the Malawi border.'

'How far is that?' Kathleen asked.

'Twenty-five miles.' He grinned. 'One day's hack if you're feeling energetic. Two to be realistic.'

Branagh said: 'It would be wiser to stick together.'

'Nico's got a head start,' Boyd said, 'but we could run into him. Best to be cautious. He could feel he's still got a score to settle.'

Branagh agreed. 'I'm certain Mulholland will feel the same way.'

'It's such a relief to be rid of them,' Kathleen said with feeling.

Boyd said: 'I suggest we leave at first light. From now on our troubles should be over.'

The bodies were laid out in a neat row at the side of the track. A Frelimo captain had his men wrap each one in a shroud purchased from the local village. He tried not to let his emotions show. He was a good soldier: honest, courageous and close to his men. In secret, he had great sympathy with their predicament. Government conscript soldiers were nearly all press-ganged into service. In the same way that Nelson's navy had recruited the drunk and unwary from the taverns in the port towns of England, government army units found their volunteers at cinema queues in the big towns.

Quite unsuitable some of them. Teachers who should have been teaching; medical students who should have been working with the sick; farmers who would have been better employed working the land. But in Mozambique you had to get who you could when you could. With the country in turmoil and almost the entire population on the move, it was nearly impossible to organise a fair method of conscription.

So, taken from their families and given rudimentary Soviet-style training, they were deployed to distant garrisons where they were underfed and infrequently paid.

No wonder they weren't winning this war, thought the captain as he surveyed the carnage of the roadblock. It was dark now, but still the wreckage of the trucks smouldered. His surviving troops stood around, watching with a mixed sense of awe and anger at who had done this thing.

Then he noticed the boy standing in the shadow at the side of the road. A young teenager dressed in torn denim trousers and a T-shirt.

The captain beckoned. For a moment the boy hesitated, then approached uncertainly.

'Who are you, boy?'

'Benjamin Matusi,' the teenager replied shyly.

The captain noticed the dull look in his eyes. So many people wore that expression nowadays – as though their spirit had been broken and their very soul destroyed by the sights they had seen. 'You are not from these parts?'

'I am seeking my family. They were taken from our village.'

'*Bandidos?*'

'Who else?' He nodded at the wreckage. 'Did *bandidos* do this?'

The captain frowned. 'Since you ask, no.' He reached into his command car and fetched out a can of beer and a can of orangeade. He offered the latter. 'You must be thirsty if you've been travelling.'

'*Obrigado*.' The boy yanked the pullring and drank greedily.

'There was an attack on a bus just ten miles from

here,' the captain said, pleased to share a confidence with a stranger of no consequence. 'A massacre. It was assumed to be *bandidos*. Then shortly after, this happened.'

Bejamin Matusi wiped his mouth with the back of his hand. 'How do you know *matsangas* did not do this?'

'I saw them. They were Europeans.' He looked up at the first stars of the night, identifying the four-pointed diadem of the Southern Cross. 'You hear these stories of South African commandos – yet I've never met anyone who has seen them. I think one of them was a woman. Strange that. But it all happened so quickly.'

The boy's eyes flickered with sudden interest; a stirring of life in the face of a zombie. 'When did this happen?'

'In the late afternoon.' Wearily.

'Which direction did they go?'

'West to the hills . . .' the captain caught himself. 'You ask many questions for one so young? What interest is it of yours?'

A shrug. 'I am only interested in finding my family.'

The captain smiled. He pointed down the road to the east. 'If you walk ten miles along here you will find a village. They will give you food and shelter. It is a safe zone. Ask there about your family. You really should not be out here at all. It is dangerous for anyone, especially a small boy.'

An answer did not come. The captain turned. The boy had vanished into the night.

Benjamin Matusi walked for a mile into the bush until he found the upside-down tree. A massive trunked baobab with short, rootlike branches beneath which he had hidden the black motorcycle.

He took a radio transmitter from his pannier and made several attempts before he found himself speaking to the leader of the column for which he was acting scout. Chande was pleased with his achievement.

His duty done, the boy spread out his bedroll. He lay back and looked up to the stars as the Frelimo captain had done. For a moment his eyes searched and found the constellation that Mikey Branagh had once pointed out to him. Lupus. The wolf, hunting in the vastness of African sky. How bright it was tonight. An appropriate omen.

In the morning, when the sun was at a low angle, he would follow the tracks to the west.

Then he was asleep, his fingers clutched around the cold gunmetal of his Kalashnikov assault rifle.

15

All day long Chande's column marched without a break, hard on the heels of their motorcycle scout.

Maraika strove not to fall behind, pounding one footstep after another, her load balanced on her head, her mind in a trance. In turn, visions of the three boy soldiers, her dead father and Benjamin Matusi revolved ghostlike before her eyes. Tears trickled unbidden down her cheeks in a constant flow like a spring stream.

'Maraika, are you all right?'

The sudden voice at her side caught her by surprise. It was the carpenter from Tumbo.

'Francisco, you shouldn't be talking to me.'

He fell in step beside her. 'I heard what happened to you last night. The *bastardos*! I should like to kill them all. I am sorry.'

'It is past.'

'I am sorry if they hurt you.'

'A woman's body is made to take a man. All they can hurt is my mind. I will not let them hurt my mind.' But even as she spoke she knew that they had.

'I am fearful they will do it again,' Francisco said earnestly. 'They take any woman of their fancy as if it is their right.'

Maraika lowered her voice. 'They will not do it again.'

'You can't be certain.'

'I can – tonight I shall escape.'

The carpenter was horrified. 'It's too dangerous. I know. I have been taken by the *bandidos* before. That is how I lost my ear. The camp will be guarded – if they catch you, you will be killed or mutilated – you know what they do to women.'

She shuddered at the very thought. 'I *have* to do it, Francisco. My brother is out there ahead of us. He is looking for Mikey Branagh.'

'What can you do?'

'I don't know. Find him, warn him.'

The carpenter glanced over his shoulder. As he had sensed, one of the bandit officers, unhindered by a pack to carry, was striding down the column. Francisco slowed his pace, dropping back from Maraika.

'Was that man bothering you?' The scar-faced officer called Sergio was at her side.

'No, sir. He was just asking after my wellbeing.' She looked sheepish. 'After last night.'

Sergio grunted. 'Well he needn't concern himself. It will not happen again. I will look after you. You will spend tonight in my care.'

She opened her mouth to protest, but he was gone. He strode forward up the line, lashing freely at the porters who were falling behind. Glumly she walked on.

As the blood-red sun set the clouds aflame in the western sky, the column found itself beyond the tea plantations. Now they were in the hills overlooking a river valley. Far below, Maraika saw the meandering silver snake of water and the burnt-out piles of a wrecked bridge. On the far side of the valley, high up beside a precipitous track, the last vestiges of sunshine dazzled on the windows of a building, hurting her eyes. It was a strange and remote place to see a villa, she thought.

But she was allowed no time to wonder. Their leader Chande selected a flattish area of dense thorn and posted his guards on the perimeter and lookouts on some of the peaks which dominated the valley. Then the women were divided into two parties, one to collect wood and light a cooking fire, the others to prepare the food.

Maraika was selected for the former and used her time picking branches to get an idea of the lie of the land and to find a route of escape. She overheard someone say there were two government villages down there, somewhere in the valley. She would make for those. Perhaps that was where Branagh was. Despair pressed down on her. Or was he in the hills? The truth was, she realised, that she did not know where she was, let alone Mikey Branagh. He could be anywhere.

Later, as she carried her heavy bundle of wood back to the thorn bushes she came across Francisco again.

'Are you still planning this madness?' he asked.

'Sssh!' She glanced around at the other women, but no one was paying attention. 'Yes – I will go tonight.'

'I will help you. You will need my help.'

She hesitated. 'If you are sure?'

'I am sure. Your courage makes me feel ashamed.'

'Ashamed? Not you of all people. Mikey used to say you had the heart of a lion.'

'Then I should fight like a lion. I will help you escape, then I will seek out and join the *Napramas*.'

She had heard of the strange religious cult, led by a man who claimed to have returned from the dead and to be possessed by the spirits of his ancestors and Jesus Christ. He led an army of followers armed only with knives and bows and arrows, yet they were reported to have struck terror into local Renamo groups. She remembered Mikey being both amused and impressed when he heard the increasing stories of their success. 'It's not all juju, Maraika. Because the *Napramas* believe vaccinations will turn bullets to water doesn't mean they hang around to test the theory. Someone's using pretty effective tactics. The important thing is, this is ordinary Mozambicans standing up for themselves.'

She said to the carpenter: 'I think Mikey would be proud if you joined them. I would be proud of you, dear Francisco. You are good with a bow and arrow.'

That irrepressible smile returned; the first time she had seen it on the march. 'Do you have a plan?' he asked.

'There is a gully at the bottom of the slope. An old riverbed,' she replied. Without watches or other means to tell the time it was going to be a hit and miss affair. 'Meet me there if you can. After everyone is asleep.'

'I will be there.'

She walked away from him, catching up with the other women. While she helped light the fire and keep it hot for the cooking pots she avoided the officer Sergio whenever he loitered close by. Time and again she sensed his eyes on her, boring into her back. She busied herself with a vengeance.

But after the bandits and the porters had been fed he at last managed to corner her.

'Are you avoiding me, Maraika?'

'No, sir.' Indignant. 'I have so much work to do and now I am exhausted.'

'Then come with me and rest.'

'I can rest here where I sit. I am almost asleep now.'

A hard edge crept into Sergio's voice. 'And do you relish being raped again by those wild louts? Next time you might not be so lucky. I have seen what they have done to some of the women . . . So come with me.'

With weary reluctance she climbed to her feet and followed him to a quiet spot surrounded by scrub. His bedroll was open on the ground.

'The grass is soft here,' he said and sat down, taking her hand. 'Come closer, I will not bite.'

She sat on the edge of the bedroll, her arms wrapped defensively around her knees.

'I couldn't help seeing you last night,' he said as he rolled a cigarette paper in his hand, filling it with ganja tobacco. 'You have a beautiful body. Very slim and muscular. Not to every man's taste, but I like it.'

'I work hard,' she muttered and keeled gently over, gathered in a tight ball like a hedgehog. 'I must sleep.'

She felt his hand, light on her buttocks. 'I am not like those boys, Maraika.'

'Am I expected to comfort you?' she mumbled into her arms.

'Only if you want to.'

'Maybe tomorrow night. I am tired now.'

She heard his sigh of disappointment and smelled the sickly aroma of his tobacco. He said: 'We have all done well today. Chande will be proud of us. Your young brother, too, does well. They say he is close to finding those South African commandos.'

But she hardly heard his words before sleep dragged her down, a heavy pressure on her eyelids. Into a nighttime world of bizarre shapes and forms, a sea of tormented black faces screaming and pleading from a fiery pit. Like a Malangatana mural. Hands frantically reaching out for help. And she could not move to help them.

She awoke to the stroke of Sergio's hand. Her eyes opened. It was pitch black; the fires were out and only the sound of snoring mixed with the nocturnal chatter of the cicadas. The hand began to knead her breast. She cursed silently; she had been hoping to slip away while he slept.

'Sir? What is it?'

'You know what, Maraika.' His voice was slurred; she assumed it was the ganja. 'I want you.'

She rolled quickly over to face him, her decision made. 'I understand – can I call you Sergio?' He nodded, smiling gently. 'You have been kind to me. Lie back and let me make *amor*.'

'Like a whore?'

'If it pleases you.'

She put her hand on his chest, easing him down onto his back. Hitching her dress around her thighs she sat astride him, feeling the hardness of his arousal against her groin. Her fingers plucked at the buttons of his shirt, played lightly on his skin like a butterfly, finding a nipple and squeezing it hard until he groaned in pleasure.

'Shut your eyes, Sergio, and let me do all the things to you you've always wanted.'

Again she squeezed and twisted; again he moaned. Unaware that her left hand was scrabbling in the grass at the side of the bedroll. Locating the webbing belt. Searching and finding the worn canvas scabbard. Her right hand slid down over his belly. The muscles contracted involuntarily at the electricity of her touch. As the fingers of one hand closed on his genitals, the fingers of her other closed round the wooden haft of the panga.

'Yes—' he gasped, driven to the edge of ecstasy.

He felt the pressure stop. His eyes opened. She was looking down at him, both hands raised high above her head. He noticed her eyes, wide and filled with fear. The panga plunged. He glimpsed only the gleam of its blade as it fell with all the strength she could muster behind it.

Blood splattered bright and warm on her thighs as the steel sliced into his abdomen, just below his breastbone. It slid in without resistance until the tip met with the earth beneath him. His eyes stared at her, his mouth contorted in an unasked question. A red froth escaped his lips. He was quite, quite still.

Her whole being trembled as she raised her leg and dismounted. Confusion and terror at what she had done numbed her brain. It refused to work. She sat sobbing at the dead man's side, waiting for some sense and clarity to return to her thinking. Anxiously she glanced around. A few metres away a man still snored, oblivious of what had happened while he slept. Somewhere someone coughed. Then all was black and still.

Aware only of her heart thudding in her chest, she reached over the dead man and picked up his assault rifle. Even the touch of it terrified her; she had no clue how to use it. But it seemed a good idea to take it. Francisco would know.

She stole into the night. In the darkness everything

426

was unfamiliar. Nothing seemed the same as it had in daylight when she had planned the route of her escape. Thorn branches tore at her skin, ripped at the tattered remnants of her red dress. She stumbled on, once almost stepping on a sleeping bandit before she realised what it was.

The ground began to fall away, she sensed the steepening gradient. Jagged rock grazed the soles of her bare feet as she tried to prevent herself from falling. She paused, straining to hear half-imagined sounds. Something flapped eerily overhead and she winced, ducking sharply. It was the spirit of the man she had just murdered. Her teeth began to chatter and she fell to the ground, protecting her head with her hands.

No, no, a voice screamed in her head. Mikey Branagh would laugh at you now. A silly village girl. It was only a bat, an owl or a nightjar.

She forced herself on, now aware of the quiet mumble of voices some distance ahead. Her heart resumed its drumbeat, blood rushing in her ears so that she could scarcely hear anything but the sound of her own body.

A rustling noise. Dead ahead. She stopped, straining to see into the utter blackness.

'Maraika!' It was Francisco, his voice low and hoarse. 'Over here.'

Relief ebbed through her. She stepped quickly across the stones that marked the gully floor. The carpenter's shape took form in the inky gloom, the glimmer of the high moon lighting the planes of his face and body.

'I am so glad to see you,' she breathed.

He pulled her roughly to him, placing his hand across her mouth. 'Do not talk,' he whispered. 'There are *bandido* guards ahead.'

She lifted the Kalashnikov and he took it. It was a relief to be rid of it.

'It is good you bring this, but it will alert everyone. Can you run?'

She grinned. 'Just watch me. I will run like the wind from this place.'

He smiled back at her, motioned her to wait and melted into the night, inching his way forward in the under-growth until he had the two bandit guards in view.

She waited, her nerves jangling, jumping at each small sound of nocturnal wildlife. The faint mumble of voices still carried from somewhere down the gully. A sudden laugh; a joke shared.

And then the noise. Two short sharp whipcracks in close succession. A sudden shuffling movement. The voices had ceased.

'Maraika! Quick!'

She sprang forward. slipping and sliding blindly on the loose pebbles, ignoring the pain in her feet. The walls of vegetation closed in on both sides of the gully as it nar-rowed.

A distant voice called out from way back at the camp. A whistle blasted. Fear spurred her on, her legs pounding over the rough streambed floor, faster and faster. Sweat broke out on her back, soaking the thin stuff of her dress.

She ran straight into him, almost knocking him off his feet. .

'Steady, Maraika!' he hissed. 'Don't panic. Come with me.'

She stared down with morbid curiosity as she edged past the bodies of the guards. They had died hugging like children in their desperation to comfort each other. She shuddered and walked on, Francisco taking her by the hand to half lead and half drag her down the steep-ening slope. Scree gave way underfoot, cascading ahead in a miniature avalanche. The bright clink of stones sounded deafeningly loud in the stillness of the night.

More whistles blew, still far away, but closer than they had been. Far pinpricks of light could be seen amidst the thorn scrub behind them. Voices shouted, the words muted by distance. It seemed as though the entire camp were after them.

Francisco gave up all pretence of caution now, slipping and sliding down the gully at an ever faster rate.

'Francisco!' Maraika yelled suddenly.

He skidded to a halt, dislodging a welter of stones.

The three bandits emerged from the bush just metres ahead. They stood and gawped, AKs hanging slackly in their grasp. It was impossible to determine who was the most surprised.

The moon's glimmer was enough for Maraika to recognise them. Perhaps it was their stance, their attitude – she just *knew* it was the three boy bandits who had raped her. Her heart sank.

Francisco fired straight from the hip. The thunder of the exploding rounds right next to her made her jump and she watched with stunned fascination as two of the bandits were blasted out of sight. Then she heard the metallic bite of the hammer falling on an empty breech. Simultaneously the muzzle flash of the surviving bandit's AK dazzled her. She ducked instinctively, and as she did she was aware of the sudden weight against her back. Turning her head she found herself looking into Francisco's eyes. There was a sadness in them, almost disappointment.

'Run,' he gasped. 'Run for your life . . .' His words faded, and she saw that his last breath had been speckled with blood.

She staggered to her feet. The oldest of the boy bandits stood unsteadily, watching to see which of the targets he had hit. There was a gleam of triumph in his eyes.

Recognition slowly dawned. 'You!' he hissed.

The stone hit him squarely in the face. He dropped his weapon and fell to his knees, his hands to his face in an attitude that could have been mistaken for shame. As he began to wail she pushed past him and ran on down the gully. Faster and faster.

Faster than she had ever run in her life. She didn't stop for a moment. All she knew was that she had to get as far away as possible. So far that they would never find her.

Branagh awoke at dawn.

It took a moment to orientate himself. The tiny hillside villa. The bedroom with the covers made up just as they must have been the day the owners left; the material mildewed and rotted, falling apart to the touch.

He raised himself on one elbow. Kathleen Coogan was lying contentedly beside him, the raw early light from the window playing along the arched spine of her naked back.

So it had been no dream. It had happened. The release of tension the previous night had been an unburdening. With Dracht and Mulholland gone, the three of them had suddenly become different people. Boyd had produced a hipflask of whisky from his rucksack and all three had shared its contents. It was the sense of freedom that had been heady, not the meagre quantity of spirit. It was as though the air itself were intoxicating. They had shared jokes; almost everything seemed ridiculously amusing. From being an avowed enemy, Anton Boyd had become a friend as they realised he had been as trapped by circumstances as they had themselves.

Branagh had taken the first four-hour stag, leaving Kathleen in the bedroom and Boyd snoozing in an armchair. He had later woken the South African, then lain beside the slumbering girl. But as he lay there, staring at the ceiling, sleep refused to come. Then he felt her hand on his chest. A movement in her unconscious, he thought. But when he looked he saw that her eyes were open, watching him.

'I'm so happy,' she whispered, and leaned across and kissed him.

That was it. Something in him perversely wanted to

resist, but he felt powerless. He didn't have to move as she knelt and crouched over him, cupped his face in her delicate hands and began to devour his mouth with her own. Such a small creature, yet the intensity of her passion shocked him. She made the running, stripping herself and then him. Running her hands over his body, exploring with an erotic curiosity.

Then she'd laughed mockingly. 'It's all right, Mike. Really. I've wanted you ever since I first arrived at Tumbo.' A giggle. 'In fact I think I've wanted you ever since I've known you – but in those days I didn't know what the feelings meant.'

His resistance crumbled then and he took her with an urgency he had not known before. Almost a frenzy. It was an animal need that drove her to convulse and gasp in response, digging her fingernails deep into his shoulder blades.

A knock on the door disturbed his memories of the night. 'Time to make a move,' Boyd called.

Branagh heard her stir. He sat up, moved to the edge of the bed and pulled on his denims. He found Boyd on the verandah, tending his naphtha stove.

'There's a brew on,' the South African explained unnecessarily. 'About five minutes.'

Branagh nodded and walked round to the back of the villa where once there must have been a vegetable garden. Water tinkled cheerfully over a narrow streambed which fed down from the hills. He splashed the cold liquid over his face and torso then looked out over the valley.

It was a breathtaking vista, even in the steely pre-dawn light. The surrounding hills floated like disembodied islands above the valley mist. The air was still crisp and invigorating, as yet unwarmed by the sun that struggled to clear the eastern peaks.

This was Maraika's land, not his. He had tried to make it his. Had fooled himself into believing it was his. All this time and he hadn't seen it. Or hadn't wanted to. What was it Mulholland had said? 'Atoning for his sins?'

Perceptive that. But then Mulholland always had been a perceptive bastard.

He had come to Africa to pay penance. If it hadn't been Africa it would have been some other remote and godforsaken part of the world. Where he could use the few skills he had. Except for the one thing he had always done best. Killing people.

He had come to hide from his past. From the dirty war. From Mulholland. But most of all from himself. Maraika had been a bonus. A blessing that made it all seem right. But he knew, too, that he could only love her in Africa. And he no longer belonged. He had begun to realise that from the very moment Kathleen had set foot on the airstrip at Tumbo.

This was Maraika's land. It had delivered her up to him as an emaciated and frightened twelve-year-old refugee. And it had taken her from him again without warning. It was the way of Mozambique. He was under no illusion that he would ever see her again. If she wasn't already dead, she would die of cholera or starvation in the forbidden Renamo zones. Or die in the attempt to escape. Die of syphilis or Aids as a forced camp prostitute. Or die on the endless bandit porter trails that crisscrossed the land.

The tragedy was that there was nothing he could do to find her. However resourceful, no one man could hope to trace her in a terrorist-infested country almost half the size of western Europe, without roads or communications, and expect to come out alive. Let alone have a hope of success.

Only if she were exceedingly lucky might Maraika one day turn up in one of the refugee camps in Malawi or Zimbabwe. One day.

And if she did, what could he offer her? More false hope and more false promises. Kathleen had been right;

in truth he'd treated her no better than a whore. Never told her or himself that they had no future beyond the compound walls of Tumbo. She deserved better than that. Love was not enough, and he realised now that it never had been.

It was time to confront his own past now. Whether she had intended to or not, Kathleen had shown him that. And Mulholland had shown him that he couldn't run away. Had it not been for Boyd's timely intervention, his failure to face up to his past had almost cost Kathleen's life as well as his own.

His mind was made up. It was time to go home.

Slowly he walked back to the verandah where Boyd handed him two mugs of coffee. He took them through to the bedroom. Kathleen was sitting up on the cushions; she made no attempt to hide her nakedness.

'We'll make tracks as soon as you're ready,' he said. 'The spring water's cold but clean if you want a splash.'

'I'm not sure I want to wash.' She smiled impishly. 'I smell of you.'

He sipped at the coffee. 'About last night . . .'

Her hair was tousled; her eyes very dark and clear. 'I hope you're not going to apologise.'

He smiled awkwardly. 'No – I think it was something we both wanted. But—'

'But?'

'I've decided I'm going home.'

She frowned. 'You told me this was your home now.'

'I'm not sure any more.'

She peered at him over the rim of the mug. 'I'm pleased you're coming back. And last night – with me – that decided you?'

'Something like that.'

'And the but?'

He stared at the cobwebbed ceiling for inspiration. How could he say it without sounding presumptuous or crass, or both? 'I don't know what the future holds. If it holds anything at all.'

'Who does? I know that.' Her eyes glistened and she stretched out her hand, taking his and drawing him towards the bed. 'Come here, you lovely man. I want you to know that everything with you feels just right. You might still think of yourself as cradle-snatching, but it's not our fault we were born a generation apart.'

He wanted her again then, that moment. Wanted to bury his head between the almost translucent marble skin of those small pert breasts. Kiss the downy hair of her belly. Sink his past and his future hopes between her lean flanks.

She said: 'You might not like it back in the Six Counties, or even in the South. Times change, people change.'

'It's possible,' he murmured, then said wistfully: 'The funny thing is for years now I've believed I'd die here in Africa.' He grinned at her. 'Buried at the foot of one of those great baobab trees.'

She laughed, sharing his mood and huddling close, playing her lips along his shoulder. 'When I was small,' she said, 'you always told me there was a world away from all the troubles in Armagh. Ironic really; I almost feel as if I'm dragging you back.' She hesitated. 'Perhaps we should both listen to your advice. Travel a bit. Maybe see how we get along?'

He nodded. 'First we've got to get out of here. And Boyd will be wondering what we're playing at.'

'Let him,' she laughed and climbed off the bed, searching for where she'd cast her clothes. As she dressed she said: 'Sure I can't tell you how glad I am that I found you. I'll let you into a secret . . . You won't be cross?'

'Try me.'

'Over the years I began to believe what my brothers said about you. Especially young Joseph. He got mixed up with the local Provies and he was so convinced you' . . .'

'I'd what?' It was so easy to lie.

She shook her head suddenly. 'No it doesn't matter.' Perhaps, he thought, she too knows how easy it is to lie. 'There's no way you'd have done the things he said you'd done. I know that now. You'd have to have been a monster. Someone like Dracht.'

'That's a thought,' he said quietly.

It was another twenty minutes before they were ready to set off in the same direction that the others had gone in the Gaz the previous evening. Without the oppressive presence of Dracht and da Gruta and with the sun beginning to warm their backs, the walk was actually enjoyable.

Yet neither man was prepared to let down his guard. Already they found they shared the professional camaraderie of old soldiers. Boyd had removed the AK47 that had belonged to Drummond from Dracht's armoury and given it to Branagh. He had also given Kathleen his Spanish automatic pistol and had watched with surprise as she had checked the breech and magazine like an expert.

'Was Mulholland telling the truth?' he had asked jokingly. 'About you being a terrorist?'

She didn't find it funny. 'No, Anton, but my brothers are paramilitaries. They taught me how to use a gun when I was fifteen. In case our farm was subject to a sectarian attack by the Proddies or an undercover Army unit.' She noticed Branagh's expression. 'Sorry, Mike, I meant nothing by it.'

He steered away from the subject. 'Mulholland rarely tells the truth, Anton. At least you'll never have to learn that the hard way.'

'But he is with the British intelligence service?'

'Is or was.'

'And you worked with him – as some sort of agent?'

435

'Special Forces, similar to you.'

Boyd nodded. 'I thought as much by the way you handled yourself back at the villa. You must have really upset that guy Mulholland for him to want you dead.'

'No comment,' Branagh said, and Boyd had accepted his answer without further question.

They had travelled about five miles when they came across the Gaz. It had been abandoned in the middle of the track, its door left hanging open.

'Careful,' Boyd warned. 'There could be bandits around.'

They told Kathleen to stay back while they approached cautiously, one on each side of the dirt road. Some fifty metres from the rear of the jeep, Branagh stopped.

He pointed to a round hole in front of the vehicle. It was some twelve inches in diameter and had been dug at the bottom of a hard-baked wheel rut in the track. The disturbed soil was darker than the surface earth, the sun not yet having fully dried it out. 'Mine?'

Boyd nodded. 'I reckon. They were lucky to spot it in the headlamp beam. But Dracht has an uncanny sixth sense about these things.'

They moved on, Boyd walking backwards, both men arcing their weapons as they advanced, covering a full three sixty degrees between them. Nothing stirred at the trackside. Boyd kept watch while Branagh peered into the vehicle.

'No sign of bullet holes. It doesn't look like an ambush.'

Boyd motioned ahead, farther up the track. It was another recently excavated hole. 'That could be our answer. More mines. They decided it was quicker to go on foot at night than risk manoeuvring through a field. Looks like they took the mines with them.'

A thought occurred to Branagh. 'Dracht wouldn't be waiting for us?'

Boyd shook his head. 'He might want to – he doesn't trust me or you. Ideally he'd prefer us dead. But his priority is to get Ngoça to where he can do some good. To be honest that's why I let them take Ngoça last night. Not very Christian—' he smiled ruefully '—but I've not much sympathy for scheming politicians. I reckoned he'd be safe enough.'

Branagh beckoned Kathleen to join them, then checked the rear cargo hold of the Gaz. 'The rocket launchers have gone.'

Boyd edged towards some flattened grass at the track-side where the hill fell sharply away to the valley. 'They slung them down there somewhere – in case they fell into the wrong hands.'

'Could we make use of this jeep?' Branagh asked. 'The mines wouldn't be such a problem in daylight, now that we know what we're looking for.'

'Depends if you want to make for somewhere in Mozambique? If you two are coming with me I'd prefer to keep away from the roads . . .' His voice trailed off. 'Wait a moment, let me take a look at something.'

He dropped to his knees and peered beneath the chassis, then reached out and pulled something free.

'What is it?'

Boyd held up the plastic cigarette lighter. 'The bastard. Just the cheapest home-made bomb known to man. Dracht's favourite trick.'

'What do you mean?' Kathleen asked.

'Tape a lighter to the exhaust pipe,' Boyd explained. 'Underneath the petrol tank. The lighter heats up and ignites. If the vehicle's tank is full it'll catch light. If it's half-empty it'll explode in a fireball. Had we travelled in it we wouldn't have had a chance. The bastard.'

'Couldn't he have booby-trapped it against bandits?' Kathleen suggested.

'Why should he? They're supposed to be on South Africa's side. Besides he was in a hurry. He did it because he knew we'd be following up the track sooner or later, and he wants me dead.'

Branagh stared at the innocuous lighter in Boyd's open palm. It was a sudden revelation, like stepping back into his own personal history. The lighter may have been a favourite trick of Dracht's, but someone else knew all about it. Someone had often promoted its use in Ulster when a killing was wanted to look like the work of the embryonic paramilitary movements of the early seventies. He could see the smiling lips now as they suggested the idea between sips of claret. The smile of the fat cats. The untouchables.

'It wasn't meant for you, Anton.' He saw it with clarity now. 'It was meant for Kathleen and me.'

'How d'you reckon that?'

'Because you wouldn't have been in the jeep. As you've just pointed out, it's only of any use if you're going somewhere in this country. Dracht knows you'll make for friendly territory. And the only country friendly with South Africa is Malawi. You'd hack it on foot and he knows it.'

Kathleen frowned. 'You mean this was Mulholland's idea?'

Branagh smiled without humour. 'It would have solved his problem of getting rid of me. And Kathleen – he can't know how much I've told you.'

She shook her head. 'I can't believe that.'

'He was happy enough to have us both killed yesterday. It's the typical Vincent approach. Always hands-off. Get someone else to do the dirty work for you.'

Boyd said: 'Then you're well shot of him.'

Branagh reached his second major decision of the morning. And the ease with which he made it sent a shudder of apprehension down his spine. 'I'm going to do exactly that. I'm going to get shot of him. Once and for all.'

'You're crazy,' Kathleen said. 'It's madness.'

'It's not madness, Kathy, it's the only way. I know Vincent. It's now twice he's tried to have us killed. He won't rest until he succeeds. If I go back to the UK or to

Ireland he'll be sure to know about it. He's plugged into the system. He's paranoid that I will give evidence against him.'

'Evidence?' Boyd asked.

'It's a long story, but I could have him put behind bars, or more likely dismissed in disgrace. He'd be a useful scapegoat for the others like him.'

Kathleen looked at him keenly. 'And would you give evidence if you could?'

'I would after this, yes.'

Boyd was puzzled. 'But if he's under some sort of investigation how could he be a threat to you?'

Branagh laughed bitterly. 'How come he's in Mozambique? He's resourceful, he's got contacts. He's part of the secret Establishment. He can call in favours. There are plenty of people willing to plant a bomb or pull a trigger if you know where to look. And Vincent knows exactly where to look.' He shielded his eyes from the sun and gazed out across the valley. 'Well if it would suit him to deal with me here – away from prying eyes – it suits me even better.'

Kathleen said: 'I don't believe this is you talking, Mike.'

'Nor do I. I thought I'd left this sort of thing behind. A long time ago.'

Boyd said: 'There are three of them.'

'I'll take my time. I only want Vincent. Will you take Kathy with you? See she gets safely to a hotel some-where?'

'Mike – you can't!' Kathleen protested. 'Not alone.'

The South African looked uncertain. 'She's right. You're no match for them. I'd like to help you, Branagh, but if it means killing Dracht, or even Armando – oppos, I don't know . . .'

Kathleen turned to him. 'Aren't you in a similar posi-tion, Anton? Won't Dracht make life difficult for you if you go back to South Africa? You know so much.'

439

'You heard him promise—' Boyd began. Then he grinned lopsidedly. 'That sounds pretty dumb, doesn't it? Believing Dracht's promises.'

'So?' Branagh pressed.

Boyd stroked his shaggy auburn moustache. 'We go after them together.'

16

'C'mon, you two,' Armando da Gruta exhorted in near desperation. With one foot raised on a rock, he leaned on his thigh and fanned his face with his bush hat.

Dracht waited impatiently, staring down the steep escarpment they had just climbed. 'A couple of bloody old women,' he agreed.

It was Mulholland who came into view first, red-faced and panting as he negotiated the boulder-strewn slope.

He stopped to gulp a lungful of air and looked back down at the climb he had just made. The river valley where the attack on the roadblock had taken place was now far distant, blurred by the midday heat haze.

'Do we have to go over these bloody mountains, old stick,' he gasped. 'Can't we just walk round them like any sensible human being?'

'It's quicker going straight over the top,' da Gruta replied without sympathy. 'We're in a hurry.'

Mulholland looked down as Ngoça appeared, stumbling like a drunkard. 'It might be quicker if you're used to it. I think chummy here's about to have a cardiac arrest.'

Da Gruta looked at Dracht. 'He's got a point, Nico. The *kaffir*'s no good to us dead. Should we take five?'

The South African was in a bad mood. 'I'm not stopping on this bare-arsed rock. There's more cover about a mile farther on. We'll stop there—'

They all heard it. They could hardly miss it. The sound of the explosion appeared to rock the hillside, reverberating from peak to peak as though emphasising the isolation of the place. A flock of birds took flight in panic.

'The jeep?' Mulholland asked eagerly.

Dracht grunted. 'Probably.' Grudging.

'Look!' da Gruta pointed. Midway down towards the valley, a coil of oily smoke wormed into the sky from the thick swathe of vegetation that marked the track. 'The position's about right. That's burning rubber. Tyres.'

A fat grin crossed Mulholland's face. 'Wonderful.'

Da Gruta cackled mirthlessly. 'You're a wicked old bastard, Vincent. Worse than the boss, you are,' he said admiringly.

But Dracht was unimpressed. 'Don't get complacent. I doubt Anton was in the vehicle and at the snail's pace we're moving, he could catch us up.'

The Portuguese commando grinned. 'I hope he does, Nico, I hope he does. It'll save us going after him later. We owe that dog.'

Dracht began to move again. 'And if that *kaffir* doesn't speed up, stick a bayonet up his arse.'

Ngoça staggered onto the shelf of level ground and slumped down at the foot of a gnarled thorn tree. His smart trousers were ripped to shreds; his shirt was sodden and sweat-stained. He regarded da Gruta with dull eyes. 'It's no good. I must rest.'

'Go on, you can make it, *Senhor President*! Just another mile.'

The Mozambican shook his head. 'I do not have the will to go on,' he said morosely.

'The will?' da Gruta queried. 'Will has nothing to do with it. Just put one foot in front of the other. Even Vincent here is managing.'

'Thank you, Armando,' Mulholland said indignantly.

But Ngoça was unmoved. Literally. 'I do not have a will for this whole thing. I've told you. Why should I do what you say any more?'

Da Gruta leaned forward, his face just inches from that

442

of the other man. 'Because if you don't, I'll fucking kill you, that's why.'

Ngoça glared defiance. 'No. I refuse.'

The commando snapped. Hadn't he been considerate to the black bastard? Coaxed him with tolerant words? Protected him from Dracht's rising anger? And this was the thanks he got. Typical *kaffir*. Give them an inch and they started taking liberties!

On impulse, he drew the Star automatic pistol from his holster. 'Get bloody moving, Senhor President. Up off your bloody arse!'

He thwacked the barrel across Ngoça's head in a glancing blow. 'Get up!' he repeated, wiping the weapon lightly back and forth across the exposed skull until the Mozambican covered his cranium with both hands and curled into a ball, starting to cry like a child.

'I say, steady on,' Mulholland protested.

Dracht slid deliberately back down the slope, scree showering out in front of him. 'All right, Armando, leave it out. Give him time to recover.'

'Bastard's taking advantage of my good nature.'

'I'm pushing too hard,' Dracht said. 'The success of this mission means too much to me. As you said, no good if the bastard has a heart attack.'

Da Gruta shrugged. 'Yeah, well, he *is* our new president.' He grinned, suddenly finding a funny side to the situation, and nudged the curled-up figure. 'Eh, Ngoça? Mustn't beat up the president, eh?'

There was no response. The man didn't move. Da Gruta nudged him again.

'What did you do?' Dracht demanded.

'Just a playful pistol whipping . . .' Panic creeping into his voice.

'It was only light,' Mulholland confirmed. 'A couple of taps on the head.'

Dracht pushed both men aside, took Ngoça by the shoulders and turned the body over to face him. The eyes were closed, the face content. The face of a man at last at peace with himself.

'Heart?' Mulholland asked, though he could scarcely believe it himself.

The commando didn't answer. He tilted Ngoça's body forward to examine the back of the head. Red liquid glistened amongst the greying curls. Tentatively, he touched the hair with his finger. There was no resistance. 'Shit!'

'What?' da Gruta demanded.

Dracht shook his head. 'I can hardly believe this. His skull is so thin, like an eggshell.'

Mulholland peered over Dracht's shoulder. 'He's dead?'

'Stone.'

'I couldn't have known!' da Gruta exclaimed. 'How was I to know that?'

'Shut up,' Dracht ordered. 'What's done is done. The first priority is to get a signal to van der Walt.'

Da Gruta stared down at the corpse. He felt a compulsive and unreasonable anger at the man for dying on him like this. As though the Mozambican had deliberately died to spite him. 'Do we bury him?'

'Why bother – he's no use to us now.'

They pushed on for another mile until they reached a dense carpet of thorns that offered reasonable cover and blessed shade. There they rigged the portable MEL set in order to contact van der Walt. The signal was picked up by the Silvermine listening station on the Cape and sent on by secure land line to the secret Military Intelligence facility on the outskirts of Phalabora in the Transvaal homeland of Gazankula. The duty signals officer decoded the message with mounting dismay. Then, after a brief consultation with the special operations commander, made a person-to-person call to the Meikles Hotel in Harare.

Willem van der Walt accepted the call in his room where he was having coffee with Veronique da Gruta.

Her small black eyes watched anxiously over the rim of her cup as she took a genteel sip. But she could read nothing in the benign, suntanned face.

At length he said quietly: 'I see.' There was just a hint of solemnity in his voice. 'What? Make sure he understands that there are to be no loose ends. He'll know what that means. Yes, of course. No wagging tongues. Thank you.'

He replaced the receiver.

'Well?' Senhora da Gruta demanded.

The smile hovered, curling uncertainly. 'I am so sorry, Veronique. They've had a signal from Dracht. Ngoça is dead.'

She closed her eyes as a lifetime's dream crumbled in an instant. Then she took a deep breath and opened them again. Carefully she placed the delicate china cup and saucer on the table. 'What happened?'

'A heart attack apparently, according to Dracht.'

'And Armando? Is there news of my son?'

'He and Dracht are well. We will continue the exfiltration as planned.'

'Exfiltration?' she flustered. It sounded awfully like execution.

'I beg your pardon, Veronique. Jargon. We will get them out as planned, just without Ngoça. We can expect them to be safely inside Malawi within forty-eight hours or less.'

'Thank God for that. And Gutala, has anyone told Armando about Gutala?'

'I doubt it,' he replied softly. 'It wouldn't be policy and, besides, we do not yet have confirmation that the government is back in control there.'

She moistened the tip of her lace handkerchief with a dart of her pink tongue and dabbed at her eyes. 'I am thankful. The news would break the poor boy's heart.' Rapidly she blinked to clear the tears. 'And Jorge, have you heard anything?'

'He is still held at Napoleão's camp until the situation is more stabilised, then he will be released. Napoleão knows better than to disobey me on that. A donation to his bank account in Swazi depends on it.'

'You will tell *them*?'

Van der Walt knew who 'them' were. The representatives of the international moneymen. 'The "heads-I-win, tails-you-lose" brigade.' Five sober-suited executives from America, Europe and the Middle East had rooms in different parts of the hotel. Each was regularly on the telephone, pestering him for news, a hint of things not going to plan, a breath of scandal, the smallest excuse to pull out. To sever connections. To keep their masters in the multinational conglomerates squeaky clean and above reproach.

The South African chuckled without humour. 'I will tell them now. Mark my words, you will not see them for dust in their unseemly rush to get to the airport.'

And so it proved. Each had checked out within the hour. Before he followed them, van der Walt made a call to Colonel Lantanga of the Malawi Army. 'I am sorry, Montgomery, it is off.'

The educated English voice gave no indication of regret. He just said, in a very English way: 'Another time, perhaps.'

Van der Walt hung up, then consulted his notebook and dialled an international call to Pretoria. While he waited to be put through, he stared out of the window at the fountains of Cecil Square. Rhodes, what would Cecil Rhodes have made of all this? If *Boeretursland* was now no more than a shattered dream, then he would have to address himself to surviving in the New South Africa with its one-man, one-vote and the inevitability of a *kaffir* government. It was time to build some bridges.

A voice crackled at the other end.

'Colonel van der Walt here. From the Directorate. I am calling from Harare. My people here have uncovered something that needs to be brought to the president's attention most urgently. I shall be back tonight and would appreciate an audience at the president's earliest convenience.'

The voice at the other end was polite, but was reluctant to alter his president's diary. 'If you could give an indication?'

Van der Walt was irritated by the lack of any sense of security. When would politicians learn the facts of life? 'Let us just say that I have managed to stop an international conspiracy that would upset our Frelimo brothers in Mozambique. Is that important enough for you?'

He got his meeting. Ten minutes later, he checked out of the hotel.

It was amazing how it all came back. Reading the signs. Branagh crouched by the side of the track and tried to make sense of the jumble of footprints in the dry dust. As he did so, Boyd and Kathleen, both armed with Kalashnikovs, stood ten metres away on each side of him, their eyes searching the brush. A person tracking was always vulnerable to sniper fire, and none of them had doubts that their quarry might seize any opportunity to turn the tables on them.

'Well, at least the four set off together,' Branagh at last decided, standing up. 'Two pairs of *veldschoen*. I guess the smaller of the two belongs to Armando.' He broke off two straightish twigs. On one he marked da Gruta's boot size and stride length with his pocket knife; on the other twig he carved Dracht's measurements. 'The other two are easier. Vincent's got new desert boots with a distinguishable tread. As we know, Ngoça's wearing most unsuitable shoes with crepe soles. See here – the pattern's gone where it's eroding away. He won't make good time in this terrain. He'll feel each sharp stone underfoot.'

'Which way?' Boyd asked.

'Up.'

The commando nodded. That would be Dracht. Up and over, a straight line between two points. The shortest route to the shore of Lake Malawi.

Using the pacing sticks, Branagh was able to find the location of each successive footfall. On the stony hillside he did not expect to find many prints. The tell-tale signs would be crushed pellets of earth or bruised and broken strands of grass. The follow-up progress was reasonably rapid. By majoring on Dracht and da Gruta he was able to ensure regular findings. The commandos would walk at a steady and reliable rate and in a straight line whilst the flagging civilians would wander at an increasingly irregular pace as they became more tired. Also, by travelling faster, the commandos would cause greater damage to grass and scrub, making the trail easier to follow.

'Chewing gum,' Branagh said, reaching down to pick up the substance. 'Still moist.'

'That's Armando.' Boyd grinned at their success. 'Filthy habit.'

They worked steadily on up the hillside, Branagh picking up clues where he could. A broken cobweb, bruised vegetation and snapped branch ends. All formed part of the picture. It was hard going, the hillside becoming steeper, its uneven rocky surface smothered with crackling dry grass and thorn, trembling in the midday haze.

'AAH!' Kathleen cried suddenly.

Branagh swung his weapon, zeroed in. 'What is it?'

She had her hand to her mouth. 'It's a body . . . Oh, my God, I think it's Ngoça!'

'Don't touch it!' Boyd shouted.

Branagh closed in swiftly. As he approached he heard the frenzied buzz of gathering blowflies. He brushed them away and leaned over the curled body. The insects had been crawling excitedly over the blood-soaked hair.

'It's him,' Branagh confirmed. 'A blow to the head – God, look at that skull bone, it's wafer-thin.'

'Do you think it was an accident?' Kathleen asked.

Branagh shrugged. 'I can't imagine why they'd *want* to kill him. Ngoça appeared to be crucial to their plans.'

'It's so sad. He was such a nice man.'

'As politicians go,' Branagh conceded. 'They all think they know better. That they can do a better job. Ngoça was no exception.'

Boyd joined them. 'We'd best be doubly careful from now on. I reckon they'll have to abort the op now. Drop the whole bloody scheme, I wouldn't be surprised. Dracht might have more time to worry about us.' He went down on his haunches. 'This proves my point. They've wired him.'

'What?' Kathleen didn't understand.

Branagh pointed to a thin transparent length of monofilament wire. 'He's been booby-trapped.'

'How awful. What a thing to do.'

Boyd traced the mine, an oblong wooden case hidden in the scrub heather behind them. 'A Soviet PMD. Antipersonnel. Must be one of those they took from the track. Enough to blow a wheel.' The monofilament wire was attached to a stout stick which propped up a heavy stone. It would have dropped straight onto the pressure plate had anyone attempted to move the body.

Branagh looked back down the hillside. The smoke from the Gaz jeep still smudged the clear, white-hot sky. 'They must have heard the explosion and seen the smoke. It might have fooled them.'

The commando laughed drily. 'Don't underestimate Dracht, Mike. He's an old pro at this game. He's not going to believe something just because we want him to. Wiring Ngoça was an insurance, just in case. He knew if we came looking, we wouldn't resist a peek at the body.'

It was in a sober mood that they continued and in an even more heightened state of alertness. Becoming jittery. Nerves jangling. At one point Boyd thought he heard the distant sound of a motorcycle. Nonsense. The mind playing tricks. They pushed on into the furnace heat.

As they neared the crest of the hill, Branagh located the area where Dracht, da Gruta and Mulholland had rested up. The grass was crushed where they had sat and wrappings from a ration pack had been hidden beneath a stone. Poor marks.

'They're getting careless,' Boyd observed. 'Or demob-happy. They should make Lake Malawi by midday tomorrow – even at their rate of travel.'

Branagh pointed to a set of toeprints. 'Vincent's having trouble with his feet. He had to take his boots off. We've got to be gaining on them.'

'I'd love to take my boots off,' Kathleen said wistfully, 'but I'd never be able to get them back on again.'

The men laughed with her; she had shown grit and stoic determination in unfamiliar and difficult circumstances. It had impressed them both.

The distant single rifleshot was unmistakable. It shook the afternoon stillness, filling the aching emptiness of the bushveld, echoing up into the hills to bounce around the lonely peaks until it spent itself. The sound had barely died when it was followed by a further quick succession of shots.

'Over the ridge,' Branagh said.

They moved on hurriedly, mounting the steep shoulder of the hill from where they had a clear view of the far side of the mountain.

The sweeping panorama was breathtaking. Through the filmy late afternoon haze, the hillside tumbled away to the yawning tract of burnished amber grass that melted into a sparkling misty shroud on the far horizon. The waters of Lake Malawi. Below them the retiring bronze sun was casting long shadows as antlike figures scurried between the green smudges of thorn bush in pursuit of their quarry. From that distance the elephant herd they hunted resembled huge grey boulders scattered at random over a mile of bushveld.

More rifle shots were followed by the faintest sound of human shouts carrying across the distance.

Boyd tugged a small pair of 8 × 21 binoculars from his pocket and put them to his eyes. 'Renamo poachers,' he decided.

Branagh and Kathleen watched with morbid fascination as the flitting ants began to encircle a number of the grey boulders. In turn, the boulders started to move, first in one direction and then another. Even at that range the animals' confusion and terror could be felt.

A volley of shots rattled across the miles; several boulders were overturned. The remnants of the herd found a gap in the ants' cordon and made a break.

Then they heard the plaintive trumpeting of an old bull, drifting up the hillside. A pitiful cry of anguish, a warning challenge.

Boyd adjusted the focus. 'I'm not certain, but it looks remarkably like that old tusker we saw at the water hole a few days back.'

'Surely not,' Kathleen said.

'Then it must be his twin brother. One good six-foot tusk and the other busted.'

'Our progress *has* been a bit haphazard,' Branagh conceded.

Boyd lowered the binoculars. 'If it is him, the lucky bastard got away. None too pleased about it, though – just listen to him.' More trumpeting carried on the air.

'More to the point,' Branagh said, 'those poachers are straddled right across our path – and Dracht's.'

'They'll take a while to hack off the ivory.' Boyd agreed. 'I reckon they'll have a feast tonight on elephant steak.'

Kathleen turned away in disgust.

It was Branagh who heard it first. For a moment he thought it was the motorcycle sound that Boyd kept hearing earlier . . . A distant, wavering drone. No. Aero engines. Indistinct at first, the noise grew until it

451

resounded around the high peaks, the aircraft itself tanta-lisingly hidden. All eyes searched in vain. The sound was deafening. Then suddenly it was there, swooping over-head.

'First one I've seen in days,' Boyd said.

Branagh squinted against the sunlight. 'It looked like a Caribou. It could be Ian Hagan's. I couldn't see if it was Arbaérea livery . . .'

The engine pitch changed and they watched as the air-craft dipped to circle low over the distant ants, sending them scurrying for cover. Sunlight refracted on its wind-shield as it straightened up and began heading back towards them.

It came in very low, its shadow flashing over them with an accompanying blast of displaced air that created a vortex of dead leaves and tumbleweed.

'I swear that was Rob D'Arcy in the cockpit,' Branagh said in astonishment.

'Who's D'Arcy?' Boyd asked.

'British contract soldier for the tobacco station in Gutala district. He's training a special force.'

Kathleen said: 'I only glimpsed the pilot. You're right, it could well have been Ian. He was wearing dark glasses. Do you think they saw us?'

The sound had receded rapidly, now reduced again to an elusive and insect-like drone that lingered in the air. The aircraft itself had vanished, hidden by the adjoining hill.

'Not necessarily,' Boyd said. 'We'd be fairly hard to pick out against the rocks in these clothes.'

Kathleen watched anxiously for a sign of its return. 'Shouldn't we try to attract attention? Light a fire or something?'

Branagh shook his head. 'With Dracht and Mulholland around, that's the last thing we want. There's nowhere they can land around here anyway.'

Hardly had the noise of the aero engines finally ceased,

than it began again, growing louder with each second that passed. They looked around in anticipation but the aircraft was nowhere to be seen. Then suddenly it appeared from behind them, gaining height to soar some hundred metres above their heads.

'Look!' Kathleen shouted.

Something plummeted earthward; a brown blur that they had no time to identify before it disappeared into a screen of withered buffalo grass. As they worked their way across to the spot, the Caribou made a final pass; a hand was glimpsed waving from the side window of the cockpit.

Boyd looked down at the shattered cardboard box. 'Provisions.'

Kathleen knelt excitedly, rummaging through the stamped tins of compo rations. 'Steak and kidney. Sponge and custard.' she read. 'Oh, wonderful, chocolate bars!'

Branagh and Boyd dropped enthusiastically at her side.

'There's a note attached,' she observed, handing it to Branagh.

As he read the words aloud, a slow grin broke on his face.

'Hey, Irish, where you been? Looking for you two days now. I was found by F patrol – presumably that's Frelimo – Leg okay, but hurts like a bugger. That Shona bastard was okay too – he disappeared like a ghost when F showed up. Fuel low now. Will return area tomorrow. Mark out LZ by 12 hours if poss. Cutala safe. Come home. All is forgiven. Love. FRED.'

Kathleen squealed with delight. 'He's safe! That's fantastic news.'

Boyd plucked two plastic bottles of water from the parcel, then drew out a third. It contained an amber liquid. Branagh didn't have to smell it to know what it was.

He grinned up at the vanishing speck in the sky. 'You lovely ugly bastard.'

The South African laughed. 'That's the sort of friend to have.'

Branagh's smile drained away. 'He didn't mention Maraika.'

Kathleen touched his shoulder. 'That doesn't mean anything, Mike. He didn't have much time to write anything down.'

'He'd have mentioned that. He's in love with her himself.'

She smiled gently. 'I think you could be right. Maybe by the time we get back . . .'

Boyd said: 'I don't want to worry you two, but if Dracht saw that drop, he'll know something is up. He'll be on his guard. Any plans you've got for Vincent Mulholland, I suggest you forget them.'

Branagh turned to him. 'No way, Anton. He'll never leave me in peace, not now. It's got to be done.' He glanced up at the sun. It was past its zenith. 'When we get to the plain, it'll be good tracking light.'

'Anyone ever tell you you're a crazy Irishman?'

'Many.' He looked towards Malawi. 'You don't have to come with me. As far as I'm concerned, all three of them are already dead.'

Kathleen watched in thoughtful silence. This was not a side of Cousin Seamus she had ever witnessed before.

Boyd said: 'Don't worry. I wouldn't miss it for the world.'

By sunset Branagh had a fix. As he had predicted, they reached the bottom of the foothills as the westering sun provided ideal low-angle conditions for tracking Dracht's party.

Although they had witnessed the gang of Renamo poachers move jubilantly off to the north, they advanced with increasing wariness. There was little doubt that the commandos and Mulholland would have been forced either to make a wide detour of the bandits or hide up until the danger had passed. It would be all too easy to stumble into them with dire consequences.

Branagh was particularly mindful that Dracht presumably still had the second PMD mine with him. He'd had no compunction about using the first to booby-trap Ngoça's body; he'd certainly not hesitate to use the other device.

At Branagh's suggestion, Boyd and Kathleen removed their boots and suffered the discomfort of proceeding barefoot. Better that than lose a foot on Dracht's mine. As explosives took the line of least resistance, the higher the footwear the greater the injury. If there was an accident when travelling barefoot, the victim might get away with no more than the loss of some toes.

There was a secondary benefit. Being without boots heightened their sense of vulnerability, making them place each footfall with more care and stealth, preventing them moving faster than was wise. Nevertheless progress remained good, with Branagh continuing to track while Boyd and Kathleen guarded each flank.

As the veiled sun finally settled like a silver medallion in the sulphurous haze that hung over the distant lake, Branagh sniffed the air.

Boyd saw him and did the same. He closed his thumb and forefinger and lifted his hand in signal. Branagh hunched down and waited until the other closed up with him.

'Ganja,' Boyd confirmed in a whisper. 'That'll be Armando. The smell doesn't carry like Virginia tobacco, so they must be close.'

They sank down into the waving grass in silence. Kathleen watched with curiosity and apprehension as the two men scoured the surrounding terrain for clues. It appeared to her that Dracht's trio could be anywhere; impossible to pinpoint.

Branagh licked his forefinger, feeling the saliva cool to

tell him in which direction the merest touch of a breeze was flowing. She saw his eyes narrow as he decided where to concentrate his attention. It became focused on a solitary mopane tree surrounded by a dense patch of scrub some fifty metres away. It would be ideal, allowing Dracht's party to move around their site in reasonable comfort without betraying their position to anyone watching.

'We'll pull back,' Branagh said quietly.

Inch by inch they retraced their footsteps, moving on all fours until they came upon a shallow depression in the land.

'It's okay here,' Branagh said. 'Say a quarter mile to that mopane tree. We'll just have to sit it out until well into the night.'

As they began the long wait, they spent the time discovering and devouring everything in Fred Petkus's surprise package that didn't require cooking. As the landscape dimmed stormheads rode majestically across the darkening sky like purple galleons, vanguards of a new weather front moving in. The long-tailed drongas were making the most of the last vestiges of daylight, swooping unusually low for insects, forced down by increasing air pressure – a sure sign that rain was imminent. The leafy smell of the land became suddenly more pungent in expectation of the first heavy drops.

They splattered singly at first, big dark starbursts on the crusted red earth. Then in a pattern, beating noisily and more regularly on the leaves of the scrub, gathering in momentum until the rattle of the foliage drowned out all other sound. Fork lightning crackled out over the lake, followed moments later by the angry grumble of a thunderclap. An elephant trumpeted in the far distance.

Boyd rigged his poncho as a makeshift tent and they huddled beneath it for warmth after the sudden drop in temperature. Kathleen succumbed to an exhausted sleep

456

while the two men waited and watched and discussed their plan in hushed voices.

When all the decisions were made they fell silent, listening to the incessant drumbeat of rain and the awesome artillery explosions of thunder all around. It was going to be an endless night until the appointed hour of one in the morning . . .

Branagh shook Kathleen awake. She peered up at him, her face pinched with the cold and wet, her hair sodden and bedraggled.

'We're going now,' he said. 'You keep this.' He handed her the Star automatic pistol. 'If anything happens to us get clear of the area, unless you know that Vincent and the others have gone. Fred will be back to search the area – he'll find you whatever it takes. When any danger is past you can find a suitable landing strip to mark out for him.'

She screwed up her eyes against the beating rain.

'Don't talk like that, Mike. As though you might not come back.'

'It's a possibility you've got to face.'

'Then don't do it. You don't *have* to do it.'

It was so dark she couldn't see his face properly when he spoke. 'I have to do it – for both our sakes.'

'You don't have to commit murder for me.'

'Murder?' He sounded surprised at her choice of words. 'Vincent knows the score. He's the one who raised the stakes. He's played this sort of game all his life.'

'Game?' Her voice was hollow. 'I don't understand you. Not at all.'

'Sometimes things must be done, however unpleasant. For years I've been trying to avoid it. Fought against it. Vincent's brought it all back. I can't go on running.'

'This isn't you.' Her eyes pleaded with him. 'Don't go.'

But he was already gone. He had just backed away, a vague half-image inked in by the night, then melted. She

457

felt suddenly alarmed, alone, twisting around for sight of Boyd. For some reassurance. But he too had gone.

Branagh heard her weep. Heard her gulp for air and the brave sniff to stifle her tears. Then the drumming of the rain closed in around him, hitting the leaves noisily and soaking his shirt and his hair. Water ran down his face in rivulets as he crawled slowly forward like a stalking leopard, the AK assault rifle gripped with both hands.

Already he had lost sight of Boyd. The commando was taking the left-hand arc of the pincer movement, a manoeuvre that would bring them both round on the far side of Dracht's temporary hide.

He settled into a slow, easy rhythm, attuning to the wet, wild world about him. Listening to the noises of insect and vegetation, any sound that was out of place. A cough, a footfall, the snap of a twig. Any smell that didn't fit. His eyes adjusted with every minute that passed, his vision penetrating the night, seizing the moment to freeze and look each time the lightning cracked with the sound of tearing canvas.

Boyd or no Boyd, it didn't matter. This was a time when a man was truly alone, when he had no friend. And as he moved on, unwanted thoughts began to crowd in on his mind. And the years rolled back.

Rain had never been so wet. Drilling down remorselessly for days. For weeks. The endless sound of dripping leaves and the nostrils filled with the peaty smell of Irish turf. A dank foxhole of a place that was your home because this was your job. Some fox. Armed to the teeth and with the very latest surveillance equipment. There with three fellow foxes because Mulholland told you to be there. Because you were a trained killer and this was your job. And Mulholland called the tune.

But this cold, wet November night in Armagh was different. This was about personal, family business. Distant family it was true, but family nonetheless. If Mulholland hadn't made the connection, hadn't recognised the possibilities, then Branagh would probably never have visited the Coogans again. Ma had always taken a shine to him as a child, her angelic step-nephew.

And he had responded in kind as any child would to an admiring aunt who held him up as a shining example to her unruly brood. But as the years passed he recognised his step-cousins for what they were. Recognised the yawning gap between the strongly Republican farmers and his own parents. Saw Ma Coogan's simmering jealousy and resentment of her own sister for what it was when she married Branagh's father – a sober, upright widower from another part of Ulster, but it might as well have been from another planet.

Yet Branagh's new stepmother had found her escape, her true place in the world, her happiness – with a six-year-old stepson as thoughtful and stiffly polite as she would have wanted any child of her own to be.

At first Ma Coogan and her sister remained close, with family visits at Easter and at Christmas. But as the years passed, the differences between the Coogans and the Gallaghers became inexorably more glaring.

As the Coogan boys grew older and more loutish and the farm went into decline, Branagh could see now the envy with which Ma Coogan must have viewed his parents – a thrifty, middle-class Catholic couple with opinions as moderate as their means. Owners of their own business, a tidy sweetshop that was open every day except Sunday when they would take their son with them to Mass. And in the afternoon his father would wash the car or clip the hedge; his stepmother would embroider or potter in the tiny back-garden greenhouse. A time for everything and everything in its place.

A far cry from the foul language and tantrums of the Coogan boys who would taunt him during those family visits that became steadily less frequent. No, apart from a lingering fondness for Ma, Branagh had no cause to go back. Would never have met Kathleen.

That was all down to Mulholland. All down to the bomb that had blown apart the corner sweetshop and Branagh's parents with it. That was how Mulholland later made the connection with the Coogan family and the SAS sergeant seconded to his special intelligence unit. Saw the possibilities.

Even now he could picture Mulholland's round smiling face, the eyes crinkled with concern. 'Listen, old stick, this is a difficult time for you. Believe me, I understand. But my people think they know who did it. No hard evidence, of course. And it's not going to be easy for you to take.' A narrowing of the eyes. 'Some people we have been after for some time . . . your own step-cousins.'

He had been hard in those days, really hard. Like Dracht was now. But he was nevertheless stunned. Speechless.

'I am sorry.' Mulholland left a decent pause. Then almost casually: 'Did you know the Coogan boys were mixed up with the Provos? Ah, of course not. Silly question.'

He had found his tongue then. Anger flared, childhood resentment rekindled. 'I could well believe it.'

Mulholland had him and he knew it. 'Just sorry it's me who has to break the news. The Int. boys in the Armagh district call them the Brothers Grim. I understand there was some animosity between the Coogan family and your parents?'

'They didn't get on, that's all. They hadn't seen each other for years.'

'The Irish can hold a grudge you know. And your parents openly supported the British presence.'

He remembered the Coogan boys all right. They would be the type to hold a grudge, he would give Mulholland that.

'Int.'s been trying to get a handle on the Coogan cell

for a couple of years. Found no way to penetrate that tightknit farming community.' He hesitated. 'I know this isn't the time, old stick, but a thought has occurred . . .'

He had taken the bait. Swallowed it whole. 'I can't think of a better time, Vincent.'

'You'd have to leave the Regiment, of course. At least, officially. Leave the Army, in fact. Just a temporary measure. I'll square everything with the Ministry of Defence.'

And he had believed the man. After all, Mulholland was a fat cat. Untouchable. Mulholland could do anything he damn well pleased.

It was naïve of him, looking back now. He should have realised Mulholland was bending the rules and that could lead to trouble. But he hadn't. The SAS had tight restrictions on the deployment of Ulstermen within its ranks. Especially if they were Catholic or had families in the Province. Yet somehow Mulholland had pulled strings in Whitehall to get round that. And Branagh knew the Regiment would pointblank refuse to allow him to spy on his own family. Ethics and morality aside, it would have been dangerous in the extreme and might have led to divided loyalties. But Branagh had been consumed with anger and was a willing pawn in Mulholland's manipulative game. He had been a different man then. A trained killer only too pleased to do his master's bidding. Especially on this occasion.

So it was that three months later he appeared on Ma Coogan's doorstep, asking for a roof over his head while he looked for a new civilian job.

Of course he didn't get one. No one in Armagh was going to give an ex-Brit soldier a job. Even if he had only been in the Engineers as he claimed. For eight long weeks he endured the taunts and jibes of the Coogan boys, again hoping they would come to like and trust him. But they never did. Only Ma Coogan and the young Kathleen treated him like a member of the human race. And, as much as he paid attention to anyone, the taciturn Pa

461

Coogan – that was when he wasn't reading his newspaper, or tending his pigeons, or playing dominoes in Liam's bar.

During those endless weeks Branagh pieced together the intelligence jigsaw, marrying up terrorist events with the movements and apparent alibis of the Coogans. Pa Coogan was uninvolved, he was certain of that. But the four boys were Provies and, by planting bugging devices in their rooms, he got wind of the planned bombing.

He passed the information on in a clandestine meeting with one of Mulholland's runners. The next day he was informed there was to be an SAS stakeout and Mulholland wanted him there to identify the gang as they planted the bomb.

For some reason he felt the first flickerings of self-doubt. A deep, nagging sense of betrayal. Not so much of the four young men whose heads had been turned by the Provies' talk and bravado, but of Ma Coogan, who had taken him in like a prodigal son without hesitation. Now he was about to deprive her of four sons for as long as the prison sentence took. Not that he had any sympathy for terrorists – it was just that it was he who had been cast in the role of Judas.

And Kathleen, of course. She had trusted him, too, when he was about to deliver her four brothers into the hands of their enemies. What would the innocent girl with the ponytail think of him then?

It had been stupid to drink so much. Stupid to go to Confession – he hadn't been in years. Stupid to feel the need. But he remembered old Father McCabe with affection from his childhood – the priest's wise and kindly words, his faint odour of pipe tobacco and whiskey, his glad eye for a pretty girl.

Branagh hadn't given anything away. He wasn't a complete fool. Just said he needed forgiveness for something he could not talk about – even in Confession.

He had not known that Father McCabe was on

Mulholland's payroll as well as that of the Provies – that Father McCabe was a double-agent.

And Branagh had not known when he left the church to join the stakeout team that the priest had sensed the anguish, had word of what was happening and had relied on a lifetime's wisdom and intuition to guess what might be about to happen. He had run through the freezing rain like a madman to ask Pa Coogan where his boys were that night. To warn them that they might be heading for trouble.

For the first time in his life, Pa Coogan made a decision – and took action. Having only the vaguest notion where to look, he took off into the sodden November night. Without stopping to grab hat or coat, he raced through the relentless downpour in shirtsleeves and braces.

Rain, rain, rain. Steam rising from his body as he ran. Ran, ran, ran. Water trickling down his face.

Rain.

Lightning spat and sizzled. It lit the bushveld like a flare in a moment of fizzling electric blue radiance, outlining the trees against the angry sky, exposing the secrets of the night.

The world was plunged back into cloying darkness and thunder detonated immediately overhead. And still the rain fell. Just as it had that November night.

Rain like this. Darkness like this. Fear and expectation, just like this.

And he'd been ready to kill if necessary, just as he was now, as he crawled to the edge of the thicket and the mopane tree. Eased off the safety catch.

But this time the kill at first light would be certain. And it would be for himself. For himself and for Kathleen.

This time there would be no mistake. No anguished Pa Coogan to burst shouting onto the scene. No confusion. No yellow card. No wild shoot-out. No mistake.

Sweat mingled with the rain on his brow, stung his eyes. He settled, patient as a leopard.

The hospital. That was where he had learned the truth, by accident. An old colleague from the Regiment bringing grapes and sympathy and black humour. He thought Branagh would want to know that a man had been charged with blowing up his parents in their sweetshop. It hadn't been remotely connected with the Coogan boys, couldn't have been. The sectarian bomber had been a Protestant from the UVF.

And Mulholland had known all along. But the lie had served its purpose and he had another feather in his cap in the prolonged squabble between SIS and its MIS rivals in Ulster. Another feather for the untouchable fat cat to boast about in the Travellers over a fine claret.

Well, this time there would be no mistakes.

Maraika opened her eyes. The rain had stopped.

Immediately she knew that Mikey Branagh was in danger. She felt it in her whole being and the certainty caused a nauseating emptiness deep in her gut.

She was tired. All she wanted to do was sleep, but her fears for Branagh were so raw and strong that she was compelled to overcome it. Her bare limbs squelched in the mud as she climbed wearily to her feet.

It was still very dark but there was a perceptible flush on the eastern horizon, a deep lilac pushing back the indigo night sky. Behind her the hills were beginning to take on form and substance, the hills from which she had somehow escaped. Where Francisco had surrendered his life for her. A shudder of cold and apprehension rippled through her and she hugged her own body for warmth and comfort. All around she heard the unnerving drip of water against leaf. The sopping earth sucked noisily at her toes as she began walking slowly through the bushveld. She did not know where she was, only that she wanted to be away from the hills and the bandits.

Someone had said there was a government safe zone somewhere in this valley. But she didn't know its name or how far it was from Tumbo. She had marched many miles since she had been abducted from the village. It would take many more days to walk back, even if she could find the way, or meet someone who by some miracle knew in which direction she should go.

At a puddle in the track she knelt and sampled the water. For once it wasn't brackish but fresh and sweet-tasting. It revived her spirits momentarily and she paused to breathe in the crisp, leafy aroma that the rains had brought to the air.

A whistle blew and the feeling of fear drained into the pit of her belly instantly. She cocked her head to one side like an antelope hearing the far-off roar of a lion.

It came from the hills. How far away she could not be certain. The bandits were not yet close enough for her to hear their voices. She must not allow them any nearer.

She started to run, splashing through the mud and the puddles, weaving round the maze of thorn bushes wherever a path offered. Time and again she was forced to change direction, rushing blindly one way and then another, following a game trail only to find it blocked by scrub. Thorns reached out to whip her as she passed. Retracing her footsteps, trying another route. And all the time the whistles, piercing the pristine air, taunting her, hunting her.

After an hour she stopped, falling back against a marula tree, her breasts heaving with the pain in her chest as she tried to draw breath. She had not heard the whistles for some time. How long? She was not good on time. There was no time in the African bush. There was only today. Today and memories of yesterday. Tomorrow was filled with fear and doubt. In Africa you never thought about tomorrow.

Her pounding heart slowed and she began to walk again, more slowly this time. The eastern sky had moved position and she tried to find a game trail that led in that direction. The ground was swampy underfoot here, the thorns thankfully replaced by tall thickets of reed. She disturbed a klipspring which leapt away in a bouncing run and disappeared from view.

Then she rounded another clump of reed, and stopped dead.

It was a small clearing of raked earth. A dome-shaped hut of woven reed stood in the centre. By its entrance sat the old man, cross-legged, stirring the contents of a blackened pot that rested on the embers of the cooking fire. He wore a linen cloth round his waist which was as white as the coating of dried mud that covered his skinny naked body and face.

He appeared not to notice her while he poked and prodded at the pot. Slowly, slowly she backed away one step, then another. Still he did not look up.

'Come, my child, you are safe here.'

The sudden sound of his voice startled her

'Come, my child,' he repeated softly in Portuguese. 'Do not be alarmed. It has been a cold, wet night. If you have been travelling you will be hungry. I don't have much, but you are welcome to share my porridge.'

She glanced around her, unsure.

A cackle of laughter. 'There are no *bandidos* here, child. Come, eat.'

Nervously she stepped forward and lowered herself to the rush mat, sitting opposite him across the fire. It was then that she saw he had no eyes and the shock of it took her breath away. There were no eyeballs and no lids, just puckered holes of flesh with dark recesses into which she could not look.

He must have heard her sharp intake of breath because he said: 'My eyes were put out by Renamo.'

She found her tongue. 'I am sorry.'

'Trees do not need eyes to grow tall and strong for a thousand years. Or flowers to bloom in beauty. You do not need eyes to see into a man's soul. Or a woman's.' He reached for the pot.

466

'Who are you, old man?'

He gave her a wooden bowl and spooned in some maize porridge with the ease of a man who could see. 'What is a name? Each of us knows who we are. That is all that matters.'

She didn't understand, but didn't say more until she'd greedily emptied the bowl with her fingers. Then, as she licked them, she asked: 'You live alone here? You are a hermit?'

'No man is ever alone.'

'A diviner, a healer?'

Those dark recesses looked at her, and she felt herself drawn into them. 'What troubles you, child?'

She didn't intend to speak, but found herself powerless to resist. Then she knew, was certain beyond doubt. She was in the presence of a *feitiçeiros*. A magician. It was as though her brain and her mouth were working without her permission. It was a strange sensation – to hear herself telling him about her life in Tumbo, her abduction, the terrible march, and her eventual escape.

'This man you speak of, this white man from across the seas. He is in danger—'

Maraika frowned. Was the hermit asking her or telling her? 'I felt it this morning. In my bones. A terrible, terrible feeling.'

'Is he a good man?'

'I love him.'

He turned his head upward, so that the dark recesses appeared to be regarding the new dawn. 'Inside each man there are two men. The man he was born, and the man he has become. This man is tormented because he doesn't know which he is.'

Still she did not understand, so she said the only thing she could think of: 'He loves me and he loves this land.'

'You ask my help?'

'I have no money.'

'Your beauty is reward enough.'

She stared at him in astonishment. 'How—?'

He raised his hand palm out. Enough. She fell silent and watched with fascination as he produced a skin bag from the hut and proceeded to pour its contents onto the rush mat. Animal bones and teeth, seashells, stones and bits of wood fell out, clinking and clattering until they came to rest. Then he took an old hollowed-out buffalo horn from the belt around his waist and filled it with the bits and pieces.

Satisfied, he sat again cross-legged before the fire and lifted up the horn with both hands, offering it like a chalice. He began to incant in one of the Mozambican languages she had rarely heard before. Maybe it was Siswati or Tongha, but she recognised enough words to know that he was invoking the ancestral spirits.

As he droned on in his coarse sing-song voice she began to experience a great weariness. Her eyelids became heavy. She felt as though she were sinking; she tried to fight it but had no strength, no willpower. Her eyes closed.

She heard the rattle of the buffalo horn and the noise as the old *feitiçeiros* tipped the sacred emblems out onto the mat.

She felt the cold rush of wind. Heard the reeds suddenly rustle together. Then the roll of thunder directly above her, so mighty and so deafening that it made her jump and hurt her ears. Her eyes opened to see the dazzling shaft of lightning so bright that it blinded her. So close that she felt the warmth of its voltage against her face, the ground itself trembling under the onslaught. Her eyes closed again in terror, her entire body shaking.

An abrupt and oddly intense silence followed.

'Child.'

She looked at the old man. Above his head the dawning sky was without a cloud. Birds were singing as they flitted about the reedbeds.

'This is an angry land,' the old man told her in a quiet

voice. 'It has become red with the blood of the old slave trails, the cruel domination of a foreign empire and now the evil alien force that has raped our country. In our ancestors' long anger there is a power. A power we mortals do not begin to understand. A power that is in the hands of every living being and beast.'

She was bewildered.

The hermit continued: 'The man of whom you speak is smiled on by our ancestors. The spirits will do what they can, but he is not one of ours.'

The old man smiled and pointed to the rush mat. The charms had fallen to form a circle. In the centre was a brown-stained enamel tooth that was so large it could only have come from an elephant.

One piece of root, gnarled into a shape that resembled a fist and finger, lay outside the circle. 'That is the way you must travel. Go, child. You will find peace and happiness before the new moon.'

17

It was time.

Even without looking at his watch Branagh knew it was time. Some instincts became so ingrained in your psyche that you never lost them. Like knowing, sensing the exact hour of the morning when waking after a night of fitful sleep. Like smelling danger when there is no outward sign.

He could smell danger now. The rancid undersmell that irritated the nostrils and sent a caterpillar creeping down the spine. This wasn't good. A bad time to sense that something was wrong.

A look at his watch confirmed what he already knew. The vast dome of the African sky had opened up like some galactic flowerhead coming into bloom, transforming the black of night into the pale blue mauve-streaked dawn of the new day.

Everything around him was taking on form and texture: the grass, the thorn bushes, the trees. A bird twittered and flew off from its roost.

He began to move, his muscles stiff after the hours of lying motionless, knowing that Boyd too would be creeping forward on a parallel line of advance. His movements were slow and easy, taking care to check the grass that parted beneath his hands. Expecting any second to see the strand of a tripwire. It was why they had waited for first light, in case one of them stumbled into it.

Then he was there, on the very edge of the scrub beneath the mopane. Again the faint smell of ganja lingered in the air as it had the night before. He heard the tell-tale hiss of a cooking stove.

A brief sound of rustling grass came from his right and he glanced over to see Boyd emerge, his clothes damp-dark from the still wet grass.

Branagh felt relief. In such a short time Boyd had become almost close. An oppo. Like the old days in the Regiment. All for one and one for all.

The man grinned. He looked content, a man who had come to terms with his conscience. A man who had decided at last to put his wife and child before the orders of men like Dracht. As a professional he was probably enjoying this, knowing this would be the last time he had to fight.

Branagh nodded and Boyd acknowledged.

The second hands on both their watches moved towards the twelve. At a time like this ten seconds was an eternity. Branagh could tell that he was years out of practice. He was letting the tension get to him. His heart like a triphammer as the adrenalin coursed. Sweat trickled down the small of his back.

He stared at the second hand, mesmerised. His grip tightened imperceptibly on the Kalashnikov. Eleven, twelve.

Now!

He'd dropped his hand in signal. 'GO!'

In unison they broke cover. Crashing into the thicket, ignoring the tenacious snagging of the thorns. Plunging into the unknown. Seconds like minutes, the crackle of snapping branches ringing in their ears, each footstep a warning of their attack.

Then they were through. In a split second Branagh had a visual image stamped in his mind – an instant photoprint: clearing of trampled grass, kettle bubbling on stove, the three men still in their sleeping bags.

This was no time for niceties. No time for recriminations or pangs of conscience. This was the old days. He squeezed the trigger, feeling the assault rifle come alive in his hands, stammering out the contents of its magazine. Boyd's weapon joined in the ear-splitting percussion, the stench of blue smoke filling the clearing, smudging their vision. But not enough to prevent them seeing the sleeping bags burst apart, the bullets tearing into the material like a crazed swarm of locusts. Down feathers spiralled into the air, gyrating madly in the sudden maelstrom.

Slowly they floated back down. A snowstorm settling over the scene of carnage. It was over.

To Branagh's bemusement he heard the angry trumpeting of an elephant nearby in the bush. A fitting last post for Dracht and da Gruta, he thought savagely.

He felt the tension flood out. Breathing heavily he lowered his assault rifle. Through eyes streaming from the cordite he surveyed the chaos.

Then he stiffened. That crawling sixth sense was back.

He watched as Boyd moved towards the nearest sleeping bag, then stopped dead in his tracks. 'Christ! It's filled with ferns—'

'Don't touch it!' Branagh warned. 'Get back!'

He swung his body, his AK arcing across the clearing to the hissing stove. Next to the empty compo tin with the smouldering pile of ganja tobacco. God, he was rusty! How had he forgotten that people can walk backwards! The tracks he'd followed the night before weren't leading to this clearing – they were going away.

He fired two rounds, a quick double-tap at the stove. The mine hidden beneath it erupted at once, the explosion rocking around the encircling thorns, a geyser of stones and shrapnel blasting out in all directions.

'He set us up,' Boyd murmured with something resembling awe. 'Crafty bastard.'

'I should have seen it.'

Then he heard the double clack of cocking handles behind him. Rounds in the breech, hammers back. They were dead.

'Tut-tut, Branagh. You took your time. I was expecting you in the night.'

It was Dracht's voice. All the time it was the South African who had been the hunter, baiting the trap, luring them in. He should have seen, should have realised.

'Turn round slow. Drop the weapons.' A mirthless laugh. 'Believe it or not, I've an aversion to shooting whites in the back.'

'Don't waste time, old stick,' Mulholland urged. 'The Irishman for one can be a tricky bugger.'

Grudgingly Branagh and Boyd obeyed, turning slowly to face Mulholland and the two commandos. But the delay cost Dracht dear.

No one had been expecting it. They'd heard the angry trumpeting of the elephant in response to the sound of gunfire, but it had meant nothing to them. But now the sudden trembling of the earth beneath their feet and the crashing cacophony of trampled brush and uprooted trees came as a total surprise.

In its maddened desire for vengeance the old tusker towered behind Mulholland and the two South Africans, its gigantic head thrown back as it uttered its bellowing war cry.

Dracht's reaction was instantaneous. He hurled himself aside, rolling head over heels out of the path of the stampeding grey juggernaut. Seizing the moment Branagh reached for the discarded AK at his feet. Armando da Gruta had half-turned his head to see the mighty beast bearing down on him – then caught sight of Branagh. It was no contest. He began to run. He'd moved three strides when Branagh's single shot rapped out, carrying him forward like a sprinter at the winning tape. He pitched ignominiously into the grass with a bullet in the centre of his spine.

The harsh bark of gunfire brought the old tusker up sharp, its massive feet skidding to a standstill, its head up to sniff the stench of cordite, its good eye wide with insane rage.

'Run, Vincent!' Branagh yelled before he could stop himself.

But Mulholland had taken root, his face ashen. Suddenly he seemed to regain control, turned awkwardly to start his run. Above him the inflamed eye caught the movement. The gnarled grey head dipped down, the tip of its single yellowed tusk scraping on the ground.

Branagh watched speechlessly as the old bull gathered speed, changing direction to follow Mulholland with agility worthy of a colt. With a snort of anger the tusk came up. Its tip gouged into Mulholland's back. Up and up, the struggling man hopelessly impaled. Screaming at the top of his voice Mulholland watched in horror as the ivory tip emerged from his own belly in a spray of blood.

There came an ear-splitting cry of victory as the tusker's huge lungs emptied and he tossed his great head in triumph. As he did, Mulholland's body detached itself and spun through the air like a discarded doll.

Branagh opened up with the remains of the magazine, half a dozen rounds emptying into the great grey flanks, tearing a path through to the animal's heart. With an almighty bellowing groan its front legs collapsed under the weight. Then, like a torpedoed battleship, it toppled slowly on its side. The earth shook as it settled.

'Mike, help!'

He turned. It was Boyd. He was lying where he had been trampled when the tusker had unexpectedly changed direction. His right leg from the knee down was crushed to a bloody pulp.

Branagh rushed to his side. 'Easy, Anton. You'll be okay.'

The South African's face was a mask of pain. 'Watch for Nico,' he gasped. 'Sort him first or we're all dead.'

It was a timely warning. Dracht was walking calmly back into the clearing as though nothing had happened. Branagh brought up his Kalashnikov, squeezed the trigger, and heard the hammer snap onto an empty breech.

Dracht smiled. 'You used them up on that old bastard, Branagh. Should have saved one for me. Didn't anyone ever tell you that man's more dangerous than any animal?'

Branagh's heart sank as Dracht raised his own AK.

'But the female's deadlier,' a small voice said.

Dracht turned. Kathleen Coogan stood to one side of him in a wide-legged stance, the automatic pistol held in a double-handed grip.

'Throw the gun down,' she said briskly. 'I know how to use this thing. I grew up in Ulster.'

A slow smile crossed Dracht's face. A fair cop; he knew when he was licked. Even if it was by a bloody woman. For spite he threw the AK deep into a thorn bush. 'Nice one, girlie.'

'Now pick up your rucksack,' she continued calmly, 'and a water canteen, and start walking. Keep walking and don't stop.'

'No, Kathy,' Branagh called. 'Finish him now.'

Her eyes darted angrily in the Irishman's direction. 'What's with you, Mike? Sure haven't you seen enough killing for one morning? Mulholland's dead – that's what you wanted.'

'Well said, girlie,' Dracht added and picked up his rucksack.

'Shut up!' she snapped. 'Just go.'

'It's a mistake,' Branagh said, watching the South African amble out of the clearing.

She looked at Branagh curiously, lowering the pistol. 'Do you *really* want to shoot him? Go on then.' She offered the pistol. 'You'd better do it.'

Branagh hesitated. What would the child in the Armagh farmhouse make of this? Dracht was a spent force now; besides the man had an urgent rendezvous at Lake Malawi. To shoot him in cold blood would be murder with vengeance as the only motive. If he did it he would have come full circle. Become again the man he once was. Another Dracht. He didn't have to do that now. Mulholland was gone; the curse was finally lifted.

'You're right,' he said resignedly, watching as the receding figure of the commando melted into the bushveld.

She smiled with relief and it lit up her face. 'God, Mike, I didn't think I was going to find you alive.' Stuffing the pistol into her belt, she ran forward and threw her arms around him. He felt the wetness of her tears on his face. 'I came running as soon as I heard the explosion and all that shooting. I knew something was wrong. And then that elephant . . .'

'That was quite something. It saved my life.' He untwined her arms from his neck. 'You're still trembling.'

She laughed nervously. 'My heart won't stop pounding.'

'We'd better see if we can do anything for the others. Boyd's hurt badly, but we might be able to keep him alive until help arrives.'

For the first time she noticed the South African half-hidden in the long grass. 'Poor Anton! What happened?'

'Trampled. Thank God Fred had the sense to include some morphine ampoules in his package.'

She rushed over to the motionless figure. 'He hardly needs morphine, Mike. He's out cold.'

'Take a look at Vincent and Armando, will you? See if there's any sign of life at all. If you've got a vanity mirror in your pack, put it over each of their mouths – see if it mists.'

As she walked off apprehensively, Branagh set to work on Boyd's leg. The most he could hope to achieve was to staunch the blood flow and splint it for support.

Disturbed by the attention Boyd's eyes flickered painfully open. 'Mike? . . . Did that really happen?'

'Yes, now don't talk. I'll give you a jab to help you sleep.'

'Is Dracht dead?'

'No, Kathy convinced me to let him go. Unarmed.'

Boyd winced. 'Bad move . . . Didn't let him take his . . . his—' The commando's befuddled mind struggled to find the word '—his pack? Not . . . his pack?'

'Why?'

Boyd shook his head in pain and maybe anger. 'He always carries a . . . a snap-down rifle . . . special lightweight job made for him.'

Branagh cursed his stupidity for not having thought to check himself. That was something he'd never have overlooked in the old days. He made light of it. 'Dracht won't be interested in us now.'

Boyd closed his eyes. 'You don't know him, Mike . . . Not just revenge . . . but that too . . . It'll be expected of him . . . We're witnesses, evidence . . . to what's happened . . .'

'We'll watch out.' Branagh lifted the syringe and squirted out the air bubbles. 'Just a shot of morphine.'

'Thanks . . .'

Before he'd even injected the full amount, Boyd had drifted back into unconsciousness.

'Mike!' Kathleen called. 'I think Armando's breathing. Come quick.'

He crossed the clearing to where the girl had the commando cradled against her chest.

'You shot him in the back!' she accused.

'It was a firefight,' Branagh answered tersely, examining the large exit wound in the man's chest. The round must have taken out his lungs and at least damaged the heart. His remaining time could be counted in minutes.

Branagh found himself staring at the man's dark, wide-open eyes. 'You? You shoot me?' Blood trickled from the corner of his mouth.

'It was you or me. You know that.'

The mouth attempted a painful smile. 'I know.' He looked down, trying to focus on the arms encircling him, then up at Kathleen's face. 'You do me a favour, Branagh.

477

I always wanted to die like this . . . in a woman's arms . . .' He broke into a racking cough, spraying blood-flecked saliva. It was some moments before he could summon the strength to talk again. 'Hey, you see my *pai*. You see Jorge, you tell him he was right all along. Not *Mãmae*. Just say I am sorry. I tried. May Dom Pedro forgive me.' He tried in vain to laugh. 'Maybe I tell my grandfather myself soon. Real soon.' An expression of anxiety came into his eyes. 'What a place to die! No priest. No absolution.'

Branagh said: 'A priest is just a man like any other.'

Da Gruta's eyelids lowered. 'Then you will have to do Irishman. Forgive me on behalf of a priest—'

It was a long time since Branagh had heard the words. From Thessalonians, wasn't it? It was a long time since they had held any meaning for him. 'We believe that Jesus died and rose again. And so it will be for those who died as Christians. God will bring them to life with Jesus. Thus we shall always be with the Lord. Comfort one another with these words . . .'

He was dead.

Kathleen lowered the body onto the grass. 'He was very handsome.'

Branagh began to go through his pockets.

'What are you doing?'

'Looking for anything that could identify him. It's better for us and for everyone that they are never found. We'll bury them here.'

She nodded. 'I suppose so. Shall I check Mulholland?'

'Do you mind?'

A shake of the head.

'I'll see if I can rig up an Indian stretcher for Anton.'

He left her to it and began the search for strong upright saplings which he hacked down with Boyd's survival knife. Between them the commandos had ample supplies of paracord to lash together the frame and cross-spars. It would be a far from comfortable ride, but at least it would

478

enable them to reach the flatter terrain nearer the lake's edge where Hagan's aircraft could make a landing.

When the task was complete he found Kathleen in a pensive mood, staring at a smouldering pile of charred paper.

'What are you doing, Kathy?'

'What does it look like?' she answered sharply, without looking up. 'Burning Vincent's passport and documents.'

Branagh felt irrationally cheated; he'd wanted to go through the papers himself first before they were destroyed. He wasn't sure why; it was just a niggling feeling that he should. 'I didn't tell you to do that.'

She looked up at him quickly and anger danced in her eyes. 'You didn't tell me!' she mimicked. 'Who the hell are you to tell me what to do, Cousin Seamus?'

He blinked in surprise at the outburst. 'What's got into you, Kathy? What's happened?'

She turned away in defiance. 'Nothing.'

'Why did you burn Vincent's papers?'

'Because you wanted to get rid of any means of identification,' she said irritably.

He took her by the shoulder, spun her around. 'What did you find?'

With an effort she forced herself to look at him. Her face wore the inconsolable expression of a disappointed child: her lower lip crumpled into a pout and her eyes were dark with unforgiving. 'My brothers were right about you all the time. More right than they ever knew. You lied to me. You lied to me then and you've been lying to me now.'

He felt the pain of her words screwing into the pit of his stomach like the twist of a knife. 'I'm sorry.' Such an apology seemed so hopelessly inadequate.

'Sorry?' Her eyes seemed to scorch into his own. 'Sorry for what? That you killed my father and my brother? Or sorry that I've found out?'

'It wasn't how you think,' he said lamely.

'Do tell me,' she invited sarcastically. 'Do tell me how it *wasn't* how I think. How didn't you murder my father and my brother, Matty? I'd like to know, because Mulholland's report was pretty convincing.'

'Report?'

'In the lining of his safari jacket.' She reached down and picked up the blood-sodden garment, thrusting it at him. There was a zippered poacher's pocket in the back flap. Had it not been for the elephant's attack it might never have been found. 'It was a photocopy of some Ministry of Defence report made after the shooting. It had "Restricted" printed all over it and it contains your verbatim confession of how you deliberately set up my father knowing he was innocent. A personal feud because you were obsessed with the idea he'd blown up your parents.'

Branagh stared in disbelief at the words he was hearing. But his eyes refused to focus on Kathleen's features. In his mind all he could see was the darkness of a November night and the lashing rain. The stumbling figure of Pa Coogan running into the stakeout to save his boys. Steam rising from his sodden white shirt. Hands suddenly to his eyes, blinded by the crossfire of dazzling light and flying bullets.

'Well?' she said.

Quietly he said: 'There was no confession, Kathy. There was no debriefing because I was hospitalised with a bullet in the lung. I was in intensive care. It was touch and go.'

'Soldiers are always debriefed after an incident, I know that,' she scorned.

'But I wasn't officially a soldier at that time, Kathy. I didn't exist. I was never there. But yes, there would have been a debriefing – strictly secret – only I bugged out. Went AWOL. Took a train to Dover, then drove to Portugal. Eventually I came here. That left Mulholland free to cover his tracks like he always did.'

480

'Cover what tracks?'

He looked across at the collapsed body now swarming with blowflies. Even in death the man wouldn't leave him alone. 'I should never have been allowed on an undercover mission against my own family. He knew that, but he bent the rules to suit himself as usual. Fed me lies about your brothers so I'd go along. I knew it was wrong too, but I co-operated because I just wanted them behind bars. Or – preferably – dead.' Even now he could vividly recall the hatred he felt then.

'Christ, you sound like Dracht.'

He rounded on her. 'I was like Dracht in those days. All I had was this burning wish to get even with your brothers.' He took a deep breath. 'But not your father. That was a terrible mistake, and Mulholland must have concocted my confession to hide another of his little blunders.'

'What was that?'

'That he'd been using Father McCabe as an informer.'

Her laugh was derisory. 'Father McCabe was a dedicated Provie.'

'That was Mulholland's blunder. McCabe warned your father that he suspected a stakeout – he was shot warning your brothers. God knows how many other lives were lost as a result of Mulholland trying to control McCabe.'

'But it was *you* who shot Pa and Matty?'

A pause. 'Yes. It was dark and raining. In the confusion . . .'

'You wanted to kill my brothers. The ones you sat at table with beside me and Ma. You wanted to kill my brothers but you killed my father instead?'

'Yes! How many more times? I'm sorry and I've had to live with it ever since.'

'You bastard.'

He felt his anger begin to rise – or was it just self-pity? 'Look, Kathy, I'm sorry you had to find out like this. In fact I'm sorry you had to find out at all. But I can't turn back the clock.' He turned away abruptly; it was pointless to try to explain. Forcing his mind back to his present situation, he said: 'Now if we don't get a move on we're going to be spending the rest of our lives stranded in the bush – and Anton is going to die. Don't forget Dracht is still out there – as well as Renamo. Fred said he'd fly over the area again at noon. We need to find a landing strip by then. There'll be plenty of time for recrimination once I've got you safely out of here.'

Kathleen watched in brooding silence while Branagh used Boyd's entrenching spade to bury Mulholland and da Gruta in shallow graves. He then dug a pit for the radio set in a different location to lessen the chance of its discovery. Next he collected a number of large white stones which he placed in arrow formation on a patch of shorter dark grass; hopefully from the air it would tell Petkus in which direction they had gone.

The work complete he struggled into the harness straps of the improvised drag-stretcher and set about trying to find a game trail that led towards the lake. Once one was found the noisy, jarring progress became a little easier.

After the night's rains the air had still been fresh, but as the sun lifted remorselessly into the azure sky it soon steamed any lingering moisture from the withered grass. At last the cruel heat reasserted itself and, as his shoulder muscles started pleading for rest, the sweat began to saturate his shirt. By mid-morning the bushveld had become a pitiless inferno. Uncannily quiet and windless. High above, white puffballs of cloud inched across the burning sky. The very air itself seemed to bake, stifling and dusty. Every footstep became an effort as the bone-dry air choked the lungs and parched the throat. Movement slowed to a snail's pace, an endless grind.

There was little water left now, and Kathleen used it periodically to squeeze droplets into Boyd's open mouth from her soaked handkerchief.

'He's getting weaker,' she reported.

Branagh nodded, finding no energy to speak. Besides there was nothing to say; they both knew the man's life was held by a thread. And it might be their turn next. A winged shadow swooped over them as a vulture glided across the sun on a thermal.

The kopje emerged from the shimmering heat haze like an island. A barren knuckle of basalt growing incongruously from the flat coastal plain.

Branagh stopped in the shade of a mopane, its leaves closed together like butterfly wings against the broiling heat. Thankfully he shrugged out of the harness, lowering Boyd's weight down to the ground. His shoulders burned with relief as the circulation returned.

Without a word Kathleen handed him the last canteen. He took two sips to soften the membrane of his mouth so that he could speak. 'It's flat enough here. Stay with Anton while I mark out a strip. Keep that AK with you at all times – you never know.'

'I will.'

It took Branagh thirty minutes to decide on a suitable stretch of well-grazed grass and a further thirty to hack away the few thorn bushes and saplings that caused obstruction. It was pushing noon by the time he'd collected six piles of brush to form marker fires on each side of the strip.

He was utterly drained by the time he returned to the meagre shade of the mopane tree where Kathleen and Boyd waited.

'How is he?'

She hardly needed to answer. Boyd was groaning, turning restlessly from side to side in a twilight world between sleep and consciousness. 'The morphine's wearing off.'

Branagh stared east towards the hills. 'We can expect the plane to show at any time.'

'Mike,' she said hesitantly, 'I've seen some sort of movement on that outcrop.'

He turned towards the kopje that rose steeply from the tawny drifts of grass some hundred metres distant. 'What sort of movement?'

'More like light reflecting on something. Just once or twice while you were away.'

Immediately he thought of Dracht, then dismissed the idea. Despite Boyd's conviction to the contrary, Branagh couldn't believe that the man would concern himself with anything but reaching Lake Malawi as fast as possible. His own survival would be paramount. To be out. Safe and clear, and to put the failed mission behind him. In his sick state Boyd was becoming understandably paranoid.

It was then he heard the sound he had been praying for. The distant noise of an aircraft wavering in the intense stillness of the air.

'It's them,' Branagh said. 'It has to be.'

Hurriedly he built the pile of gathered brushwood on a circle of earth he'd cleared. He struck a match, then threw a rubberised groundsheet into the catching flames. Within seconds a dense column of greasy black smoke was snaking its way into the white-hot sky.

He started to run then, back to the strip to fire the marker beacons. As he lit the last one the drone of the air-craft reached an ear-splitting crescendo. The machine roared low over his head so that he ducked on reflex. He watched with mounting relief as the pilot began to bank, turning in a wide circle to line up his first pass for an inspection of the strip.

Throttling back, the aircraft came in just above stalling speed, wheels only feet from the ground. Anxious faces peered down.

The sound of the gunshot was just audible. It cracked, hard and sharp, several decibels above the clamour of the aero engines.

Instantly the aircraft veered. A round had smashed clean through the cockpit windshield. It took the startled pilot several seconds to recover. As it dawned that they were under fire the engines gathered sudden momentum, the pitch rising while the blades fought for purchase. The machine peeled away abruptly, gaining rapid height.

Two more shots. The first kicked a hole in the dirt by Branagh's feet, but he was already on the move when the second followed. Had his reactions not been instinctive, had he hesitated for a second, the bullet would have found its mark. As he ran a wild, zigzag course an instant picture formed in his mind. He could see Dracht on the kopje. His own figure in the cross hairs of the telescopic sight, partially obscured by the smoke from the beacons. Even as he dived for cover he felt the sharp sting of pain in his bicep. He fought to ignore it until he was safely sheltered in a shallow depression. He sat down and examined the wound. Blood came away on his fingers. The bullet had creased the skin leaving a groove of raw exposed flesh. A mere irritation, but it was no more than twelve inches from his heart.

Ripping one sleeve from his shirt, he tied the material tight around his arm to prevent further bleeding. As he did so he watched with sinking spirits as the aircraft receded into the distance.

It was a difficult crawl back to the mopane tree. He could see now that Dracht had a commanding view from the kopje. If they made any attempt to cross open country he would be able to pick them off at will.

'Why is he doing this?' Kathleen asked plaintively.

Branagh helped himself to Boyd's binoculars. 'Anton was right. Dracht's orders must be to get rid of anyone who knows about the mission.'

'Us as well? I can hardly believe that.'

'South African Military Intelligence has got a world-wide reputation. Ruthless and secretive. That's how they've managed to keep their activities in Mozambique quiet all this time. Everyone knows, but evidence is hard to come by.'

'We should have believed Anton.'

Branagh zeroed in the binoculars on the kopje. 'Yes, he knows his own people. Mind you, there wouldn't have been much else we could have done. Dracht's the hunter now.'

She shivered. 'What are we going to do? Wait for nightfall?'

'Anton will be dead if we do. No, it's my guess that Fred will be flying back to the nearest source of fuel to top up. There's enough daylight hours left for him to make one more attempt to land today.'

'You can't be certain.'

'I know him. He'll try again.'

Kathleen looked anxious. 'Dracht will shoot at him again.'

Branagh lowered the binoculars. 'Then I must try to stop Dracht. He's probably planning to keep us here until nightfall before he moves in. He'll be planning to pick us off at leisure.'

'How can you get up there? He'd have a clear view of you if you tried.'

Branagh regarded the buttress for several moments. 'That's the obvious way, up the slope to the rear. I had in mind a more direct approach. Frontal.'

Kathleen's mouth dropped. 'That's impossible. It's nearly vertical.'

The Irishman smiled uneasily; it was a long time since he'd done anything like this. 'Sure that's why he wouldn't be expecting it.'

'It's crazy.'

'But it's crazier to play it Dracht's way. He wants us dead and he knows how to do it. He nearly got me out on the strip. If he had, what chance would you and Boyd have then?' The expression on her face told him that the desperation of their predicament was sinking in. He added: 'I'll need some help.'

She viewed him coldly. 'Do I have any choice?'

'Not if you want to get out of this alive.' He hesitated. 'There'll be some risk.'

Kathleen nodded. 'I realise that.'

Branagh moved to Boyd's side. 'How are you, old son?'

The commando's eyes were closed and his face glittered with the sweat of fever. He appeared to be concentrating his mind, fighting the pain. Without opening his eyes he bared his teeth in an attempted smile. 'Never better . . .'

'The weapon Dracht keeps in his rucksack, what is it?'

Boyd's head rolled from side to side. 'I don't know . . . can't think . . .'

'You said it was a special conversion.'

'. . . Ah, yes . . . It breaks down to fit a backpack.'

'Think, man. Try.'

The commando was visibly willing himself to remember. After a few moments he moistened his lips. 'I know . . . a Ruger Mini-14 . . . converted by a friend of his . . . Stock removed, fibreglass handguard . . .'

Branagh recalled the weapons trials at the SAS headquarters in Hereford in the past. The Mini-14 had created some interest. Very lightweight. An adapted model wouldn't weigh much more than a bag of sugar. It was basically a scaled-down M1 Garand designed to take modern small calibre 5.56 mm rounds. That, at least, was good news. Dracht had been using an AK on this mission. 7.62 mm calibre. That meant the only likely ammunition supplies he had were confined to a single magazine. Most likely just twenty rounds as he used it only as an emergency weapon.

On the other hand Branagh had da Gruta's M48 submachine-gun and Boyd's AK47. And no shortage of rounds.

'How are you going to get to the outcrop?' Kathleen's words cut across his thoughts.

'The sun's in our favour. It's a trick I've heard the Royal Navy used in the Falklands. Blinding enemy pilots with lasers. This idea's a bit more primitive. We'll use Anton's heliograph and blind him with the mirror.'

'Won't he shoot at the reflection?'

'Of course, but it won't be easy. It also means you'll have to change position frequently, but there's a useful gully or old streambed running across his field of fire.' He pointed to the way he had returned from the strip. 'You can move up and down there in reasonable safety. But one hit from that Ruger would very likely kill you. It's dangerous.'

She nodded, accepting her fate.

'I'll leave the AK with you. Combine that with the blinding technique to keep him guessing. Don't use auto, you'll likely get a jam. Never more than two shots in quick succession before you change position. I want to encourage him to waste as much ammunition as possible.' He looked into her eyes. She seemed very calm, very cold. 'Have you got that?'

He went carefully over the workings of Boyd's Kalashnikov until he was certain she could handle any problems, including the drill for clearing a jam. Then he removed his blue denim shirt and replaced it with a khaki one from Boyd's pack. It was several sizes too large but it would have to suffice. Using some of the last precious drops of water he mixed up a mud paste and began smearing it over his face and hands. Finally he wrapped a camouflaged scrim scarf around his head like a turban and added quantities of grass and small branches to both it and the rest of his clothes.

'I expect this reminds you of old times,' Kathleen said icily.

He regarded her calmly. 'Let's save the fighting for Dracht. Are you ready?'

'Yes.'

'I'll start advancing when I see the mirror reflecting.' He put Boyd's pencil flare in the map pocket of his trousers. 'When I fire this you'll know it's safe. You can stop shooting.'

He took the commando's combat knife and da Gruta's M48 and slid away into the undergrowth. Without rushing he began a careful crawl away from the kopje on a route that was obscured by the mopane tree. Then he worked around in a wide loop which brought him to a position where he could begin his advance, two hundred metres parallel to the tree. If Dracht was concentrating on Kathleen, the South African should have little time to examine the rest of his field of fire. Any giveaway movement from Branagh would be on the periphery of Dracht's line-of-sight.

Crouching behind a termite hill, Branagh raised his binoculars to study the outcrop where Dracht had concealed himself. He concentrated on a ledge some metres below the blunt top. It took him some moments before he was satisfied that Dracht was there. Very little of the commando showed, presenting an impossibly small target given his advantage of height.

Then Branagh saw the flash of the heliograph, a bright spot of light dancing on the syrup-yellow walls of the kopje as Kathleen steered the beam towards the ledge.

She was taking too long, giving Dracht time to locate the source through his telescopic sight. Through his own binoculars Branagh saw a movement, saw the barrel of the Ruger protrude to take aim.

The spotlight found its mark. He winced as he imagined the effect of the knifelike shaft of light magnified down the scope. Just as Dracht was thinking he'd found a careless reflection, the spotlight had found its target.

The expected shots came quickly. Three in rapid succession, trying to hit the light source. Kathleen held steady; the beam didn't waver.

Dracht would have to find a new position, away from its glare. While he did it was Branagh's time to move.

Keeping his head and backside low he moved forward on knees and elbows with the wriggling gait of a lizard.

He halted when he'd closed the gap between himself and the kopje wall to just a hundred metres.

Another sharp report echoed across the bushveld.

He stopped and again took up his binoculars. He watched with detached fascination as a return of fire came from the gully. On the kopje ledge he saw the rounds kicking up dust inches from Dracht's new position. She was a good shot, he admitted grudgingly. The man might have height advantage, but if he wanted to maintain it he would be confined to the ledge. He was an easy target for the beam to find. Again the spotlight moved in.

Branagh found a screen of thorn bushes to offer cover and sprinted some fifty metres before dropping to his hands and knees again. Panting heavily, he looked up to see that now the ledge was hidden from view. Only if Dracht leaned out and over would he be able to witness Branagh's approach. And that was something he was unlikely to try while coming under fire from Kathleen.

Branagh moved faster now, breaking cover to race the last fifty metres to the foot of the kopje. When he arrived he gave a brief thumbs-up signal to Kathleen, then secured the M48 sub-machine-gun across his back in order to leave his hands free. Looking up, the wall of the outcrop was an intimidating sight. Wind-smoothed basalt towered above his head, offering little in the way of hand or footholds. He studied the surface, trying to relate it to the climbing route he'd decided on earlier through the binoculars. Close to it didn't look so promising.

The only possibility offered for the first twenty metres was a funnel of vertical groove in the surface. It began some three metres wide before eventually narrowing to a point.

He faced the rock square on and selected the first meagre holds. Taking a deep breath he started to move, one hold at a time. Right hand, left foot, left hand, right foot. Think ahead at all times. Always keeping the back

490

straight, always keeping three holds secure whilst moving the fourth. Golden rules. The instructor's voice, speaking to him over the years. From days when he was a fitter, younger man. Days when he knew no fear.

But now his heart was pounding in his chest, his breathing was short and his fingertips screamed with the strain of holding his weight on some hairline crack and smooth indentation.

Faith-holds, no more. He heard the training sergeant's words. *'Faith-holds – you can do it if you believe you can do it.'* They hadn't impressed him then, and they didn't impress him now. Not when he could feel the sole of his boot swivel on the glasslike surface of some shallow hold. Knowing that only his muscle pressure held him fast, like a limpet defying gravity. Muscles that burned with the pain of unrelenting effort. Muscles he hadn't used for years.

Up, you bastard, up. You've started this, you've got to finish it. You can't ask Dracht to throw down a rope. Up, you bastard, up!

Another move, edging ever higher. To a hold out of reach of his outstretched hand. Extending his body, willing his tendons to give like elastic until the ball-joint of his shoulder felt as though it was parting from the socket. Push up on the balls of the feet. Gotcha! Fingers finding the dusty fissure, mere millimetres of grip.

Faith-hold. Go for it!

Push and up. Move the left leg. Test. Foot secure. Up with the right leg. Stance level. Holding. He pushed his forehead against the sun-baked rock and closed his eyes. Heaving lungfuls of warm air. Trying to calm himself, to steady his thudding heart. He relaxed his shoulders and flexed his knees, reviving the cramped muscles as best he could.

He was drenched in sweat. The sweat of exertion, the sweat of fear and the sweat from the anvil beat of the African sun on his back. Sweat that was making his palms slippery. Sweat that was running into his eyes to blind him.

Again he looked up. Through smarting eyes, he saw that the funnel was narrowing above his head. Keep at it, he told himself. Just a little more. You can do it.

Reluctantly he again began the same pattern. One hold at a time. Repeat and repeat. Would it never end?

Then, suddenly, he was there. The funnel had closed sufficiently for him to twist awkwardly so that his back was jammed against one side and his feet against the other. Perched safely, for the moment. A forty foot drop below and an arch meeting overhead.

Roughly he wiped the sweat from his face with his forearm and dried his sticky palms on his clothes.

Blessed relief for his tortured muscles as he massaged them as best he could. Recharging his mental batteries for what was to come.

For the first time he was able to view the sunlit plain spread out before him. He could clearly see the mopane where Boyd had been left. Then he saw a flash of light from the gully. But this time Dracht didn't take the bait. No firing came from above. In fact now he couldn't recall if there had been any shooting at all during his ascent.

Could Kathleen have fired a lucky round? Would he finish this climb only to find himself face to face with a corpse?

As though in answer he heard gunfire from somewhere high over his head. He smiled grimly to himself. That's what you get for wishful thinking. That was how his prayers had always been answered.

No, it was Kathleen who was in danger the longer it took him to reach the top. Dracht had the patience and cunning of a wildcat. This was his territory where for years he had been the king of predators.

The thought spurred Branagh on. His pulse was steadier now, his concentration sharper after the short respite. By twisting round he was now able to face into the funnel

492

with his feet astride the opposing walls. The confined space supplied the pressure for even meagre holds, easing the muscle pain and making the steady upward progress almost leisurely. Inch by inch he edged up until the funnel sides finally met above his head.

He leaned out to inspect the overhang. It didn't look inviting. Smooth, crumbling basalt forming a crude ledge which protruded some two feet. One slip and he would plunge sixty feet to almost certain death.

Choosing a route to the right, he left behind the safety and shade of the funnel, the sun-scorched rock once again burning under his palms. Back to the regular pattern. Right hand, left foot, left hand, right foot . . . Slowly he manoeuvred up under the overhang. He leaned out as far as he dared and reached up an exploratory hand. Over the edge of the shelf, fingers scrabbling blindly for a hold.

Then the bird took off.

Flapping noisily it suddenly hoisted its great weight off the hidden nest and took flight. All Branagh heard was the panicky explosion of sound; all he saw and felt was the shadow pass inches above his head.

In the shock of the moment his right foot slipped from its hold and for the longest second of his life he swung precariously like a pendulum, held only by one hand and one foot.

Pain seared through his fingertips and wrist, sparks of agony shooting down his arm and shoulder as he clung for dear life. Then, miraculously, his wildly thrashing foot found a new hold and he breathed again.

He renewed his concentration and reached up, fingers exploring the upper side of the ledge like a blind man reading braille. He could find only one indentation, just wide enough to allow a three-finger purchase. The rest of the shelf offered nothing but a smooth surface that sloped towards him.

He was going to need the worst kind of faith-hold, and he began to feel physically sick at the very thought. The only way he was going to surmount the overhang was to propel himself up, grab the one hold he'd found. And pray to God he could find another hold in the split second before gravity pulled him back down.

It was the hardest decision of his life. Yet it was hardly a decision, he realised. There really was no other choice.

He flexed his knees, feeling the pressure of his toes on the rock. Tensed the muscles of his calves and thighs like a coiled spring. A deep breath. Wait. This was the moment. No going back. Go!

His legs straightened, the relaxed muscle power driving him up and out, clearing the shelf top for the first time. Giving him his first and only view. Perhaps half a second. perhaps less.

The image that registered was of a shelf no more than two feet wide and the nest from which the bird had flown. His right hand snatched at the indentation he'd found – the left simply reached as far in as possible. To claw the bare rock. Only to feel himself being dragged down by the weight of his own body.

It was a long moment while he slid inexorably back, the skin of his fingertips burning with friction against the coarse surface. Finding no hold.

Below, the bushveld spun crazily, the horizon at a curious angle. Everything was a mad blur as he swung from one hand . . . He let go.

He grabbed at the rock wall as he fell. His left hand found something, and held it. The violent jarring almost dislocated his shoulder. His other hand desperately sought to share the grip while his legs scrabbled with a will of their own to find a purchase.

Shaking and awash with sweat he clung on with eyes tight shut, his lungs heaving. Loose shale showered down the rockface.

He opened his eyes. His white-knuckled fingers were clasped around six inches of exposed tree root. Tree root! Halfway up a bloody kopje. A tree root. As he looked up he saw the small seringa, its green head waving against the sky. A miracle of nature. It always amazed him how some trees managed to grow out of what appeared to be solid rock.

He glanced back up to the ledge. Somehow he had fallen to one side. It hadn't been intentional. But now he saw with growing relief that he had landed on a surface that was far easier to climb, but that would have been impossible to reach from below. It had been an unnerving answer to his prayers.

With renewed vigour he began to power up the incline, this time the hand and footholds offering themselves at regular intervals. After only a few minutes of fast scaling he found himself approaching Dracht's eyrie, just metres below the summit.

Gingerly Branagh reached for the ledge. Using both hands he lifted himself high enough to see over.

Dracht was crouched some twenty metres away, staring straight at him.

It was impossible to know who was most surprised. Probably it was the South African because his Ruger rifle was still pointed out over the bushveld. The noise of Branagh's fall must have alerted him that something could be happening. Yet it was clear he wasn't expecting his adversary to appear where he did.

As Branagh struggled to free the M48 from his back, the Ruger swung to face him. Too late. Dracht had seconds of advantage.

Then a volley of shots suddenly peppered the ridge. From her distant viewpoint Kathleen had been able to monitor events clearly. Ignoring Branagh's earlier advice, she showered the basalt ridge with rounds. They whined and ricocheted off the rock wall above Dracht's head.

Branagh read the sudden panic in his eyes. Caught off balance, not knowing that the Irishman was unable to shoot. His interest was for self-preservation. He leapt back into the boulder debris, seeking cover. Branagh swung up onto the ridge and unstrapped the M48.

Now they were equal. Man against man, gun against gun. Each the hunter, each the hunted.

Branagh heard the clatter of disturbed scree as Dracht hurriedly negotiated a way through the maze of boulders, moving towards the rear of the kopje where it tumbled slowly down to ground level.

Height, Branagh told himself, gain height. An urgent breathless scramble took him to the summit. Reaching it on all fours he moved towards the rim of the flattened top. He was greeted by the singsong whine of a ricochet as Dracht fired up at the offered head.

Now Branagh had what he wanted. Had Dracht's position fixed, hidden between two boulders on the lower slope.

He slid swiftly back down, scrambling over the lower rock stacks as he worked his way behind the South African. Then he slowed, progressing cautiously. Move, listen. Move, listen. The slightest clink of pebbles underfoot, the careless scrape of gunmetal against basalt. Any such giveaway would hand the advantage to the other. Might decide the bloody outcome.

It was tiring on the eyes. The deep shadows between the boulders were in sharp contrast to the sun-bleached rock. Branagh tiptoed forward another few paces.

Then he heard the sudden rustling movement – behind him. Christ!

As he turned he saw Dracht step out of the shadows, the Ruger raised, his huge box shoulders silhouetted against the sky. A smirk of satisfaction crossed the South African's face. Then the smile crumbled as he heard the hammer fall and nothing happened. A jam. He turned and ran.

Branagh fired from the hip. A wild shot. A kick of dust testimony to how close it was. Close but not close enough. There was no time for more, but it was too late anyway. Dracht had darted back into the shadows.

Branagh was at his heels, pausing at the dark passage formed by two huge basalt buttresses. Daylight at the other end. Dracht at the other end.

Branagh proceeded at a crouch down the gloomy passage that had never seen the sun. The air smelled dank and stale. A lizard scurried from his path.

The aperture of brilliant sunlight came ever closer, filling his vision, refracting off the outside rocks with dazzling intensity.

He didn't see or hear Dracht. Just felt the hammerblow to his head as he emerged. Flashing lights and stars sparkling in a red void. He was vaguely aware that his fingers had lost their grip, powerless to stop the M48 flying from his hands before he landed on the rocks.

He shook his head. Tried to ignore the pain, clear his vision. Crawled forward to reclaim the weapon. But brain and body refused to coordinate and he fell back to the ground. He looked down to see the blood dripping in starbursts on the earth.

It was too late. Dracht was there, casually picking up the M48 as though he had all the time in the world. King of the predators. Master of the bushveld.

Branagh reached down to the map pocket of his trousers.

Dracht inspected the M48, checked the breech and catch, then pointed it at Branagh. 'You're a fighter, Irishman, I'll say that for you. Mulholland said you were SAS once.'

Branagh palmed the pencil flare, shifted his position slightly on the ground. 'I've lost my touch.'

'You did pretty well.'

'This is stupid. Let's talk.'

'No time. I've a boat to catch.' The gun didn't waver.

Branagh moved one hand up along his body, using it to lift himself up. 'Leave the girl – she's nothing to you.'

Nico Dracht smiled. 'Sorry. Orders. You know how it is.'

I know how it is. Orders – orders in Armagh in the pouring rain and the dark. His thumb found the springloaded trigger on the pencil flare in his clenched fist.

The explosion was ear-splitting in the confines of the rocky maze, the noise like cannon fire as the flare discharged. Barely an inch of lead casing but it had the power and velocity of a rocket, streaking flame as it shot across the short distance between them. The flat head acted like a dumdum, taking Dracht full in the chest. The force of the impact created its own fiery cavity, slamming him off his feet and several feet backwards.

There was no movement after, there couldn't be. The flare had burned its way through his heart and lungs and smashed a path through to the spinal column.

As Branagh rose to his feet the flare was lifting limply into the sky – a spent force, still fizzing and trailing an arc of green smoke. He looked down at Dracht's stricken body, his face frozen in a death mask of horror that he would take to the grave.

It was over. The South African had failed his last mission. The dream was dead.

Suddenly Branagh felt drained. Exhaustion crowded in on him; all he wanted was sleep. He dragged the corpse into the passage between the boulders and threw on stones until the body was covered. Then he shouldered the M48 and began to find a path down to level ground.

Twenty minutes later he was approaching the mopane tree. The coppery sun was losing its strength now. All he could think of doing was to lie in the shade. To sleep for a million years.

Kathleen was waiting. The expression on her face suggested she didn't trust the evidence of her own eyes. 'You did it?'

He threw down the M48. 'Dracht's dead.'

'I saw the flare. I couldn't believe it.'

He noticed she didn't smile; it obviously hadn't sunk in yet. 'How's Anton?'

'Unconscious. I don't know if he'll make it.'

Branagh ran a hand through his hair. 'He'll make it. He's a tough bastard. They all were.'

'Like you were.' There was a chill tone to her voice.

'What?' he asked distractedly. There was a faint hum of aero engines on the light breeze that had picked up. He squinted towards the hills but couldn't make the aircraft out.

'Like you were,' she repeated. 'A tough bastard.'

He looked back at her. She held the Star automatic pistol in a double-handed grip. 'Kathy?'

'A tough bastard and a liar.' The gunmetal snout kept pointing. 'And a cold-blooded killer. You were then and you are now. No, don't move an inch.'

Branagh froze, still not comprehending what he saw. The hatred in her eyes, the mouth he had kissed contorted as she spoke the words. 'You lied to me when I was a child and I believed you. You lied to me again here – and I still believed you. I thought the work you were doing here was selfless and wonderful. I think I even started to fall in love with you. And you let me – knowing all the time you killed my father and my brother.'

He couldn't believe she meant what she was saying. Couldn't believe she would pull the trigger. 'I explained all that to you, Kathy. It was a terrible mistake.'

'It was the worst mistake you ever made.' Each syllable dripped ice. 'Mulholland knew – or more likely guessed. Unfortunately for you he never told you. I guess he had his own reasons. Hoped I'd do the job for him.'

'Knew what, Kathy?' His voice had dropped to a whisper.

'That I came to Mozambique to kill you.'

In the moment's brittle silence the drone of the distant aircraft became more distinct.

Branagh said: 'You've taken your time.'

Her smile was cold. 'I had to wait for the moment. You can't just waltz into Mozambique with a gun in your luggage. Besides, I wanted to be sure.'

'Tell me.'

'It was my brothers' idea. After Matty and my father were murdered we'd all watched Ma's health deteriorate. She was being treated for cancer within a year. It was thought to be cured but it kept recurring. She suffered a long and slow decline. It was painful to see. The last three years were the worst. I was visiting Nial and Joseph in the Maze. I told them about your letter. They vowed to come and find you eventually, but they've got years left to serve. So I said I'd go. As a journalist it would be easier for me in all respects. Besides, I wanted to be sure myself. I could never believe you'd had a hand in Pa's murder – let alone pulled the trigger.' There was a sudden look of sadness in her eyes. 'How wrong I turned out to be. I thought I would be able just to warn you of my brothers' intentions, then go back home to convince them of your innocence. That's what I thought would happen.'

'And Vincent guessed this?'

'He had an idea. There was something else with that report I found in his pocket. Some sort of memo from the British Embassy in Pretoria. It said I'd visited my other brother in Johannesburg on my way here.'

'Padraig.' The bomb-maker.

'He's been working as an engineer here. At least that's his cover. He's a Provie adviser to the African National Congress – the ANC. They see themselves as political allies, you see. I saw him to ask what to do – he has African friends who knew all about Mozambique. Obviously British Intelligence had him under surveillance.'

Branagh was still stunned and it was difficult to bring some order to his thinking. 'So Vincent knew your visit here wasn't all it seemed? That you were part of an IRA hit team?'

She shook her head vehemently. 'Not IRA, Cousin Seamus. This is personal. Family business. But Mulholland must have had a suspicion that you could be in danger – after all *he* knew what happened when you killed Pa and Matty. Maybe he'd have warned you if you'd played along with him.' A pause. 'Or maybe he just thought a naïve farmer's daughter didn't represent any real threat. That I would never pull the trigger.'

Branagh narrowed his eyes. 'Was he right?'

Her voice was low to match his own. 'He couldn't have been more wrong. I told you once before – I am not the little girl you once knew. I've grown up. All the horrors you have here – shootings and mines and massacres – I've seen them all back home. It's not so different, only we think we know better. I've reported them. Been there! Even my own father and brother. I'm sick of it – because it seems to me it just goes on and on. Everything you told me then was lies. My brothers were right about the occupying Brits. Right about you. There is no justice.'

He indicated the gun. 'And this?'

'This is my justice. One small piece of justice, Cousin Seamus. You condemned yourself with words from your own mouth.'

The noise of the approaching aircraft changed pitch as it settled into a search pattern. As Kathleen's eyes flickered sideways in the direction of the sound, Branagh took a step forward.

'Don't move!' she hissed.

His voice was very measured, very level. 'This is madness, Kathy. They're about to land – you'd never get away with it. Give me the gun.'

She took a step back. 'I'll say it was bandits – or Dracht. Boyd won't know, and no one's going to hang around to check.'

It was then that he saw the boy over her shoulder. He stood in the hazy afternoon sunshine like a mirage amid the swaying grass. The Kalashnikov he held in his small black hands was almost as long as he was tall.

'Kathy!' Branagh called.

The double report was virtually simultaneous.

Benjamin Matusi had no way of knowing who shot first. No way of knowing whether the dark-haired woman had shot Mikey Branagh before he shot her, or the other way round.

All he knew was that the tall white man who had once been his friend had been blown backwards into the grass by the closeness of the impact. The woman had dropped the pistol instantly and stood for a second staring down in astonishment at the bloodstain spreading from her heart. Then she too collapsed. Hidden beneath the rippling yellow carpet of buffalo grass.

He walked slowly forward through the bushveld as he had walked for the past two days. From the little Portuguese villa on the far side of the hills, across the hills themselves after the abandoned jeep, and then to this place near the lone kopje.

It had been a strange journey. For two days he had travelled alone without other bandits for company. In his anxiety not to lose or alert his quarry he had eventually hidden his motorcycle and continued stealthily on foot. Alone with his thoughts. Alone with the words his sister had spoken to him when last they met. '*You belong with us, not here. We forgive you as God forgives you, little brother.*'

Those had been her words. That was what Maraika had said after he had told her he had killed his own brother. Had killed young Jaime in order to save himself. He did not understand. How could she say such a thing after he had committed such a shameful sin? After he had pledged himself to the devil that was Renamo?

These and many other things he pondered on his lonely vigil, tracking the spoor of the white people. Repeating his sister's words over and over again in his head. Feeling the slow, growing warmth of comfort at what she had said.

Then that morning he had found the body of an ancient elephant and the shallow graves of two white men, both of whom had been shot. Something had happened there which he did not begin to comprehend.

That afternoon he had heard gunfire from afar and had seen a trail of green smoke in the sky above the distant kopje. He had hurried then – only to be confronted by the strange sight of a white woman about to shoot his one-time friend.

'*He has always loved you as I have loved you.*' Again Maraika's words echoed in his head. '*Whatever happens you must spare Mikey.*'

He brushed apart the grass and looked down at the woman he had killed. She seemed very small and pale, very beautiful. Her eyes were closed as though she were just asleep.

A few feet from her Branagh stirred. Benjamin looked down with a sense of horror at the gaping chest wound. As he rushed to the man's side it did not occur to him that he had not felt such compassion, or anything like it, for almost two years. He unstrapped the water canteen from his side and, propping Branagh against his knee, put it to the man's parched lips.

He barely had strength to swallow and his eyelids opened only with the greatest effort.

'Senhor Mike,' Benjamin said earnestly.

A painful smile forced itself to Branagh's lips. 'Benjy? This is a dream . . . Is that really you?'

An irrepressible grin broke across the boy's face. He could not believe that anyone could be so pleased to see him. 'It is me, Senhor Mike. You do not dream.'

'. . . I never thought . . . we'd see you again.' He coughed and a thin trickle of blood escaped from the corner of his mouth. '. . . You must get . . . back to Gutala . . . the aircraft up there . . . Take the wounded

503

South African . . . He is a good man, believe me . . . Fred Petkus will look after you . . . I am afraid your sister . . . has been taken . . .' He shut his eyes. 'So sorry.'

'I know. I see her.'

Despite the pain Branagh's eyes fluttered open again. 'Alive?'

'She is alive.'

'. . . Thank God. She will be so pleased to know . . .' Again the pain rushed at him and he was powerless to resist. He was so tired. So, so tired. He must sleep.

'Senhor Mike – why did you tell me lies?'

Lies? Lies? The words tumbled through Branagh's brain. Why did everyone accuse him of lies? He moved his mouth, but he could not hear any words.

Benjamin said thoughtfully: 'You say to me once – at Sunday school – that Jesus loves children. He will look after us. If we have faith, we will be saved.'

'. . .I said that?' Scarcely audible.

'I had faith, Senhor Mike. I prayed for forgiveness. Jesus did not save me.' He looked down at the gold crucifix at Branagh's throat. The crucifix that had always fascinated him as a child. 'I think that I will burn in hell.'

Branagh said something the boy could not hear. He leaned closer as the parched lips moved imperceptibly.'. . . Sometimes a man must learn to forgive himself—'

Benjamin Matusi lowered the Irishman's head to the ground. Very gently he undid the clasp of the chain around his friend's neck and held the carved gold crucifix in his palm so that the sun flashed and glittered on its surface.

Thoughtfully he rose to his feet and looked up into the dulling sky and watched as the pilot of the aircraft gave up the search pattern and decided to land as a last resort. Seeking out the charred grass where Branagh had lit the strip earlier, the machine inched down for a bumpy landing.

The boy looked around him, beyond the golden beauty of the bushveld to the stark outline of the hills from which Renamo would be coming. And he felt a shudder of apprehension.

But he took comfort in the noisy clatter of the taxiing aircraft. It would be able to take off again before nightfall. Which was just as well, because everyone knew that the night belonged to the bandits.

EPILOGUE

The big limousine with its tinted windows did not take kindly to the rutted surface of the farm track in the eastern Transvaal. And the weight of the sole passenger in the rear seat contributed to his own discomfort, straining the butter-soft suspension to its limit.

Peering out at the neatly ordered pastures and crop fields the passenger felt more than a little uneasy. This was the heart of Boer country. He did not belong here. Here the white man was king and anything could happen to the likes of him. No one would turn a hair if a black man were found in a field ditch with a bullet in his head.

At last the trackside avenue of fan palms gave way to a sweep of gravel drive that ran between close-shaven lawns. The limousine glided to a halt before an impressively large bungalow of magnolia-coloured stucco. The white chauffeur held open the door impassively, but made no attempt to assist as the passenger struggled to climb out with some dignity.

Perspiring heavily, the big man made it to the front door. Despite the light material of his vast grey silk suit he was hot and bothered, far more used to the short sleeves and open throat of his bush fatigues.

Even when Willem van der Walt threw wide the front door and greeted him with his usual enigmatic smile and laughing blue eyes, the big man felt nervous. Warily he glanced behind him in case the chauffeur should have a gun at his back.

'Come in,' the South African said and quickly closed

the door. 'I will really have to get used to calling you Sozinko. It wouldn't do to use the name Napoleão here.'

He waited patiently whilst the gigantic Mozambican waddled through to the lounge. Beyond the open French windows fairy lights illuminated the swimming pool and white plastic patio furniture. The smell of barbecued meat hung succulently in the air. 'I've a few like-minded friends over for a *braai* – mostly chums from the Directorate. But I wanted to talk to you first.'

'It is a pleasure, Senhor van der Walt.' Feeling a little more relaxed.

'Willem, please. A drink?'

'Just a beer – Willem.'

As the South African attended the drinks cabinet Ashton Smythe sauntered in from the garden. The Englishman wore his usual crumpled alpaca suit and had his equally usual gin in hand.

Alarm spread across Napoleão's face.

'Of course, you know Ashton – my Mr Fixit.'

The Mozambican inclined his head; Smythe smirked disdainfully.

Van der Walt smiled lightly. 'Something is worrying you?'

Napoleão cleared his throat. 'The money. You do not want the money back?'

The South African looked at him directly for several long moments before speaking. 'No.' The ghost smile rematerialised. 'No, Operation El Dorado is over. We must learn to accept that and put it behind us. There will be no new Afrikaner homeland in Mozambique – well, for the present. Instead we must mend bridges with the Renamo leadership – support them as best we can with our dwindling resources.'

Napoleão gestured round the room. 'But this is your *retirement* home, is it not?'

Van der Walt nodded. '*Enforced* retirement, that is true. But I am still not without influence. At the party tonight you will meet many famous faces. All my long-term friends. The people who have made South Africa what it is today. And we need your help. Your special skills.'

Napoleão frowned. 'How can I help you? I am even scorned amongst the Renamo leadership after my involvement with your plans.'

The South African smiled sympathetically and, placing a hand on the big man's back, led him to a quiet corner, out of earshot of Smythe. 'With El Dorado failed, we must look again to our own country. Mandela is out of prison and the liberals are anxious to do deals for one-man, one-vote and all that nonsense. We need to illustrate to the world that these politically motivated young blacks are not fit to govern, are not ready. There is no love lost between the ANC Xhosas and their rival Inkatha Zulus. It would not take much to get them at each other's throats, fighting like wild dogs. In such chaos it would be impossible for the liberals to go ahead with their plans for the new South Africa. It will give us time, maybe until there can be another plan like El Dorado.'

Napoleã's eyes began to twinkle and he emptied his Castle lager into a glass. 'Willem – I think I begin to understand.'

'You will remember your training camp at Phalaborwa,' van der Walt said.

'It is not far from here, I remember.'

'We have a special unit from 5 Recce. Many Mozambicans. I want you to train them and deploy them quickly. At a private facility we will provide.'

'Deploy them? What do you have in mind?'

'Perhaps an attack on the Johannesburg commuter train to Soweto,' van der Walt replied. 'A massacre carried out by professionals. No warnings. No survivors. Kill a few ANC supporters and the Zulus will be blamed. Then an attack on the Zulus and the ANC are blamed.'

'I can train such people,' Napoleão said proudly.

'There is a suburban station at Benrose. My people

think it would be an ideal spot.' Then he saw the look in the Mozambican's eyes, the unasked question. 'Ashton Smythe will look after the necessary false passports and identity papers for your men. And the money.'

'Dom Pedro would never forgive you for what you are about to do,' Senhora da Gruta pronounced. It was her last defiant word, yet she knew it was a waste of time.

Her husband pulled up the handbrake of the Toyota and climbed out. He poked his head back inside. 'Dom Pedro has been dead two years, Veronique. Leave him, and his memories, and his grandiose ideas to rot. Because of him our son is dead.'

'I do not believe he is dead, Jorge.'

Senhor da Gruta sighed. 'You have read the press reports. That South African commando in the hospital in Harare. He even named van der Walt and Dracht. He was there.'

'He is a publicity seeker. Making it all up to create a sensation. Willem wouldn't lie to me.'

'As always, Veronique, you only believe what you want to believe.'

She pouted, folded her arms and stared straight ahead. 'Anyway, if he doesn't watch his mouth Willem's people will be paying him a visit.'

Shaking his head in exasperation, Jorge da Gruta took the dynamite charge from the back of the truck and picked his way through the slag heaps to the mouth of the Shangaan Queen.

Quarter of an hour later he was back. 'A ten-minute fuse. Next time it will not be so easy to reopen. Perhaps it will be less of a temptation now.' He started the engine. 'Forget about what used to be, Veronique. Learn to accept it. Mozambique is for the Mozambicans now. Come back and stay in Gutala.'

But she hardly heard as the Toyota rolled forward. She leaned back in the comfort of her seat. 'There is one

509

consolation, Jorge. We may not have the Shangaan Queen now, but neither does the Frelimo government.'

'It gets lonely at Gutala without you there.'

She walked alone, holding herself proudly erect, looking neither left nor right.

No one on the bustling streets of Gutala paid her a second glance. Even when the woman came nearer and they realised that she was covered only in baked white mud that created the illusion of clothing, no one turned to look.

She was naked. Like hundreds of thousands of others she literally had nothing. Just another *affectado*. The affected ones. The dispossessed. It was not unusual.

Her pace quickened as she approached the square. Her eyes began to dart back and forth across the street, seeking a familiar face. To see life going on as normal lightened her spirits. She hardly dared believe that once again government troops were patrolling the streets, that destroyed huts were being painstakingly rebuilt. The smell of peace and normality was like a balm in the warm air.

A few more paces and she would be at the square. The sun was low in the sky, so she knew where she would find him. As always at that time he would be seated on the verandah of the *cantina* with Fred Petkus. A Jameson and a vodka on the white metal table.

Then she was there, in the shadow of the hotel, shouldering her way urgently through the market shoppers.

Her heart skipped as she saw the distant table and the bulky frame of the Russian stretched out in his chair. A frown creased the smooth surface of her brow. The other chair was empty. The Russian was alone.

He saw her then, his eyes attracted like a magnet, zeroing in through the confusing hustle of people. He sat up, pulling up his legs, reaching for the verandah rail.

'Maraika!' he bellowed like a foghorn and all heads turned.

She saw that his leg was in plaster but it hardly slowed him as he began limping awkwardly towards her, pushing people aside in his haste. She started to run, finding a sudden source of energy from deep within her emaciated body.

Then she was home. Crushed in the Russian's powerful arms, squeezed to his great chest, feeling the warmth of his tears on her head.

'You are safe! You are safe!' he mumbled into her hair. 'The most beautiful woman in Africa is home!' He pulled back, taking her hand and leading her the last few steps to the *cantina* verandah. He took the leather flying jacket from the back of his seat and draped it round her shoulders and made her sit on the chair.

'Mikey is not here yet? You wait for Mikey?'

A look of sadness filled the Russian's eyes. 'I do not wait for Irish, my little one.'

'He is not here?'

'Irish is dead.'

'No!'

Petkus swallowed hard. 'I bury him myself. In the bush not far from the shore of Lake Malawi.'

She stared at him, her eyes wide and pleading. 'Tell me this is not true. Mikey cannot be dead.'

'It was me who finds his body. And the body of the girl he called his kissing cousin.'

'She?'

'They are both shot.' He reached across and squeezed her hand. 'We think it was *matsangas*, but no one knows. Even the other person I find there. He says he knows nothing.'

'Other person?'

Petkus turned towards the door of the *cantina* and whistled. 'I get him a job here. Maybe now there is quicker service.'

But Maraika hardly heard. 'What am I to do? Mikey is dead.'

He looked at her earnestly. 'Do not cry. And do not worry. I will look after you. Now you are safe.'

The boy stepped out of the *cantina* and onto the verandah, and stopped dead in his tracks.

Her mouth opened. 'Benjamin.'

He regarded her sheepishly, fearing her reaction. But she only thought how different he looked from the last time she had seen him. The sullen, haunted expression had gone. Then he wore military fatigues like a little man; now he had on a clean shirt and shorts. Branagh's gold crucifix glinted at his chest.

Petkus leaned forward to whisper with a chuckle. 'He says he is going to be a priest.'

The tattered notebooks belonging to journalist Kathleen Coogan were found in Tumbo village and were eventually forwarded to the London magazine for which they had been intended.

But the poignant story was incomplete and the editor judged that the subject of Mozambique lacked popular appeal.

It was never published.

POCKET
BOOKS

Terence Strong
Deadwater Deep

As Britain hands over Hong Kong, a secret long-term intelligence plan is revealed to the new Prime Minister in London. A plan to overcome Communist China's hundred-year strategy for world domination and its frightening growth in military and ecomomic might. A plan to set free one-fifth of the world's population.

The instruments on which success depends are John Dancer, the laconic CIA agent who's been in China too long and seen too much, and Project Deadwater, which pushes combined Anglo-American stealth submarine technology to its limits, and demands total dedication from the special forces SBS, SAS and SEAL teams it will put ashore.

The most audacious power-broking game in history is about to be played out. Only problem is, no one has yet told the US president . . .

ISBN 978-1-84739-032-5
PRICE £6.99

SIMON &
SCHUSTER

Terence Strong
President Down

Former intelligence officer and one-time instructor at the
British Army School of Sniping, Phil Mason is struggling to
make ends meet as a private investigator when he's contacted
by his former M15 liaison officer.

The overstretched security service needs all the help it can get
hunting down members of al-Qaeda terror cells in the UK –
and Mason needs the cash.

But in the murky intelligence world of smoke and mirrors,
nothing is what it seems. As a routine surveillance operation
escalates into a full-blown international crisis, Mason must
come to terms with the unthinkable: there must be a traitor
within Britain's security forces.

Entering a desperate race against time to identify and avert a
major terrorist threat, Mason must hastily re-hone his old
counter-sniper skills as he returns to the business he swore he
had left behind forever. The killing game.

'Relentless energy from a man who knows his tradecraft,
survival skills, muzzle velocities and conspiracy theory as
well as anyone in the business' *Guardian*

ISBN 978-0-7432-8564-3
PRICE £12.99

POCKET
BOOKS

Terence Strong
Sons of Heaven

They are the Pessarane Behesht. Sons of Heaven. The
secret sword of Islam. Spawned in war-torn Beirut, nurtured
in revolutionary Iran to wreak vengeance on the enemies
of Allah.

When the freighter Clarion Call disappears mysteriously in the
Gulf, she is carrying a secret consignment of French arms for
the Pessarane Behesht in return for the release of a diplomat
held hostage.

And ex-SAS Major Robert D'Arcy, whose international
security firm was protecting the ship, finds himself in the
midst of a deadly battle of wills between state-sponsored
terrorists and rival Western intelligence agencies with
conflicting interests.

As the Iranians resort to kidnap and assassination in their thirst
for revenge, and the lives of an innocent woman and her child
hang in the balance, D'Arcy must act alone to prevent a
horrifying carnage.

ISBN 978-1-84739-257-2
PRICE £6.99

POCKET
BOOKS

Terence Strong

White Viper

Where do you find a man to send beyond the reach of
international law? To fight state tyranny, terrorism and
traffickers in the world's deadliest narcotics?

The Z file – the last resort.

When vast quantities of White Viper – an exceptionally pure
and branded cocaine – threaten to flood Britain, Europe and
the USA, the authorities are forced to look beyond the
conventional forces of law and order to tackle the crisis. Enter
Kurt Mallory, former SAS. Infiltrator, investigator and
sometime executioner, he's the natural choice to head up a
covert search-and-destroy operation. One that will force him
to face the demons of his past. And take him to the depths of
inhumanity on the most unnerving mission of his life . . .

'The tension is razor-sharp' *Daily Telegraph*

ISBN 978-1-84739-033-2
PRICE £6.99

POCKET
BOOKS

This book and other titles are available from your local bookshop or can be ordered direct from the publisher.

978-0-74328-564-3	President Down	£12.99
978-1-84739-256-5	This Angry Land	£6.99
978-1-84739-257-2	Sons of Heaven	£6.99
978-1-84739-032-5	Deadwater Deep	£6.99
978-1-84739-033-2	White Viper	£6.99

Please send cheque or postal order for the value of the book, **free postage and packing within the UK**, to
SIMON & SCHUSTER CASH SALES
PO Box 29, Douglas Isle of Man, IM99 1BQ
Tel: 01624 677237, Fax: 01624 670923
Email: bookshop@enterprise.net
www.bookpost.co.uk

Please allow 14 days for delivery. Prices and availability subject to change without notice